NIGHTBLADE

BY: RYAN KIRK

NIGHTBLADE

Copyright © 2015 by Ryan Kirk

ISBN-13: 978-0692530160
ISBN-10: 0692530169

Cover art by Armin Numanović
Interior design by Ryan Kirk

www.waterstonemedia.net

Give feedback on the book at:
contact@waterstonemedia.net

Twitter: @waterstonebooks

First Edition

Printed in the U.S.A

For Katie.

The most amazing person I know.
You make this all possible.

PROLOGUE

I am crawling, silent as a shadow, through the tall grass, each prolonged moment bleeding into the next. The full moon is rising as bright as the sun to my night-adapted eyes. It pierces through the leaves of the new forest, clearly illuminating the way forward. Tonight I count the moon among my enemies, assisting the archers scanning the grass and the trees for signs of my presence. I have no need of the moon's light and curse the necessity to act on this night, but my enemy is no doubt grateful for its near omnipresent light.

The night is blissfully cool, a strong breeze coming in from the north, portending rain. Despite the chill of the night sweat pours from my body, drenching my loose black robes. My conditioning is excellent, but stealth is exhausting. The breeze which slices through the top of the grass does not penetrate down to my level. Fortunately, I can sense that the security and relative darkness of the forest is getting closer one agonizing pace at a time, marking the end of my slow crawl through the grass.

I halt my crawl, just for few moments, to focus my sense. The closer I get to the outpost, the closer I am to the danger that sits patiently within. Even now I can sense him nibbling at the edges of my awareness. I should know everything that is happening around me, the movement of all living beings. But there is a hole, a sense of darkness where darkness shouldn't exist. It's near the center of the outpost, and my experience identifies that darkness as the man who is out to end my life.

The grass is just tall enough for me to sit on my calves without being detected, a relief my body thanks me for. With my head higher, I begin to feel the wind brush through my short hair. Breathing deep and filling my lungs, the tension in my body dissolves and I empty my mind just as I was taught many cycles ago.

With stillness comes the sharpening of the sense, and I drink in everything that it whispers. Behind me, two archers have taken up posts in the trees I emerged from just as the moon was beginning to rise. They haven't seen me yet and their eyes and ears are focused outward, not knowing that I'm already behind them. It must be terrifying sometimes, not being able to sense others. To rely only on sight and sound. To know, with the animal instincts we always try to deny, that danger was approaching, but to be unable to detect anything but the peaceful passing of an evening in the woods. The not knowing seems impossible to live with.

But if the archers are afraid, they are professional soldiers, and they do not show it. They are still, arrows loosely nocked in bowstrings, waiting for the slightest hint of unnatural movement in the grass. One of them, higher than his partner, is scanning the grass and surrounding forest in quick sweeps. In other, happier circumstances, I might have laughed. Tonight I am grimly content. He will not find me. I am completely within myself, a ghost, and he does not have the senses necessary to locate the small emptiness only twenty paces ahead of him.

The archers are a threat, but one that can be dealt with. I cautiously expand my senses outward, towards the outpost. Soon I will re-enter the wood and be safe from the wandering eyes of the archers. Then a very short hike to the clearing which surrounds the outpost. This place was designed with secrecy and defense in mind, unique among the southern lands. Beyond the clearing is the wall, twice as high as a man. The south has seen nothing like it before, but more will be built as Lord Akira continues his plans for the expansion of his kingdom.

Everything inside the wall is glowing with life. There are more than thirty soldiers stationed in this outpost, but no women, no children. The signs of fear are overwhelming, palpable against the soothing backdrop of the peaceful woods. They have heard the rumors and they know whom they hunt. Everywhere is the fear of death, of the terror that grips even a courageous heart when it knows that it faces impossible odds.

I know all too well what those soldiers are feeling, for I feel it as well, although not because of the difference in numbers. It is because of who sits in the center of that outpost. I can sense him only as emptiness, blackness at the center of activity. He is also perfectly still, searching for me. I am unsure if he can sense me this far out. In this, at least, I am his superior. But it is in this and this only. By the time I make it to the wall, he will know me, and he will come.

I push aside the darkness, if only for a moment. Our fight is fated to occur whether I want it to or not, and so there is no point in worrying. I expand my sense one more time, seeking out the other two, the reasons I am here. They are both there, even though they are both hard to find. One, because she has camouflaged herself so well, the other because she is barely alive, and is close enough to the Great Cycle that she is almost beyond my sense.

I bring my senses back and let my fingers brush lightly against the hilt of my sword. This sword and I have come a long way to be here, and the sword has been constant, with me from before I had even taken a life.

When the dawn breaks she will be unsheathed again, and although I hold out little hope for myself, I hope that she will taste the blood of the shadow tonight.

CHAPTER 1

The afternoon was cold, a cold that seeped into your bones. In the wide plains of the South Kingdom there were no trees to block the wind, and it tore through the small caravan heedless of the suffering that it caused. The cold spring air was bad enough, but the wind sliced through the travelers' clothing, driving daggers of ice into their skin. Snow whipped around the villagers, creating the illusion of a blizzard, even though the sun burned brightly and helplessly above them in a cloudless sky.

The caravan was barely large enough to be called one, a group of traders from a small village who had walked for four days to reach New Haven, the capitol of the Southern Kingdom. They had been returning home, celebrating an unexpected level of success in the city, when the winds picked up. Trapped in the middle of the plains, just over half-way home, they had no easy choices. Their unofficial guide, the local blacksmith who spent as much time wandering the plains as smithing, believed that they were only a hard day's journey from home. But no one was sure of their exact location anymore. In the wind and blowing snow, the signs that marked the trail were no longer visible, and the plains that were visible appeared the same no matter which direction they looked.

There were only a dozen people in the caravan. Three elders, who had come along to aid in the bargaining, the blacksmith and two families. The first family was a merchant who had brought textiles and weavings from the village as well as his wife and son. The boy was thirteen cycles of age and rebelled against his surname. The whole trip he had been nothing but a nuisance. He wanted to be a great warrior, and so followed without end the two soldiers who had been hired as an escort. This often caused him to wander away from the events that his father had planned for him, an introduction to the business of trading in New Haven.

A farming family rounded out the group, a relatively young but well respected couple whose first and only son was with them. He had just seen the passing of his fifth cycle, and the trip to the big city had been his first, a late gift from his family.

The travelers brought warm clothes, but they were not prepared for a storm of this ferocity and duration. Spring in their village was a fickle time. There were plenty of storms, some severe, but they occurred infrequently enough that the elders, hardened by cycles and cycles of life, ignored the potential threat. Travel to the city was somewhat rare during the spring, but the weather had been calm, if cold, and an early start to trading would increase the revenue throughout the village. It had been a calculated risk, but one that had backfired. The travelers did not often see storms like the one they were caught in, and as the wind continued to howl with no end in sight, worry began to build into fear. Death by freezing seemed like a much more likely possibility the longer the storm lasted.

After following the blacksmith through the afternoon, dissension rose among the group. No one recognized any landmarks even though the smith assured them they continued to get closer to home. Seeing no end to the storm's fury, the travelers decided to stop and try to maintain a fire. After the herculean efforts of four of the men of the party, a small fire was started, and all twelve of the caravan huddled together for warmth. Even the soldiers, who had stood firm against the brunt of the storm, decided it wisest to be as close as possible to the burning wood.

The travelers could not see the sun set, but as it grew darker discussion of their options became more cynical and more heated. Fear was growing, gnawing its way into the stoutest hearts of the group, and rationality crumbled before heightened emotions. The blacksmith continued to swear that they were close, and that it was no more than half a day's journey to home. He looked to continue the journey by night, to make it to the village before daybreak. The elders were hesitant and divided, and the soldiers were of no help at all.

It was the merchant who became the strongest proponent of continued travel. He didn't like being away from the comforts of hearth and home, and his growing nervousness made him restless to move on. "These are not safe lands. We are in the open and defenseless, with goods and gold to tempt any traveling band of raiders. The best way to minimize our risk is to be out on the road for as short a time as possible. We should continue."

The soldiers quietly added their assent. Part of the regional militia, they had only been blooded earlier this cycle, and eager to avoid conflict. The elders also nodded. Although the merchant was the wealthiest of the group, and the unofficial leader of the caravan, tradition and honor demanded that the elders make the final decision.

The farmer looked around the group and saw that no one dared contradict the merchant. The man was powerful in town, and speaking against him was an expensive proposition. But the farmer worried about his family, and he viewed the dangers of being lost in the open during a blizzard to be far more threatening than a band of raiders in this weather. After a moment's hesitation, he spoke, "I worry that we are not as close as we believe. I live on the land that approaches our village, and I do not recognize these surroundings at all. To leave the fire is to endanger the health of my son and wife. Let us instead camp by the fire. This same blizzard which pins us down surely keeps the bandits in the holes they dig for themselves. It is safer to travel by day, warmed by what heat the sun can give us. The young, and the old," he added, with a meaningful glance to the elders, "would be unwise to travel in such cold conditions, away from the warmth of camp."

The elders, sitting together, took their time conferring. The merchant and blacksmith exchanged chagrined looks as the farmer looked on. They were well used to the deliberation of elders. Their caravan was filled with younger people and waiting patiently for the elders did not come naturally. The merchant and blacksmith exchanged some whispers, but the farmer held his tongue. It was a common practice to malign the indecisiveness and slowness of the elders, but the farmer didn't join in. Someday he'd be an elder, and would rather have respect than half-hidden whispers.

The elders reached a decision before frostbite settled in. The oldest of the elders acted as their spokesperson as tradition mandated. "The farmer is right. Traveling in these conditions is more dangerous than the risk of bandits. We will leave at first light, assuming that the storm has abated."

The merchant stepped forward, his mouth half open in protest before his wife's hand on his arm restrained him. The elders' decision was final, and the soldiers were bound to the will of the elders. Although upset by the decision, launching a public protest would do him no good and only hurt his trade upon their return to the village. He had two options open to him. He could either take his family and leave without the support of the soldiers, or he could abide by the decision of the elders.

The farmer watched the merchant closely out of the corner of his eye. Although outward appearances suggested he was a simple peasant, a man tied to the land, he was well known in the village for his quick intellect and insight. When he had been younger, growing up, the elders had suspected he possessed some degree of sense ability, but he had always denied any affinity for it, and he had never passed the tests the monks administered to all children throughout the Three Kingdoms. The farmer knew he had made an enemy of the merchant, at least for a time. Rates of exchange would be unfavorable at the merchant's, and he would have to trade in other villages. The information was filed away with the rest of the tidbits of information he kept in his head.

The farmer's gaze lingered upon the merchant for a moment more, then moved back to his family. His worries melted like the snow around the fire when he saw his son. The boy was too young to understand the disagreement that had just taken place, and he was content to be nestled between his mother and the fire. The farmer was proud of his son on this trip. The child was a prodigy, apparent to everyone who met him. He had learned to speak well much faster than any child the elders remembered. At the age of five he asked questions of everyone and everything, and his recollection was impeccable. The farmer had been hesitant to bring his son to New Haven, but his fears had been ungrounded, and the trade he had bargained for had been much better than what he would have gotten if he had relied on the merchant to sell their goods.

The farmer had always been quick to encourage his son's curiosity, indulging any pastime and interest with genuine encouragement. He never lied to his son and let him ask whatever was on his mind. But in the city they had not made much progress through the streets as the boy stopped every two steps to ask questions of anyone who would listen, and several of the questions had bordered on inappropriate. It marked the first time the farmer asked his son to hold his questions for a while so they could conduct their business. The boy had, true to character, asked why, and the father hadn't been able to decide whether to be frustrated or laugh in submission to his son's undying curiosity. Fortunately, the son heeded the father, and he asked only the burning questions until they left the city outskirts. Almost as soon as they passed the final houses, he started rattling off question after question.

The farmer forced his attention to the present. The camp was in motion, preparing shelter for the evening. Since the matter had been decided, it only took the group a short time to build up the fire and collect more wood from the caravan's stores. Watches were decided for each of the soldiers, and both the merchant and farmer agreed to stand a watch.

In time they all fell asleep in a ring around the fire, sheltered by wagons and beasts. The watches went by without incident, and before long the darkness gave way to the gentle but insistent push of the rising sun. As was their custom, the farmer's family was up to greet the daylight. At home there was always much work to be done, and daylight was the most precious of resources. The soldiers woke next, accustomed to the routine of the garrison, while the merchants and the elders were last to rouse themselves.

The dawning of the new day raised the spirits of everyone in the party. Doubts of survival were laid to rest as a strengthening sunlight broke through the clouds. All the men had maintained a stoic exterior throughout the night, but each of them, at least once, had wondered if the snow and wind would overpower the fire and their ability to stay warm.

Hopes gave way to a creeping unease as it was discovered that the blacksmith had left camp. The soldier who had been on watch last said the blacksmith had woken up early, just before the breaking of the sun, to find the way. The farmer and merchant set aside their differences and agreed that even if that was the case, he should have returned by the time the camp was up and ready.

The news sparked another round of discussion between the traders. The elders believed the blacksmith had found his way home and decided the comfort of hearth and home were more important than the well-being of the travelers. The events of the past few days had convinced them that the man had been a poor choice for a guide. The village must be nearby and the blacksmith must have assumed the rest could find their way easily.

Another possibility was the blacksmith himself had gotten lost. The elders were quick to point out that if the blacksmith had not made it home this was the other most logical explanation. Although the elders didn't know the blacksmith's fate, they were certain whatever occurred was due to the ineptitude of the blacksmith. It was a consensus the merchant quickly agreed with.

The final option, voiced by the farmer but dreaded by all, was that the blacksmith had been attacked by bandits. The elders and merchant were quick to dismiss this idea, to the hearty agreement of the soldiers. No bandits would venture out in this weather. Any problems were certainly of the blacksmith's own making.

The farmer did not argue, but saw the eyes of the elders dart back and forth. The farmer reflected that fear was always based in the unknown, and there was enough unknown to cause anyone to fear. He sympathized. The farmer had known the blacksmith for many cycles, and although he was not known for his competence in metalwork, the farmer did have to admit that no one knew the land better. It seemed much more likely to the farmer that the blacksmith had come to harm, either accidental or intentional. He held out hope he was wrong, but felt in his heart he wasn't.

After the options were debated, the elders decided that the farmer, knowing the land the best of those left, would be the one to take them home. The farmer objected, claiming he did not know the area they were in, and to depart would be even more dangerous than staying. However, the elders were insistent, and they wanted to be home. The farmer had no choice but to accept the position of guide.

The farmer shared his concerns softly with his wife, who said little. The farmer always appreciated that detail about her. His wife did not complain about the burdens of daily life, or even those that transcended the day-to-day. Instead of complaining and evaluating, she acted. Often listening to her husband's observations and internal debate, she would silence him with a quick gesture and ask, "So what are you going to do?"

She would not let him over-think too much, and whatever his answer was, she set about to putting it in motion. The same was true today. Staying or going, if there were bandits, there wouldn't be any safety. There was no complaint or overt fear in her eyes. She instinctively brushed her right hand over the belt that held her winter garb together. Cleverly hidden behind it was a small, exceptionally sharp dagger. The farmer knew she had no training, but was certain she would not hesitate to use it well if the situation required.

The party, now eleven, moved forward as best as the farmer could determine. He knew which way they had been heading last night and figured his best bet would be to follow in the same direction. He was optimistic that soon they would be in lands he would recognize.

For a moment the farmer allowed himself to hope. The sun, although low, was shining brightly, reflecting off the snow, creating a bright, clear day. The fresh snow crunched underneath their feet, and for a while everything seemed perfectly right with the world.

The farmer's feeling of perfect contentment passed like the sun behind a storm cloud as he came over a rise. On the other side stood eight men with dark, ragged cloaks, standing in the intended path of the party as if they didn't possess a care in the world. Although the bandits were outnumbered, the farmer knew the trading party had no chance. They only had two swords to the bandit's eight. He turned around, and his last act in life was to attempt to tell his wife to run. The cloaks moved with incredible speed through the snow, and cold steel was through his heart before he could finish his yell.

There was a moment of complete shock when nobody in the caravan moved. It happened too suddenly for them to process. But within moments the scene erupted into mass, uncontrollable panic. The two soldiers, green as fresh spring grass, stood tall against the assault, but were cut down without even drawing blood. The rest of the group attempted to scatter to no avail as they were rapidly rounded up by the dark cloaks who corralled them into a small circle. They encountered no resistance besides the guards. None in the caravan were warriors and shock had stolen any rationality they possessed. Resistance was the quickest path to death, and it is always better to lose one's money than one's life. There was hope among the group that the bandits would not want further blood on their hands.

The bandits had no such thoughts. They had already committed murder, and murder was always punishable by death in the South Kingdom. They knew they were safer with no survivors. It took them only moments to seize possession of all the travelers' goods, so next they took the merchant's wife. Although older than the farmer's wife, her skin was not cracked and hardened from cycles toiling in the sun. She was soft, and even after two brutal days on the road, retained some semblance of the sensuality that had drawn the merchant's eye many cycles ago.

It was too much for the woman, and she began to cry, fight, and scream. She could bear to lose her money, but not this. They grabbed her, treating her no better than an animal. She knew her future and refused to accept it. She was queen of their little village in all but title, and she believed herself noble. This happened to peasants. She pointed at the farmer's wife and yelled at her captors to take her instead. She yelled and kicked until one bandit struck her with enough force to daze her. As she recovered her senses her eyes pleaded desperately for her husband to take some action to stop what was about to happen, but he couldn't see.

The merchant kept his head down, trying to shut out the sights and sounds surrounding him. His wife saw the ultimate cowardice of her husband, and she lost all tension in her body as though dead. Her eyes flickered from pleading and desperation to fury and finally to resignation. Twenty cycles together and the merchant would not even raise his head to comfort his wife, much less risk his life.

But their son would. One of the militia soldiers had fallen only a couple of paces away from the boy, and the bandits were more focused on the merchant's wife than on their prisoners. Over the past days, the soldiers thought there could be no end of the boy's dreams of becoming a great warrior. His head was full of the stories of the nightblades in the Great War, and he saw himself as the second coming of those legendary warriors. The militiamen had allowed him to take part in their morning exercises, and went so far as to pretend he was a great swordsman, a natural talent. They saw it as a kindness, and the boy knew it as fate. Today he saw his chance, saw himself rising as a hero to the village, saving the elders and his father and mother from the bandits. He had heard the stories of swordsmen defeating groups of twenty to thirty men, so he thought nothing of only eight.

The boy rushed to the fallen sword. He swung it up and made his first cut before the bandits realized their danger. By then it was too late, and to the boy's credit, his cut was true. He almost severed a bandit's neck, getting his new sword stuck in between the bones of the spine. The three bandits who had taken the wife held her still to watch while the remaining four bandits drew their swords and cautiously circled the boy. Every one of the villagers was speechless. In the village, the child was well-known as a spoiled brat, mocked by the elders and his own parents for his foolish dream. Sons of merchants did not become warriors. But his last day proved them all wrong although none would remember it. The boy's bravery far surpassed his father's. He did not back down and defended himself well, though the outcome was never in question. It took several strikes from different swords before the boy finally fell, bleeding from several cuts that should have been immediately fatal.

The merchant seemed not to notice what had transpired, so frightened he was unable to even lift his head. His wife couldn't tear her eyes away from her son's battle. She had felt him too spoiled, but was proud to have been wrong. She took one last glance at her husband and knew there was nothing left for her in this world. She was eager to join her son in the Great Cycle. She stopped struggling against her captors, and in the moment they relaxed their grip, she broke free, grabbed one of their daggers and ran it roughly across her own neck.

The rapid chain of events left everyone, including the bandits, in a state of surprise. They had lost one of their friends and a defenseless woman in the space of a few heartbeats. Their leader, a man larger and stronger than the others, calmed them, directing them to get the prisoners in a tighter circle. Order reasserted itself, and the leader took stock of the situation. They had their loot, but the boys were still eager for more. It had been a long, hard winter, and with the spring their libidos and blood lust were as high as he had ever seen them. And they had just lost their prize. There was still one woman, and although she wasn't as pretty, the boys wouldn't care. They were safe enough out here in the middle of nowhere. He motioned to the farmer's wife, and the bandits grabbed her without hesitation. She didn't have the soft skin of the merchant's wife, but she was a woman, and that was enough.

Her son, so curious and so brave, rushed towards his mother in an incoherent attempt to do something, anything. He was picked up easily by one of the bandits and restrained without problem. None of the men, none of the elders, no one so much as raised their voice to protest the crime which happened next. They still believed that silence was their greatest defense. The boy was made to watch as the bandits took his mother on the cold ground. He didn't know about her knife, but other men held her arms still while another was between her legs. They were taking no chances. When all willing were satiated, the bandits pulled the mother over to the boy by her hair.

Unable to move her legs, she tried to stand but had to be thrown through the snow the last remaining paces to her son. She did not say anything, couldn't say anything, but she somehow held on to the last shred of her dignity and pride, the piece that no violence could take away. Her eyes did not burn with hatred, nor did they reflect the calmness of resignation. If the boy didn't know any better, he'd say that his mother's eyes were smiling. Later in life he would see that same look, and he would realize it was hope. Hope that despite everything, he would have a better life. He would never forget her final moments.

One of the bandits casually stuck his sword down through her, pulling it out slowly. He laughed as he watched her life blood flow out of her as though he'd just heard a joke that was kind of funny. With a quick flick of his wrist, he snapped the blood on his sword onto the boy. He chuckled, but left the boy alone. The boy watched the life leave his mother's eyes. But even in his shock, the boy's mind was working, and he cataloged his mother's killer as the leader.

The rest of the work happened quickly. The bandits were seasoned and went around slicing the throats of the rest of the party with a ruthless lack of concern. It was quick work, done without hatred or malice. It was business, no different than slaughtering cows. The farmer's boy understood the truth the other villagers did not. The bandits had killed already. To leave witnesses increased the odds of capture and prosecution. Robbery was one matter; murder another, with much stricter penalties. Killing the rest was just good practice – safety first.

The boy was held tightly by one of the bandits and was unable to move against the much stronger grip. Forced into the role of a spectator, the boy could not help but bring his power of observation to bear on the unbearable scene taking place before his eyes. Of the elders, the oldest was resigned to his fate. In a last show of bravery, he bared his neck and stared his killer in the eyes. He died without a sound. The other two elders whimpered and tried to scamper away, but were easily caught and killed before they could get more than a few paces.

The merchant was the most interesting to the boy. He, whose hope for life had made him a coward, found his strength in the face of certain death. With no other option he raged, attempting to defeat his captors. But with no weapon and no training in defense he was beaten and mocked by the bandits before he was finally silenced for good. They held the man in disdain, the man who wouldn't fight for what was his.

After all was done, it was only the boy left. The bandit the boy had identified as the leader walked up to him. "Well, boy, this is business." His voice held a trace of an apology, a tone the boy found strange considering the circumstances.

The boy looked his murderer in the eyes. He would show no fear to this man.

The leader, despite his cruelty, was observant. "The boy is brave. Do you wish to join us? We could use someone to keep camp for us. We can train you how to fight."

The boy's mind was racing, thinking of the answers and the consequences. Looking from the corpses strewn around him to the leader, he spoke with a soft voice. There was no defiance, none of the hatred the bandit leader had observed before. "No."

The bandit leader studied the boy. He was not trying to stare him down or offer foolish intimidation or threats. He was only a couple of cycles old, but he knew the cost of his answer, and was unwavering. For a young boy, he seemed much older than he was. The risk of taking on a personality that strong was not worth the potential benefits of trying to convert him.

Turning to the boy, he spoke again. "It was well said, son. I respect that." He looked up to the man holding the boy. "Kill him."

The boy did not close his eyes. He had seen the cowardice of many in the group and swore that he would represent his family with honor. There was a soft rush of air past his head, and the boy waited for the transition to the Great Cycle. But there was no pain. After a moment of confusion the boy discerned that the grip which had been holding him in place was loosening. He glanced up and saw a throwing knife lodged deep into his captor's throat. His captor, suitably surprised, dropped to his knees unable to breathe.

A man appeared out of nowhere. He was of average height and wore clothes of white that blended in with the snow in the background. He spoke, and his voice, while deep, still seemed soft to the boy. "That's enough."

The bandits all turned to face the stranger. Disbelief was etched on the leader's face, mirrored by the boy's. There were still six bandits left. It was suicidal to go against those odds. No one fought six men and lived to tell the story. It was great for the storytellers, but the young boy wasn't fooled by stories like the merchant's son had been. It didn't happen in the real world. But the stranger was calm, as if he'd stopped by on a morning walk to say hello to a neighbor. His sword was sheathed, and his hands were open and relaxed at his sides.

The leader spoke with confusion and a trace of nervousness in his voice, "Who are you?"

"Shigeru. I've been tracking your group since the last farmstead you raided. I was asked by the girl you barely left alive to kill you."

The bandit nodded. "Should have killed that bitch quickly. What is your family name? A man of your confidence must come from one of the Great Houses."

"I have none."

The boy saw the tension in the leader's shoulders dissipate. No last name meant an outcast, a bandit or rogue with no formal training. The stranger standing in front of him may be an excellent throw with a knife, but would be dead within minutes. With a nod of his head the five remaining bandits rushed at the stranger, swords drawn. The boy watched with open eyes, unable to turn away. Something about the stranger's attitude drew all of his attention.

The stranger stepped forward into the rush, moving with calm steps. What struck the boy as unusual was that the stranger did not seem to move much. His cuts all blended into one beautiful motion. There was never even the clang of steel on steel. When he stepped out of the back end of the rush of bandits, the boy would have sworn that they had been play-fighting, unwilling to actually meet steel.

The impression vanished with the spirits of the bandits. The five men collapsed, and within the space of a couple of breaths they had stopped moving altogether. Their leader was the only one standing, and although he stood tall, the boy could almost smell the fear radiating off of him. He was much bigger than the stranger dressed in white, but size wasn't going to save him.

"Who are you?" The bandit leader asked again.

"Shigeru," stated the enigmatic man.

"Your name is no answer, where did you learn how to do that? I have never seen moves like that."

"Nor will you again." The statement was made without a change in inflection.

The bandit held his sword out in a defensive stance as the stranger took two paces forward. The boy stared, intent on watching what happened. He thought for a heartbeat that he felt the movement of the stranger. He blinked, and it was untrue. The two warriors had not moved. They stood two paces apart, the stranger with his sword held low and behind him, the bandit with his blade held straight in front of him.

The boy wondered if they would stand that way forever. The bandit held his stance, as firm as he could, while the stranger was relaxed. In time, the bandit's stance began to falter, but he was without options. Turning his back would mean immediate execution, but an aggressive cut seemed equally unlikely to succeed. He was most safe as he stood, but he couldn't lower his guard without risk.

The outcome was inevitable. The bandit, either out of frustration or the realization that there was no other option, switched to an offensive stance and stepped forward. The stranger, as relaxed as ever, moved forward as well. Again there was no clang of steel, but the bandit fell without a sound. The stranger flicked his wrist, and blood snapped off his blade. He withdrew a cloth from the folds of his robe and wiped down his blade before sheathing it in one smooth motion. He was unhurried and thorough. The boy got the impression he had done this many times before.

The process only took a couple of breaths, and when he was done he turned his attention to the boy. The boy, earlier fascinated, now felt the slow but steady growth of the taste of fear in his mouth. He had never seen anybody like the stranger. He thought quickly. Behind him the stranger's throwing knife was embedded in the bandit who once held him captive. It wasn't much, but it was a hope. He could grab the knife and throw before the stranger reached him.

The stranger stopped where he was. "You need not worry about me, boy. I have no intent to harm you. Leave the knife where it is."

The boy started. He had made no motion towards the knife and was confident he hadn't even glanced towards it. The pieces fell into place in his head, and the boy found his natural curiosity overwhelming his fear. "You can sense, can't you?" He put a strong emphasis on the word sense, savoring the sound of it like a rare dessert, something one got to experience only occasionally, if ever.

The man let the hint of a smile creep into the corners of his mouth. The boy found that with the smile, the stranger who had just slaughtered a group of bandits was kind and warm. The stranger nodded. "My name is Shigeru. What is your name?"

For some reason the question gave the boy pause. He was five, and of course he knew his name, but he couldn't bring himself to speak it. Some quality in this man wouldn't allow him to speak. His tongue, always quick with questions, was thick and heavy. His mind, quick and sharp, could not form a coherent thought.

The stranger examined him head to toe, and for the first time in the boy's life, he felt like he was no longer the one who was asking the questions. Without saying a word, the stranger managed to look into him. It wasn't that he was being stripped naked, but that somehow this Shigeru was able to look straight into him, unraveling all the paradoxes which defined him as a child. Shigeru held the boy in his gaze and seemed to come to a conclusion. Without warning the boy felt like he had been folded back up into the box of himself. It was disorienting, and it took him a couple of breaths to recover.

"Your name is Ryuu." The stranger mentioned this matter-of-factly, confusing the boy even further. From a literal perspective, the man was wrong, but there was some quality in the name that seemed so right. The boy nodded, implicit agreement with a new reality defined by his new name.

The stranger sat down, calm and unmoving. Ryuu watched Shigeru as he pulled out dried fruit and ate. He offered some calmly to Ryuu, who took it without saying a word. The food tasted wonderful to the boy, who hadn't realized how hungry he was until he started eating. He realized as he ate he didn't recognize all the fruits he tasted. He filed the information away. Wherever Shigeru had come from, it wasn't near here.

Seeing that Shigeru wasn't moving, Ryuu turned to his parents. They lay unmoving on the snow, and for the first time the reality of what had happened started to sink into Ryuu. The grief rose over him and crested like a wave, almost knocking him to his knees. He stood through it, pondering his next move. The first was clear. He needed to take care of his parents.

Shigeru watched without speaking as Ryuu brought his parents together over some straw from the caravan. The work was slow and his parents were heavy, but Shigeru did not offer help and Ryuu didn't ask. He laid them in repose and quickly said a prayer to the Cycle. He took a moment to reflect on all that his parents had given him. Grateful, he took the embers from the caravan's forgotten fire, stoked them back to life, lit a torch, and then carefully touched the flame to his parents' pyre, which was slowly consumed by the fire.

Ryuu watched them burn, but could not bring himself to cry. Not yet.

After the bodies were fully consumed, Shigeru stood up. He re-arranged his limited clothing. Without a word, he turned around and started walking away. Ryuu understood. After one last glance at his parents, Ryuu followed him.

CHAPTER 2

The sounds of battle died away, leaving behind an eerie silence, a natural honoring of the dead. But the smells lingered, impossible to forget. It was the smells that haunted him day in and day out. If he wasn't watched like a hawk by so many, he would have thrown up. But that was not a possibility here.

Prince Akira sat on a horse, his balance and poise reflecting the cycles of training he'd already accumulated despite having only seen ten cycles. He followed his father as they inspected the troops recovering from the battle. They were trying to retake the Three Sisters, the single large pass that exited the south of the Kingdom. To hear his father tell the stories, this battle was just one of a much larger cycle. Ever since the collapse of the Great Kingdom over a thousand cycles ago this pass had been controlled by the Southern Kingdom. It was only in the past fifty cycles that it had become a site of contention between the Southern Kingdom and Azaria, the people to the south of the mountains.

Akira would have loved to see an actual Azarian. The one people, although divided into three kingdoms now, were all the same heritage. Azarians were different. They were supposed to be taller and darker skinned. Every man and woman of their people was said to be equal in battle skill to three of the Southern Kingdom troops. Akira had quizzed his father on the Azarians relentlessly when he had been younger, but his father had always pushed aside his questions. It wasn't until two moons ago he realized it was because his father hadn't known the answers. They only ever encountered the warrior class, and neither nation had managed to push far into the other, due in large part to the Three Sisters.

The Three Sisters was so named because of the triple peaks that rose almost exactly in the middle of the pass, which was a three days journey for an army. The pass was the sole route wide enough to march an army through, but it was still narrow. It was easy to defend and hard to take, which made it a target of prime importance both for the Azarians and for the Southern Kingdom.

According to his father, Lord Azuma, the pass had belonged to the Southern Kingdom for as long as their records lasted. The Southern Kingdom had never pushed south beyond the mountains. The mountains were a natural defense, and the land to the south was desolate. They hadn't even known the Azarians existed until they took the pass for the first time. It kicked off an endless pattern of violence. One side would spend an enormous amount of troops to retake the pass. It was always brutal and slow, and often it would take entire cycles. There was never enough time to establish more than a foothold on the other side of the pass before winter would set in and the pass would close down.

The rulers of each nation had come to realize this, and major offensives in the pass were now rare. There was an unspoken agreement between the two nations, an understanding that the pass could be the death of either nation. The Southern Kingdom faced constant, unrelenting pressure from the Northern and Western Kingdoms, and couldn't spare enough troops to retake the pass and launch a major offensive into Azaria. Besides that, no one was sure Azaria was even worth conquering. No spy or scout had returned yet, another mystery that needed solving someday.

This lack of knowledge intrigued Akira, who was relentless about acquiring knowledge of his world. He knew that someday he would be the Lord of the Southern Kingdom, but even at the age of ten, the idea didn't interest him in the least. He wanted to understand this world, know the people and the places, and see it all.

Azuma had inconveniently interpreted his son's curiosity about the Azarians as the battle dreams of a future Lord. Akira's father had been made on the battlefield and he expected the same from his son. Every day Akira trained in the use of the sword and already was well known for his skill even though he never wished to use it in battle. He had already decided, although he never told his father, that if he did become Lord he would be a diplomatic Lord.

Despite his gentle protests, Akira landed here at the front line of the largest campaign the Southern Kingdom had seen in a generation. The Azarians had held the pass now for almost thirty cycles, defending it against the force which was sent against it every year. But Azuma was passionate about retaking the pass. It had been many cycles in the preparation, but the day had come at last.

Every step they took was bloody, harried by archers and ambushes, but their progress was relentless. The sheer number of troops Akira's father was pouring into the pass was terrifying, and the Azarians were retreating, step by blood-soaked step.

Akira's father predicted that within the next quarter moon the Azarians would abandon the pass.

But that was a quarter-moon more to sit through this experience. Akira found that there were parts of battles that were beautiful. The flight of arrows through the air was mesmerizing if one could ignore their intended destination. The order and sound of an army on the march was also thrilling if their steps didn't end at the steel points of their enemies.

Akira maintained a brave face. Even at ten his father had well drilled into him the importance of appearance. He mimicked the same stern expression that was his father's face, and did not allow himself to display any of the emotions that were coursing through his mind. When he and his father were alone, they could talk and speak with refreshing honesty, but if even a servant was nearby the masks fell into place. At ten, Akira couldn't imagine any other way of living.

They finished their inspection even though there wasn't much to inspect. Azuma's army was always in perfect condition. The real purpose was to be out among the troops, build their morale. Lord Azuma was held in mixed regard by the people. Order ruled the Southern Kingdom, but it was a harsh order which rankled many who saw their lifetimes as a time of peace. They were removed from the fighting at the pass and didn't realize the full extent of the effort that went into taking and holding the pass and protecting their borders.

While the civilians had doubts, the army did not. Azuma wasn't just a Lord, but was one of the top generals in the Three Kingdoms. While he was stern he was also fair and kind to his troops. After every major battle or skirmish he was out among them, spreading an encouraging word here, a compliment there. While the people of the Southern Kingdom may have mixed feelings about their Lord, the troops adored him, and Azuma taught Akira it was the troops who kept any ruler in power. Akira could recite the lesson from memory.

Arriving back at the tent was a relief. Akira could shut out a small part of the smell of the battlefield. Incense was lit in the tent, and Akira welcomed its pungent scent.

Akira's father dismissed everyone, including the servants. He finished preparing the tea that had been started for them and served himself and his son. "How are you, son?"

Akira never lied to his father, a lesson he had learned at an early age. His father was a hard man, but a man who believed in truth. Akira had always been punished for lying. He had been punished at times for telling the truth as well, but to a much lesser degree. "It's hard, father."

Akira's father nodded, and Akira was relieved. "It can be, yes. Do you know why we are fighting for this pass?"

Every day, always a test. Ten cycles and he was already sick of it. But Akira answered, "Because then we control the flow of troops. If we control the pass, we take an important step in defending the Southern Kingdom."

Akira's father leaned in. "Yes, but do you get it?"

He didn't.

The Lord of the Southern Kingdom leaned back. "You're not wrong. We need to control the pass to protect our kingdom. But you see only the blood of the soldiers in front of you. That's good. You should always know the cost of what you do. But try to understand the greater implications. The Azarians have held the pass for many cycles, and every cycle we have to launch a bloody campaign to keep them from establishing a sizable foothold. If we can control the pass, we can save hundreds, if not thousands, of lives which are lost every year. Defending the pass is much simpler than taking it. What could you do with thousands of extra troops every cycle?"

He paused, to make sure his son understood. "So it may cost us many lives to retake this pass, but it costs far less over the cycles, and that gives us an advantage in this world. It's hard for me to see good men die as well, but their sacrifice means safety and opportunity for us all. Even though there is a part of me that hates it, I will continue to send men to their deaths as long as I live, so long as it means the safety of those in my Kingdom. Do you understand now?"

Akira couldn't do anything but nod. He had never thought of it in that way, but it made sense.

"Good. It's only through death that we can keep this kingdom alive, son. Remember that, because some day you too will be called on to send men to their graves."

CHAPTER 3

The first time Ryuu laid his head down in the same place two nights in a row was almost a half-moon later. He had never journeyed like this. Every day they walked further than Ryuu's little legs had ever been. Though he had been raised in the fields, his feet grew even more calloused and he stopped asking when they would rest for the night. They walked as long as the sun was up and sometimes longer. Ryuu wanted to complain but wanted Shigeru's respect even more. Every time he formed the thought, he reminded himself that he was traveling with a nightblade! He shut his mouth and focused on putting one foot in front of the other until Shigeru would tell him to stop.

After the first few days Ryuu adapted to the pace. He had never been a heavy child, farm work and little food guaranteed that, but he could feel himself getting lighter and stronger every day. Each day it was just a little easier to keep up with Shigeru. With his parents he had complained about bedtime, but with Shigeru falling asleep was sweet relief.

Every morning was the same routine. Shigeru would shake Ryuu awake, unaware of how strong the shaking was. While Ryuu wiped the sleep from his eyes Shigeru went through his morning movements. The movements were beautiful in a way Ryuu found hard to describe. In some movements he held his sword. Others were empty handed. Ryuu had never seen movements like these before. He had watched the militia guards train, but Shigeru's practice seemed something else entirely. His cuts were quick and blended together into one flawless blur of movement. Ryuu knew it was combat practice, but how it applied to real world combat was beyond him. Whenever he heard Shigeru moving in the morning he would watch through slitted eyelids.

Shigeru never talked about his practice or what the movements meant. Ryuu was burning up with questions, but Shigeru's demeanor restrained him. Shigeru was private and quiet. He was a man you didn't disturb no matter how important your question was. But Ryuu's unwillingness to ask questions fueled his imagination. Coupled with what he had already seen, he was convinced that Shigeru could destroy an army by himself. Sometimes to distract his mind from the relentless walking he would imagine an army over the next rise. His imagination painted vivid scenes of battle in which Shigeru emerged victorious.

Somewhat to his disappointment, danger never materialized. If it did Ryuu wasn't old enough to recognize it. All he knew was that when he was in the company of Shigeru, he felt safe, even from his imaginary armies. He did not worry about food or bandits or any of the dangers of the trail his parents had impressed into him. In his young eyes, Shigeru could do no wrong.

The impression was only strengthened by the types of conversation Shigeru held. He was private but when he spoke he used imagery that Ryuu was unable to process. He would talk as if he wasn't sure what he was supposed to say next. It was as if he had never spoken to a child. On the fifth morning of their journey, Shigeru said, "Our lives are like water, always flowing forward in the streams of time. When we encounter what is unexpected, our best choice is to flow around the obstacle." Then he looked at Ryuu as if he expected a response.

Ryuu, unable to decipher the Shigeru's meaning, nodded his head enthusiastically, hoping that it would pass as comprehension. It had often worked with his parents. Shigeru gave him a knowing smile and let the subject drop. Though he didn't understand, Ryuu would repeat the words to himself over and over, committing them to memory. He was certain that there was wisdom in his words and wanted to be able to understand them one day.

The days cycled in a routine that Ryuu soon relaxed into. They would walk all day, keeping the same pace, stopping only when the sun began to set. They avoided all towns and ate on the move. When the sun began to dip, Shigeru would motion them to a halt. If they were near some trees or brush they would start a small fire. Otherwise they would simply settle down, eat some food, and be asleep by the time the sun went below the horizon.

The days passed in silence, which Ryuu found himself comfortable with. He believed Shigeru did not like to talk, and that was fine. Try as he might, he couldn't stop thinking about what had happened, but he couldn't bring himself to talk about it. The scenes replayed themselves over and over in his head, and his fear of the visions mounted. But then he would glance at Shigeru and the fear would be replaced by anger. Anger at himself. He should have done more to protect his parents, especially his mother. He visualized himself picking up a sword and slaying the bandits by himself. But every time he did, he remembered what had happened to the merchant's son. He had seen firsthand what became of boys who thought they were warriors. But he believed the merchant's boy had died an honorable death and was now relaxing with his parents in the afterlife. Ryuu wondered at times if it would be better if he was dead as well.

After three more days of walking his thoughts turned again, replaced by comforting thoughts of Shigeru and the future. He realized that he was learning a lot from Shigeru just by walking with him. Often they would stop so Shigeru could point to something interesting about the world they were passing through. It was the beginning of Ryuu's education under Shigeru, but it was also the beginning of his healing. He was relearning there was more in the world than death.

Shigeru would point to a flower that if chewed would bring quick relief from minor pains. He could tell where animals were before Ryuu could see them, and the two of them delighted in sneaking up on unsuspecting deer. They weren't successful at it when they started. Ryuu couldn't move without sound like Shigeru could, but by the time they reached Shigeru's hut, Ryuu could make it within twenty paces before the deer would startle. It was some of the most fun he could ever remember having. He loved moving silently, but even though he could sneak up on a deer, he could never get close to Shigeru.

Ryuu realized that Shigeru knew about an entire world he had never known about. It was more than just plants and animals. Shigeru knew the cycles of the stars, and at night he would tell stories about the constellations. Ryuu had heard some stories from his father, but Shigeru's stories were different. They were stories of loss and heroic deeds and hope that transcended life. Even the constellations he pointed out were different. When Ryuu asked why he hadn't heard any of Shigeru's stories, Shigeru replied that his were old stories not told in the Three Kingdoms anymore.

When Shigeru spoke like that, Ryuu wondered where they were going. Shigeru often spoke of the Three Kingdoms as something less than the whole. Ryuu had never heard about anyplace besides the Three Kingdoms, and his mind would flash back to the fruit Shigeru carried. Were they leaving the Three Kingdoms?

As they traveled, the land began to change. Ryuu had grown up farming and knew the land around the farm. The trip to New Haven had been the furthest he had been from home, but the land was much the same, rolling plains that stretched on as far as the eye could see. His young mind imagined all the Southern Kingdom the same, but he found out he was wrong. The plains gave way to dotted woods until they were traveling among young cottonwoods and elms. Ryuu had never seen a forest before, but he felt comfortable in the confined spaces and the trees which muffled the sounds of their footsteps.

Food was never an issue. Almost every day Shigeru would motion them to a halt and pull out a throwing blade. Ryuu noticed that every time he drew a throwing blade, he would dip it in a small hide that was tied into one of the myriad knots of his belt. Ryuu didn't know what was in the bag, but he knew every time Shigeru hit his target, which was every time he threw, the animal stopped moving. He also discovered when he tried to touch the blades that Shigeru wouldn't let him near the blades until he had wiped them clean.

It was during a hunt that Ryuu began to get a clearer idea of the man he was traveling with. When Shigeru would motion for him to stop he would keep moving forward, and Ryuu, despite his best efforts, couldn't even hear a whisper in the grass as he moved. It was rare that Ryuu even saw what Shigeru was throwing at. His hand would snap forward, always surprising Ryuu, and wherever the knife landed they would inevitably find small game, a hare or squirrel. Ryuu realized he was with someone who wasn't even supposed to exist in the Three Kingdoms anymore.

It was the hunting that pushed Ryuu's curiosity past the breaking point, and he began asking questions as he had of his parents. He wanted to know how Shigeru found the prey, how he moved without a sound, and how he threw so well. Although they never stopped walking, Shigeru would often take the time to explain, at least in basic terms, what he was able to do. Shigeru talked about the sense and what it was, how it worked. Ryuu didn't understand what Shigeru was saying, but he listened to every word, doing his best to memorize everything. He didn't understand it today, but he figured it might save his life tomorrow.

Their journey continued, taking them from the new woods Ryuu had fallen in love with to older woods. Where the young woods maintained an atmosphere of welcoming embrace, Ryuu felt claustrophobic among the old trees. Their branches extended impossibly high into the sky, blocking out light and sound. The creatures made noises Ryuu did not recognize, and every shadow held danger. Again, Ryuu wondered where their final destination would be.

It came without warning or fanfare at a small hut. The building was small and had been built not too long ago. Ryuu had some small practice taking care of their farm and recognized that the hut was well built. The wood had been joined together well and there weren't seams what would allow rain or snow to get in. The thatching was well done. It was apparent that great care had been taken in the construction of the building.

Even after living in the open plains, the hut was more secluded than any place Ryuu had ever been. He had known little but the farm and was used to empty space, but this was different.

Once they had entered the old woods any trace of humanity disappeared. It was more than not seeing a town or house. They hadn't even seen footpaths that denoted human travel. Ryuu, his curiosity overflowing, hounded Shigeru. Even at five, Ryuu could tell that it was excellent land and that there should be people everywhere.

Shigeru grinned at Ryuu's curiosity. Ryuu had noticed that his attitude was more relaxed now. "Most people avoid the old woods. Throughout the Three Kingdoms there are stories told to scare people from going in. People still fear them. These trees have seen more of our lives than we can imagine. These were old woods before your grandfather's grandfather was even born. They are full of darkness and shadows, and people believe that these woods are haunted. They fear what they don't understand."

As Shigeru explained, Ryuu glanced around and believed he could feel a chill in the air. He chided himself for letting his imagination get the better of him, but the shadows cast by the trees still seemed threatening. The question had to be asked. "Don't you believe in the ghosts?"

Shigeru laughed, the first time Ryuu had heard him do so. The sound startled him in his already nervous state. "I'm not sure. I'm open to the possibility. I've never encountered anything that would provide proof of ghosts. The old woods have their dangers, but ghosts aren't one of them. That being said, I do sometimes help the nearby villages believe in the superstitions. My privacy keeps me safe."

"No one knows you're here?"

"No. I only go to the villages occasionly, but I go to different villages, only returning to one after many moons have passed. They believe I'm a traveling doctor. I sell some mixtures that I make here, heal when I can. It's nothing special, but my techniques are effective and some are beyond what is practiced here in the Three Kingdoms. It provides me some money when I have need of it."

Shigeru brought Ryuu into the hut. He wasn't surprised that it was bare. A small collection of cooking necessities was stacked near a wall, but otherwise the space was empty save for a mat on the floor. Ryuu looked around and was bored in a moment. He had hoped for more weapons.

The next few days were uneventful. The hut and the surrounding forest was a young boy's perfect playground, and Ryuu took full advantage of the space. He explored the woods as far as he dared and was delighted to find a small waterfall only a short walk through the forest from the cottage. Shigeru told him not to wander beyond the distance of the waterfall and let him know that the evening meal would be just after dusk each evening. Beyond that he gave no further rules and allowed Ryuu to do as he pleased. He let Ryuu have the mattress and slept sitting up against the wall of the hut, his sword held in front of him.

The lack of interaction suited Ryuu perfectly. He had always been fascinated by the world around him and the new environment provided countless days of exploration and wonder. He hated chores at home not because he hated work, but because they took away his freedom to explore. Here he spent his days as he wished, digging under rocks and studying plants and animals he had never seen before. When that became boring he allowed his imagination to take the best of him, and he was Shigeru, slaying groups of bandits and making them serve him at his leisure. Innumerable trees felt the sting of a sword shaped branch against their trunks as Ryuu reenacted battle after battle.

Shigeru stayed near the hut, working in the garden and going through his movements every morning. Sometimes he would leave for a short time, but Ryuu didn't ask why. Despite his growing familiarity with Shigeru he still wasn't comfortable. Shigeru was so strong and quiet it was hard not to be a little intimidated even if Ryuu knew it was foolish. He accepted that Shigeru was some sort of nomadic wanderer, and he always reappeared in the evenings in time for the meal, which was all that mattered to Ryuu.

When the sun set Ryuu struggled to maintain the illusion of control he felt during the day. Evenings reminded Ryuu of his family. Night had been the time when his family would come together for their meal and share the events of the day. It hadn't always been fun, but it had always been family, and Ryuu didn't realize what that meant until he didn't have one anymore.

During the day he convinced himself that he was fine and he just had a couple of days off from chores to run around and be a child. He kept himself active enough that it was easy to do. Being busy and throwing himself into a new environment kept his mind off of what had happened. But at night there was little to do except speak with Shigeru. And while Shigeru was certainly polite and the most interesting man Ryuu had ever met, he wasn't mother and father. It was at night that Ryuu remembered the images burned into his memory: the death and corpses of his mother and father, the last stand of the merchant's son. He kept seeing his father turn around with his last breath, trying to warn his loved ones, but it was too late.

It was at night he would cry. It would start as a single tear, but he knew from experience that once the first tear fell, he would lose all control. His sobs wracked his body, but he didn't dare make a sound. He didn't want Shigeru to know this weakness. He knew Shigeru was a man who had withstood everything that had been against him in life. And although Ryuu had only been with Shigeru for about a moon, he knew that Shigeru had never cried.

The days began to pass in a manner that could almost be called routine, if life after trauma can ever be considered routine. Ryuu spent the days outside wandering in the wilderness or helping Shigeru tend the gardens. As he settled into the routine he started to help out with more of the chores. Not because Shigeru asked, but because it was the right thing for him to do. Shigeru had taken him in and saved his life. The nights, despite the heat of the fire in the hut, were cold and lonely, and Ryuu felt every minute of them, tears falling down his cheeks in silence.

While Ryuu passed the days in relative peace, Shigeru was busy. His life for almost ten cycles had been structured. He raised enough food for one. He wasn't worried about more food, but it did require more work. It was another mouth to feed and another body to clothe. The garden which he maintained was larger than he needed, but could not support two through the cycle. It would have to be enlarged. Clothes would not be an issue. He had more money than he would ever be able to spend from selling medicine in surrounding communities.

Shigeru also had to gather more information. The journey had taken him much longer than he had expected. Of course, he hadn't expected to come back with a child in tow. He needed to make a circuit of the surrounding villages, both to ensure the safety of his hut and to gather the latest news in the Southern Kingdom. He stayed alive by staying silent and aware of everything happening around him.

Spring was dawning on the land, which meant war. The Three Kingdoms remained at relative peace although there continued to be talk of unusual troop movements. The Lord of the Southern Kingdom, Lord Azuma, was well known as a cunning leader. He ruled by strength, and although there was often talk against him, the Kingdom was peaceful and prosperous. Yes, those who spoke too loudly against the Lord had a tendency to disappear, but the Kingdom was stable. It was that very stability that brought Shigeru to the Southern Kingdom in the first place.

Last fall, Lord Azuma hadn't allowed his men to return from their annual campaign in the Three Sisters. Talk in the village closest to Shigeru was that Azuma had moved the deployment schedule. Typically troops returned from the Sisters in the fall, allowing families to be together and the harvest to get finished. Shigeru noted that having the young men back in the fall always seemed to produce a strong batch of offspring the following summer. Shigeru doubted that was an accident. Rumors were that the troops would now be coming home in the spring, but Shigeru didn't believe that. Azuma was massing for a campaign.

Last fall there had been nothing to do but wait and see. Odd troop movements by themselves didn't concern Shigeru. However, if Azuma was plotting a major action in the Three Sisters, Shigeru would consider leaving the Southern Kingdom. Stability was part of his cloak. If there was a chance of the Kingdom falling into outright warfare, he would need to leave. Caution was the better part of valor.

Despite Shigeru's need for information, the actions of a Lord hundreds of leagues away did not concern him as much as Ryuu did. Taking him in had been an impulsive move, the sudden and unexpected culmination of his journey. The boy was different. He possessed the gift of the sense. That much was obvious in the first few moments Shigeru had laid eyes on him. But the boy didn't know it. He watched the boy from a distance as he played in the woods. He observed the boy's reenactment of battles, slaying all the trees surrounding the hut in the process. He assessed the boy's intelligence through conversations at meals and while in the garden. Ryuu had an impressive thirst for knowledge, a trait Shigeru assumed had been cultivated by his parents. Shigeru appreciated the constant stream of questions even though he wasn't ready to answer many of them yet. He had much still to decide.

It was the evenings that were most difficult. Shigeru sensed the boy at night while he cried. It was almost impossible for him not to. The boy was quiet, and even Shigeru's practiced ear could barely catch the sound of the boy sobbing night after night. But his sense was almost overwhelmed by the boy's power. The boy had the gift of the sense, but it manifested in the old way, a way Shigeru hadn't sensed since coming to the mainland. Most with the gift shone like bright candles, burning the space around them with their abilities until they learned the rudimentary levels of control taught in the monasteries. Any individual attuned to the sense could feel them coming from leagues away.

The boy was an anomaly, at least here. Shigeru could feel the overwhelming strength of the boy's sense, but instead of a burning ball of energy, it was as if he was extending whip-like tentacles of energy around his body. They were faint but at the same time stronger than any lines of sense Shigeru had felt in many cycles. The boy was gathering in more information than he could imagine, he just had to open his mind to it. Shigeru knew the boy was five cycles old. He should have been tested by the monks by now. At first it was difficult to believe that Ryuu had not been taken by the monks, but Shigeru wondered if the very nature of Ryuu's sense hid him from a monk's rudimentary tests. What Shigeru would have given to meet Ryuu's father and mother.

Regardless, Shigeru was faced with the most significant decision he had faced since he escaped the island. The boy had no family, immediate or extended, that he could be returned to. Shigeru knew people that would welcome the boy into their arms. He could grow up to live a more normal life. But Shigeru sensed something greater unfolding before him. Shigeru wasn't a big believer in fate, but it could not be a coincidence that when he left on his journey this boy was at the end of his path. Fate seemed to be twisted around this boy, leaving little doubt in Shigeru's mind that this was meant to be.

The decision would impact him beyond just training the boy. It would mean stepping out of the shadows some day. He had avoided the Blademasters for so many cycles by disappearing. He did not hunt for bandits or display his skill in the courts. Every part of his life was structured around the practice of not arousing attention. Adding a second life to that mix complicated matters and left the door open for circumstances beyond his control. Taking on a student who could carry on his legacy could be the very act that killed them both. That fear prevented him from acting decisively. Instead, he continued to watch from afar, giving Ryuu as little direction as possible. If he believed in anything, Shigeru believed in the power of choice.

The choice was too big for him to make by himself and wasn't really his choice to make at all. Instead he would follow the Path of the Blademasters. The boy would be given his own choice to make. Shigeru would explain everything as clearly as possible and Ryuu would have to decide. It was a lot to ask of one who had only seen five cycles, but it was the only clear path forward. The decision made, Shigeru didn't hesitate, but brought it up at that evening's meal.

At supper that night, Shigeru found he was more nervous than he had been in many cycles. Despite the thought put into his decision, he wasn't sure it was correct. Giving the boy a choice was uncertain and Shigeru found that in the course of the past moon he had developed a certain level of affection for the child. He tried to hide his indecision, but apparently wasn't succeeding. His young companion was able to pick up on it. Although, Shigeru argued in his own defense, Ryuu wasn't a typical child.

"Shigeru, what's wrong?"

Shigeru hesitated. He had rehearsed this moment over and over through the day, but the words no longer seemed right. He struggled to articulate what he wanted to say. Struggled to find the tone he wanted to say it with.

Ryuu looked up from his bowl of noodles. He waited patiently for Shigeru. Shigeru respected that about the boy.

"Ryuu, what do you know about me?" Mentally, Shigeru shook his head. He had wanted to start assertively, to come from a place of power and responsibility. Instead, he had come forward with a question that only indirectly led to what he really wanted to ask. When his own Blademaster had given him this choice, it had seemed much more formal.

The boy looked up. He paused before answering, considering what he had put together. "You're a nightblade, even if they are supposed to be gone from the Three Kingdoms."

Shigeru was surprised to feel an unknown weight lift off his shoulders. The boy spoke without a hint of judgment in his voice. It had been almost ten cycles since anyone had known the truth about him. In this land his kind were hunted without end, the public convinced they were the monsters responsible for the collapse of the Kingdom. In time, stories which had held the truth had become legends and propaganda with little regard to historical events. But Ryuu knew and didn't care. He was the child of farmers though, so perhaps he had never been exposed to the prevailing attitudes. Shigeru hadn't expected such relief at the revelation of his secret. It solidified his resolve.

"Ryuu, you have the skills to become like me. There is a path forward which I can offer. It is one choice out of many. I will offer them to you today, and if you choose to stay with me, I will offer the same choices twice more. It was the same for me when I was growing up. Everyone has three choices, three chances to walk away."

Ryuu answered with conviction, "I would like to stay here with you."

Although Shigeru had expected this, hearing it out loud sent a surge of emotion through him. He checked himself. He had been away from people for far too long. Too much attachment to the boy would cause problems for both of them.

"I understand that, but I want you to understand the choice you will be making. You are young, but the decision must be yours."

Shigeru took a few heartbeats to pause, collecting his thoughts. "Your first choice is to leave this place," Ryuu started, but Shigeru held up his hand for silence. "I know you don't want to leave now, but hear me out. I know people, good families who would love to have a child, or another child. You would be treated as one of theirs and you could live a normal life in relative peace, comfort and prosperity. You could choose your future as you see fit. You would have a last name and status in this world as you grow older."

"And my other choice?"

"You can stay here and I will take you on as my apprentice." Once again Shigeru had to hold up his hand before Ryuu could commit. "You must understand what that means. I myself am masterless, hunted and an outcast both from the people of this land and my own people. I have no last name, nor would you. Life would not proceed as it has this past moon. Training will be difficult. You will wake up early and train mentally and physically all day. There are no breaks and no second chances. You will be cut and you will bleed. I will not abuse you, but neither will I take it easy on you. You succeed or fail on your own terms, and you may die. If you do succeed in the training, you will be hunted and hated for the rest of your life."

"You also need to know this. The nightblades are hated within the Southern Kingdom and throughout all three Kingdoms. Perhaps someday that will change, but it will not happen for many cycles, if at all. If you follow me, you will never have a normal life, a life with friends and family who care for you."

"Finally, there is one other truth that I believe in. Nightblades have always lived by the sword, and throughout history, we have died by the sword. It is very likely that you will die young, cut down by one stronger than you. Or by thirty scared of what you may become. Regardless, very few of us die peacefully in our sleep."

Shigeru gave the boy credit. He didn't jump to one decision or another. He sat in silence and thought. Although the boy didn't know what he was doing, Shigeru could sense the battle of emotions running though his mind. For a moment, Shigeru thought that he might have overdone it and he might have lost the best chance at a pupil he'd ever had.

His fears proved ungrounded.

"I will stay here and train with you."

Shigeru did not reply, but instead offered a bow that went halfway to the ground. The boy bowed all the way to the ground, forehead against the wooden floor of the hut.

The rest of the meal was eaten in uncharacteristic silence. Shigeru had half-expected a fresh barrage of questions regarding training and what was to come next, but none came. Ryuu sat pondering his future, and Shigeru could see on his face that the journey was one that was part over-hopeful imagination, part sadness, and part anger. Shigeru was pleased. He didn't want to train a boy who believed that swordsmanship was only fun and games. It was a hard way of life and an easy way to die.

It was the way of the sword. It was the way of death.

When the meal was finished Shigeru urged the boy to go to bed, even though Ryuu couldn't contain his excitement. His fears had been overwhelmed by his dreams of training. He only got the boy to sleep by repeating, "It will be the hardest thing you have ever done in your life. You will need your sleep."

When Ryuu was awoken in the morning he found that Shigeru had not exaggerated. As the child of a farmer he was used to waking up with the sun, but the sun wasn't even up yet. He was still bleary-eyed from sleep when Shigeru pushed him out of the hut. Ryuu watched as Shigeru lashed two wooden swords to his back in addition to the steel swords which were his constant companions. Together they took off at a trot. For Ryuu, who was only five and much shorter than Shigeru, the trot felt a lot more like a sprint.

Shigeru made it into a game, teasing and prodding Ryuu to try to catch him. As Ryuu's body started to wake up he fell in love with the game. Even though he was quickly exhausted, he found that he was always willing to sprint just one more time with the belief that this would be the time it worked, this would be the time he caught Shigeru. When the game was over Ryuu found they had left behind any terrain he recognized as familiar. His legs agreed. He could feel them wobbling with the effort it had taken him to come this far.

They were still in the old woods in a clearing that was only twenty paces wide at any point. Given the chance to observe his surroundings, Ryuu imagined the clearing as a fort in the woods. The woods they had traveled through had been dense, even thicker than the considerable growth around Shigeru's hut. For a boy of the plains to be enclosed by the majestic trees of the old woods was novel. It excited his imagination.

Forgetting how exhausted he was, Ryuu ran around the clearing, trying to find the best vantage point for spying on the outside world. No matter where he looked, he couldn't see more than a couple of paces in any direction. Even the hint of a footpath they had followed into the clearing twisted in such a manner that it didn't provide a view out of the clearing.

"How did you find this spot?" Ryuu asked, admiration in his voice.

Shigeru did not reply, and Ryuu saw he had taken the wooden swords off his back. A surge of energy and excitement ran through him. Today he would learn how to be a swordsman like Shigeru.

The excitement lasted only as long as it took Shigeru to give Ryuu his first instructions. To Ryuu's great disappointment, he learned that his sword lessons were not to begin right away. Shigeru stood in front of him performing a series of moves that Ryuu was supposed to follow. Almost a cycle ago Ryuu had seen dancers who had visited his village. To him the moves seemed equivalent. What was the purpose of moving without a sword when you were learning how to fight with a sword?

After what felt like a hundred repetitions Shigeru stood back and had Ryuu perform the actions on his own. After several more repetitions Shigeru attacked in the middle of a repetition. Ryuu was caught completely off guard, but his body had become so focused on repetition it was stuck in a rut. His reaction was to finish the movement Shigeru had taught him. He blocked all of Shigeru's light punches.

When the surprise of being attacked had worn off, Ryuu realized that Shigeru was teaching him defensive combinations. What at first seemed to be a dance without purpose was instead a new way of showing his body how to move, how to be effective. Once Ryuu had put the pieces together he threw himself into mirroring and learning Shigeru's movements.

They broke for a quick lunch of berries, dried meat, and rice and then returned to their training. This time Shigeru picked up the wooden swords which had rested so peacefully throughout the morning. The same practice was employed. Shigeru demonstrated a technique. Ryuu copied the technique under Shigeru's critical eye. The sword tip always had to be in a specific spot. His foot placement was just a little off. Ryuu soon realized that Shigeru's only expectation was perfection.

Ryuu learned that there was an exact spot where the sword should be at any given time. If the sword was at the correct point everything fell into place. If the sword was positioned well he could block and cut faster, and all swordsmanship seemed to be about speed and accuracy. Over the course of the afternoon his body responded in less and less time. Ryuu mentioned this once after a practice cut.

"There is a movement to all things in this world. Nothing stands still. Even this planet we are on moves, which is why the sun rises and sets every day. What you are feeling is called centering. Memorize the feeling, make it your home. It applies not just to swordsmanship but to life. A centered opponent is a fearsome enemy. Stay centered and stay alive." Shigeru paused, noticing the puzzled expression on Ryuu's face. "Don't worry, after a couple of cycles of hard training, you will understand what

I am talking about. But it is good to recognize that some things feel right."

Ryuu simply nodded, lost right after Shigeru began speaking. The planet was moving? That was silly.

Shigeru's eyes sparkled, and if Ryuu had thought to guess, he would have guessed that Shigeru was laughing at him. But Shigeru's face betrayed no other emotion and Ryuu was too young to understand his new-found master.

The training went through the day. When they finished, Shigeru again took Ryuu trotting through the woods in a friendly game. When they got back to the hut it was almost dark, and they had just enough time to get a quick meal started before the sun set. Ryuu asked if he could miss the evening meal. He wanted nothing more than to get to bed. His arms and back were sore from swinging the wooden sword, his legs were sore from running, and everything else hurt from the light blows he had taken throughout training.

Shigeru made him eat. Training would be hard every day, but he had to keep his body well conditioned. Ryuu knew Shigeru was right, so he forced food down his throat as well as the tea Shigeru had prepared. As he ate, he realized that the food tasted better than anything he had ever eaten, and he said as much.

"It's because food has become more important to your body, so your body treats it with more respect now."

Ryuu shook his head. He wondered if Shigeru realized he was speaking to a child who had no idea what he was talking about.

The next morning was brutal. Ryuu woke up at dawn as usual, but his body seemed to be several heartbeats behind his mind's commands. He was sluggish and could almost hear the screams of his limbs as he willed them to motion. There had been hard days helping his father in the field, but never anything like this.

His pain disappeared when he stumbled outside to catch Shigeru in his morning practice. The early morning sunlight glinted off Shigeru's blade, glinting like a crazed firefly in the daylight. Ryuu couldn't track the quick motions of the blade, only see the flashes of lightning as the sunlight reflected off the shining sword. Shigeru's movement was otherworldly, his feet and arms moving in a graceful, deadly, beautiful dance. Ryuu imagined he heard Shigeru's sword sing.

Ryuu could see that Shigeru had noticed him right away. He thought he saw Shigeru's eyes glance his way for the briefest of moments, but his awareness was formed more by the knowledge that it was impossible to sneak up on Shigeru. He was always aware of everything. Ryuu accepted it. It was just the way of being a nightblade.

Despite his awareness, Shigeru did not halt his morning routine. He completed the movements with a simple, effective sheathing of his blade. One moment the cold steel was flashing in the sunlight, the next it was resting in the warm embrace of its sheath. Ryuu hadn't even noticed the movement.

Shigeru took a deep breath and Ryuu could sense that he was being examined. Shigeru's conclusions drawn, he spoke, "You are young, and training to handle a sword is difficult work. Later, we will train every day. But today we rest."

Ryuu felt relief wash over his tired body. Everything hurt to move, he couldn't discover a single exception. His feet were sore from running and standing all day. His legs were sore from holding positions. His core and arms and chest and back hurt from handling the sword and the hand-to-hand combat. A day of rest meant the opportunity to go back to bed and sleep the rest of the day away.

But as he turned to go back to bed he heard Shigeru's voice behind him, a hint of laughter in his words. "Not that way, Ryuu. We're going for a hike through the woods."

Ryuu wanted to groan, or scream, or cry, but even at his young age he knew that none of those responses would make any difference to Shigeru. They would go on a hike and it would end when Shigeru said. Ryuu wondered for a moment if it was worth even trying to resist, to put up a token argument. A moment's reflection confirmed that it wouldn't and he dutifully followed Shigeru away from the hut with one last, longing glance at the corner where he knew his bed to be, still warm from his deep slumber.

They did not walk very far, only to the stream and small waterfall that Ryuu had discovered on his first adventures around the hut. Once there, Shigeru lay down his swords and began to stretch, bouncing on some occasions and holding still on others. To Ryuu's young eyes, Shigeru looked silly, and he tried to contain his laughter. With a flick of his head, Shigeru made it clear that Ryuu was to join him in imitating the movements.

Ryuu had no energy left to protest even though a small part of his mind argued that it was silly. He mimicked Shigeru's moves as well as he could and noticed the effects right away. Every move stretched specific muscle groups. When he bent over to touch his toes he could feel the back of his legs complain and fight back against him. But he persisted, and soon he felt them relax and stretch out.

As he learned the purpose of the movements he became more enthusiastic. They hurt at first, but as his body stretched and relaxed he could feel the pain from the previous day's training slipping away. It was fascinating that by just moving his body he could find relief.

A memory came unbidden to his mind. His father in the house at night, unable to move from the agony of a day in the fields. He sometimes moved like an older man, but he had only seen twenty-four cycles. He had been discreet, moving little once he sat in the house at night, but Ryuu was observant enough to know he was hurting every time he moved. What if he had known what Shigeru knew? Would he have suffered the pain he did?

The thoughts distracted him from his practice for a moment, but if Shigeru noticed it he did not let on. They continued to move through the exercises for a while before Shigeru stood up straight.

"What still hurts?"

Ryuu thought about it before mentioning a few places on his body. His shoulders, arms, and back were still painful, a throbbing ache that refused to go away. Shigeru nodded. "Lie down."

Ryuu hesitated. He knew that Shigeru was going to do something to his body, but the thought of another person close to him bothered him. He remembered his mother's embrace on cold nights and the rough hands of his father. Their warm memories clashed violently with the reality of his present moment and tears came to his eyes.

Shigeru watched every emotion cross the boy's face. Not for the first time, Ryuu felt like Shigeru knew everything in his mind. He said nothing, allowing Ryuu to process the conflict by himself, offering only quiet support. In a while the feelings passed, and Ryuu nodded his assent. He laid down on the soft grass near the waterfall. The sun was falling on the spot he chose, and sleepiness overwhelmed him.

"This may hurt."

Ryuu nodded and gritted his teeth. He still wasn't above trying to get Shigeru to show some sympathy. He felt Shigeru's hands running over his back, quick and sure. Despite the coolness of the late spring breeze, Shigeru's hands were warm. They were also as firm as steel. His father's hands had been rough, weathered with creases and valleys. Shigeru's were smoother but his hands had more focused callouses. They were as hard and unbending as the sword sitting in the grass next to them.

Without giving a warning, Shigeru pressed his thumb into a spot on Ryuu's back. All thoughts of bearing the pain left with Ryuu's voiceless scream. It took a couple of breaths, but he was managed to regain his composure, and when he did he could feel that his back was already feeling better. Despite the pain he was fascinated, his insatiable curiosity overwhelming his natural response.

Shigeru continued, pressing on spot after spot, each one sending new waves of pain through Ryuu's small body. He couldn't help but gasp each time, but when it was over Ryuu felt a lightness new to his experience. He felt like he could jump forever.

Ryuu experimented with his brand-new body by running around for a while without purpose. It was enough to enjoy the sensation of moving without pain. But his body knew things it hadn't before. It was more balanced, more ready to strike. It wasn't much, but it was noticeable. The elation that Ryuu felt gave him energy he hadn't known he possessed.

Shigeru waited for Ryuu to run through his burst of excitement and newfound lightness. After Ryuu had run through his initial energy, Shigeru motioned for him to sit.

"How do you feel now?"

"Great!"

"Good."

"How did you do that? It hurt so much, but now it feels so good. You weren't even pressing on the spots that hurt. How does that work?"

Shigeru raised his hand to halt the flow of questions. "I will teach you everything I know, and before long you will be able to do this all on your own. Have you heard of the dayblades?"

Ryuu nodded. Everyone knew the legends of the dayblades and the nightblades. They had been two separate halves of the group of people known as the Blades, over a thousand cycles ago. Both groups had been destroyed in the Kingdom. The dayblades were healers, but everyone knew they were just as dangerous as the nightblades. In the stories that Ryuu had grown up with, all the blades had been killed, but Shigeru was still here.

Shigeru continued, "Remember yesterday how I said that it is good when you notice that things feel right?"

Ryuu nodded.

"The same energy that you feel when you are in tune with your swordsmanship also applies to your own body and everything in the world. This is the very foundation of what you know as the sense. You can use this knowledge both to heal and to harm a person, but it takes cycles of practice. The dayblades are experts at using their knowledge to heal. The nightblades are experts at using their knowledge to kill."

Shigeru paused. "The divisions aren't as clean as the legends would have you believe. The two groups draw upon the same body of knowledge, but physically manifest their skills in different ways. That being said, a dayblade can be an excellent warrior even if they are an even better healer. Likewise a nightblade can heal as you just experienced."

Ryuu sat and pondered what Shigeru was saying. It was different than the stories he remembered. The nightblades were evil men who had destroyed the Kingdom, and the dayblades had kept them alive. But if Shigeru was a nightblade that meant he was evil, but he had saved Ryuu. His thoughts running in circles, Ryuu's confusion was evident. Shigeru saw the confusion, but didn't guess the reasoning behind it.

"I'm not going to try to teach you about it now; you're not ready to learn yet. But I will tell you that everything you experience, from the woods you walk through, the trees you climb and the people you meet, everything is connected. What is true of the outside world is true inside your body as well."

As was often the case, Ryuu was lost at Shigeru's explanation, but he filed it away for further use.

Shigeru let out one of his wide open grins, the one that made Ryuu believe, however momentarily, that this was an open man with no defenses. "Now, I see I've confused you again. I'm sorry, but I don't know how to talk to someone who has only seen a handful of cycles. It wasn't a part of any training I received. However, I do know that this pond is wonderful to swim in, and it will help your body feel even better. Care to join me?"

Without any more warning Shigeru dove into the pond, a small ripple the sole evidence of his dive.

Surprise halted him only for a moment. Ryuu jumped in, lacking the grace that Shigeru brought to his dive. The water was cold, but it felt wonderful to swim around. Shigeru splashed him, and Ryuu tried to pick him up underwater.

The two of them continued to swim for most of the afternoon, returning to the hut just in time to cook a meal before the sun came down. It was the best day Ryuu could remember having.

CHAPTER 4

Takako had been to New Haven several times. At the age of ten she was old enough to have accompanied her parents on more than one trip. New Haven was the biggest city in the Southern Kingdom, but it was five days of travel from their home village. A trip to New Haven was for the most serious business or the greatest celebrations. This was Takako's fifth trip into the city of unfamiliar lights and sounds.

Takako was ten, but even the most observant bystanders would have guessed her closer to fourteen or fifteen. Her breasts were too small to be average for the age, but all other standards she met or exceeded. She was exceptionally tall for her age, towering over even her older male friends. Her father was a struggling merchant working to make ends meet in a village that didn't have many needs. There were many mouths to feed in their house and the business, while consistent, was not enough to put more than the minimum of food into the family's stomachs every evening when they gathered around the table.

It was not hunger that bothered Takako. She had grown up eating little and knew little else. What she hated not having a teacher. She was the oldest of four, but the only girl. Her father felt that there was no need to provide her more than the basics, but even his judgmental mind acknowledged she was excellent at everything she put her mind to. She was gifted with both numbers and letters, but despite her recognized aptitude her father paid her no mind, focusing instead on educating his three sons. They were the children that would take over the business.

Which made this trip all the more unusual. Takako didn't know why they had come, but her father's demeanor made it clear to her young mind that this was a business trip. If it was a celebration he would have brought the whole family, or at least been in a good mood. But if it had been a business trip he would have brought the boys despite their lesser age and gifts. It didn't fit Takako's paradigms for pleasure or business, but her father had been serious the entire trip, so it had to be business. Takako was beside herself with curiosity although the thrill of being in New Haven overwhelmed her desire to barrage her father with questions.

New Haven suited Takako well. She had been born with a positive attitude, and her mother told Takako that she had come out of the womb with a smile on her face. Takako thought the story seemed a bit of an exaggeration, but she liked it anyway. She did not like the manner in which her father treated her and her mother, but there was nothing she could do about it. So she did what was required of her and looked forward to the future. When she was in New Haven she felt like the future was right in front of her, beckoning her into a warm embrace. The city was big, with room for a woman to grow. She had seen women who ran businesses and tried to picture herself as one of them. She knew she was capable, she just didn't know why nobody else would acknowledge it.

One of Takako's most pressing questions in life was how her mother put up with being treated like less than Takako's father.

Takako knew that her mother and father had been married for over twelve cycles. Her mother was a quiet woman who possessed an inner steel that displayed itself in very rare circumstances. But to hear the neighbors talk her mother had not always been quiet. She used to be the life of the village, beautiful and full of energy. One of their neighbors once told Takako that her mother had been quick to tell her mind, even to the elders of the village, who allowed her to get away with it on account of her beauty and charm.

She was still beautiful, but cycles of marriage to Takako's father had smothered her fire. She loved him and worked hard to keep him happy. In the beginning it was said that their marriage had been picture perfect and the two of them were ranked among the most respected people in the community. But then the children came. Takako was first, followed by twin brothers and then one more. The business did not grow in proportion to the size of their family. What had been a comfortable existence slid into one of daily struggle. Takako's father once had dreams, but the never-ending monotony of trying to produce enough to survive wore him down to a shadow of the man he had been.

Even Takako's mother could not keep his spirits up. There were still days where everything seemed to be as it should. They would both smile and laugh and the children were all too willing to follow suit. But it could not last and it never did. The periods of happiness would dissipate like the morning fog leaving nothing but the cold reality of day to day survival.

None of the children were ever abused or neglected. Their father worked hard so they could all be fed and the mother spent every day with her children doing her best to educate them and prepare them for their futures. They all helped with the business doing whatever they could. When they weren't at the shop they were home cooking and cleaning. Their mother's willingness to make her husband happy was contagious. Every evening rotated around the whims of the father. Takako's mother became like one of the children, hanging on to his every word, trying to find a measure of his infrequent approval.

As the cycles passed, everything worsened and life decayed like an old piece of paper. Takako's father began gambling with some friends. Until that day he had abstained, knowing there wasn't enough money for the family to be frivolous with any of it. But one night something had changed his mind, and he adopted the belief that it was his hard-earned money to spend as he desired. He talked it over with his wife and she agreed that it might be good for him to relax with friends and do as he pleased. They ran over the numbers, and figured on a suitable amount for him to take to the halls, expecting and planning for him to lose everything. They would have to trim a couple of corners for the next few days but they figured they could make ends meet without too much difficulty.

That night Takako saw her father the happiest he had ever been. He came back flush with winnings. He brought treats for everyone and still brought home much more money than he had left with. That night the family celebrated their good fortune with an opulent meal and games. The night became forever etched in Takako's memory, a colorful, vivid memory against a backdrop of black and white images.

The happiness of that evening lasted for a while. Both Takako's mother and father were by nature careful spenders and for almost a full moon the air around the house was jovial. It never reached the heights of the first night, but her parents did not seem as worried as usual and the mood was palpably more relaxed than it had been.

But Takako had been taught that all things in life travel in a great cycle, and the good fortune experienced by the family slowly returned to the day-to-day drudgery the family knew so well. The day-to-day drudgery uncovered the same tension that had consumed the family earlier. Once again, the merchant went out to gamble, but this time it wasn't for fun or pleasure. It was to earn money for his family. His wife tried to dissuade him, but only half-heartedly, fearful hope instilled in her as well. The joy of that night was still flush in her mind, and although part of her knew that luck didn't visit the same person twice in the gambling halls, she wanted to believe it enough she was willing to ignore her intuition and put her trust in her husband's confidence.

The whole family waited up filled with expectation, but when the merchant returned, he returned with less money. It wasn't much less. He had runs of both good and bad luck but had quit before he lost too much. A little less money meant a little less food and a little more tension around the house. But it was manageable, and life moved forward, the great wheel slowly spinning.

The cycle continued, inevitable as the rising of the sun. Her parents started fighting more. Takako didn't always know what was said. Her parents always argued in hushed tones at night so they wouldn't wake or disturb the children. Takako could sometimes make out snippets of conversation, but rarely enough to put together a coherent picture of what was happening. She assumed that it was about money. She was old enough to know that her father's business wasn't doing as well as they needed, which was why they didn't have very much food.

Takako wondered if all the arguing had to do with why only she and her father had come to New Haven. She didn't understand why they were here by themselves. A visit to the city was always a big deal and always involved the whole family. For business or celebration, everyone came together. Still, she was happy to be here, feeling special that her father had recognized her for something unique. But her father wouldn't answer her questions. That made her nervous.

In between her excited observations of her surroundings Takako would steal glances over at her father. He smiled at her whenever he caught her looking at him, but he also seemed like he was about to cry at any minute. She didn't understand. They had made a long journey but her father brought nothing to trade. If this was a business trip it was unlike any trip she had been on before. Instead of leading her to a specific destination her father kept asking her what she would like to do, and then they would do it. Takako tried to select activities that didn't cost too much, but her father spent money on her without complaint. His newfound generosity scared her most.

Takako didn't feel like she should complain about the treatment, but it was out of character for the father she knew. Her father was by nature a frugal man. He had grown up the son of a poor merchant and couldn't move forward his entire life despite his constant efforts. Spending money without question on his daughter was unheard of.

As the sun set her father asked her if she would like a special treat. She said yes, and they wandered until they found a small out-of-the-way candy merchant. Takako's father looked through the candy as if it was the most important purchase he had ever made and selected one for his daughter. Takako watched, amazed by how much money her father had handed over to the merchant. He didn't receive change.

They sat down on the side of a street, watching the passerby as Takako savored the candy. She had never eaten anything like it before, and seeing how much it had cost, she was set on making the most out of the experience. As she ate her father watched her, his eyes never leaving her face. She was so absorbed in her treat she didn't even notice when he began to cry.

"You know, when I was a child that was my favorite candy. I don't remember how I got it for the first time. I imagine my father bought me some on a special occasion, just as I bought it for you today. But I loved it so much that every time we came back to New Haven, I had to have a piece."

Takako looked up at her father. "How did you get it? You didn't have much money growing up."

Her father looked down at her, surprised. It made Takako angry. It was as though he didn't realize she could put things together for herself. "You saw how much it cost." He sounded resigned, like he had known his one attempt to be secretly generous would fail. "I worked very hard for those candies. I was about the same age you are now and I worked all the time for my father. He didn't give me very much because we didn't have much, but he felt I should be paid like a regular employee. He thought it would teach me hard work would be rewarded, so he always gave me a small percentage of the profits as an allowance. It was clever parenting. If I worked hard and business improved then I would earn more. If I was lazy and business dropped I didn't earn anything. It was a good lesson," his voice turned bitter, "even if it was a lie."

Takako nodded She didn't understand the last part of his thoughts, but she too had dreamed about working in the store. She wondered if her father would ever let her work in the business. She was more than old enough to help out, and often did small odds and ends, but she didn't have anything important to do with the business. Her father used all the boys even if they were younger and dumber. She was left tending the house with her mother. She would have loved the same treatment her father received from his father. The idea of having money of her own was very appealing.

Her father didn't give her the chance to interrupt, continuing his story as though lost in thought. "I worked very hard and the business, while it didn't improve too much, it made enough money that I was able to save up a little. Like our family, we didn't go to New Haven often, so by the time we would make it around to going, I almost always had enough to buy one of these candies. And every time it was the best one. It was never disappointing, not after working for it for so many seasons."

Takako's father laughed, a short laugh, and shook his head. "Father never did understand. He considered it a terrible waste of money, and I think he started to believe me a lost cause then. But it was worth every piece of wealth I had, just like it is today."

Takako cocked her head to one side. It seemed like an out-of-place thing to say, and sounded ominous. The questions, driven out of her mind by the candy, came back into her thoughts.

Her father didn't give her long to wonder. "Takako, we're here because I had to find work for you."

Takako's heart leapt with sudden joy. A job meant money, and it meant she would stay here in New Haven to work. No more endless days spent tending house. She felt like a hawk escaping from the cage of her life into the bright sunlight of a new day.

"Takako, I want you to know that I'm not happy with having to find you a job here. In fact, I feel horrible. If it wasn't for me, my failures, you wouldn't have to work at all, and you could live with your mother and me until you found a husband, just like we'd planned. But that's not what happened. You may hate me forever, but I want you to know I love you. I love you like I love your mother, and although neither of you will ever forgive me, please try and remember me kindly."

Her father's words echoed through her mind, unable to find any purchase there. Everything he said drifted by her like a leaf blown quickly away by the wind. Takako was lost in her new vision of the future, managing her own store, sending money back to her family. She would show them all! She would be the one who saved her family, the one who brought honor back to their house. And she loved her father more than she ever had before.

Takako shared the last bites of candy with her father as they sat together for the last time. When the candy was gone they stood and walked to a neighborhood Takako had never been to before. The streets were illuminated by a soft red light. It was enough to see by, but it was dark and foreboding. Takako was used to seeing swords. All the soldiers had them, and many others in the city had them as well. But in this neighborhood everyone wore a sword even if they didn't wear a uniform, and many of the men were having trouble walking and talking. As she glanced around again, she also realized she was the only woman on the streets of any age.

She held on to her father's hand, afraid to let go in this neighborhood. But she didn't show any other fear. If she was going to be shown to her first job, she wanted to make a good impression. Takako's father led them in straight lines. He walked straight to a three story building with dim red lanterns hanging outside of it. It seemed to be the quietest place in this busy neighborhood. Men walked in and out of the building, but were always subdued They were also dressed quite well. Takako's clothing was rags in comparison.

The first detail Takako noticed were the two men at the door. They were standing on either side, but something about them made them different than men she had seen before. She stared at them without shame until she figured it out. They were still. For as long as she stared at them, they did not move unless it was to serve a purpose. At first she wondered if it was some sort of childlike game, a competition to see who could stand still the longest. But unlike her childhood games these men were not tense from the effort of remaining still. Their bodies were relaxed, not tense like hers would be if she tried to stand still. Although she couldn't say why, she knew that these men were dangerous. Her excitement about her new job faded as doubts overcame her.

Her father spoke in hushed tones to one of the men and was given directions. He motioned Takako to follow and took her up the stairs into a room on the second floor. As she walked through the building she saw this was where all the women in the area had been hiding. They were all beautiful. Takako had never seen so many women in one place. Each one wore a gorgeous, unique dress. Takako wanted to be just like them, the envy of men everywhere.

Takako couldn't help but stare, but each of the women she stared at had no trouble meeting her gaze. They each returned Takako's stare in a different fashion. Some seemed angry at her while others gave her generous smiles. There were a few who looked at her with sadness in their eyes. Once again Takako felt like she was full of questions she didn't know how to articulate.

Her father led her into a small room which was dark but quiet. The room was different than the rest of the building. Everywhere else was quiet but busy. This was peaceful. Takako and her father sat and after a short wait another woman came in. As soon as she entered the room the whole atmosphere changed. It felt like a block of ice had been moved into the room. Everything got colder and Takako wanted to reach for a blanket. The woman was unique in that she wore no make-up. Her face couldn't be called beautiful, but neither could it be called plain.

The woman was older than the others. Takako guessed she was about forty. She was still attractive, but Takako guessed when she was younger she had been even more so. Her figure was tall and slim, but even under her layers of clothing it was obvious she was strong. She moved with a grace that demonstrated decades of practice. Power and control radiated from her.

The woman offered tea which was accepted by both Takako and her father. She sat and studied Takako and her father, but spent more of her time on Takako. Takako felt naked under her gaze. It wasn't a harsh stare or judgmental. It was all-encompassing, taking all of Takako in within the space of a few breaths. There was something about this woman that unsettled Takako. It wasn't anything about her appearance. The stranger continued to smile as if it was the most natural expression anyone could make. But her gaze made Takako shiver a little on the inside. There was something cold at the center of the woman.

The woman broke the nervous silence. "I very much appreciate you two coming today. I know that this is often a difficult day, but I assure you that in this house the girls are treated much better than in any other house."

Takako's father nodded. "I have heard of your reputation and am glad that you agreed to take on my daughter for so generous a sum. The reputation of your women's condition brings great relief to my heart."

The woman's smile increased just slightly in a manner that Takako found sinister. "My girls are consorts to the highest men in the land. They need to be intelligent, beautiful, and well-educated. Your daughter, according to the people I have asked, possesses at least two of these qualities. The third we can provide."

There was a momentary silence. Neither Takako nor her father knew what to say. The woman continued after subjecting Takako to another visual examination.

"It is also my experience that the quicker this goes the better off everyone is. As stated before, this is a difficult day. I have here all of the papers required to be signed for our deal to be concluded. For your convenience I have made two copies, both of which we will sign. In this way, you will also have the agreement in case there are any arguments down the road."

The woman took out the papers as she spoke, laying them on a low table that sat between her and Takako's father. She offered him a quill, which he took hesitantly. He looked over at his daughter one more time, and the sight of her seemed to take all the energy out of him.

The woman spoke, her soft voice firm in the darkness, "I understand the pain you are going through. I would be much more concerned if you did not hesitate. This business is what it is, and I will make no lies to you about it. However, your daughter will receive the best care possible here. She will be well-fed and educated as well."

Her strong voice seemed to reassure Takako's father, and in two quick movements he signed both the papers in front of him. The woman took the papers, turned them around, and signed them herself. She folded up one copy and gave it to Takako's father. The other she rolled up and hid somewhere in her kimono. The woman bowed slightly and stood up. "I will take my leave now. I will give you a little while to say good-bye. Once again, I stress that it is easier both for the girl and for you if it goes more quickly but I will not rush you beyond that. Takako, once your father leaves, please remain in this room. I will return shortly to give you a quick tour of the house and then we will find you a bed so you may get some rest."

The woman left, her bare feet not making a sound on the polished wooden floor, and Takako's father came over to his firstborn daughter. He wrapped her up so in an embrace that squeezed the breath out of her. He continued to hold her for a long time. Takako soon realized that her father was crying as his tears ran down into her hair.

"Please forgive me. I know you don't know what is happening right now, but when you do figure it out, please forgive me. I swear to you that if there was another path I would have taken it."

He turned around and started walking out the door. Takako thought she had never seen her father so defeated. Shouldn't her first employment be a joyful day? Takako regained her senses long enough to rush up to him to embrace him again before he left. She didn't know what was happening, but she did know that she wasn't going to be seeing her father for a very long time.

Moments after her father left the woman came back into the room. Even closing her eyes, Takako imagined that she could sense the woman's presence. It was difficult to tell what type of woman she was. On the outside she continued to smile and was the perfect image of a caring woman. But Takako couldn't shake the feeling that something wasn't right about her. It was as if a flexible mask had been placed over a demon trying to convince the world of its goodness.

Unfortunately Takako had no proof of her feelings. The woman was polite, and even with her father gone the woman's attitude did not change. She continued to be kind and gentle, leaving no room to suspect any wrongdoing.

Her reverie was interrupted by the woman. "You may call me 'Madame.' All the ladies do, and that is sufficient. I run this business. There is one more piece of business I need to take care of before letting you rest tonight. I need you to take off all of your clothes and lie down."

Takako stared ahead. "What do you mean?"

"I need you to take off your clothes so that I may examine you. I need to make sure you are healthy and in the condition you were promised. If not your father will not leave this building."

Takako misunderstood. A glimmer of hope flickered in her heart. Perhaps she wouldn't be right, and her father would come and get her back. She had to bring honor to her house though, so her hopes remained silent. "My father says that I never get sick. He is proud of that. He says it is unusual for a girl to never get sick."

"I'm sure that your father is a very smart man, but I need to see for myself so I can take the best care of you."

Takako took a couple of breaths to think about it. For some reason the men at the door occurred to her. She had a vision, just a fleeting thought, that this wasn't so much a house as it was a prison. Whatever this woman said was law here. She started undressing. Madame watched her with eyes that never seemed to blink, making Takako uncomfortable.

When she was done Madame moved with a practiced ease. She looked her up and down, spending a lot of time peering between Takako's legs. Takako felt like she was being judged, even though Madame gave no expression, no hint of what was passing through her mind.

Madame drew back slowly. "How old are you?"

"I've seen ten cycles, but soon I'll turn eleven."

"Did you know your father said you were older than that?"

"No. He knows I'm ten. I'm often told I look older than I am though because I am so tall."

"Do you have any idea why you're here?"

Takako hung her head. "No."

The woman stepped away from Takako and started pacing through the room. She kept glancing at Takako. Even Takako knew that the woman was trying to figure out what to do with her. Her father had lied, and this woman's plans had not gone as she had expected.

"Not what I expected, but this could work out well. You are too perfect to be used up at ten. Ten is too young. Not that there aren't men who would pay very handsomely for your work, but it would wear you out too quickly. You need to be older if I'm going to get the most out of you."

When Madame said "work" Takako had the impression that she was referring to something else. Madame came to a decision.

"I think you will become very valuable to me. You will start out as a house assistant. You will cook, clean, and assist the other women with their needs. When you turn fifteen I will sell your maidenhead. With your exposure in the house, I should be able to fetch a pretty sum. What do you think of that?"

"I am here to work for you. I need to bring honor back to our house."

Madame laughed. "Well, I don't think that's going to happen here, but I will take care of you. Every woman is important to me because you will work for me for a very long time."

The woman stood up and motioned for Takako to follow her. She led Takako up to the third floor to another room which had a comfortable bed, dresser, and mirror. "Go to sleep Takako. Tomorrow is the first day of the rest of your life."

CHAPTER 5

Moriko's family had always lived on the boundary between forest and farmland. Although Moriko was only seven she already knew the story. Her great-great-grandfather had selected this land after a long process. Her ancestor had been a soldier in the militia but was looking for an out of the way place to settle down in peace and raise a family. He had chosen well. Throughout the generations the family had alternated between two incomes. They brought in money both from farming and from the lumber they cut. When times were good, Moriko's family did quite well. When times were bad they still survived without suffering.

For Moriko and her family it was timber which made the most profit. Moriko's father still planted the land, but most of it was saved for the family to decrease their expenses during the cold months. It was a large family with six children, four boys and two girls. Moriko was the fourth oldest after two of the boys and her older sister. The family all pitched in. Moriko's two older brothers helped their father in the forest cutting down the trees. Moriko, her sister, and her two younger brothers kept the fields and the house. Moriko was envious of her older brothers. She wanted to be out in the forest with her father.

Even at seven Moriko knew she was different from the rest of her family. It was true that the rest of her family was loud and boisterous, but her differences went much deeper. She was always curious and always wanted to learn, often receiving long talks from their father because she was the only child who would listen.

A few days ago Moriko had been out in the forest with her father. They spent most of the day doing business, her father teaching her what trees should be cut next and for what purpose. Moriko's mother didn't approve of her getting such an education, but Moriko's father knew how much it meant to her, and he didn't see any reason why she couldn't learn the business as well as a son. As the late afternoon approached her father took her deeper into the woods, into the old forest. Her father, though a practical man, still kept to the old ways. The edges of the forest with the younger trees were excellent places to ply his trade. But he always planted new trees to replace the ones he had cut. He never cut more than was needed, and he never, never, harmed an old tree.

Moriko had asked him about it once, but all he said was that the old trees were special and that to cut them down would be a terrible thing to do.

Like her father, Moriko held a reverence for the old forest. She loved how it was quiet and dark. She couldn't help but feel these were the kinds of places where the stories she grew up with occurred. She imagined she could feel all the different animals around her, and at times she even believed she could feel the trees, like old men and women watching over the passing of the world.

Throughout their walk Moriko asked her father about all the animals. It didn't take her long to realize that her father, who always seemed to know so much more about the forest than anyone else, didn't always notice the animals she did. Moriko would often ask about an animal, point in the general direction of the creature, and ask her father a question about it. But he didn't always see it and sometimes didn't even know it was there.

Moriko didn't think much on it until they returned home. Her mother and father exchanged the usual pleasantries, but the conversation was about Moriko. She couldn't hear them, but they cast frequent glances her way while talking in hushed tones. She wondered what they were saying, but she had the impression she had done something wrong.

Moriko was not given much free time, but what she had she used in wandering through the woods. It was a habit that frustrated her mother, but her father always said that Moriko knew the forest so well it was the other predators that should be afraid of her. Moriko's mother didn't laugh at the joke but followed her husband's wishes.

The old forest was a second home to Moriko. It was quiet and gave her time to think about whatever she wanted to think about. There was never anyone waiting impatiently for an answer or response. Moriko wasn't a slow thinker, but she always thought deeply. The unwillingness of people to wait for an answer always struck her as unfair and rude. If someone asked a question they should be willing to wait for the best possible answer.

One night Moriko's family had a guest, an unusual occurrence. When Moriko's ancestor had chosen the land he had chosen it well out of the way of those who would pass by. People only came to their house with intent, so visitors were rare. This visitor was a complete stranger. Moriko had never seen anyone like him before. His clothes were not rough like the ones her entire family wore. They were fine and did not show the wear that her father's did. The man's head was shaved, and he wore a permanent grin on his face that Moriko was convinced was false. But it was the first time she had ever seen her father bow his head in submission. She had seen him do it politely before, but never to the degree he did when the strange man entered their house.

Moriko decided she didn't like the man. It was more than just his clothes. It was his demeanor and presence. Moriko had never felt what she was experiencing when she looked at him. She felt like he was somehow glowing. She didn't understand it. No one else seemed to think anything was strange about him, but he seemed brighter than anyone else in the room. Moriko wanted to ask her father why the man was brighter, but knew the interruption wouldn't be welcome. She sat on her questions, fear and curiosity burning through her.

The conversation was brief but serious. Moriko heard enough to know what was happening. It was a monk from the nearest monastery who had heard about the household. No one from the monastery ever came this way, but he had come to rectify the situation. He would test each of the children to see if any had the sense. He looked directly at Moriko as he spoke.

Moriko was too young to know why her father didn't protest. She didn't know that the monasteries were backed by the full military might of the Kingdom, and she didn't know that her father had no choice. All she knew was that her father was doing whatever this man was asking.

When the monk began his testing Moriko's fears began to dissolve. All he would do was hold his hand up to the child's forehead. Whatever kind of test it was, Moriko was confident she could pass it. They went by age. Her two brothers and sister went ahead of her and each returned to their place at the table.

When it was her turn Moriko walked up without fear, confident she would pass as they did.

The monk rested his hand against her forehead. She was surprised by the cold firmness of the man's hand. It was as though he didn't have a heartbeat. Moriko looked up at the monk. His eyes were as wide as saucers. Moriko became scared again, even more so when the man smiled at her. "Your daughter is blessed."

Moriko watched her parents closely. Her mother held her hand to her mouth, but her father just nodded as if it was the news he had been expecting all along. "I will pack her things."

The stranger held up his hand. "It will not be necessary. Everything she needs will be provided. She will be safe, and we will protect her from others and herself."

Her father bowed again. "Thank you."

Moriko's mind was racing. She didn't know what was happening underneath the surface of the conversation. It sounded like she was going to leave with this man, but why didn't her father fight? There was no way he would let her go. She was his favorite.

Moriko started to protest, but the sounds died in her throat when she saw the expression on her family's faces. There was no love anywhere around the table. They had all shifted away from her. They were scared. And angry at her. Why? Even her father, who had always been so kind to her, had a cautious look in his eyes. None spoke up to convince the man to leave her here at home.

She looked from face to face, seeking support, seeking someone who would ask her to stay. Just the previous night they had all been laughing at her faces around the table. Today she was a stranger who had wandered into their house.

Moriko started to cry. No one was going to help her. No one did help her.

There was silence in the room until Moriko felt a hand on her shoulder. She looked up, expecting to see the smiling face of her father telling her it would all be fine.

But it wasn't. It was the strange man. He was smiling a smile that wasn't a smile, telling her it would all be fine.

Moriko followed the man meekly out of the door. She didn't want to, but she also knew that there was no way to get away from this man without the help of her family. She climbed on the man's horse, her quick mind numb. As they started their journey away from the only home Moriko had ever known, she risked one glance back towards her home, hoping that maybe someone had come to wish her farewell. The house looked warm and inviting, but not one family member was outside watching her leave.

The journey to the monastery was uneventful. The monk, whose name Moriko discovered was Goro, tried to engage her in conversation, but was stymied by her persistent silence.

She thought about trying to escape. There were opportunities, but Moriko didn't know what she would do after. Her family was the only comfort she had ever known. There were no relatives or friends to escape to. Her only home had already closed its doors to her. The only open doors were to the monastery.

In her silence Moriko wondered what the monastery would look like. She imagined it as a grand castle with buildings rising high in the sky. It would be filled with wonderful people. The monks were very brave. All the stories said so. Maybe she just got a bad monk.

Her heart sank when they crested a small hill and the monastery came into view. It was a gray and dreary day, and the monastery itself was remarkable only for how unremarkable it was. The most distinguishing feature it possessed was a solid wall just higher than the height of an average man. The wall was made of wood, and as they passed through the gates Moriko was struck by how peaceful everything appeared. She had expected the monastery to be larger, more alive. The grounds were almost as dead as the barren plains outside the walls. The compound wasn't large, and Moriko saw that it would be a short and easy sprint from one wall to the other. In one corner a group of youths about her age were exercising under the supervision of one of the monks. None of them appeared happy to be moving, but they also didn't seem sad or angry. Moriko reserved her judgment, although the place wasn't as exciting as she'd hoped.

They came to a stop and dismounted. A monk who had been working on some chores walked over to Moriko. He smiled a genuine smile, and Moriko's heart lifted. Not all monks were like Goro. It was going to be fine. "Welcome to Perseverance." Moriko looked at the monk with a question in her eyes, which was enough for him to elaborate. "I forget that not everyone is a monk. Although the monasteries don't have names according to the outside world, the earliest monks after the war found it necessary to have some naming system to distinguish them. Monasteries were named after qualities the monks treasured. Although there aren't many monasteries anymore the practice is still maintained."

Moriko nodded, her attention still focused on her surroundings. One building stood out above the rest, located as far away from the gate as was possible. It was the only building with more than one level and it was decorated with some of the most impressive and ornate woodwork she had ever seen. She assumed it was the most important building. There were four others, all of which were simple, unremarkable, and efficient.

The monk spoke again, and there was a new edge in his voice that caused Moriko to focus. "Don't think about escape. I realize it's all you're going to think about for the next few weeks, but please try to avoid it. As you can see, the walls aren't tall. The gate is shut at night, but it isn't much more than an ornament. Our strength comes from our powers, and you can't escape from them. Trust me."

Moriko surprised herself by blurting out, "Why should I?"

"Because many cycles ago I was in your shoes thinking the exact same things. I tried to escape. I had a brilliant plan for getting away. The night of my escape I ran and put my plan into action. They didn't stop me from leaving. Looking back on it now, I'm pretty sure that one of them watched me as I left, although I thought I'd gotten away without notice. They didn't even try to chase me. They let me get a head start, just so I knew what I was up against. I never stopped moving, trying to get out of the range of their senses. I ran for two days, forfeiting sleep. But it didn't matter. Two days later, after I thought I was safe, they came for me and brought me back. I still carry the marks from the punishment to this day."

Moriko thought over his words. She decided that it was a good story, but she didn't believe him. He noticed it too.

"Don't worry. I know you'll try to come up with your own plan, and you won't listen to me. Few people do. But listen to the others. They've been through the same things, and some of them have tried to escape. Listen to their stories and then see if you will believe mine. I'm just trying to help." The monk halted for moment, as if he had just noticed something that he hadn't before. "Now, I must take you to the Abbot, for he wants to meet you."

Moriko followed the monk without argument. As she suspected, they went to the large building at the back of the monastery. The inside was even more impressive than the outside. The carvings were elaborate and stretched throughout the entire frame and all the woodwork. There was more gold than Moriko had ever seen in one place before. Moriko, despite herself, was fascinated by the carvings and etchings and wished she could have the opportunity to look at them and study them. Sometimes in her spare time she enjoyed carving, but this was far beyond her ability.

She almost didn't notice the man who sat in the center of the room. He was a small man, but when Moriko turned her attention to him, she knew immediately why he was the leader of the monks. Goro had been stronger than anyone she had ever met. Through their entire journey he never stopped glowing, and Moriko came to accept this was what monks were like. This was stronger. She had adjusted to being around Goro, reaching the state where she only noticed his glow if she searched for it. Facing the Abbot she felt her heart begin to beat faster and her palms begin to sweat.

The Abbot sat cross-legged, engaged in meditation. Moriko almost jumped when he spoke. He had been sitting so still she had wondered if he was awake. "Moriko, I am glad you are able to be with us. I can tell that you are scared and angry and thinking about your family. I want you to know everything is going to be fine. We are going to take care of you here, and we're going to teach you how to be the best person you can be so you can go around helping people like we do. I hope you think that sounds nice."

Moriko thought that the Abbot's monotone voice sounded more creepy than nice, but even her young mind was able to see the wisdom in going along with this man. "Yes, it does."

"I know you're going to think about running away, but please don't. What you don't understand is we need you here. People like us are special, and for the good of the Kingdom we need to take care of each other. There are rules here that will help keep you safe and happy. The first one, and one of the most important, is to never leave without permission. The world is a dangerous place, but in here you will be safe, and we will take care of you. The other students will let you know the other rules."

Moriko nodded, unsure of what else she could do.

"There's another reason we ask you not to leave. The world doesn't understand the power you have. They are scared of you. It's much safer for you to be here with others who understand you. If you go out into the world again before you are ready, I don't know what would happen to you."

Moriko thought of her family, not even seeing her off. The moment she had been tested she had been torn from her family as though she had never existed. They had let her go. They had wanted her to leave. She understood now.

"I'm the Abbot of this monastery. I want you to think of me both as a teacher and as a friend. I will make sure that the rules are followed so everyone stays safe, but if there is something bad happening, or if you need help for whatever reason, rest assured that I will be here to help you out. You can always come talk to me."

Moriko nodded again. She was confused. Everything about the monastery was wrong, and she felt like unknown horrors were heading towards her, but she couldn't figure out what they could be. Everyone here seemed kind if a little weird. She didn't like Goro at all, but he seemed to be the exception. Everyone else had been very nice to her. They had been nicer than her family.

Moriko's head swam. She didn't know what was right and wrong. The abbot saw her distress and decided to conclude the interview.

"I apologize for taking up so much of your time at such an inopportune moment. Of course, you must be exhausted after all the traveling you have done. You should get some rest. Some of the students will show you where to sleep, and after you have gotten some rest, we can help you write a letter home to your parents so you can tell them you are safe."

Moriko shook her head. If there was one thing she was certain of, it was that she didn't want to write to her family. They wanted her gone and so she would disappear.

The kind monk who had brought her to the Abbot escorted her out of the building. He didn't say anything, but he seemed happy to have Moriko there. The monk led her to one of the less elegant buildings Moriko had noticed upon her arrival. Inside she found a communal living space with a small kitchen, a dining area, and a number of beds. The monk motioned over one of the other students who was cleaning their area. "Tomotsu, get over here."

Tomotsu stopped cleaning his space and came over, giving both the monk and Moriko a quick bow. "Yes, sir?"

Moriko's heart fluttered for a moment. Even with a shaved head and the plain robes of the Monastery, the boy was cute. He was very cute.

"Moriko, this is Tomotsu. Tomotsu, Moriko. Moriko is going to be our newest student. I would like you to take her around the monastery, tell her about life here, share with her the rules, and get her settled in."

Moriko looked at Tomotsu curiously, her childish heart leaping to fantasies her head knew were silly. She wanted to ride out of the monastery with him. She guessed he was a couple of cycles older than her, maybe three or four. But he was tall and his shoulders were already broad. Even with the small age difference it looked like he could pick her up easily and throw her around. He could be the boy who rescued her. They could live together and raise a big family in a nice house. . .

"Moriko?"

Moriko startled. She had gotten lost in her dreams and didn't realize the boy had been trying to get her attention. She looked at him and nodded.

"So, they got you too?"

Moriko nodded. She was finding it challenging to know which words to use around the boy. It was much harder than talking with her brothers.

"It's tough. I know. We've all been through the same here. We were all taken from our families at one point or another, although usually younger than you. But don't worry, life here isn't bad. The rules are simple. Listen to the monks and don't try to leave."

Moriko gave the boy a hostile stare. She felt like her newly woven dream was fraying at the edges.

"It's not something they tell us to say to newcomers. It's something I've experienced, something a lot of us have experienced. Almost everyone tries. It's scary at first. A couple of cycles ago, when I first got here, a couple of us tried to run away. We made it quite a ways, but they always get you in the end. The Abbot, he's really strong in the sense, and he can always find you no matter how far away you get. When I got back, he gave me these." Tomotsu turned around and raised his robes a little to display his back, which had narrow raised scars crisscrossing all over it.

Moriko shuddered. "Did it hurt?"

Tomotsu lowered his head and his voice. "Yes."

"I'm sorry."

"Don't be. I'm not. I still think about escaping sometimes, but there's no way. Sure, you can get outside the walls, but they'll find you. They can sense you no matter where you are. But life here isn't too bad. The food is good and as long as you follow what the monks say, life is pretty comfortable. We don't really want for anything, and they do make us stronger. Both physically and with the sense."

Tomotsu took her out into the grounds. The five buildings were arranged in an arc opening towards the main gate. One building was a supply building, holding all the food and goods for the monastery. The other building closest to the gate was a training center than was used during the winter and during inclement weather. The next two buildings in were living quarters, one for the students and one for the monks. Each held about fifteen to twenty people, so the monastery never had more than forty residents.

The main building was, as she had guessed, the home of the Abbot. It served several ceremonial purposes and was the center of all activity in the monastery. Students were not allowed in without permission until they became blood-sworn monks.

Moriko suffered from a sense of claustrophobia. Every day of her life the world had been open to her. She had explored woods and forests, free to go as she pleased. The world was large and wide. The monastery was small and confining. She couldn't see over the walls. She wanted the trees more than anything else right now.

At the end of their tour, which didn't take very long, Tomotsu offered her a bed next to his own. Nobody else was using it and he told her he'd watch over her and keep her safe as she got used to her new place. Moriko gladly accepted, childish love warming her heart in a cold place.

As Moriko was being shown around the monastery, Goro made a visit to the Abbot's quarters. The girl concerned him. He needed the guidance of the Abbot. When Goro entered the sanctuary he saw the Abbot was in conference. He walked silently to a corner, knelt and bowed his head to the ground, his forehead resting against the earth. Nervous, he waited for the Abbot to speak to him.

The Abbot was finishing a meeting with a local official. Goro tried to listen in, but the two were close and the conversation hushed. He couldn't make out what was being said over the other noises of training trickling in from the grounds, but it was easy to see the Abbot ruled the conversation. The local official was bowing and nodding his head while the Abbot radiated an air of authority. Goro loved to watch the Abbot work.

Goro tried to keep his smile to himself, but when he failed he didn't worry. No one would see with his face pressed to the ground, the perfect image of obedience. Almost everyone who came to the monastery, no matter how great, was humbled by their visit. Although different monasteries operated differently, Goro was pleased to be part of one whose respect and knowledge were so well preserved. He knew from his travels that some other monasteries sealed their doors to the world.

He thought the idea repugnant. There was always a debate about the role of the monastic system occurring between the Abbots. The monasteries faced a unique set of challenges. They were the sole proprietors of the sense, a power coveted and feared by all governments and people. They were also mandated to remain out of secular affairs, which in practice meant staying out of politics. It was this mandate which caused consternation at the Abbots' council. Some Abbots believed that the monasteries should remain separate, opening their doors only when necessary.

Perseverance, to Goro's delight, was involved in the affairs of the world. Not in a way that broke the letter of the mandate, but other abbots had questioned the spirit of the work. The Abbot of Perseverance made himself available to the locals on a limited basis and the monks were often dispatched to local regions. A monastic escort ensured safety from bandits in the region, and the Abbot supported local leaders who would keep the monastery well-supported. Perseverance's Abbot did not get directly involved in the affairs of government, but he was without doubt the most powerful person in the region.

Goro was grateful. He knew he was special. He was gifted in the ways of the sense. He knew it was their role to shape the course of future. If not for the monks, Goro was convinced the Three Kingdoms would have been wrecked beyond repair. Through their interventions they would bring back the One Kingdom. It was their destiny.

Goro's reverie was interrupted when he felt the Abbot's energy flow over him. He looked up and saw that the local official was being dismissed. The official, who Goro thought he recognized as a vice-mayor, made several awkward bows and walked backwards out of the room. Even after the nuisance was gone, Goro waited until he was summoned.

After a couple of moments of silence had passed, Goro felt the Abbot focus his entire attention on him. It was a disconcerting feeling. Even individuals who didn't have the sense reported being able to feel the Abbot's power. For those who were trained it felt like being overwhelmed by wave after wave of attention and energy. It was strong enough to take your breath away, and even then it was just a fraction of his total power. Goro tried to remain focused despite the attention.

The Abbot spoke, "I can see that something troubles you, Goro. Tell me, what happened?"

"Abbot, the girl concerns me. She is different than anyone I have ever met."

The Abbot listened politely. Goro knew he appreciated brevity, but it was also important to him that he explain why he felt how he did.

"I can barely feel her. When I touched her I was shocked by the amount of energy she was putting out. I had heard rumors in the neighborhood. Stories of being able to see things that no one else could. I went to the house just to test her."

Goro looked up. The Abbot seemed disinterested. Goro didn't understand. He sped up his retelling.

"I was convinced the rumors were without basis. I didn't feel anything from her as I approached. Even when I was right next to her she didn't seem to be anything special. I thought there was no way she could be one of us. But then I touched her, she's stronger than I ever believed. You're the only person I've ever met who is stronger."

Goro risked another glance. The Abbot seemed unconcerned.

"Abbot, I need your guidance. Please, let me know what is happening."

The Abbot waved his hand dismissively. "The girl has the power of the old ones. I have seen it before. Train her as you would any other. She will find her way on the new paths, or she will die."

Goro bowed again. He had heard of the powers of the old ones, but he had never experienced it. But he trusted the Abbot with his life. He would do as ordered. He always did.

CHAPTER 6

He still wasn't used to the golden crown on his forehead. The new Lord of the Southern Kingdom, Lord Akira, looked upon his army as they marched in front of him. He tried to ignore his itching scalp and imagined himself as a stone within a crashing river, solid and unmoving in the torrential chaos of life. He straightened his posture even further and wiped any hint of emotion from his face. Stone in a river.

The parade was the beginning of Lord Azuma's funeral march. He had died as he had lived, on the battlefield swearing both at his own generals and his enemy. The stories were already becoming legend, and as he thought about them they almost brought a smile to Akira's face. Almost. But fate had been too cruel. A lone archer, lost in the chaos of battle, had managed to get close enough to the Lord who rode upon his horse. It was a shot legends would someday be written about, but more likely it had been sheer luck. When the archer had been captured he had been nothing but a second-rate soldier, lost behind the front lines when his own troops retreated. His death had been slow and painful. Akira's anger had guaranteed that.

Azuma had lived long enough to see the defenses of the pass solidified. His campaign had pushed through the Three Sisters, and they now had built a foothold, a fort on the other side. After cycles of warfare a truce had been reached, and the Kingdom was at peace again, at least for today.

Akira ran his eyes over the assembled crowd. It seemed as though everyone in the Kingdom had made an appearance, and Akira was struck for a moment by the scope of his responsibility. He knew the people assembled were a minuscule proportion of the people under his rule, but the tide of faces stretched out forever. His father had been right about one thing. Ruling this many people was not an easy task. Those who killed for the responsibility were fools.

Akira held back his tears. There would be time later. Today he had a Kingdom to rule, and a Kingdom was not strong when its ruler wept.

He allowed his eyes to wander over the people again, picking out faces at random. His father had been many things to different people, and as Akira's glance passed from face to face he could see a spread of reactions. Some were angry, some sad. Some were cheerful, and some were plotting. Akira took it all in. His father had been many things. He had been a hard man and a hard ruler. More blood than seemed possible was on his hands and that blood had passed from the father to the son. Not all the blood was foreign either.

The young lord knew all this, but Azuma had also been his father. A strict and demanding, often absent father, but a father whose love and wisdom were never in question. Azuma hadn't always had time for his son, but when he was with Akira, Akira felt as though he were the only person in Azuma's world. Azuma had shown him the demands of power. He had never hidden the shadows of the power he wielded. He admitted to his son that he had killed his own people. He wasn't proud of it, but the only way to control the people was with an unyielding fist. Akira had thought it brutal growing up, and he still did, but he saw the wisdom in it now.

He brought his mind back to focus. He had a problem in front of him already, and his reflection had made the path clear. One of his father's favorite generals, a man well-respected in the military, was planning a coup. Akira had only seen twenty cycles and the belief among the old guard was that he was too young and too weak to lead. Akira understood their concern. Despite their treason, they had the interests of the Kingdom at heart, which made his choice more difficult.

The generals had never known the full extent of Akira's trainings. His father had made sure from his son's earliest days he would be groomed to rule. He was an only child, much to the dismay of those who wished for smooth continuation of the royal bloodlines. But Azuma had always fought with a close guard. Akira was twenty, yes, but he had the knowledge and training of a man twice his age. The generals didn't know about the thousands of hours of military history and physical training Akira had been subjected to. Azuma had once said that Akira would be the best-trained Lord the Kingdom had ever seen, and Akira didn't doubt the truth of the statement.

Akira calmed himself and thought through his moves, analyzing potential consequences. There was risk. But risk carried reward. In this case, great reward. The risk was his life, but better he controlled it than wait and be passive. The best defense was a strong offense.

Akira turned around and faced the audience behind him. General Yano, commander of the Second Army, was standing next to the visiting Lords from the Northern and Western Kingdoms. Both Sen, the Lord of the Northern Kingdom, and

Tanak, the Lord of the Western Kingdom, were in attendance. Tanak and Yano had been conversing in hushed tones throughout the parade. Sen, almost a grandfather figure to Akira, had been a silent if attentive neighbor.

Akira glanced at the other men nearby. General Nori, the commander of the First Army of the Southern Kingdom, was separated from the others. Akira's spies knew Nori was the true ringleader of the coup, but he wasn't a man to get his own hands dirty. He was a brilliant commander, one of the best generals the Southern Kingdom had ever seen, but his honor wouldn't allow him to do the hands-on dirty work a coup required. If he was concerned about Akira's strength, his concerns would be laid to rest soon.

Next to Nori was Toro, the youngest of Azuma's generals and commander of the Third. He watched the area around him like an eagle. Toro had just seen his forty-second cycle, and he and Azuma had been as close as brothers. They had served together for many cycles. Akira's spies reported that Toro did not collude with the other two generals, but he didn't turn them in either. Reports said that he was trying to play both sides of the field, but Akira found it hard to believe. Toro was too honorable of a man. He hadn't decided on the best course of action for the Three Kingdoms.

"General Yano."

The general stood up and snapped to attention. "Yes, Lord."

Akira lowered his voice. "I, in the presence of all these witnesses, charge you with treason. By law and custom I challenge you to a duel. Do you deny these charges?"

Yano was surprised. Akira didn't blame him. They had underestimated him. He had thought it through.

Yano bowed in recognition of the move. Nori was higher up in the chain of command and was a better commander. Yano was the stronger swordsman, providing Akira a more difficult challenge. If Akira could prove his strength, Nori might back down and support the young Lord. Challenging Yano in public left him with no options. If he denied the charges the other Lords would see a man without honor. If he accepted them, he kept the honor of his name but was still branded a traitor.

Yano glanced at Nori, who nodded almost imperceptibly. Yano returned his gaze to meet Akira's.

"No, Lord, I do not. I accept your challenge."

Akira stepped back to a proper dueling distance, studying his opponent with care. He had a small advantage in that he had watched Yano train many times. Yano had never seen him. Despite Yano's ability, he didn't know how fast or strong Akira was. It was a small advantage, but might be enough. Akira was confident, but not certain of his victory.

Yano returned Akira's studious gaze. He appreciated Akira's solid stance.

"Lord, accept my apology. It is not personal, but for the Kingdom. Know that I loved both you and your father. Please say tell him as much when you meet him in the Great Cycle."

Akira filed away the information. He was being underestimated. Yano wasn't prone to boasting, so he believed he would win.

Yano moved in to attack. He moved with grace and speed, but Akira was sure he had seen Yano move faster before. He was overconfident, trying to make a statement about how weak Akira was.

It was a fatal mistake. Akira deflected the cut and was within Yano's guard in one move. Akira hesitated just a moment. He had never killed before. It was just long enough for Yano to realize what had happened. There was no sadness in his eyes, just satisfaction at the surprising strength of his Lord. Akira cut and Yano's life was ended.

Akira looked straight at Nori, who returned the stare without flinching.

"Would anyone else care to claim responsibility for this attempt on the throne?"

Nori almost seemed to smile. Akira was no mind reader but his thoughts were obvious. He approved. Akira turned his back. It was done then. Better one life than civil war. He sheathed his sword and turned back to the funeral procession. All eyes had been on him. It would be a story that would pass through the land like wildfire. They wouldn't know why, not for a while. But it was for the best. He would start with fear, then move to respect if he could.

Akira caught sight of his father's funeral pyre, being carried by his honor guard. A single tear rolled down his eye, but he didn't think anyone saw. As his father's body passed by, Akira could only think about how much he missed his father.

CHAPTER 7

Ryuu was getting frustrated. He had been training with Shigeru for a full cycle. A whole cycle and he hadn't yet been made a nightblade. He tried to remind himself it would take many cycles, but he wasn't patient and training was slow. He hadn't learned anything useful about the sense skills that made the nightblades and the dayblades legendary.

They maintained a regular pattern of combat and physical training. There were rest days, but they were rest in the way that there was no particular training for that day. Shigeru encouraged Ryuu to play outside and to help out with chores around the house. Ryuu was glad to oblige. Shigeru's gentle encouragement was the same as a lesser man's orders in Ryuu's eyes.

As the morning sun rose Ryuu tried to keep his spirits up. He would learn. He knew he would. Shigeru wouldn't lie to him about that. The two rose as usual and Shigeru led them out into the woods, Ryuu following along, his frustration fueling his run. It wasn't as hard to keep up with Shigeru anymore. As he jogged behind, he wondered what training would be like today.

They had done physical training yesterday, but today Shigeru didn't carry any weapons beyond the sword and handful of throwing knives that never left his person. When they got to their usual clearing Ryuu stopped but Shigeru kept running without pause. Ryuu followed, going deeper into the old woods than he had ever been before. He wouldn't admit it, but being deep in the old woods alone still frightened him. Everyone knew that you stayed away from the old woods. They were thick and dark and damp, and his boyish imagination didn't have any difficulty creating monsters to populate it with.

But with Shigeru in the lead he followed without question. He wasn't scared, not when Shigeru was around.

They didn't go too far into the old woods. He tried not to show his emotions, but he was relieved. He trusted Shigeru, but people just didn't go into the old woods. It wasn't smart. Ryuu wasn't too good at estimating distance or time, but he felt like they were only deep enough in that they were completely surrounded by the old wood. The trees and plants he was used to were nowhere to be found.

Shigeru grinned at him and asked, "How are your climbing skills?"

He pointed upwards.

Ryuu followed his finger and saw that in one of the trees there was a platform. It was maybe only three times Shigeru's height, but to the boy it was a very long way up.

"There's no way that I can make it up to there."

"I thought as much. There's a rope up there I can toss down to you." Ryuu didn't know how anyone could climb the tree. The nearest branches were half again as high as Shigeru. To Ryuu's amazement, Shigeru took a couple of steps back and ran at the tree. He leapt, planting his right foot on the tree. To Ryuu, it looked like he pushed off that foot, and in the space of that single move he was able to get himself up to the lowest branch, and with his momentum, on top of it. From there he was able to climb branch to branch until he reached the top. It took him a couple of moments at most. If Ryuu hadn't been watching he might have missed it.

Ryuu stood at the bottom with his mouth hanging open. He trained a lot with Shigeru, and he always knew Shigeru was holding back when they trained together. But he had forgotten just how capable Shigeru was.

Shigeru lowered a rope and Ryuu was able to climb up. He was impressed by his own climbing skills as well. He figured that a cycle ago he never would have been able to pull himself up so easily. Training with Shigeru was making him stronger. It was a concrete reminder he was making progress.

When he pulled himself to the top, Shigeru invited him to stand for a moment and look around. The view was incredible. They weren't too close to the top of the tree, but their vantage point did allow them to see quite a ways through the forest. Ryuu forgot he was supposed to be afraid of the deep woods. The trees here were different, wrapped in vines or other growth. Some had different plants growing out from and around them. Ryuu could hear birds and other small animals although he could not see them. Ryuu wondered if all the stories his father had told him when he was younger were wrong. He had thought at first the old forest was dying and scary, haunted by spirits, ghosts, and monsters. Instead, it was even more alive than the forest he played in every day.

His reverie was broken by Shigeru, speaking quietly and with a sense of awe. "You know, I used to come here often, and I almost took it for granted. Not anymore though. Life has been hectic this past cycle, but it is wonderful to be back here again. Can you guess why I built this stand?"

Ryuu examined the surroundings with a more careful eye. While the view was amazing, he couldn't see anything that would recommend this particular spot as a stand. Shigeru wasn't using it to spy on someone else, that much was certain. Nothing else came to his mind, and he shrugged.

"It's because I used to hunt here in the woods. See the path that runs there?" He pointed, and what Ryuu hadn't seen before became as clear as day. It wasn't much, but there were thin worn paths running underneath their feet, places where the vegetation had been disturbed on a regular basis.

Inspiration struck Ryuu as he examined the space around him. "A lot of the paths come together here. This was a spot where you had a good chance of seeing different animals if they walked by here."

Shigeru was pleased by the deduction of his pupil. "That's right. But I've also always liked climbing, so part of it was for fun too. Do you have any idea why we came out here today?"

"To hunt?"

Shigeru shook his head. "That will come later. There are some more skills I want you to develop before we attempt to hunt together. Today I brought you out here because I'm going to start trying to teach you about the sense."

Ryuu's breath caught in his throat. It was hard for him to admit how much he wanted to learn.

After his initial excitement faded Ryuu was confused. There was no way he could be a nightblade. The monks had come and tested him just like they tested everyone around his age. Ryuu had tried his best. He wanted to impress the monks, to show them he was the great warrior they had been searching for. But they had simply shaken their heads and Ryuu remembered being held tightly by his mother after.

He tried to wipe the image from his mind. Every time that he thought of his mother his vision started to swim with memories of blood. It was easier to try to forget, to push it down into places where he couldn't remember.

After the flood of emotions had washed through him, all that was left was the despair of failing to reach his dream and the anger he felt at losing his parents. It caused him to react bitterly. "You can teach me about it, but I can't do it. The monks said that I would never be a great nightblade."

Shigeru laughed out loud, which only served to increase Ryuu's irritation. "It's not funny." He crossed his arms and attempted to stomp his feet, although his position on a barely steady tree stand limited him to shuffling his feet in childish anger.

Shigeru continued laughing. It was only Ryuu's prolonged angry stare that caused Shigeru to calm down.

"I'm sorry. . . I realize it's not funny to you." Shigeru had his hands on his knees. "Oh, to see your face. I'm sorry, that was priceless. I forget sometimes how respected the monks are here. What if I told you that the monks that you know are less intelligent than your average piece of rabbit droppings?"

Ryuu glanced at Shigeru to see if he was joking. He seemed serious, but there was a glint in his eye. "They can't be dumb. They are responsible for making sure that the sense is protected and that they protect all of our kingdoms, making sure that there is never another great war again!"

Shigeru chuckled again, but held himself better than before.

"Trust me when I say that none of that is true, but for now I am willing to let it rest. There are larger problems afoot, and the first is that we need to teach you how to use the sense."

Ryuu's respect for Shigeru clashed with the deeply ingrained fear and respect of the monks.

"I'm going to be a nightblade? Even if the monks said I never would?"

"I think you will be. I hope you will be. At least, most of me does. In the end, the decision is up to you. It's not always going to be easy or fun, but it's up to you to decide whether or not you keep training."

There was no hesitation on Ryuu's part. He had feared the monks, but he trusted Shigeru. "Let's get started then."

Shigeru nodded and motioned for him to lie down. "It's easiest to begin when you are relaxed and focused."

Ryuu lay down and did his best to relax. It was difficult with the excitement running though his body.

"The first and most important thing you must know is this: the whole world around us is alive. I'm not saying that the moss in the stream have feelings or that the trees have thoughts like you do. But there is energy, a connection between all things. Simply put, your ability with the sense is the ability to be aware of that energy, to know where living things are and to know how things are going to move. In reality, the sense is nothing more than the ability to have a little bit more information than the others around you."

Ryuu didn't understand what Shigeru was talking about. In his head he imagined everything being connected by a rope, but everything was stuck in place because it was connected to everything else, the whole world stuck in one large spider web. The imaginary picture almost made him giggle, but he caught it in time. Shigeru was speaking very softly and with reverence. This was not the time for laughter.

Shigeru paused for a moment as if deciding what to say next. He stopped talking about the sense and switched to giving Ryuu concrete instructions. As he lay down on the tree stand, Shigeru tried to get him to focus on his breathing.

Ryuu had never thought about his breathing before. Shigeru coached him in taking deep breaths, slowing him down until Ryuu thought he wasn't getting enough air. "If you can hear yourself breathing through your nose, you are breathing too quickly." It took a little practice, but soon Ryuu was maintaining a perfect breathing rhythm.

As Ryuu narrowed his attention on his breath, he experienced the strangest sensations. It was like he was trying to close a window in his imagination, but the more he focused, the more he shut out his thoughts, the more the light came in. Something was happening, but he lacked the words to describe his experience.

His eyes were closed per Shigeru's instructions, and his mind relaxed on his breathing. He felt emptied. A part of his mind was aware of the brush of the wind moving through the trees and the sounds of the forest, but he paid no attention to any sensation except his breath. He knew the deer approaching the tree below was a young buck.

Something clicked in his mind and realization hit him. There was no deer below them. He hadn't seen or heard a deer, but he knew that a deer was present nearby. He sat up and opened his eyes to see Shigeru studying him, a knowing smile on his face.

"I saw a deer. Did I imagine it?"

Shigeru didn't say anything. He had just the slightest trace of a smile as he pointed with his left hand. Approaching below them was the same deer Ryuu had just seen. Ryuu's disbelief and excitement quarreled with each other, but the excitement overpowered doubt like water breaking through a dam.

Possibilities ran through his mind. In a moon he would be killing bandits with ease! He imagined glory and battles and helping those weaker than him with his skills. He could find lost animals! He would hunt like Shigeru, for now Ryuu knew how he did it. If you knew where the animal was going to be every time hunting would be a simple task.

Shigeru attempted to get Ryuu to focus, but he saw he was fighting a battle he couldn't win. Ryuu tried, but he might as well have tried to stop a thunderstorm. Ryuu laid back down on the stand and attempted to focus once more, but his excitement was too great. Shigeru tried to hide his disappointment. No one ever succeeded on their first attempt. That much he knew. The boy had, but he lacked the ability to replicate the feat. Shigeru had felt Ryuu's sphere of attention expand. His sense had expanded out in all directions, like tendrils searching for any life they could find. To be able to use the sense in a manner that was so natural would serve the boy well. He hoped that the initial success wasn't just a fluke.

It was clear no more success would visit them today. Shigeru could feel the boy trying to focus, but he was six and didn't have such a high level of control. He sighed inwardly. He was beginning to realize just how patient his own tutors had been with him. No man could ever accuse Shigeru of being impatient, but even the simple training of a young boy was enough to push his limits.

The problem was his potential. If the boy had been ordinary, just another boy, or even the type of boy the monasteries found and trained, Shigeru wouldn't have had such high expectations. But the boy was special. He interacted with the sense in the old ways, in the ways that Shigeru himself had been trained. It was the natural way, the stronger path, but here on the mainland, no one followed the old ways anymore. The monasteries, corrupted by political influence and crippled by the knowledge lost in the

Purge, had lost the way, and the sense was passed down in a new way, a shell of the power it had once possessed. Ryuu had potential to be great. Possibly even greater than Shigeru if he worked hard enough at it.

But Shigeru, like the boy, had to remind himself success did not come overnight. He wanted the boy to be great almost as much as the boy himself wanted it.

The following moons and cycles passed by in a blur. Ryuu thought the previous training had been a dream come true, but the new training, which included instruction in the sense and combat, was pure bliss. It wasn't to say it was easy. It was the hardest task Ryuu ever set himself to. There were days of physical training, conditioning, and combat. Mixed in was training in the sense. Over and over Shigeru brought Ryuu to the edge of complete exhaustion and then brought him back, giving him a day of rest while they focused on developing his sense.

The days were filled and busy. Chores, studies, training, more chores. Ryuu was never bored with his environment. He learned how to cook, garden, hunt, understand the importance of the stars in the sky and the different ways to navigate through the world. He learned the geography and history of the Three Kingdoms and could recite distinguished bloodlines while performing challenging workouts.

One technique Shigeru often employed was mixing learning with physical tasks. They would work with numbers while out running, or Ryuu would have to answer questions about the world while sparring. He became an expert at thinking on his feet while the world spun around him.

Shigeru sharpened Ryuu's love of observation. Before he met Shigeru, Ryuu had been curious about his surroundings, but through his new master he learned how to turn that curiosity into useful information. He learned how to tell if people were lying, how to mix his visual observations with what he learned about his environment through the sense and most importantly, he learned how to be aware of everything happening around him at every moment. The training even extended into his sleep as Shigeru taught him how to maintain a relaxed sense-awareness at night. As his sense skill grew he became like Shigeru, impossible to sneak up on.

Two cycles went by in this manner. Winter had turned to spring long ago, and spring turned into summer, fall, and winter again. Ryuu had determined where he lived now was more temperate than the village where he had been born. There was still snow during the winter, but it didn't blow and drift at Shigeru's home the way it did on the plains of his early childhood. In the same way summer wasn't too warm. The trees and the terrain kept much of the land shaded and cool.

Ryuu had never had much, but with Shigeru he learned how to do with less. They possessed little. Shigeru carried his weapons everywhere, but besides garden implements and cookware, there was nothing else in the house. At times Shigeru would make journeys and return with reading materials for Ryuu to practice with, but Ryuu didn't have the toys of his younger days.

It was spring when Shigeru began to act distracted. Ryuu could tell there was something on his mind but decided not to ask He would discover in due time if he was supposed to. If Shigeru never spoke of it, it wasn't for him to know. Whatever it was, it distracted him every day. Often Ryuu would catch Shigeru staring off into the distance as if the horizon was hiding the answer he was looking for.

One evening over supper it finally broke.

"Ryuu, in a couple of days I am going to leave. I'll leave on the new moon, just for tracking time's sake. I plan on being gone for several days, but it may be longer. I'd like you to stay here."

Ryuu accepted the news without comment. He had been expecting something of the sort. He had often been left alone at the hut but never for more than a few days. His childhood fears began to surface, bubbling through the protective layer he had hidden them under.

Shigeru weighed his words. "I believe that it is time for me to take a journey. It touches on my own past, and I haven't been sure about it, but I've made up my mind. I thought about taking you with me, but there is some danger involved and I would rather you remain here."

"Will I be fine here without you?" There was a hint of doubt in Ryuu's voice.

Shigeru flashed a smile at the question. "I don't think you realize it yet, but though you're only eight you're probably the strongest warrior besides myself in the area. I'm sure you'll be able to handle yourself, and I don't expect anyone to show up here. I'll make sure supplies are taken care of. I don't want your training to change. You know how to push yourself. You've been doing it now for several cycles, it will just be up to you to motivate yourself to keep training for the next couple of days."

The morning after the moon turned, Shigeru prepared to leave.

"I'm hoping I will only be gone for a half moon, but if you see a full moon before I return, you need to accept something might have happened to me. Go down to the village just like I've talked about in the past. You need to tell them I was your uncle but that I disappeared. Pretty much anyone in the village would be willing to help you. Just stay away from the monks. If I'm alive, I will find you."

Ryuu nodded his consent, but couldn't help running up to Shigeru and embracing him. The move caught Shigeru by surprise. The two of them weren't given to hugging. Still, Shigeru returned the embrace and tussled Ryuu's hair. Then he turned around and was off without a backwards glance.

Shigeru's absence didn't affect Ryuu as much as he expected. He followed Shigeru's instructions to the letter. Being busy allowed him to forget he was alone in the world. Every morning he did chores and trained. He would play for a while and then finish the day with more chores and more training. He even pictured Shigeru's stares of disapproval anytime he made a small error. It wasn't hard to do.

It was only at night that his fears manifested. Ryuu still had occasional nightmares. When he was awake he couldn't remember his mother's face anymore. He wished that he had a painting or something he could use to remember her, but she existed in his memories, locked away during the day. Every time she came to mind all Ryuu could think of was the final look she gave him, but even that look was was decaying in his memory, leaving only the feelings of her death, exaggerated with every remembrance.

Ryuu took to getting up and walking out of the little cabin at night when the nightmares would wake him. Walking naked in the night, he would come out into the cool air surrounding the hut and would look up at the night sky. On the cloudy nights there was no relief, but on the clear nights Ryuu would stare at the moon. As the days passed it stopped fading and began to grow, a little more each night. As it grew Ryuu would look at it and think, "Shigeru will be on his way back soon. Just a few more days and he will be back. I just need to be strong until then. He would make fun of me if he knew how much trouble I had when he wasn't around." Repeating this mantra over and over, Ryuu would succumb to sleep.

Shigeru returned two evenings before the full moon. Their meeting was a warm one. Ryuu sensed him coming from quite a distance away. He broke from the house and met him while he was still deep in the woods. Ryuu had expected to get in some trouble for his rashness, but Shigeru said nothing, answering Ryuu's enthusiasm with his own grin. The two left much unspoken in a tight embrace.

Shigeru didn't speak to the purpose of his journey, but he was carrying a large package on his back. It was long and narrow, wrapped in a cloth that was covered in dirt and grime. It didn't seem like something someone traveled many leagues to find. When they got back to the hut, Shigeru kicked Ryuu out to go play. Ryuu knew he was being sent away because of the package. His curiosity was overwhelming, and he tried several times to sneak back to the cabin, but Shigeru's sense couldn't be fooled, and he was yelled at from behind the closed door every time. Ryuu finally gave up and ran to play in the woods.

When Ryuu returned closer to evening Shigeru was more prepared for him. There were a couple of new items around the cabin, but Ryuu knew that something more was still afoot. The package had been too large and the new items Ryuu could see around the house did not add up to the space of the package. A new pot and some spices did not a long journey make. Shigeru, as always, knew what Ryuu was thinking. He laughed out loud. "There's really no use in trying to hide anything from you, is there?"

Ryuu shook his head. Shigeru groaned to himself and thought for a minute, giving Ryuu the look he always dreaded. It was as if Shigeru was trying to stare right into his soul. Finally

Shigeru seemed to reach a decision. "Fine, I think you're ready, at least for the gift itself. I'll show you the real purpose of my trip tomorrow. What I am going to do is something that should be done during the daylight, and so you'll have to content yourself with one more night of waiting."

It turned out one more night of waiting wasn't a problem at all for Ryuu. He was so tired from his sleepless nights he fell asleep early and slept in late. He awoke disoriented. It was unlike Shigeru to let him sleep in. The truth was apparent when he looked over and saw Shigeru asleep himself.

Ryuu determined he was going to get a jump on the day. He did his best to complete his chores as quickly as possible, and much to his frustration Shigeru seemed content to try to sleep the entire day away. Ryuu had done all his chores and completed his morning training before Shigeru stirred from his slumber.

To Ryuu's dismay, Shigeru went about his morning routine as if nothing was different. He awoke, ate a light breakfast and went through his own morning routine. Having nothing to do, Ryuu watched his master, his father. He was so fast, and even though Ryuu had been training with him for almost three cycles, there was still no way for Ryuu to track all of his movements, although he was getting better.

Shigeru finished his training and went into the house. Ryuu sat, pretending patience. When Shigeru reappeared Ryuu saw he was carrying a large bundle wrapped in the dirty cloth again. Shigeru nodded and the two of them went walking. It didn't take Ryuu long to realize they were going back to the small clearing in the woods.

The arrived and Shigeru knelt down to the ground, placing the package in front of him. Ryuu followed his master's lead, facing him from three paces away.

Ryuu's breath caught as Shigeru unwrapped the package. His actions were deliberate and Ryuu thought he wouldn't be more careful if he was unpacking a baby. It was a pair of swords, both the long and the short. The sheaths were simple black but beautiful. They were similar to Shigeru's. The hilt was simple, but when Shigeru pulled the blade from its home, Ryuu knew he had been given an incredible gift. The blade was as fine as Shigeru's, which Ryuu knew was unique in the Southern Kingdom. It was a sword fit for a prince.

Ryuu bowed forehead to the ground as Shigeru presented him the sword.

"These blades belonged to a dear friend of mine. I think she would be glad for you to have them."

Ryuu's ears perked up at the mention of a "she." Shigeru never spoke of women. He filed it away as his eyes continued to drink in the vision of his gift.

"Take care of them, please."

Ryuu looked up. There was a surprising amount of emotion in Shigeru's face.

"I will."

Shigeru nodded. After a few moments of silence he composed himself again.

"Always remember. You hold a weapon designed to take the life of another. It is a tool for killing. Never forget that. However, perhaps through one man's death you can protect another. I pray you will succeed in your responsibility."

Ryuu was overwhelmed with gratitude and joy and excitement, but he just managed to catch what Shigeru said under his breath to no one in particular.

"I pray that you'll do better than me."

CHAPTER 8

The first three cycles of Takako's servitude were as pleasant as growing up in a brothel could be. Parting from her father had been difficult, but she had always looked on the bright side and it didn't take her long to settle into her new life. Madame did not push. She checked in every day. Despite Takako's attempts to demonize her, it was hard not to like and respect her. When she came in she was warm and maternal, asking questions and listening to Takako's answers. She frowned when Takako was upset and smiled when Takako let herself relax.

Takako was always on the lookout for that inner steel she had felt upon her first meeting with Madame. But it never reappeared and Takako began to wonder if she had imagined it all. Madame was nothing but caring and concerned. Perhaps she had judged Madame too soon?

She decided to wait and see. If Madame was kind, Takako could be kind as well. But she wouldn't let down her guard. After her first four days as a self-imposed prisoner she decided to face what was in store for her. She couldn't put it off forever even if she wanted to.

Madame put her to work the moment she stepped out and from then on Takako was too busy to be depressed. She was up early every morning to do chores, cleaning and repairing the place from the night previous. Sheets needed to be washed and rooms needed to be picked up. The chores took her most of the morning. When she was done she reported to the kitchen to learn and work. She learned how to cook and bake breads. She learned about spices and how to combine them to create savory, sweet, or sour dishes. Beyond the techniques, she learned about food: where different plants came from, how much meals would cost, and other areas of conversation with men who might be interested in food.

Lessons were always practical. Every instruction she received related to the satisfaction of the men and women she would one day serve. The thought never bothered her when she knew she would get a small portion of her culinary efforts for her own mid-day meal.

After lunch Takako received the education she'd always dreamed of. Although the work was difficult it was one of her favorite parts of the day. Learning how to read, how to write, and learning about numbers was satisfying. She liked being able to write her thoughts down. It was powerful to think she could write something down and someone else could share in her experience in a different time or in a different location. But what she enjoyed most was the history and her lessons about the Three Kingdoms. Growing up she had learned about her village's history, but even that was limited. There were stories and rumors about the world outside, but in general everyone kept to their own business. Survival was hard enough. It was exciting to hear the stories of old, of heroes and villains who had changed the course of history. Every once in a while her instructors would catch her daydreaming, imagining being caught in one of the stories read to her.

Takako learned about the Great War and how the wickedness of the nightblades had been forever wiped out from society. Like all in the Three Kingdoms, she had heard of them before, but now she learned why the Purge had been necessary. She learned about the monasteries and how they worked to protect the Three Kingdoms.

After the afternoon study sessions Takako was given a little time to relax. She had toys to play with, and as she learned how to read she was given books. It was in the evening when the house was most busy, so the hours between her afternoon studying and evening chores became some of her most precious time. She was also given paper to write on although never too much. Paper was expensive and Takako was always grateful to Madame for allowing her to write. She wrote letters to her father in small neat handwriting so she could fit as much on the page as possible. She never asked if she could send them for fear that Madame would say no. When she had filled a piece of paper back and front with her small handwriting she would fold it up and put it with the rest of her meager possessions.

Evenings were another round of chores and learning. Some nights she would shadow a particular client or one of the women. Takako was taught how to be a keen observer, to notice how the women made men comfortable, made them want the women. Madame's women were the best in the city. They were educated and could talk of philosophy, theology, politics, history, food, drink, whatever the man was interested in. The men who came knew this. Sex was easy to find in New Haven. There were many brothels and even more street-women. Men came to Madame's because they wanted something more and were willing to pay for it. They wanted the illusion of a relationship, the comforting world of having someone to talk to whose only concern was their well-being. Takako found it sickening. Many of the men who came in were married, many of them middle-aged or older.

Over time Takako learned not just the secrets of the women who worked for Madame, but she learned the secrets of the city as well. She realized almost anybody important in New Haven had a relationship with Madame. She knew most of the appointed officials, generals, soldiers, and spies. She even knew the Abbot of the nearest monastery. Takako was young, but she understood the power of the knowledge Madame's women brought to her.

Over the course of her first three cycles Takako came to meet and know almost everyone important in the city, and it seemed at times like almost everyone knew her. Although it had never been spoken of in Takako's presence, no man tried to buy her services. They would often greet her warmly, and a couple of the older gentlemen would bring her small gifts like she was a surrogate grand-daughter. She was a servant in the house, but her fate was known to all. Already she had overheard whispers of the future. Men were offering ridiculous sums of money for Takako's first time. Madame was pleased and she let them wait.

Her reception from the women who worked in the house was varied. Some attempted to bring her under their wing, showing her the ropes and how to be more successful at the house. The majority were not interested in her. She was an additional presence, easy to be ignored. She was not yet one of them, so not worthy of their time and attention. They did not treat her poorly, but they did not treat her well either. The final group of women were those who seemed hostile to her presence among them. The friendlier women claimed it was because Takako was young, beautiful, and unspoiled. The other women were jealous. Whatever the reason, Takako learned to keep her distance from them. They gave her extra chores and let snide comments slide when she was just at the edge of hearing.

Those women had to be careful though. At the end of the day the house was Madame's and her word was law. She had accepted Takako, and so long as Takako abided by the rules of the house she was to be given all the respect that any of the women received. The women could toe the line, but none of them dared cross it. Their profession may be one of the lowest, but they were the top of the bottom rung and none of them wanted to endanger their position.

The only aspect of Takako's life which was odious was her interactions with General Nori. Takako had heard the stories which followed him like a shadow. From what she could tell he was the most powerful man in the region. He was the general of the Southern Kingdom's second army, making him one of the four most powerful men in the Kingdom. He was also a frequent customer of Madame's.

He was unlike the others. Most customers came to be with someone, to take and pretend they were with a person who cared about them. To Nori, a trip to Madame's was no different than a trip to the lowest class whorehouse. He had a wife back many cycles ago who had given him a male heir. The wife had died in her childbirth to the boy. Since then Nori frequented Madame's whenever he was near the city.

None of the women liked him. Regardless of their relationship to Takako, every one of them did their best to keep her away from him. She was the adopted daughter of the house and he was rougher with the women than anyone else. If Nori had been anyone else Madame would have had him killed. But a general of the Southern Kingdom was untouchable, and he took advantage of the fact by treating the women at Madame's the way he wanted. The General was the only person who could bend Madame to her knee. There was no recourse for her and Takako had heard some of the women say he didn't even pay full price.

It was unbearable because the General had his eyes on Takako. Every time he came by he would send an invitation to her she could not refuse. She would come to him and serve him drinks while he spent his time with another woman. He did not attempt to sleep with her, which was both a relief and source of confusion to Takako. He did not come to enjoy the company of any woman at the house. He came for sex alone, so why antagonize her?

His non-sexual interest in her was worse. Sometimes Takako caught herself thinking it would just be easier if he would take her to bed and get it over with. There was something intimidating in a man who wasn't interested in sex with you when you were in a brothel.

Nori was also unique in that he saw Madame frequently. Madame was very concerned about her privacy and few men were ever allowed to see her face. It protected her house and her women, but Nori had demanded. He could have the place burned to the ground and no one would question his right to do so. Every time he visited he had tea with Madame, an action Takako suspected was akin to gloating.

Every time the General had tea he requested Takako serve. This afternoon was no different. General Nori hadn't even announced his intention to visit. Despite the rudeness, Madame wasn't caught off guard. There were enough ears around that she often heard all she needed to know. She knew Nori was in town, and if he was in town he always visited. It was only a matter of when. She had warned all the girls and had canceled the appointments of the girls he liked best.

For Takako the dreadful news did have a silver lining. She had to be ready to serve tea on short notice and so was able to skip the more physically demanding chores for the days they were on watch. She still had lessons and light chores to keep her occupied, but she wasn't running around the house sweating so it was a definite improvement.

Takako felt like waiting for Nori to visit was akin to waiting for death. You knew it was coming, and the fear of it could paralyze you, but there was no way to avoid it. So you just kept going forward. And so she did. She decided to make herself as happy as possible and did her best to ignore her impending fate.

Nori's arrival was just as inevitable as one's journey to the Great Cycle, and when he did arrive it was no great surprise to anyone. Takako changed into her clothes to receive him and went down to the kitchen to grab the tea.

Takako could not enter the reception room without thinking about her father and their parting. It had been three full cycles and the memory of that day still burned like it had happened yesterday. She passed the exact spot she and her father had their last embrace as she carefully approached with the tea, smiling so all the world could know she was happy to be here serving this man.

General Nori was an imposing figure. He stood taller than most other men and had the physical size to match. He had been one of the strongest men in the world at one time, it was said. As he had aged his body had decayed, but he was still the strongest man Takako had ever seen. He could have broken her father in half, and she suspected that he could even best the younger guards who vigilantly watched the house. It was rumored that he was still the best swordsman in the Three Kingdoms.

General Nori's hair was starting to grey, which only terrified Takako more. There was something about an older man who had the habits of a killer that made shivers run up her spine. Soldiering and killing seemed to be something young men did, not something older men should be adept at.

Nori bowed his head a small fraction of an inch when Takako entered. Coming from him it was an impressive sign of respect, although Takako didn't trust it. Takako served the tea, trying to perform the actions as with as much grace as she could manage at high speed. She hoped to escape before having to spend too much time in the General's company.

As she moved to stand and leave, Nori gestured for her to sit. Takako glanced at Madame, who made no motion to counteract the General's request. Her stomach sinking, Takako knelt down off to the side and slightly closer to Madame's side as required of her station.

Satisfied, Nori and Madame resumed their conversation. Takako's stomach twisted as she tried to fathom the layers of meaning to their conversation. She knew from all her training that Madame and those she interacted with rarely spoke of what they meant. Takako tried to decipher the hidden meanings, but was too distracted to focus.

Despite Takako's inability to follow the conversation the topics seemed rather mundane. There was talk about the weather, the General's health, his recent activity and the such. Takako found herself flustered, convinced something more was being said, but being bored by the conversation itself.

She was caught by surprise when Nori turned and spoke to her.

"How are you finding Madame's hospitality?"

Takako bowed her head towards Madame in a gesture of respect. "Madame has been very kind to me, and she has taught me much about the world that I didn't know before."

Although Takako had been referencing her book studies, her comment brought the barest hint of a smile to the General's face. Takako realized the general had understood a different meaning. She found herself even more nervous, a feat she hadn't imagined possible a few moments ago.

"Tell me, Takako, what have you learned while you have been here?"

"I have learned much. I have learned how to read and write, how to cook, and how to prepare the tea. And I have learned about people."

"What can you tell me about me?"

"You are a general without equal in these parts. You are one of the top advisors to the Lord and command the largest contingent of men under his control. You have been victorious in battle, and while your men fear you, they also respect you."

Nori smiled at that summary. It was the most terrifying face that Takako had ever seen. "I appreciate the directness of your answer even if it does lack a certain amount of tact. But all you have proven to me thus far is that you have studied history and have listened to rumors about me. What do you know about me?"

Takako glanced over to Madame for guidance but her face was completely neutral. No help there. She had been taught in these moments to be honest. It was a lesson Madame hadn't been able to replace from Takako's childhood.

"You are a controlling man who is not used to either rejection or failure. You believe that you can control not just yourself but others as well. You have had no experience yet which contradicts the belief. It makes you strong, but like many strengths, also doubles as your weakness. You feel you are given the authority to punish those who do not please you and enjoy being able to exert power over others. You believe you make the laws that govern the land but are not answerable to them."

The silence in the room was deafening. Takako noticed Nori with his hand on the hilt of his sword. Perhaps she had gone too far this time.

The moment stretched, and Takako let out the deep breath she didn't even realize she had been holding when Nori relaxed his hand and brought it back to his lap.

"You are a very observant girl, and very clever as well. I do not know if anyone has ever spoken as directly as you have. Certainly no one that lived to tell about it." He paused for effect. "However, I shall allow you to leave with your life today."

Takako bowed her forehead to the floor and exited the room. Her heart was pounding, and it took all the courage she possessed to control her breathing and facial expression. Stupid! She could have been killed and Madame never would have done anything to protect her. She cursed herself and her fate as she went back to her room.

In her absence the room she had just left remained quiet. Madame did not show any expression of concern or care. But, Nori thought, she never did. If she had been a man and a warrior she would have been a very dangerous enemy. As it was she was still be a force to be reckoned with, but Nori felt she thought too highly of herself. She valued information over strength. Information was valuable but the ability and will to take life had no equal on this world.

Madame resumed their conversation. Nori appreciated one thing about the woman. She was intelligent. Their conversations were always interesting. In time the conversation turned to Nori's son, Akio. Nori was proud of his son, who was nearing the age of manhood.

"My son is young and untried in battle, but I am confident his skills will be of great use to him as he enters manhood."

"I am sure he will bring honor to your family name, much like you have."

"It is very much my wish that this be so. I wish to put him on the path and provide for him any opportunities that will lead to his success."

Madame nodded, already guessing the turn that this conversation was going. "It is as much as any parent would hope to provide."

"You don't have any children, do you?"

Madame felt her heart drop, a familiar sensation to this question. How had Nori known? "No. I am not able. But the women here are as my own daughters."

Nori laughed. "You are a horrible mother to whore out your children."

Madame shook with rage. It wasn't much, but it was a better fate than these women would have had elsewhere. But Nori wasn't done.

"I came today to ask for a consort for him for the spring season when we go to war."

Madame was taken aback. The question itself was beyond rude, beyond being socially acceptable. The request was impossible. No woman had ever left Madame's house. They were her daughters of misfortune. The work was what it was, but it was safe. Madame always made it so. Sending a woman off to war was wrong.

"I'm sorry, general, but as you know the women of this house aren't allowed to leave the premises except under escort, and are never allowed to leave the city."

The general waved away her excuses as though he were brushing away a fly. "I'm sorry that you feel that way. I have long been a supporter of this little endeavor of yours. It has always been a quality establishment. But I will have a woman for my son."

Madame felt a flush of anger and struggled to suppress it. She had to remain calm and decide how to deal with this man. If a man, any man, could come in here and leave with one of the girls she would soon be dealing with mutiny. Her mission would be ruined. She couldn't let it happen but couldn't think of a way to stop it.

The general continued. "It is my desire that my son have a consort who will instruct him and be available to him without reservation so he may maintain his focus on the campaign. As a young man in a position of privilege, it would not be unheard of for unscrupulous women to approach him and attempt to get him to divulge information. A consort would protect him against such indiscretions. I believe Takako will serve him well."

Madame felt her stomach drop even further. She had always assumed Takako would become the general's favorite when she came of age. Already her beauty was well known around the region, and Madame had looked forward to grooming her to be the consort of the most powerful men in the city. Information was power, and Takako would acquire much of it.

Madame's mind raced as she sipped her tea. She thought about attempting to kill Nori. He had been a well-known swordsman back in his day, but she hadn't heard anything about his skill since he had taken to commanding the army. Her guards were superb, but she had no way of knowing. She was not a fighter and couldn't judge. It was too risky and difficult to hide or frame. Nori was one of the most powerful men in the realm and his death was sure to have more consequences than Madame could calculate.

On the other hand she feared for the reputation of her house and the women who worked for her. Working at Madame's was safe. Their work was dangerous for many women and deaths, beatings, and maiming were common stories on the streets. As long as they lived under Madame's house, her women were safe and protected. Every day they turned away desperate women. Madame had a reputation around the city for defending her women and no men dared try their luck, no matter their level of intoxication. To risk her reputation risked everything. Madame felt her future unraveling.

Accept or resist, neither option put Madame in a better place. There was a good deal of time left before spring season, and it was worth playing with Nori while she tried to figure out alternatives.

Nori was tired of waiting. "Madame, I know you believe your house is different. That although you live richly, you are somehow the protector of these women. But make no mistake, at the end of the day your girls are whores. They are the best whores in the whole region, and whatever lies you tell yourself to make them so are fine by me. But Takako will come with me in the spring to accompany my son. Prepare her, and your house will stand. Cross me, and your house will burn with you and your girls inside."

All Madame could do was nod her assent. She would protect her girls, no matter the cost, but she did not know how.

CHAPTER 9

Despite her desire, Moriko did not try to escape. Her inability to work up the courage to try infuriated her. She wanted to see the outside world more than she desired food. But she believed the monks and she believed her new friends, if they could be called friends. Her courage failed her, vanished like a shadow in the night. Everyone she asked had the same story. The easy escape, the first few days of freedom. The inevitable capture and lashes. Moriko understood. You could escape the monastery but you couldn't escape the monks.

Life wasn't all bad though. Tomotsu was a welcome presence in Moriko's life the first few seasons of her time at Perseverance. He was an optimist and never gave up hope of escape even though his first attempt had been so unsuccessful. Moriko doubted he would ever get around to escaping again. He talked a lot about it, but he never planned anything, never took any concrete actions. Life in the monastery was difficult but food was always provided, the fires always burned at night, and the life of a monk was one of privilege in society. Although the life may be severe at times, it seemed worthwhile to all the monks who trained them. They were believers.

There was always plenty of talk about the outside world. Moriko remembered being treated as an odd child by her family, but other children had stories that made her realize how lucky she had been. Once people found out they possessed the sense they were shunned from society, often beaten or hunted. The monastery could be hard, but it was safe compared to a life outside the walls.

Monastic life was nothing if not routine. Rise with the sun, morning exercise, chores, classes, lunch, combat training, sense training, supper, more classes, bed. At least, Moriko thought, it was not hard to fall asleep at night. The first few nights had been more difficult. Moriko missed the old forest, the sounds and peace and serenity that she experienced while she lived there. She missed her father and their journeys into the old woods. She missed listening to the sound of his voice as he explained the things she didn't know. But busy days and physical exhaustion kept her from lamenting too much.

As the seasons changed Moriko's attitude began to change, so subtly she didn't notice the change at first. When she had first arrived Tomotsu talked daily of escape, but as the seasons passed the talk became less frequent as he became more involved in his training. Moriko would sometimes try to remind him of his former passion, but it was a risky proposition. She worried she was losing her one confidant inside the monastery walls. As Tomotsu grew older and more comfortable in his life his desire for change and freedom diminished. He grew stronger and more powerful, more attached to the life and privilege of a monk. Moriko took small comfort in knowing at least he didn't report her to the Abbot or to the monks.

She found that despite his cooling passions, she still adored him. It was unrequited, and a part of her understood and was fine with it. He was nice to her and he made her laugh, and in a place where her surroundings never changed it was a priceless gift. He was the older brother she had always wanted, one who cared and listened and tried to help.

The part of the day Moriko enjoyed most was combat training. On her first day she discovered she had a natural aptitude for it. Perseverance had its own combat training system that was a derivative of a style designed for monasteries throughout the Three Kingdoms. The style emphasized circular movements in both attack and defense and Moriko found the movements very natural.

It wasn't long before Moriko was top of the class in combat training even though she was the youngest and the newest initiate. The pleasure she derived from throwing the larger boys around the practice yard was intense and often made up for the monotony of the rest of the day.

Chores were dirty, repetitive and soul-crushing, and training in the sense meant time in meditation which Moriko struggled with. She loved to be active and to move. The prolonged sitting was torturous and she could only sometimes create the results the monks were expecting of her. Ironically, she thought, the sense did not make any sense to her. Sometimes she believed she could feel others around her, and she could always tell when the Abbot was around, but the monks told her stories of abilities that made her doubt her own experiences. There was always a glimmer of hope in her heart. Perhaps she wasn't meant to be a monk after all.

The worst part of her life was Goro, the monk who had taken her from her family. She didn't have any strong feelings about any of the other monks. They were all nice enough when she behaved and stern enough when she didn't. But ever since she had come to the monastery Goro had taken a unique interest in her. He was the only monk who didn't teach. All the classes were taught in rotation by the monks depending on who was available and who was most competent in the area being taught. But despite Goro not being a teacher, he always seemed to be in Moriko's space, looking over her shoulder.

During chores he would stand behind her, ordering her to repeat whatever task she had just completed. During combat training he would often sneak up behind her and use a pole to knock her off-balance just in time for her to be unable to deflect an incoming strike or throw. Even during sense training he would walk by with his switch and strike her, telling her to focus, regardless of her state of concentration.

She asked Tomotsu about it one time and he told her she was imagining him as an enemy because Goro was the one who brought her in. Life in the monastery was tough for everyone, and he implied she shouldn't be complaining when all the other students were undergoing similar punishments. Moriko tried to convince him this was unique, more focused than anything the other students were experiencing, but Tomotsu didn't believe her and told her she'd have to be stronger.

Through everything, Moriko managed to control herself and not act out. She tolerated his pokes and jabs until one afternoon of combat training when Goro poked her with his staff just in time for her to take a fist to the face from one of the oldest and strongest boys. She wasn't sure why, maybe it was the look of satisfaction on the older boy's face, but Moriko was furious and swore she would never let Goro sneak up on her again.

Their training continued and Moriko tried to split her attention between Goro, who circled the perimeter of the practice area, and pay attention to her opponent. She realized in short order she wouldn't be able to keep track of both, and with the more immediate threat being an older boy trying to redeem his pride from an earlier defeat, she was forced to pay more attention to the attacker right in front of her.

When it happened it came without warning or conscious effort. Moriko felt the end of Goro's staff coming towards her lower back. The world seemed to slow down and everything became clear to her. Without looking she knew where the staff was and where it was going to be. She took in the whole situation in less than the space of a breath. The pole was behind her, creeping with frustrating accuracy towards the base of her spine. In front of her the older boy had seen an opportunity and was lunging forward, off balance with the whole weight of his body behind his right fist. He had seen the opening and was committing everything to redeeming himself by crushing this small girl.

Her response felt natural, the extension of all her training in combat. She pivoted, using her left hand to guide the pole and direct it down and to the side. At the same time she caught her partner's wrist in her right hand and brought her center of gravity down, throwing him as though she was tossing a sack of vegetables onto the ground. As soon as she let him fly, she reversed her pivot, gripped the pole with both hands and shoved it back towards Goro, who was also off-balance and unprepared for a counterattack. With a little twist, Moriko was able to direct the other end of the pole straight into Goro's throat.

The strike hadn't been too strong, but the surprise and the strike were enough to drop Goro to the ground, clutching his throat and struggling for air. The effect wouldn't have been greater if Lord Akira himself had materialized in the center of the practice ground, everyone stopping their sparring to stare open-mouthed at the sight before them. Monks demonstrated techniques and supervised sparring. None of the initiates had seen the monks fight in real combat, but they were very good, and they trained by themselves, sometimes allowing the initiates to watch in amazement. None of the initiates would have guessed that any one of them could take out a full-fledged monk. But the evidence was right in front of them.

Moriko was flooded by a quick succession of conflicting thoughts. Her first reaction was to smile, which made her realize this was probably the first time she had smiled since arriving at the monastery. Whatever the reason, it felt wonderful to have taken Goro down. She wondered about herself. Being happy to have committed violence against another. She used to feel so bad anytime she had hurt anyone.

Goro was standing up, catching his breath in fits and starts. Anger swirled around him like a dust storm, but Moriko did not see him. She saw nothing in her excitement. She felt as if she were born to fight. It fulfilled her. The power inside of her was fantastic.

Moriko didn't notice when Goro motioned to two other monks who moved to Moriko's side and grabbed her arms. She followed them, unresisting, as her mind struggled to deal with the implications of her thoughts. If she beat Goro with so little problem perhaps she could leave the Monastery. Perhaps no one could stop her, no one could hold her back. Her soul burned like wildfire through dry prairie, consuming all logic.

A sharp jab in her back brought her mind back to her current situation. Each monk had a firm grip on one of her wrists. They were almost picking her up, moving quickly, not letting her get any firm contact with the ground. There was nothing she could do. She began to think her situation wasn't as positive as she thought it had been. Her hope began vanished like a ghost with the coming of the morning light. She glanced around, searching for exit, escape, or relief, but none was to be found. The Abbot's building loomed larger and larger and Moriko could sense he already knew what had happened.

When they got her in front of the Abbot the two monks forced her to the ground, her forehead slamming against the hard stone, each of her arms in a severe joint lock that made her want to scream in pain with every slight movement. She couldn't see the Abbot, but she sure could feel him. But she doubted her sense for the first time since learning about it. The Abbot didn't seem angry so much as curious. She could feel him extend his power toward her, focusing it on her. It felt like her skin was being torn off, burned by the power of an exploding sun, exposing everything underneath. The monks holding her relaxed their grip as they were overpowered by the Abbot's focus on her. Moriko tried to move, but her body wasn't responding to her commands.

Moriko went inside herself, focusing on her own body and doing everything in her power to ignore the incredible energies being brought to bear upon her. She could hear her captors wheezing in pain from just being too close to the object of the Abbot's undivided attention. Whatever she did had some effect, because the Abbot relaxed his focus, unable to find whatever he had been looking for. Moriko moved to escape, but the monks had recovered faster and had renewed their joint locks on her arms. There wasn't any hope.

Goro spoke without permission, "Abbot, this girl just attacked . . ."

He was cut off by an abrupt motion by the Abbot. "Shut up, Goro. I know what happened."

Goro obliged, quivering in his own fear. He was a pathetic piece of trash.

The Abbot spoke again, "How did you do this?"

Moriko couldn't resist being rude. It was her last layer of defense. "I only did what I've been taught in my classes."

The Abbot smiled. "Unless my monks have made incredible progress without my knowledge, I think we both know that's not true. Give me the truth, child."

Moriko remained silent. She didn't know how she had pulled off what she had done. It had come naturally to her. She wasn't even sure how it was special.

The Abbot stared at her for several breaths before coming to a decision. "Goro, grab two staffs please."

Goro, although confused, acquired them from a weapons rack near the side of the Abbot's quarters. He brought them to the Abbot, who tossed one in front of Moriko. "Get up, girl."

Moriko obeyed, rubbing her shoulders to return some feeling back to them after the monks let her go. She looked around for an exit, but they were well guarded.

The Abbot tossed the second staff to Goro. "Attack the girl." The Abbot returned to his chair to watch the proceedings.

Moriko was slow to respond, still afraid of the Abbot's wrath. She suspected she didn't know everything that the Abbot was capable of. Goro had no such problems, the lap-dog always ready to do whatever his master commanded. He leapt forward and landed a crushing blow on Moriko's shoulder, bringing her down to one knee.

The blow shocked her to her senses and her training took over. Goro never paused his attack, but she automatically deflected his next swing, which was slow and powerful. She flinched as their staffs cracked even on the deflection. Goro wasn't trying to do anything complicated. He was too angry and embarrassed to do anything unexpected. He would attack straight on until she was down.

Goro paused his series of attacks to glance at the Abbot. Moriko glanced as well. The Abbot didn't care about Goro. All of his attention was on Moriko.

Goro took this as permission to give Moriko his full attention. He stepped back and spun his staff around in a complicated pattern. Moriko was reminded of the fact that he was older and much better trained than she was. She knew better than to fight the monks. They were so fast and so strong. It was nothing but pride which told her she had a chance.

Goro moved forward, his first steps so fast Moriko almost didn't realize what was happening. His staff blurred in her vision.

Without warning the feeling of moving in slow motion returned and Moriko clearly saw the pattern Goro was tracing with his staff. She knew he was going to try to use a big swing to knock her off balance and then come in with another big swing to knock her out or kill her. She didn't give him the chance. His moves were quick, but she knew his move, and knew the precise spot she needed to strike. She didn't hesitate, a quick jab with the end of her staff inside his guard.

Goro didn't react to her movement, not even making the slightest attempt to block. She struck him in his stomach and he collapsed into himself.

Faster than it began, it was over. The monks appeared to be in a state of shock, but the Abbot's gaze had never faltered. He was still acting like a curious child. The Abbot stood up, went over to Goro, and picked up the fallen staff. He spoke to Moriko as he approached. His voice was so soft Moriko wondered if anyone else could hear what he said.

"Goro was a fool. Fool someone once, shame on you. Fool someone twice, shame on them. He should have known what we were dealing with."

Moriko didn't understand. What were they dealing with? What seemed so serious?

The Abbot turned on Moriko with the staff and he was even faster than Goro. Moriko had been paying attention though and was able to move just fast enough to block most of his strikes. She chose, taking the hits that seemed like they wouldn't be too bad while blocking and deflecting those that would have been more damaging. She felt him focus his energy and felt it wash over her as she moved through it. She began to hope that she had a chance of escape. Perhaps she was the strongest!

Her hope was fleeting. Not even sure how, she found herself the focus of all the Abbot's energy and attention, and it forced her backwards one step at a time. It was like standing too close to a fire, a fire that was focused only on burning her. Her sense was blinded, and she began to take too many strikes. Every hit knocked her a bit more off balance, and before long it was over, a jab to the stomach similar to the one that had taken Goro out of commission.

The world wavered in front of Moriko. She was hurt and exhausted, her mind and body spent. The Abbot looked at her one last time, shook his head, and brought his staff around, striking her across the head and causing her world to go completely black.

Moriko was surprised when she awoke. She had half-expected in the last moment of consciousness to never wake up again. On her next breath, she started to wish she hadn't woken up again.

Her head felt like it had been cracked open and her mind was leaking out. She tried to bring her hands to her head to feel the damage, only to realize she was tightly bound to the monastery wall. Her arms were stretched out to each side and tied to anchors in the wall. Moriko had always wondered why those anchors had been there. She tried to move her arms, but there was no give at all. She was bound facing the wall, so her backside was facing the courtyard. Fear entered her heart, pushing away the blackness at the edges of her pain-filled vision.

Moriko turned her head to look around and immediately a wave of pain and nausea washed over her. Her legs gave out, but she only fell the tiniest distance. Her arms stretched out searing in pain, unwilling to take the strain of all her weight. She put her feet down and tried to stand. It was a small improvement.

As her mind caught up with her surroundings, Moriko felt the fear gnawing its way through her stomach. She had beaten Goro, not once, but twice. The Abbot had defeated her without a problem. What was the punishment for fighting with the Abbot? Why did everyone seem to be scared of what she had done? She thought backwards. The pieces started to connect. She had used the sense in combat.

Nightblade.

The words cut through the fog in her mind. It wasn't supposed to be possible. The monks were trained to use the sense, but not with combat. It didn't work. The sense was used for information gathering and activities that were slow and methodical. The ability to fight while using the sense was punishable by death. There weren't any nightblades any more, and for good reason. They had destroyed the Kingdom. She deserved to die.

A monk training nearby noticed she was awake and ran to ring a gong outside of the Abbot's quarters. It was only struck on important occasions, usually holidays or funerals. Moriko wondered if it was ringing for her own funeral. There was a bustle of activity, and soon Moriko sensed almost every monk in the complex was standing to attention behind her. She felt like she should be self-conscious with everyone standing behind her. But she could only focus on the pain and the fear.

She sensed the Abbot behind her. She took a deep breath and tried not to be scared. It was easier than she expected. At the end of all things she found she just didn't care. Not happy or sad, she missed her old woods, the feel of the trees and the tranquility of solitude. She was thinking about the giant trees when the Abbot approached and ripped the robes off the top of her body.

Moriko instinctively tried to cover herself with her arms, forgetting for a moment she was immobile. But once the shock passed away she didn't care about her nudity either. She was facing the wall anyway. There wasn't much for anyone to see. She sensed the whip coming at her bare back, but didn't have enough time to tense.

The pain was surprising even though she knew it was coming. The whip felt like a small line of fire burning its way across her skin. The fire did not ease with time, but intensified as it was joined by more lashings. Soon it felt like her entire back was burning, red hot lines of flame everywhere. Every breath, movement and thought seemed to drag out as the pain ravaged her mind and body. She had never experienced anything of the sort. She came to the point where she almost welcomed the lashes as they gave her a single point of pain to focus on.

She had planned on being defiant but the pain was too much. She collapsed, screaming and crying as the Abbot went to work with the whip. She hoped it would bring some relief, but every breath she took to cry burned across her body. She wanted to die, wanted the pain to end. Why wouldn't he just kill her?

A small part of her, the part attuned to combat, realized the Abbot was an expert in applying the whip. No strike landed in the same place. Sometimes he allowed the whip to curl around her torso, arms, or legs. The worst was when it lashed around and cut into the side of her breasts. That was a new and horrible sort of pain.

Moriko tried to focus, tried to find an inner sanctuary, someplace where she could shut out the pain. In between strikes she remembered the stories she had heard about monks who could withstand incredible pain without losing face. But the Abbot was a master at what he was doing and Moriko had no experience to draw on. He never gave her enough time between strikes to focus. They came one after the other and blurred together into one continuous experience of hell.

Time became endless, and she struggled to remember a time when her life wasn't filled with pain and suffering. She had become so senseless she didn't even realize her punishment had ended. There were no more lashes, just the unending torment of breath. A moment later her hearing returned to her, and she realized that the Abbot was speaking to the congregated monks.

". . . violation of the rules of our order. Today I bring my sword, the ultimate symbol of the warriors which we are descended from. We are men and women with a sacred task, a task to protect the world we live in from all threats. If we are not united, the world itself falls. If we do not recognize the corruption, even within our own ranks, the Three Kingdoms would burn."

The Abbot paused for effect. "We recognize in the sword the ultimate paradox. It is the protector of life, yet it brings death. Like the great warriors of old, we live in that paradox daily, struggling always to understand it. Today the sword decides the fate of the one who violated our precepts."

Moriko's sense returned to her just in time for her to sense the blade's approach. Time slowed down, just as it had before, but there was nothing for her to do. No way to react. She was tied tightly and had no desire to live. She sensed it approach, unfeeling and uncaring. When it entered her, she couldn't even distinguish it from the other levels of agony she was already suffering. But when she looked down and saw the point of the blade protruding from her torso, her blood sparkling in the evening sunlight, she couldn't take anymore. For the second and final time that day, Moriko's vision went black, and she went willingly into darkness' cold, comforting embrace.

CHAPTER 10

Ryuu was no longer a boy. Several cycles had passed, and it was clear to any observer he was now a young man. He was of average height, but his musculature set him apart from others. The young man was lean, the muscles of his arms, torso and legs clearly defined, with no vestiges of childhood fat left. He walked tall and without hurry, taking in the world around him. Shigeru could always sense the faint tendrils of Ryuu's sense expanding throughout whatever environment he was in, and it made him proud. Ryuu's sense would be almost undetectable to the monks.

Just as important to Shigeru were Ryuu's eyes. They never rested but were always moving back and forth, using every sense available to bring in information about his world. Many trainees, when they were young, relied on their sense too much. Shigeru knew there were ways to fool the sense, but not all six. Shigeru often told Ryuu no one could sneak up on him and it was probably true. Ryuu paid attention to people when they spoke, focusing exclusively on them. When he did his eyes would light up with the delight of conversation. It was obvious to all who encountered him he was focused on the present, always curious about everything around him. But what only Shigeru could sense was that even though Ryuu's eyes might be focused on one person, his sense tendrils spread out even further. The boy was a marvel of awareness.

His swordsmanship was also excellent. Even if he hadn't been sense-gifted Ryuu might have been one of the best in the Southern Kingdom. In conjunction with his sense, Shigeru suspected his student was one of the best warriors in the Three Kingdoms. And he had only seen fourteen cycles. His swordsmanship would improve as he gained more experience. The boy wasn't anywhere close to his limits. There were warriors that could beat him, but all of them existed in a different life. Shigeru had a suspicion that in two or three cycles, if the boy's path continued, he would be much stronger than his master. Their meeting had been incredible and Shigeru felt the subtle threads of the Great Cycle in everything the boy did. There was a convergence approaching, and Shigeru feared the consequences. They were not known as pleasant occasions.

Shigeru was apprehensive about the boy's second resolution. He had sworn he would honor the proper training methods in the raising of the boy, but he had grown fond of the boy's company. Shigeru had resigned himself long ago to a solitary, hunted life. He had never expected a son, and never one so unique. Ryuu was a cheerful, optimistic young man who balanced out Shigeru's natural pessimism and cynicism. Shigeru knew what came next. It was, perhaps, the hardest of the choices a young nightblade made, but it was also the most necessary. It would be easy to justify another path, to say a new way would better. Some nights as Shigeru was relaxing in the evening with Ryuu, reading by the fire, he would think of all the ways it could be done differently.

But in the light of day Shigeru's thinking was more clear. The training methods had the balance of history behind them.

Shigeru himself hadn't progressed far enough to understand the reasoning behind all the methods, but he never questioned the pure intent behind them. The old way was not the easy way, but it was true.

It was the dead of winter when Shigeru announced they would be going on a trip. Ryuu looked up at his master, grinning. "You mean we're going to the village? I thought you were looking forward to not going back for a while."

Shigeru shook his head. "No. Not to the village. It's time for you to go to a city. Winter is the perfect time for it with many of the people inside because of the cold. We won't be bothered and you will have to develop your sense there so you are prepared for using your abilities in crowded spaces."

Ryuu felt his stomach tighten up at the mention of a city. His parents had died returning from a city in winter, and he hadn't been back in the intervening nine cycles. Winter was bandit season in the region, picking off travelers struggling with the weather. He didn't want to go. "I already know how to handle the sense in a crowd of people. We've been to the village, and it has almost one hundred people."

"Yes, and the fact you can allow your sense to spread as far as you do in the village is an impressive feat. But you need to find your limits. In New Haven there are tens of thousands of people and you'll need to control your sense so the information doesn't overwhelm your mind or distract you from your more immediate surroundings."

"Why can't we go in spring and blend in with the tourist crowd? That would be better practice."

Shigeru's look changed, and Ryuu could tell he had finally figured out Ryuu's reluctance.

"You'll be fine. We're going together and we'll stay together. Anyhow, you have a sword now and are more than capable of protecting yourself from any danger. Face your fear and you will discover it has no hold over you anymore."

Ryuu nodded. Facing his fears sounded like an excellent plan, but his mind and body disagreed. His sleep was restless and his nightmares came back. He dreamed of blood, of the face of his mother, blurred with time. Even unclear her face still haunted him. He hadn't had the dreams for cycles, and the memories made him sullen in the mornings leading up to their trip.

Shigeru noticed his attitude but pretended to ignore it. He was overly cheerful, and Ryuu considered more than once poking him with the pointy end of his sword. "Come on, let's get started. It should only take us four or five days if we make good time."

"I remember the trip as being a lot longer than that."

"The last time we made it, it was. But you were also five then and didn't walk as fast as you do now. I also found you several days east of the city."

Ryuu chastised himself. Of course. He gathered his belongings in a pack and took off with Shigeru. As promised, the trip only took four days. It was uneventful, but Ryuu felt like he was being reborn. He remembered clearly parts of his first journey with Shigeru. Her remembered the plains turning into forests, and now the forests turned back into plains. It was like re-entering the real world after a long absence in a make believe land. Now and then he glanced up to make sure Shigeru was still in front of him and real.

As they approached New Haven, Ryuu began to sense not just the enormity, but the density of the place. People were stacked on top of other people and they mixed and tore apart in innumerable ways. In just the space of a heartbeat Ryuu could sense people making love, people fighting, selling, bartering, begging, bribing, coercing, threatening, and laughing. In the unconscious monotony of the journey, Ryuu had spread his sense out much too far, and the sudden awareness of too much information overwhelmed him. He brought his sense back in, trying to find the ideal balance.

He was doing well until they entered the limits of the city. On the outskirts, Ryuu's mind felt like it snapped. There were too many people, too much to keep track of. He couldn't distinguish an enemy from a salesperson. He fell to his knees and clutched his head between his hands, rocking back and forth in an effort to get the information out of his head. In the past he had never had to restrict his sense. He had always allowed it to roam and to wander.

Shigeru's voice penetrated the chaos surrounding his mind. He could hear the concern. Shigeru was repeating himself. He probably had been for a while. He was repeating Ryuu's name. Ryuu glanced up and tried to focus on Shigeru's face.

Shigeru noticed. "Focus on my voice. Think only about my voice. I'm right here for you."

It took a tremendous effort, but Ryuu soon brought all of his focus to Shigeru's voice. Shigeru kept speaking to him softly, reassuring him. As he focused, the pain in his head started to recede, replaced by an overwhelming numbness. He was tired, but it was better than being on the ground in pain. He saw the looks of the few passersby on the street.

Still focusing on Shigeru's voice, Ryuu found his feet and stood up, supported by Shigeru's shoulder.

From Shigeru's voice, Ryuu focused on meditating on his own center. The drills came back to him, drilled over cycles of practice. Ryuu had found them meaningless in training, but understood now. After a couple of breaths, he was back, his sense limited to just a pace or two around him. He and Shigeru could have been the only people in the world at that moment.

He smiled uncertainly. "I'm back. That was. . . a lot."

Shigeru nodded. The two of them stood in the center of the street as Ryuu tentatively expanded his sense once again. He let it expand a pace at a time, sipping at the extra information it provided. Once it got to be too much he backed off, limiting himself. It was tiring, but Shigeru had put him through much worse in training. He could handle it.

As they continued into the city, Ryuu continued to experiment. He would push out his sense until his head started to hurt, then bring it in close for a time. He practiced pulsing his sense out versus keeping it extended all the time. He was looking for balance, and every step into the city was more natural than the one preceding it. Like all challenges, he would overcome.

Shigeru led Ryuu through the city, allowing him the time and space to experiment with his sense. It was a cold day and most people did not travel slowly. People were bundled in layers, rushing from one house to the next, seeking warmth wherever it could be found. As a young man who had lived his entire life outside, Ryuu was confused. He didn't notice the cold the way others seemed to. He asked Shigeru about it as he also seemed to be unaffected.

Shigeru would only provide one of his cryptic answers. "Our minds protect us."

There was little to be gained from a visual inspection of their surroundings. There was nothing to see in the midst of the winter season. The buildings were drab and lifeless. They were bigger than Ryuu had seen in the villages near the forest, but besides size, there was little to distinguish them from anything else. As he lifted his gaze to the center of the city he saw buildings which were much larger and more ornate. Those he was interested in.

His memories were vague, but he recalled that New Haven was a place of lights and activity. The signs were everywhere, but the cold had shut the city down. Market stalls were empty and restaurants had their doors sealed tight against the blowing snow. If not for the sense, Ryuu almost could have convinced himself they were alone in the city.

Ryuu did notice no one his age wore a sword, at least with any ease. There were a few young men who seemed to carry swords as a symbol of status. But Ryuu could tell in a glance they were not actual swordsmen. Their bodies told him from the way they walked, the way they held themselves, their lack of muscle and awareness. He felt a revulsion towards them. Shigeru had taught him nothing but respect for the sword and the path which it cut. To wear a sword and not be prepared to use it made Ryuu sick. A sword was a weapon, not a fashion accessory. To wear one without skill was demeaning and dishonorable.

Ryuu felt the glances several of the adult men gave him. He couldn't read their minds, but he suspected they felt about him much the same way he felt about the other boys carrying swords. They suspected him of being undeserving, of being a boy playing in a man's world. A small piece of him shouted out, angry. He did not like being misjudged. He knew how to use a sword. He was nothing like these pretenders. But he kept his hand far from his sword. Shigeru had well drilled into him the importance of secrecy. He didn't like being underestimated, but it was better than being killed.

On this journey they had changed from their typical disguise. Shigeru pretended to be a down-on-his-luck minor lord, and

Ryuu his son. It allowed them to wear their swords out in the open.

Ryuu's thoughts were further diverted by the sudden discovery of someone else using the sense. It felt like someone was trying to shine a light into a dark room, overpowering the shadows with light. Ryuu had never felt the sense used like this. It felt crude. The man using it was a ways off, but his path would cross with theirs. Ryuu glanced at Shigeru, but Shigeru kept to his path. Ryuu followed suit. It was always another test. The monk passed them, offering no acknowledgment of their presence. Ryuu didn't need the sense to observe the fear the monk inspired in the people. Empty streets managed to become even more deserted as the monk passed.

Ryuu couldn't help himself. The monk carried himself better than most, but Ryuu felt he had nothing to fear from the man. His use of the sense was rudimentary, like a child. He sent out his sense, contrary to everything Shigeru had ever told him to do.

The monk continued on without seeming to notice them. Ryuu saw the tension seep out of Shigeru's shoulders. Shigeru had been ready to draw his blade at a moment's notice.

"Don't ever do that again."

"I could have beat him."

"I know. That's not the point. It brings attention to us, and attention brings armies to our doorstep. Secrecy is our best defense."

Ryuu struggled. He had all these powers and no outlet to use them. Shigeru made it clear if he did, he would die. It was unfair.

"He didn't even know I was sensing him."

"They weren't trained as you were. I don't want you to tempt fate. Don't worry. I have the feeling you'll run into them soon enough."

Ryuu disagreed. He wanted to use his powers. Now wasn't soon enough.

After the monk was gone Ryuu was able to relax and take in more of his surroundings. They weren't heading into the center of the city but were staying near the outskirts. Ryuu observed they were getting into parts of town with more and more businesses. It took him only a quick breath with his sense to figure out they were moving into the section of New Haven that dealt in prostitution.

Ryuu was confused. He knew about sex even if it wasn't something he and Shigeru spoke about. He was a young man and his needs were growing, but it had always been academic to him given that he lived in a hut in the woods with only his surrogate father for company. He wondered if they had come for sex or if they had another purpose. His teenage imagination began to run away from him, fantasies clouding his reality. He was also nervous. He didn't have a lot of experience with girls. There were a handful in the nearby village, but Ryuu had little to do with them.

Shigeru, after having known Ryuu a lifetime, must have sensed his apprentice's thoughts. "It's not what you think." He gave a small half-smile. "At least, not quite."

Ryuu relaxed a little, but was also disappointed. If not for sex why were they here? His curiosity and imagination ran far ahead of reality, stopping only when they reached a three story building with red lanterns on the outside. Shigeru led him inside. There were two guards whom Ryuu reached out to sense. They were strong, stronger than anyone he had encountered in the streets thus far, but he thought he could still kill them if he had to.

Shigeru knew where he was going and the guards didn't bother to stop him or give him directions. Ryuu followed him to the second floor where they knelt in a small receiving room. They were greeted by a middle-aged woman who moved with power and precision. Ryuu didn't sense anything special about her, but she was strong in her own way. Ryuu caught Shigeru's glance of disapproval and immediately withdrew his sense. He still wasn't sure when it was appropriate to use his powers.

The woman, although she moved with grace, was conflicted about something. She kept glancing at Ryuu with the slightest hint of suspicion in her eyes.

After pleasantries that seemed to last forever, Shigeru spoke. "You got my letter?"

"I did. Your offer was a very unique one, and coming from anyone else, I would have doubted the sincerity of it," she paused. "Frankly, even coming from you, I doubt your motives. The girl is worth a fortune."

Shigeru bowed his head in understanding. "I know she is spoken for. If nothing else, trust I would not cross Nori."

Madame inclined her head. Something in his inflection had caught her attention. "That's the first time you've ever lied to me. I don't know what kind of man you are to be so bold, but I accept your offer. Perhaps it will benefit both of us."

Shigeru nodded and addressed Ryuu for the first time since entering the room. "I'm going to leave you for a while. I'd prefer it if you don't try to go looking for me and instead spend your time focusing on your education here."

Ryuu understood. Shigeru didn't want Ryuu trying to sense him although that might be difficult. Ryuu was so sensitive, so used to Shigeru's presence he couldn't help but sense him. But he'd try, at least. He was very interested to see what his "education" would look like in the next few watches.

Madame struck a small gong softly and a young woman, probably five to ten cycles older than Ryuu, came gracefully into the room. She was without doubt the most beautiful woman Ryuu had ever seen. The village they lived near didn't have anyone that compared to her. She was tall and slender, but her gown only masked her lithe strength. Her hair shone and her almond eyes looked calm and peaceful, like you could look into them and lose your concerns forever. She bowed to Madame and to the guests, and Shigeru nodded one last time at Ryuu and left the room

Ryuu had to stifle his laughter. Shigeru's energy had spiked to incredible levels when the woman had walked in. He had initially thought Shigeru didn't want him sensing him because he was going to do something secret. Ryuu supposed what happened in a bedroom should be secret, but he had expected something different. If Shigeru didn't get himself under control, there wasn't going to be anything Ryuu could do about it though. His mentor was throwing off enough energy to heat a block of this city in the winter.

Ryuu's musings were interrupted when Madame struck the small gong again. Ryuu's world closed in on itself as Takako entered the room. A couple of moments ago Ryuu would have claimed the woman with Shigeru was the most beautiful person he had ever met. He couldn't believe he had been so wrong. Takako was a slender beauty and Ryuu couldn't imagine her equal.

She looked to be a little older than Ryuu, maybe by two or three cycles. She was tall with long dark hair that put the night to shame. Her physical beauty was incredible, but it was her eyes that drew Ryuu to her. For no concrete reason he could explain, he knew she had seen much sadness. But despite the sorrow her eyes were lively and excited and nervous. She seemed vulnerable but strong, someone who could use his protection but wasn't helpless. A reason for him to be strong.

Madame introduced the two of them and nodded slightly to Takako. She offered her hand to Ryuu, which he took after a moment's hesitation. Her touch was softer than anyone, her fingers delicate yet strong. She led him to a small room with a bed, some mats to sit on and a low table. The room had a slight sweet scent and was warm although not uncomfortable. In short, it seemed like the perfect place to enjoy Madame's ladies' company.

They knelt by the table. Ryuu didn't have the slightest clue how to proceed but was determined not to look like a fool in front of this girl. He knew she was a prostitute and was paid for her services, but he still wanted to prove himself to her. It was irrational, but he wanted to impress her. He tried to shake himself out of the train of thought, but rationality did not rule his actions as long as her eyes were on him.

Takako prepared the tea and Ryuu noticed a slight tremble in her fingers. He frowned and tenderly extended his sense. Shigeru seemed to think he shouldn't, but Shigeru was distracted and there was no harm. He was surprised. She was more afraid and more nervous than he was. She lacked clear intention. Her actions were muddled because of her fear. Given what he was sensing he was surprised she was able to serve him at all.

His boyhood curiosity crashed through his facade. He dropped any pretense of knowing what he was doing. "Why are you so afraid?"

Takako's eyes shot up, fearful. "How do you know?" She stopped herself as she realized she had just confirmed his question and lost control of the situation. Ryuu could see her berating herself.

Ryuu laughed at the awkwardness of the situation. Everything fell into place in his mind. The sense was a tool, but it didn't give the answers. Shigeru and he trained often on interpreting what the sense was telling him.

"Let's just say I'm pretty observant. Let's have some tea and you can tell me what's going on here."

Takako gave him a look which he couldn't decipher, but Ryuu knew that behind that face her mind was churning, considering alternatives, figuring out how to act next. But then her mask dropped and Ryuu knew he was looking at Takako as she was, not as she was expected to be. Her trembling stopped, and she poured the tea, speaking as she did so. "This is my first time with a man alone, but Madame told me I am not to sleep with you. The agreement was only for us to spend time together."

Ryuu nodded. He suspected something similar although he was disappointed sex wasn't going to be a part of his afternoon.

Takako pulled a small slip of paper out of her kimono. "She gave me this packet to put in your tea."

Ryuu sniffed at the packet. He recognized the smell as part of his training with Shigeru. It was a mixture that wouldn't leave a taste when mixed with tea. He would have felt fine for long enough to have a decent conversation, but then he would have been fast asleep with no ill effects when he awoke. Shigeru had taught him how to use it to put a target to sleep for a time without the target suspecting anything was amiss. The time it took the powder to take effect usually masked your own guilt.

"So you were to converse with me for a while but make sure I was asleep before the evening became sexual?"

Takako turned a little red. Ryuu had thought she couldn't have gotten any more attractive, but he had been wrong. "Yes."

Ryuu sighed. But it was hard to be upset with a girl so beautiful. "Well, I can do better. We can talk for as long as you like and I won't try anything untoward."

Takako giggled, then immediately tried to stifle it. "I don't think you'd have a chance. It's cute you have a sword, but I am promised to another man. If you try anything I'm supposed to give a signal and the guard outside will be here in a heartbeat. Unfortunately, I'm afraid you'd be cut to little pieces."

Ryuu restrained himself. Being so consistently underestimated was frustrating. But his training held. Shigeru had drilled it into his head that his abilities were not for bragging even if it meant sacrificing the chance to impress this girl.

Ryuu began asking questions, curious about this new person in his life. He hadn't realized how desperate he was for company besides Shigeru. How old was she? Where did she originally come from? How did she get here? Ryuu had always assumed prostitution was something one wanted to do, or something lower castes did as a way to advance their social standing. He had never really thought there might be other stories, stories where people didn't have the chance to choose their path. The reality tugged at him in a way he couldn't understand.

It was because Shigeru had always given him choices. When they were training Shigeru would give him orders, but in day to day life he never did. Ryuu knew he always had a choice. Even the training was a choice he had made. It got under his skin as he listened to a story where choice wasn't an option.

It was when Takako got to the part where she was promised to Nori's son that he couldn't take anymore. He stood up and paced the room. He was agitated and found he wanted something better for this girl. He tried to remind himself she was a prostitute, but she was also a person, and Ryuu couldn't process it. The warmth of the room grew constricting. He wanted to draw his sword and cut something, just to act. But he knew better and stayed his hand.

He sat back down, angry. "It isn't fair! You've never done anything wrong and yet you are promised to a man who doesn't even know you. You should have a choice! There is always a choice!"

Takako held up her hand to calm him as she shook her head. "You may be right, but that is the way of the world. We don't all have the options to choose. I have no choice and there is no escape for me. If I left the house, I would be killed, and my family also for not paying their debts. This is the only thing left, so my only choice is to act honorably and attempt to make the best of it."

"No! You have to fight!"

"I have nothing to fight with."

"There has to be another option. Can't you buy yourself back or something?"

Takako laughed. "You really shouldn't worry about this. Thank you for caring, but my fate is as inevitable as all fate, simply just a bit more apparent than most people's. It is not yours to be worried about me."

Ryuu couldn't leave the subject alone, and in time it managed to irritate Takako. Ryuu could see his anger grated against her acceptance, but he couldn't stop. He was too angry.

In frustration, she leaned forward and kissed him quickly on the lips. It was so fast he couldn't process it, but it shut him up as he tried.

"Look, I'm thankful that you care so much. It says a lot about you, but you need to be able to let it go. It's an important lesson I'm still learning. You need to be able to understand what you can change and what you can't. You shouldn't even care for someone like me. You're rich and have the world in your hands. I don't know exactly what your father intended from this exchange, but I suspect this isn't going to be a meeting that will be repeated. Let's not worry about what the future will hold and instead spend some good time together. I enjoy your company very much – it's been the most refreshing experience I've had in many cycles."

Ryuu capitulated and allowed himself to be entertained by Takako. He found that like Shigeru, she had a strength in listening to what other people said. It made her easy to talk to and Ryuu began to wish he could talk to her day after day, pouring out his one big secret.

Their time ended too soon as Shigeru knocked on the door. Ryuu bowed all the way to the floor when he left, and he felt both Shigeru's and Takako's shock at his gesture. He left with his head held high even though he was torn up inside and realized his outlook on life wouldn't ever be the same.

After leaving Madame's they loaded up on supplies in haste and with a minimal of conversation. Ryuu found he wanted nothing more than to be at home with his thoughts. As they left New Haven Shigeru allowed Ryuu to spill out his story. When he was finished Shigeru continued walking without saying a word. Ryuu followed him for a ways but then stopped. "It's not supposed to be this way."

Shigeru turned. "It never is. The world doesn't listen to us and it doesn't follow any order. To believe this world cares, to believe that nature will somehow protect us, is utter foolishness. Nature is not good or evil. It just is. Takako is trapped by circumstance, and as it stands, I believe her attitude is noble."

Ryuu was ready to explode on his master. How could Shigeru argue the world didn't care? He could feel the pulse of the land through his sense just as well as Ryuu. Ryuu couldn't believe in a world without purpose. It meant his parents had died for no reason, a meaningless death.

"But what is our strength for if we don't help those who are need helping?"

Shigeru didn't respond right away and Ryuu realized he was arguing a very personal topic. He saw Shigeru's shoulders tense. Not for the first time he wished he knew more about his master's history.

Shigeru spoke, his soft voice barely carrying to Ryuu's well-honed ears. "I don't have a good answer for you. Ever since I took you in I've been asking myself what I'm doing. When we return home, I believe it's time for me to tell you my story and how I came to be here. It's not a good story, but I continue to hope it will turn out well. Perhaps that's an empty hope. I don't know how to fix the world, or even the problems of one young girl in New Haven. Perhaps I'm a coward for not trying, but maybe my purpose was to set you on the path. I don't know. Ryuu."

Shigeru paused, trying to find the next words, the perfect next words. Nothing came.

"I just don't know. I don't know what to do any better than the next person, and I hope you are old enough to understand."

Ryuu was silent. Shigeru had never seemed so human to Ryuu. He had never displayed any weakness in almost ten cycles. Ryuu was thrown off balance. The world seemed to be spinning around him even though it stood still.

They continued their walk in silence. Ryuu was having trouble thinking straight. It was difficult to hold on to thoughts for more than a few breaths at a time. He had never really thought about his future, not with any seriousness. He already possessed enough strength to best almost anyone who might challenge him, but he didn't know what he would do with his strength. A part of him dreamed about being a hero, saving people in distress. But who could he save, who was in distress? Was Takako?

Ryuu asked Shigeru if they could take a break for a little while. Shigeru studied him for a moment and assented, although with a warning.

"There's a storm coming in. We should find shelter sooner rather than later."

Ryuu looked into the sky and felt the wind against his skin. He agreed with Shigeru. There was a storm coming in, and it felt like it might be strong. But he needed to get his head on straight first.

They sat and Ryuu began by focusing on his breath the way Shigeru had taught him so many cycles ago. From there he pushed his sense outwards until he felt connected with the world again. Allowing his sense to roam was like being released from the tight confines of a cage. He felt like he could breathe again.

Ryuu's meditation also revealed other interesting information. There were four men following them, in a depression out of sight. They intended violence. Ryuu stood up and informed Shigeru. He nodded. He had already known. Ryuu berated himself for becoming so distracted he didn't notice bandits.

"They are waiting for the storm to set in and then attack. It's common for bandits. It makes it more difficult for survivors to reach safety and makes them almost impossible to track after."

A wave of fear washed over Ryuu which he fought to control with rationality. Memories of his mother and the blood threatened to overwhelm him. It was just like when he was five. But this was what he had trained for. Shigeru had assured him over and over again he was strong. But doubt and fear assailed him. Not even Shigeru's presence calmed him as the storm came in.

Ryuu thought of Takako, unjustly held in a house of prostitution. His fear dissipated. If he couldn't protect her, what good was he? It was time to know. He collected his gear and continued on his way as the snow came blowing in.

Shigeru followed, pleased with this decision. Ryuu asked if Shigeru could find their way home even through a storm, and Shigeru replied in the affirmative. Ryuu tried to draw strength from Shigeru's calm. If nothing else, he had Shigeru here to protect him.

The snow and wind reduced visibility to a few dozen paces. Ryuu found the lack of sight didn't bother him much. He could feel the bandits starting to approach closer, preparing to make their move. When they finally appeared in front of Shigeru and Ryuu, Ryuu was glad the wait was over.

As the four shadows materialized Ryuu noticed that Shigeru made no attempt to get his sword ready. The message was clear. This fight was Ryuu's. Ryuu focused and sensed it wasn't entirely true. Shigeru was ready to spring, but was trying to create the impression it was Ryuu's fight.

Fair enough. As he surveyed his enemies a flicker of fear sparked to life. There were four, all much larger than Ryuu. They looked like they had killed before. There was no joy, just the grim determination of survival on their faces. He tried to focus, but he couldn't quite push away the thought of his mother dying in a storm much like this. It threatened to overwhelm his thoughts and focus.

No words were exchanged, and the conflict was decided in an instant. Ryuu sensed the movement of the bandit on his far left and the near simultaneous response of his partner far to the right. There was no honor or fairness in this fight. All four were moving for Ryuu, planning to kill him and move to Shigeru, four versus one as often as they could.

The movements snapped Ryuu back in sync with his sense. Without thought he knew where each cut would come from and where it was aimed. He knew where to strike and saw the entire battle unravel even before his sword was drawn. All that was left to do was act, and Shigeru's training had been comprehensive in that regard.

The next conscious thought Ryuu had was that he was unharmed. No blade had come close to him and the four bandits were dying or dead on the ground around him. Ryuu slowly looked around, taking it all in and realizing what had happened. He looked down at his hands and saw them holding a bloody sword.

His power sickened him. The bandits never had a chance against the skills he had developed. He had believed on the day he actually had to use his skills it would be a noble contest, but instead it just seemed unfair. It was too easy to take a human life. It had taken just a couple of movements and four men no longer walked the cycle on this planet. These men probably had families, people that cared for them, and they had been killed by a boy without a thought. Ryuu clutched his sword as he knelt to the ground and threw up.

When he was done, he noticed Shigeru hadn't moved at all. He hadn't said anything. The only hint he wasn't a statue was he was no longer close to drawing his own sword. Ryuu looked desperately at Shigeru, pleading for some form of absolution, some comfort that would make the world make sense again.

Shigeru returned his look without flinching. "If I were to tell you it was self-defense, it would be true. They attacked us first and made a choice with consequences. But this is also a lesson I cannot teach. At the setting of the sun you are one of the most powerful warriors in the Three Kingdoms. I know only a handful who are your equal. The power I've helped you develop is yours to use. It can be a force for good, where you protect those who need protecting from evil men, or it can be evil when you use your power for selfish reasons. That power, your strength, is only a tool. How you decide to wield it will determine the type of man you will become. The only person who can make that decision is you."

So much for comfort.

Shigeru wasn't quite finished. "While these men did attack us, you always have a choice. You could have let them kill you. I don't want to ever see you hide behind false justifications. You always have a choice. Today you made one."

Ryuu knelt in the gathering snow, attempting to make sense of it all. In time, Ryuu's forces of habit took over and he cleaned his blade and sheathed it. He stood up and Shigeru led him towards an abandoned cabin for the night. Ryuu was completely inside himself and if not for Shigeru's guidance would have been lost and unaware. He could have been beaten by a child with a kitchen knife. Shigeru got them both inside as the storm picked up in intensity.

While Ryuu recovered, Shigeru found an old and dry wood pile and built up a small, warm fire they sat next to. Shigeru sat silently, offering his company as Ryuu came to terms with what he was capable of. Ryuu had always dreamed of being a strong warrior, but in the company of Shigeru, he hadn't realized just how strong he had become. Until today, it had been an academic exercise to see who he could beat by trying to sense their strength. He had no idea he'd become so strong he could kill four men without breaking a sweat.

Ryuu forced himself to remember the cuts he had made to bring down each opponent. He walked through every move again. His moves had been almost perfect. But as the memories of combat ran through his mind they began to twist and darken until the images of his victims blended with the red nightmares of his mother, and he felt like he was going to throw up again. Was he any better than the men that had murdered his mother?

As the fire began to die down, Shigeru spoke, breaking his long silence. "Today is an important day. I had hoped it would come later, in another cycle or two, but fate has decreed. Do you remember when we first met and I brought you home? Do you remember the offer of a real home, a last name?"

Ryuu nodded. He remembered every day with Shigeru. There had been many days when he had wished he had chosen the other path, but on the whole he thought he had made the right choice.

"Tonight I offer you the same choice again. If you like, I can introduce you to a family as a new member. They would accept you, share their last name. You would be a farmer. It would be a hard life, but it would be honest labor and you would have a family. This choice is always offered on the day a pupil learns the consequences of their violence. I think now you realize the full extent of what your training will make you. You can stay with me and continue your training, or you can go on to a new life. The choice will be yours to make by morning."

Ryuu looked at Shigeru. "What do you think I should do?"

"It's not for me to say, boy. I must remain as neutral as possible, so the decision is yours and yours alone. You are the one who has to live with it."

Ryuu nodded, and Shigeru turned in. Ryuu threw another couple of logs on the fire and let his thoughts wander. He was torn in half. He didn't want to be anything like the men who murdered his parents, and a part of him yearned for the life of a farmer. But Shigeru was family too even if he didn't recognize it. He had protected Ryuu, brought him up as his own. He had given everything to train Ryuu. The cycles had been hard, but Shigeru had never lied about the challenges. Farming would seem easy by comparison.

This decision was about him though. He didn't want to be somebody he wasn't just because he felt like he owed it to Shigeru. No, this decision had to be about what he wanted.

He was a murderer now. When he had ended the lives of four men, he had murdered. He tried to imagine himself as a gardener, trying to grow new life. Was he even worthy? How could he justify growing life if he had already made a choice to take it? Perhaps he would bring bad luck to the farmer willing to take him in, the plants would sense the blood on his hands and wilt and die.

Then there was Takako, searing into his memory. There were people who needed protecting. It would make him a murderer, but was it worth it? With his strength he could save her and all those like her. He was strong. If anyone could save her from her fate it would be him. She didn't have anyone else. The price was high, but training with Shigeru gave him the ability to make the world better for others.

The image of his mother's face flashed across his memory again, settling in to stay. Ryuu felt the familiar sensation of fear growing inside him, but suddenly became tired of the back-and-forth. It was time to decide. He needed to settle the nightmare of his parents' death, and there was only one way he could think of to do so. He believed his mother would understand his choice, and when he thought about it, he believed she would be happy with it.

Ryuu crashed to sleep. He slept soundly. When he awoke there was no need to speak with Shigeru. There was never any need to speak with Shigeru. He knew. The two of them ate a quick breakfast and were on their way.

CHAPTER 11

Ryuu had managed to get underneath Takako's skin. Despite her best efforts she couldn't forget his visit and she couldn't decide if that was good or bad. On one hand he was a ray of sunlight poking through the cloudy existence of Takako's life. She would catch herself thinking of him and smiling, daydreaming of him while doing her chores. Try as she might, she couldn't help herself.

She liked that Ryuu was a mystery. Everything else about her life felt preordained, but Ryuu had come from nowhere. Takako couldn't shake the feeling he was different than he appeared. He dressed like the son of a lord who had lost his fortune, but he didn't act like any of the men or boys who came into the house. He didn't act entitled like the world owed him a favor. Most rich boys seemed to. He had also been surprised by her situation as if it never occurred to him that not all prostitutes were volunteers. It was a rather refreshing level of naivete. He was also strong. He hadn't acted like it, but Takako had learned to discern much about a person based on the way they wore clothes. Ryuu didn't have an ounce of fat on his body. Rich boys always did. There was a secret to Ryuu, she just didn't know what it could be.

Despite the secret, and maybe because of it, Takako found herself drawn to him in a way she hadn't dared since her arrival at Madame's house. He was a genuine and nice young man interested in talking to her without the pressures associated with sexual liaison. It had been apparent he didn't know what he had been getting into, but he hid his obvious disappointment well. It had been pleasant conversing with him and watching him as he observed the world around him. He had a funny habit. When you talked to him he looked right at you, almost staring but not quite, but whenever you weren't talking with him, his eyes would begin a slow wander around the room. She had noticed it early in their meeting and had tested her theory as their day had gone on. It was always true.

Even though her situation was inescapable there was still something about Ryuu that gave her hope. She knew it was foolish, but she enjoyed contemplating what a life outside Madame's walls would be like. She didn't believe Ryuu would save her from Akio, but he reminded her there was another life out there and it gave her hope. One time she tried to imagine Ryuu coming in and saving her with his decorative sword, but the thought saddened her. Takako suspected Madame's guards would stomp Ryuu like a bug, probably without even drawing their swords. He seemed nice, and she didn't want to see him getting hurt doing something foolish.

But he gave her a sense that not everything in life was meaningless. She had enjoyed her time in his company. She wondered if there was any chance of another visit from him, simply to break the monotonous dread she felt regarding her future. During his visit she had been able to focus on the present. For just a short afternoon she believed everything would be fine. It wasn't much, but it was more than she had previously.

On the other hand, his positive influence in her life wasn't always a good thing. One lesson she had first been taught by Madame was that hope was dangerous. It wasn't until she met Ryuu she realized just how honest that lesson from Madame had been. Any time she began to hope she remembered there was no way out of her situation. He reminded her she was innocent and there should have been a choice. Once her thoughts began running in that direction she would become more and more gloomy.

Daily she began to think about clever escapes. She considered faking her own death or even committing suicide. She dreamed up schemes to find the money to buy back her freedom, each one more ridiculous than the last. She would meticulously think through each of these plans, only to run up against some wall, some inescapable fact that prevented her from acting upon her dreams. Her responsibility to her family weighed on her mind even though she hadn't heard a word from them since her arrival. The mere threat of violence against them was enough to motivate her to stay in place.

Every time she hit that wall, that inescapable fact, there was a moment she hated Ryuu for making her life more difficult. Resignation was easier than hope, less emotional. She thought about some of the older ladies in the house, how often their days off were spent intoxicated by the cheap wine Madame supplied for her girls. She understood now why those women chose that path. It was easier and less painful in the long run.

But then her mood would change and she realized that she still liked Ryuu, and it wasn't his fault her life was as it was. If blame had to be placed it would be on her father, but Takako couldn't bring herself hate her father, not even then. So instead she did as her nature directed her and strove to make the best out of her situation.

It took all her courage to go to Madame one afternoon to ask for permission to write to Ryuu.

Madame stared at her warily. Takako didn't shrink from the attention.

"I've been worrying about the effect his visit had on you. Your mood has been much more unpredictable since his arrival."

Takako didn't say anything.

"Why?"

She had thought carefully about this. "It is good practice for me. But most importantly, it would make me happy."

Takako had spent the past several days deciding how to defend her decision. There was no hope in lying to Madame. No one could. Madame frequently spoke about wanting to care for her women, wanting to keep them happy. Takako was betting it wasn't all a lie.

But Madame had let Ryuu come in the first place, which meant there was something else going on as well. Takako was sure the money was good, but Takako was dangerous right now. All of her potential clients had dried up as soon as word of Nori's request had spread. Letting any male near her was dangerous for the house.

No, there was something else, some threads Takako didn't see. Whatever the case, she had rolled the dice. There had been no other option.

"Fine. But I expect to read all correspondence both ways."

Takako had expected nothing less. "Thank you."

So Takako wrote to Ryuu, keeping the first letter short and meaningless. She didn't know if it would get to Ryuu and didn't know if he would respond. Takako didn't even know if Ryuu could read or write. She didn't want to invest too much of herself into the letter if her plan backfired. When she looked over it, she almost wondered if it was too bland. Thank you for your visit, I enjoyed your company, I hope you will look us up the next time you are in town, hope that your journey back to the village was safe, et cetera. She worried that even if he could read he might consider it a polite thank you all customers received. In a small act of rebellion and freedom she kissed her signature on the page and gave it to Madame to be sent.

A full moon passed, and she did not hear back from Ryuu. Madame had cautioned her about getting her hopes up. Although the letter had been addressed to the village nearest where he lived, Madame mentioned in passing she wasn't sure exactly where Shigeru was from and that he may not stop into town for a while to pick it up. She also wasn't sure either Shigeru or Ryuu could read. This was all news to Takako. Although Madame wouldn't speak about it, it was clear she knew more about Shigeru than she let on.

Takako's high hopes began to plummet despite her best efforts at not investing herself in the letter. Ryuu wasn't much, but he was the only thing she had. But maybe she had been wrong about that. After a while her natural optimism reasserted itself, but she knew even that dimmed a little every day.

Takako almost jumped for joy when she received a letter written in small, neat handwriting. The seal had been ripped open, but that had been the deal. Madame had made herself clear. Just as she was about to open the letter she stopped. Better to hold on to it. She set it aside in her room to treasure until that evening.

When the day's work was done Takako prepared herself for bed and her last action of the day was to open Ryuu's letter. His handwriting was dense as if every inch of paper was valuable to him.

Takako read through the letter once quickly and then went back to read it, savoring every word. Then she read it through a third time. Like her letter to him it was full of meaningless discussion. There was a short description of one of his favorite places to relax, some details from his journey, and greetings and well-wishes from Shigeru.

Takako pondered the letter. Although there was a lot written there, she could tell almost nothing about Ryuu from the message. The tone was friendly, conversational, and kind, but she learned nothing meaningful about him. No hint of what his family did for a living, why he carried a sword, or even where he lived. Takako had to look up the village on a map. Even once she found the village, which was in the middle of nowhere, she had no idea where Ryuu lived relative to the village.

Frustrated, Takako decided she would try to use these letters to draw out the mysterious Ryuu. She fell asleep committed to replying the very next day. She fell to her task with ardor and the next day Takako watched as the daily messenger left carrying her letter among others.

The second response from Ryuu came more quickly than the first, just over a half-moon from the day she sent the message. She saw in Ryuu's letter that he promised to stop by the village as often as possible to check for messages. He hoped it would decrease the necessary delay between contact.

Once again though the message didn't reveal anything personal about Ryuu. He seemed to be an expert at deflecting any attention away from himself. He answered all of her questions about him in vague generalities and redirected the conversation back to her with his questions. Takako almost laughed at the pattern once she recognized it, but couldn't bring herself to use the same tactics on him. She vowed to continue trying to draw him out of his shell while revealing herself naturally.

The messages continued throughout the rest of the winter season. Another meeting was arranged for the beginning of the snow melt, and Takako realized she had something to look forward to. Many of the ladies in the house commented on her positive demeanor, and she replied kindly to them all, believing that perhaps her fortunes had changed. If Ryuu was rich, perhaps he could buy her before Akio. It didn't seem likely, but perhaps it was possible.

The snow couldn't melt fast enough for Takako's liking and at times Madame would remind Takako the snow melt also signaled the beginning of spring when Nori would bring his son to the house to buy her. Takako determined not to let the news bother her and fought to remain positive and look forward to Ryuu's visit.

Finally, a letter came from Shigeru, which Madame let Takako read. It stated the two of them were to come four days hence and their hospitality would be much appreciated for the night. Takako continued to read the letter beyond the pertinent information, realizing Madame was charging an exorbitant fee for a night of conversation for Ryuu and a night for Shigeru. Takako didn't realize Madame's income was quite so high. It forced a new perspective on her.

The wait was interminable. The four days seemed to pass one extended breath at a time. Chores were difficult to focus on and complete and Madame frequently scolded her for her poor manners and behavior around the house. Takako found she couldn't help it. The thought of being with Ryuu again, even if it was just to have a conversation, was so pleasing that daily tasks seemed monotonous and difficult to complete.

The day of Ryuu's arrival was a bright and sunny spring day. The snows had yet to melt which meant Takako had at least a moon or two of freedom left. She enjoyed being outside, the warmth of the sun not eliminating the cold but still melting snow. Despite the brief respite and the beautiful weather, Takako was anything but cheerful. She rarely blamed Madame for her problems, but she did today. Takako's list of assigned chores was almost unbearable. She suspected Madame was assigning her so many chores on purpose, to remind her why she was here.

Takako wanted none of it. Her plan for the day had been to spend all day making herself look nice for Ryuu. Not seductive, just nice. She found herself wanting to impress him even if he was younger than her. He was hope, but Madame saw him as a distraction from her chores. Takako did sloppy work that morning, being ordered by Madame to try and try again until her areas were spotless.

Madame, realizing that there was no fighting the emotions of the young, relented and released her from her daily duties with a threat tomorrow would be worse. Takako was so overjoyed she almost hugged Madame before remembering herself and scampering back to her room. Time seemed to snap forward. Every moment which had gone by at a snail's pace now seemed to fly by and Takako found herself pressed for time. The letter hadn't specified what time they would arrive, but Takako guessed they would show up when the sun was high.

Her instincts proved to be right. Shigeru and Ryuu arrived at mid-day looking much fresher on this journey than last time. She greeted Ryuu warmly, and although he returned her greeting in kind, Takako thought there was a new hardness in him that hadn't existed before, a new mask on top of the others. It fueled Takako's curiosity. She needed to know who this young man was.

All of those thoughts faded as they began to converse. It was like the last time. As they talked she faded into blissful contentment. She forgot that in the whole story of her life Ryuu would just be a small positive part of it. She would still be given to Akio for an end that was still unimaginable. She forgot it all and enjoyed these moments. She relaxed and focused on the present, all of her worries drifting away to the soft cadence of Ryuu's voice.

He still avoided any direct conversation about himself. As their meeting drew to a close, Takako was alternately frustrated and amazed. All the other women spoke of the men they were with. Takako got the impression men were capable of doing little but speaking about themselves.

Ryuu was different. Ryuu was focused on her, and Takako swam in the peace he provided. He didn't get angry at her, no matter what she said to tease him or provoke him. He too was lost in the present and enjoying the time together. They talked about the weather, about Takako's impending doom and what life was like for her. Ryuu seemed to be fascinated by her life and said as much. His interest was both refreshing and disturbing. It was nice to feel like she had a life story worth telling, but if her story was interesting to someone who was the son of a lord, what did that say about Ryuu? Was he defective?

The time seemed to pass in a heartbeat and Takako soon noticed it was late afternoon. She hadn't even noticed the time passing. She smiled at the thought and it caused Ryuu to stop speaking. She turned to him. "I'm sorry, I wasn't reacting to something you said, I got lost in my own thoughts."

"I think you are beautiful when you smile. You don't do it often. Not for real."

Takako burst out in a huge smile. "I know you find me beautiful, but I appreciate you saying it, it's very kind of you."

Ryuu smiled then too, and Takako believed for the first time she was seeing Ryuu actually smile, not a grin that came from the mask and mind, but from the heart. She felt a warmth in her stomach she'd never experienced before, and the moment hung suspended for one fragile instant.

The moment was cut short. Ryuu became very serious, his hand going down to his sword. In that moment Takako felt something else slip away, another layer of protection Ryuu maintained throughout their time together. She had pictured him as a young man of affluence who carried a sword as a status symbol. In that instant she knew Ryuu knew how to use his sword very well. She accepted the intuition without question, not being able to process it in time.

"What's wrong?"

"There's a group of armed men approaching the house."

Takako frowned. There was no way to know that. They were in private chambers well protected from the outside. When one became accustomed to the house they could tell when somebody entered, but Ryuu had said "approaching," not "in."

The door to the house opened and Takako caught a hint of argument between Madame's guards and a group of men. She looked at Ryuu with a sudden fear. There was no way he could have known! Who was he? Takako realized again she had pinned her hopes on a man she knew nothing meaningful about. His deception seemed much more sinister now.

Takako looked at Ryuu trying to find some answers written somewhere on his face. But there was nothing to be found. His face was emotionless and calm. He was thinking fast, trying to decide what to do, even though he hadn't moved a muscle. Almost as soon as the moment came it passed and Ryuu relaxed his grip on his sword and became the same Ryuu she had known throughout their brief encounters. He apologized and asked for more tea. Takako doubted her sanity. It was as if two young men were trading places in front of her. As she poured the tea she could hear the footsteps of the group come closer to her door. She started to panic. It shouldn't have been possible. It was too soon.

Her door opened and all her fears were realized at once. The man who opened it was young, a couple of cycles older than her. He could have been handsome if not for the look of anger upon his face. Takako had seen a lot of men pass through the doors of Madame's house over the cycles in a lot of different ways, but she had never seen a man whose face could be twisted in so much rage.

He took one glance around the room and pointed at her. "Grab the whore and makes sure she is placed somewhere that she can't throw herself at another man."

Four men followed his command, and Takako felt herself picked up by each limb. She thrashed about in terror, screaming for Madame to do something until part of her clothing was jammed roughly into her mouth. She tried to bite the hand holding it in, but there was too much cloth in the way and she couldn't even begin to close her jaw.

Takako tried to turn around to look at Ryuu, managing to grab the edges of the doorway, fighting to see what transpired between the two men. She could only assume the angry man was Nori's son, Akio. Her fears were confirmed when Madame reached the scene with all of her guards of the house behind her.

"Akio! What are you doing here? This is a place of business! Let down Takako now and take that damned gag out of her mouth."

Akio looked around and examined the situation. He motioned to the guards, who dropped her none too gently to the ground.

She pulled the gag out of her mouth and started to cry silently, not wanting to risk Madame's displeasure which was now squarely focused on Akio.

"The girl is yours, what do you mean by coming in here and trying to take her by force?"

Akio wasn't bothered in the least by Madame. "I should be asking you the same thing. I came here, hoping to surprise my consort with some new gifts I had picked up in town. I desired to properly introduce myself to her before we are to leave in a couple of days time. But when I get here, your guards tell me Takako has another appointment, and she can't see me right now. The agreement my father made with you demanded she be untouched. I come in, just once, and I find her with this dog," he said, jabbing his finger at Ryuu.

"The girl is still untouched, boy, so don't go making accusations of me. You can feel free to check, but I will vouch for her. She is teaching the tea ceremony to this young man while his father enjoys the pleasures of this house. Do not assume a conspiracy where there is none."

Madame's response only seemed to flame the fans of Akio's rage further. "Tea ceremony! You must think me foolish to believe that. I should have both this cunt and dog killed." Akio drew his sword, starting a chain reaction of swords being drawn. The building echoed with the ring of steel being loosed.

Madame motioned for her guards to bring their swords down. "There is no need for violence here, Akio. The girl is yours as promised. Any killings here would bring dishonor to both you and your father. No harm has been done and you will know she is untouched yourself in due time. It would not be wise to take this any further."

Takako watched everything with rapt attention, a captive audience of one. Madame stood tall, calm in the face of danger, her guard behind her ready to defend and attack at a moment's notice. Akio and Madame had about an equal number of retainers present, so it would be a close fight. Akio was still angry, but Takako could see Madame's words had gotten to him. He was scared of his father. The realization came like a lightning bolt on a clear day, but Takako recognized the truth of it immediately. And in her room sat Ryuu, still surrounded in mystery. Was he a warrior or a child? Takako couldn't decide, even knowing him better than anybody else in the situation. He didn't seem worried, but Takako guessed she looked fairly normal too, frozen in complete fear as she was.

Takako was only thrown into more confusion as Akio made his decision. He sheathed his sword and walked over to Ryuu. "You must be a rich kid to be carrying that sword like it's something you know how to use." He picked Ryuu up with one arm, and Takako saw firsthand just how strong Nori's son was. Ryuu dangled there, feet scraping the ground. But Ryuu didn't struggle. Akio continued insulting him. "Come on, if you can use that sword, now is a good time. Otherwise I'm going to bring more pain down on you than you've ever experienced before. I might even cut off one of your hands. That will teach you to touch other people's women."

Ryuu looked at Akio calmly. Takako saw there was no fear in his eyes, but he took no steps to save himself. Who was he? Why wasn't he scared? Akio laughed and head butted Ryuu. Takako swore she saw Ryuu move enough to deflect the blow, but she couldn't be sure, everything happened so fast. Akio started raining blows down on Ryuu as Ryuu protected his face and groin. Akio punched and kicked him over and over, and Takako saw the blood starting to splatter over her private space. Takako screamed for Akio to stop, but that just caused him to kick Ryuu with renewed vigor.

Madame held her guards back with one hand and Takako begged her and pleaded with her to make it stop, but she took no action. With one final, incredible kick that lifted Ryuu's smaller body off the ground, Akio reached a point of exhaustion. He turned around and looked at Takako. "This is the least that will happen to any man I see you with even if you are just teaching him the tea ceremony. Are we clear?"

It was all Takako could do to nod her head. As Akio motioned his guards to take her with them, she managed to steal one last glance at Ryuu. His face looked unharmed, and he was looking at her with the same mask he always wore. Takako would have sworn he was fine, and as she was pulled out of sight, she thought just for the briefest of moments she saw him smile. Even as she was being thrown in a cart she couldn't help but wonder, who was Ryuu?

CHAPTER 12

Moriko awoke confused. She was dead. But dead should be
. . . different. She was awake, and awake wasn't right. Her mind
was a blank slate for a couple of breaths before memory exploded
through her. She remembered the combat with the Abbot, being
whipped against the monastery wall. But what she couldn't forget
was the sword through her abdomen. She could still see the drip
of blood from the tip of the blade.

The pain came blasting through on the heels of her memory. She
was lying on her stomach with her head being supported by a rather
clever arrangement of pillows and blankets. Without even moving
she could feel the tenderness of her back. She tried making just
the slightest movement and the pain that shot throughout her back
dimmed her peripheral vision. She bit herself trying not to scream.
Every welt seemed to be connected to the next one, and movement of
one seemed to light them all up. If the Abbot had done it on purpose
there was no way he could have done a better job of it.

Moriko was worried about the cut from the sword but she
couldn't bring herself to try to find it. If she was alive now, she
would be alive when it was fine to move her arm and find out.
There was no rush, not right now.

She heard a soft movement. As her head continued to clear her sense returned to her. She was in the monastery which wasn't surprising, and seemed to be in her own bed. She heard Tomotsu's voice and it sounded like the sweetest music she had ever heard. Even through everything he had watched over her. Perhaps there was some good in the world. "How are you feeling?"

Moriko gently moved her jaw and determined it would be okay to speak, "Horrible."

"That doesn't surprise me." There wasn't much sympathy in Tomotsu's voice and her heart sank. "I'm surprised the Abbot let you live. I thought he meant to kill you."

"I am too. I saw the sword. Why am I not dead?"

"The Abbot is one of the best warriors in the region, something you should have known before pulling your stunt. He was able to place the blade in a safe place, not cutting any organs. It was an incredible strike."

The tent of hope she had raised collapsed to the ground. Her only hope at sympathy and support was instead complimenting the Abbot on his incredible swordsmanship against a bound girl. Tomotsu didn't care. He had been assigned to take care of her. She was alone. Moriko swore to herself and wished for death, or at least the quiet of the forest. She decided in that moment she was done with people for good.

If Tomotsu didn't sense that, he at least understood she didn't want to talk to him. He stepped away from her bed. "I will let you get some rest. The Abbot will want to see you when you are stronger."

Moriko cried, the pillows bunched around her face drinking her tears. There was nothing left for her in this life.

Moriko's recovery was agonizing and slow. Although her body did its best to try to stitch together all the cuts every small movement she made ripped open a new scab. It was almost a full moon before Moriko was able to sit up in bed and try walking around without pain. It was a small achievement, but being able to move again was an incredible relief to Moriko. She was more scared of paralysis and losing her ability to move than she was of death.

Tomotsu made it clear she wasn't to leave her quarters. He told her the Abbot wanted her healed before she would be allowed to wander the monastery grounds again. Moriko accepted the orders without comment. She was too weak to do anything useful anyway, so the order was to her liking.

Moriko spent many of her waking hours thinking of trees. She imagined them whispering in the breeze, the shade and the sun making exquisite patterns on her skin. There was something so natural, so primal about the woods. Life made a lot more sense there than in the monastery cut off from all nature except the sky.

At least she had plenty of time to think about what had happened. The offenses she had committed were punishable up to death by their monastic code. While not a required punishment, common belief held an offense of her magnitude was almost always met with death. Moriko struggled to figure out why she hadn't been killed. Her mind could only come up with two unpleasant possibilities: either she was being healed just to be tortured again, or the Abbot felt like she could be rehabilitated.

Moriko dismissed the first possibility for two reasons. The first was that although Perseverance was a strict place, it was not unnecessarily cruel. Although she would be delighted to escape at a moment's notice, monasteries were beacons of light in a dark world. If the Abbot wanted that belief to continue, he couldn't torture girls at will. The second reason was that if it was true, Moriko could do nothing about it, so it was no use to even worry about it. Better to focus on more positive outcomes and hope for the best.

Which left only the possibility the Abbot had some greater plan for her. It left her more options but was also much more terrifying. Moriko examined the situation from every angle. She was the only one who knew how desperate she was to escape, who knew how much she detested living in the monastery. Perhaps the Abbot was looking to use her as a warrior for the monastery. He couldn't know her disloyalty extended to the whole monastic system.

Although Moriko couldn't guess what the Abbot was thinking, she knew she had a choice to make. To continue her show of defiance would lead to her death. To submit to the Abbot held the possibility of future life. Defiance seemed preferable, but submission meant life. For many days the wish for life and death fought within her soul, and her final decision was not one she was proud of.

She decided to submit and follow the Abbot's orders and plan for her life. It felt like a coward's decision, but she did not want to die. She missed her family, and she missed the woods. She would give anything to wander through those woods again, to use her new powers to sense the life that flowed through the area. Life meant opportunity and hope. She would never give in to the Abbot's manipulations but would always be looking for her opportunity to escape.

Her resolution set, Moriko set about fulfilling her plans. She pushed her rehabilitation as far as it would go. It wasn't pleasant, but she wasn't sure what was next and her body needed to be prepared. She had been letting it heal slowly but she hadn't been keeping her body in shape. It was time to do so. She began exercising a bit at a time as her body would allow her. Combined with frequent stretching, Moriko found within another moon's time she was starting to feel almost at the level she had been at before the torture. The skin on her back still felt tight sometimes but overall she felt like her body was ready for new challenges.

Moriko was proud of her body. She was proud of what it was capable of, how strong it was. As her fingers traced over the parts of her back she could reach, she found she was even proud of her scars. She would finger the scar on her abdomen where she had been stabbed and swore to herself she would never forget what she had endured at the hands of the Abbot.

Her relationships with the other students also changed. Where she had used to be shy, she now almost didn't speak at all. The other students ostracized her which was perfectly fine to her. She had seen the pattern begin with Tomotsu and saw it develop in all the other students as well. She was unclean, to be avoided. The other students were becoming content and comfortable.

The initial adjustment to the monastery was difficult as most students were taken from their families. But as they adjusted to a comfortable existence, the desire to escape shrank more and more. Comfort was the nemesis of change and within a few cycles most students became attached to the monastic routine and way of life. There was power and privilege here, and no one willingly turned away from that. Moriko labeled them all cowards and refused to deal with them.

Tomotsu continued to check on her daily. She tried to delay the inevitable, but she knew it was only a matter of time before she was summoned to the Abbot's chambers. Moriko had been expecting the summons for a while by the time it came. She was as healed as she was going to get while resting.

Tomotsu had returned her sword several days ago. It was a clear message. Even armed, she posed no threat to the Abbot. She was thankful for its unyielding presence. The blade was cool and solid as she ran her hand over the blade before resting it in its sheath and preparing herself for the meeting. She imagined herself as the steel of her sword, folded upon itself hundreds of times, the core a secret to all.

For the first time in almost two moons, Moriko stepped out into the monastery courtyard. It hadn't changed since her fight with Goro. Her breath caught in her throat when she saw the rings she had been tied to while whipped. She pushed the reaction down and forced herself to stare. There was no blood under the spot. The monks had cleaned well.

Inside the Abbot's chambers was stillness. The typical bustle surrounding the Abbot was nowhere to be found, replaced by a quiet, meditative silence. Moriko filled herself with the silence. Emptiness was safety. If she kept herself empty she could face the Abbot without fear. She did not underestimate his sense. She kept herself as still as the room.

Moriko put her plan into action. She approached, getting on her knees and bowing her face all the way to the floor. She did not move and willed her body to relax as the Abbot's sense washed over her. He would find nothing but emptiness. Emptiness and silence, a soul ready to be tamed.

Although she couldn't see him, she could almost sense his broad smile. She quenched the flicker of hope and anger that threatened to spark the forest-sized rage she felt. She had to stay empty, to let him believe he had conquered her spirit.

"I'm glad to see you have learned some respect, little Moriko."

The spark was alive inside of her, threatening to burn her plans to the ground. She wanted to stand, fight her last fight and welcome death like an old friend. But her face remained stone, her posture unchanged, her muscles empty. She felt like she weighed as much as ten men.

She felt and heard the Abbot approach. "Sit up, my child, and let's take tea together." Moriko obeyed and found herself face to face with the Abbot. Typically one saw him from a few paces away and on his pedestal. He had never seemed this human to her.

"Your lesson was not a pleasant one for me to teach, but I see the effects were worth the cost. I hope in time you will come to see why I had to take such drastic measures."

Moriko remained silent. She didn't know what to say and didn't trust herself to speak without anger. Fortunately, the Abbot seemed to respect her silence. As the tea was served he was content not to speak. He played the role of a kind and gentle father whose daughter had misbehaved. Moriko reigned in her thoughts. She focused on the scar in her abdomen and the fatherly image blinked out of her mind, replaced with her truth of what he was.

Silence persisted throughout their first cup of tea, but as the Abbot signaled for a second cup, he asked her a question, his voice gentle in the silence. "Tell me, Moriko, what do you know of the history of the Three Kingdoms?"

Moriko had come into the chambers prepared for many outcomes, but not one of them included a history question. She took a few moments to put her thoughts together. "Only what I've been taught. There used to be a single Kingdom which had lasted for many, many generations. About one thousand cycles ago there was an attempted coup by several of the King's advisers and the nightblades. The coup was unsuccessful and led to a civil war between the King and the families and holdings of two of the advisers. Even though the King's forces were by far the strongest, the conflict raged for ten cycles, resulting in the truce which currently holds between the Three Kingdoms. The truce calls for coordination on matters of defense against outsiders, but leave the Kingdoms separate in all else."

The Abbot nodded. "That is the version that is taught, yes. But there is a fact withheld from these teachings, a fact only the elite in society know about. What do you know of the nightblades?"

That seemed like a silly question. Everyone had heard of the nightblades. How else did parents get their children to behave when they wouldn't listen?

She warmed up to the conversation despite herself. It was pleasant to talk to someone else even if it was the Abbot. For two moons she hadn't had a meaningful conversation. She didn't drop her guard though. "The nightblades were legendary fighters. It was said in the day of the one Kingdom they were wanderers beholden only to the King's justice. They traveled through the countryside acting both as diplomats and as warriors. They were respected and are often credited with maintaining the One Kingdom for as long as it lasted. However, after the Great War people began to realize how dangerous and evil they were, and they were all hunted down and killed."

The Abbot nodded his agreement. "As always, there is a truth to the legends. If there was not a truth, they wouldn't exist in our collective psyche as long as they have. Would you like to know the truth of that conflict?"

Meekly, Moriko nodded. She didn't want to show the Abbot just how curious she was. All the great stories came from the Great War.

The Abbot started his story. "There are several facts you don't know about. The first is that the Great War was started solely by the nightblades. It is well-documented that a collective of nightblades poisoned the minds of the advisers. It was this failed attempt that led to the Great War. Apparently the nightblades were not content with their lot in life as wanderers and strove to take positions of power in the Kingdom. The King at the time had many nightblades and dayblades who were loyal to him and stayed in his court, but they were far outnumbered by those who wandered the country."

He checked to see if Moriko was still paying attention. She didn't have to pretend. The story was fascinating to her. She had never heard any of this before. The Abbot continued. "The reason that the Kingdom was split in three is because of the nightblades. Even though the King commanded a large army, the nightblades could and would change the tide of a battle, both as commanders and as soldiers. It was a case of greater numbers versus greater skill, and in the end there was no victor. When the advisers met with the King to create the treaty of the Three Kingdoms even they realized they had been duped, and it was decided that the nightblades were too dangerous for the Kingdoms to handle."

"Thus, the system which has lasted since the Great War was created. Those dayblades who were loyal to the King founded the monastic system that lasts even today. We can trace our own history back to one of the King's original retainers. Every nightblade and the dayblades who were not loyal to the King had several options. Many were killed in the treacheries of the following cycles. Some went into self-imposed exile, leaving this land for parts unknown. Another group, maybe a third of all blades by some estimates, opted to give up their swords and settle down as peasants. They were stripped of all honor and title, were given a small plot of land and nothing more. They were observed and spied on by those loyal to the King. This is why there are so many people today who still use the sense. It is passed down from parent to child."

The Abbot paused in his story. He took a sip of tea and studied Moriko. She got the idea he was at the crux of the story, the reason he asked her here, and the reason she was still alive. "Moriko, do you know why the monasteries were created?"

"To protect the Three Kingdoms."

"Yes, but do you know how small monasteries like ours protect the Three Kingdoms?"

Moriko stopped mid-answer. At first she thought it was because the monasteries created excellent warriors, but that wasn't necessarily true. Their martial skills were excellent, but they rarely saw actual combat, and couldn't be any better than those in elite military units. It was the sense which distinguished them, but she didn't know how it made a difference. They weren't nightblades. Everyone in the monasteries was descended from Dayblades. She shrugged.

"The answer has two parts. First is that we help control the public and the peasants. The capitols of the Three Kingdoms are far apart and the lands they hold are wide. It would take almost two moons for some capitols to get a main armed force to a revolt. The monasteries are symbols of power throughout the Kingdoms. Even though you know we aren't nightblades, the sense is still a mythical power to peasants. We work to keep it that way by keeping the paths of the sense secret. Peasants are much less likely to revolt when they believe a supernatural power could be raised against them at any time."

Moriko understood that concept all too well. She remembered how others had spoken in hushed whispers about her when they thought she couldn't hear them. Having the sense was a great gift, but it was also a curse among the people as they looked upon those gifted with it as supernatural outcasts.

"The second purpose is to control the sense. Not the power itself, but how it manifests itself in society. This is our main purpose, and the one your actions two moons ago endangered. We find all the individuals in the world who are sense-gifted and we bring them into our monasteries. Here we are safe and powerful. If we find someone who has the sense outside our walls, we always bring them into our walls because we believe, and the Great War has taught us that the sense is a power far too great to be released into society uncontrolled. The effects it could have on society can be no less than disastrous. History teaches us this as a fact and we always strive to maintain this order. It is why our monks are always out traveling the land, trying to find those who are gifted and bring them here to safety."

Moriko struggled to remain critical of the Abbot. Everything he said made sense. If nightblades had started the Great War they were too dangerous to be loose. Everyone wanted the one Kingdom to return. It meant certain sacrifices for many children, but wasn't that better than a war which killed thousands of people? She thought over the story while trying to maintain an empty expression. She found she couldn't do it. Too much was at stake and she was too interested. She blurted out, "How does this apply to me?"

"Here at Perseverance, as in all monasteries, we guide students in the sense, and we train them in martial skills, but we train dayblades, not nightblades. Do you know why?"

Moriko shook her head. It was starting to crystallize for her now. When she had attacked Goro, she had acted as a nightblade, not a dayblade. But she doubted herself. Everything she had done seemed as natural as running naked through the woods. It had been liberating, freeing, primal.

"Nightblades are too dangerous, both for the monastery and for the Kingdoms. When I saw you starting down the path I feared not just for you but for all of us. Dayblades can't use the sense in combat, but we can use it to bring healing. What you did was wrong, perverse. I thought you might try to kill all of us."

Moriko held her head low. She felt like crying. Would she have been able to kill everyone? Maybe. She had felt so strong, so free. Was it wrong?

"Don't cry, Moriko. I had to be stern, because your crime was severe, but I see great promise in you. You can be a great asset to this community which is why I let you live. Everything is going to be fine. You need to trust me though."

Moriko was torn. She had come to the Abbot's quarters with a sense of purpose, a knowledge found through suffering. Her own experience taught her the monastery was an evil place, but the words of the Abbot were very convincing. Although she had never heard his version of history before, she felt it had the ring of truth. Harnessing the power of a nightblade had felt so right, like it was the culmination of all the cycles of training she had been through. It was like reaching the top of the tallest tree she could find in the old woods. It was scary, exhilarating, but freeing.

The Abbot's tale didn't deny her the power of her experience, but showed Moriko the long-term error of her ways. Perhaps the monastery was a difficult place to survive, but Moriko was beginning to realize they sat on the edge of a blade trying to both understand and control the sense. That kind of balance couldn't always be achieved by gentle means. Moriko felt her resolution waver and dissipate like smoke from a fire. She struggled not to cry. It was anger that had given her a purpose to survive, to recover. Without anger she had nothing left.

"Why did you let me live?"

The Abbot smiled and Moriko felt an uncomfortable chill begin to sneak back through her body.

"I was wondering when you would come to that question. The punishment for your offense is typically death, but since the day you came through those doors with Goro, I have believed fate holds an incredible promise for you. I believe you are talented and may be one of the strongest people to come to this monastery in my time here. I needed you to know the truth and for you to make your own decision before I destroy what is a rare gift."

Moriko's thoughts raced by, too slippery to hold onto. She had been right in assuming there was something more to the Abbot's mercy. For the moment she was grateful. Perhaps she had been too rash and had made her judgments too quickly. If the Abbot spoke the truth he had nothing but her best interests in mind.

"Moriko, it is time I introduce you to somebody very important. His name is Orochi, and I believe he will have much to teach you in the coming cycles."

She recoiled when a shadow unfurled itself at the edges of her sight. Realization struck her like a hammer to the head. In her time at Perseverance she had become used to living with the sense. She used it all the time, in the background of her mind, gathering information on everything transpiring around her. But she hadn't sensed anyone else was in the room with them. She could sense everybody. That was the point of the sense. She had been under the impression it was only her and the Abbot throughout their conversation. But there were no entrances behind the Abbot's chair. He had been back there in the shadows the entire time and Moriko had never known.

Orochi was intimidating, his figure larger than life due to Moriko's surprise and inability to process what she wasn't sensing. He was tall, at least two heads taller than Moriko, and he was big. Not fat. It looked like it would be impossible to find fat on him, but every muscle in his body seemed like it had been inflated beyond what was possible. He had broad shoulders and his head was shaven.

Of all his impressive features, Moriko was drawn most to the way he moved. It was graceful and silent. She had never seen anybody walk like him. She had heard of giant mountain cats that killed unwary travelers and she imagined Orochi to be their human manifestation. Moriko knew this was a man who could kill anyone. Even the Abbot's power was nothing but a paper-thin shield compared to what this man was capable of.

The scariest part was that Moriko couldn't sense him at all. If she focused hard enough she could sense a spider across the monastery, but this man standing in front of her gave off nothing. It was fascinating and terrifying. She could only sense the nothingness faint against the background of life she had become used to. She could locate him, but just barely, and only when he was a pace or two away.

The Abbot was grinning ear-to-ear. Moriko thought of him as an overgrown boy, a bully who existed to make others suffer. Moriko's terror was apparent. There was no mask that could cover her shock at meeting someone she couldn't sense. She imagined it was the same expression one would have if they saw a ghost.

The Abbot could barely contain his glee. "As you can tell, Orochi has a special power. It's not unique in the world, there are a handful of people in the Three Kingdoms who have the ability, but it is useful to this system. Every once in a while, a nightblade develops out in the world. Evolution and chance make even accidental nightblades a certainty given enough time. It may be a militia member with the sense or even a bar-room brawler. Whatever the case, when they develop, it is up to individuals like Orochi here to take care of the situation."

Although the Abbot didn't say what "take care of the situation" meant, there was little doubt in Moriko's mind. Orochi was a killer, an assassin hired by the monasteries to take care of people like Moriko who accidentally discovered their full potential. Moriko's former resolve hardened in a moment, forged even stronger by the Abbot's behavior. The Abbot believed he was telling the truth, but Moriko knew there was still more to the story. A man like Orochi didn't work for the monasteries. Her mask slipped on again and she became obedient as the Abbot hoped and expected. Her face didn't even twitch when the Abbot revealed his plan, though her mind felt like it had been uprooted and thrown away.

"Moriko, I let you live because I want you to become Orochi's apprentice."

CHAPTER 13

Shigeru and Ryuu sat across from each other in the hut. Ryuu felt the room contracting around him, his sense focused on his master, the focus of his anger. He clenched and released his fists, the repetitive movement his only release. If screaming or drawing his sword would have helped he would have. But he was old enough to know better. He pushed his anger down with more anger and forced himself to focus on the conversation thickening the air between them. Shigeru was speaking, slowly and deliberately.

"What will you do if I don't grant you permission? I am not your father or family, but your master. You have sworn obedience."

Ryuu shook his head. Shigeru was grasping at straws, trying to bluff his way forward.

"You are my father as much as I am your son." The words refocused his mind and his anger flashed out, snuffed like a fire with no air. He had said it himself. Shigeru was everything to him. He couldn't deny it. When he spoke again he felt resigned. "I want your permission. I'm not sure what I will do if you don't grant it."

The two sat in silence. Ryuu had been tossing ideas back and forth since they left Madame's. His anger burned against the wall of rationality he had built over the cycles of training with Shigeru. He craved decision and action.

Shigeru seemed calm but Ryuu could see the emotions toiling beneath the surface. He knew Shigeru too well. A small facial twitch was all he needed to know Shigeru's mind about anything. Shigeru shared Ryuu's anger but could bury it under more blankets of rationality. He had more practice.

After days of war between rationality and passion Ryuu made a decision. He was going to go after Takako. She didn't deserve her fate. He had come to Shigeru in the evening to ask for permission. Shigeru was doing all he could to talk Ryuu out of it.

"You know if you do this you might be making the choice to kill another person. You wouldn't even be able to use the flimsy excuse of self-defense. This time you are consciously making the choice to kill. Are you ready to make that choice? Is this worth it?"

Ryuu did not respond right away. They were valid questions, and he had spent most of the journey back to the hut thinking about them.

"I'm already a killer, and this feels like a much better reason to take life than self-defense. It's what you trained me for and what I am."

Ryuu wanted to bring the words back as soon as he said them. Ryuu didn't mean to attack Shigeru, but he was frustrated by Shigeru's argument. This was what he had been training for since he had seen five cycles. Shigeru trained him to be a warrior but wouldn't let him fight. It felt weak, like the training was the end in itself. Ryuu felt Shigeru lacked the courage to continue to move forward.

An uncomfortable silence stretched for a few breaths. Ryuu realized he'd never argued with Shigeru over anything important before. They were treading new ground together. He took a deep breath to keep his wits and logic about him.

"I'm sorry, I didn't mean . . ."

Shigeru held up his hand for silence. Ryuu took another deep breath. Shigeru had come to a decision. "No, you're right. I know what I've done. Some days I'm not sure my decisions were the best, but they are the ones I've made. If you're going to do this I'll support you, but I want you to understand the full effect of your decision. There is no going back after this. We may never be able to return here."

Ryuu perked up at the mention of "we." He had never thought Shigeru would come with him. But then Shigeru's words sunk into his heart. He hadn't thought about the consequences. In his head he imagined he would come back with Takako and everything would be great. He never thought about what it meant to be hunted and pursued. The thoughts saddened him. He loved his life here with Shigeru. His resolution wavered, just for a moment. But he steeled himself. Just moments ago he had been telling himself he was willing to sacrifice life itself. He wouldn't be hypocritical. If he was willing to give up his life he had to give up his home too. It was time to mend the broken fences.

"Shigeru, don't question what you did. My path was set the moment those bandits killed my parents. There was never any turning back, despite your hopes I might lead a normal life. I'm proud of who I am, and because I am proud of my skills I must use them to save Takako. I know I don't know her that well, but if I'm not willing to help someone whom I am convinced is innocent, what is my life and training worth?"

Ryuu could see Shigeru was overcome. He couldn't guess what was running through his master's head.

"I will be proud to accompany you. Even though tracking an army is easy, I believe I will be able to provide some valuable lessons along the way. My presence too close to the army may jeopardize your mission, but I can take you most of the way. In the end it will still be up to you."

Ryuu nodded and their decision was made. They spent the next day preparing, closing up the hut in case they weren't able to return. Everything they needed was packed with them even though it amounted to very little. Ryuu understood a truth as they packed. Shigeru had always been prepared for this, regardless of his comments otherwise. They didn't own anything superfluous. Their only possessions were a pot, a pan, and some bare utensils. There had never been a need for anything else.

They left early the next morning as the sun was starting to hint it was about to peek over the trees. After a few hundred paces they came to the last spot they could see the hut from. They took a moment to look back at it. Each experienced a strong emotion although it was different for each of them. Ryuu was nostalgic but hopeful. This hut was where he had grown up and where he had felt safe and cared for most of his life. He was leaving it, but he took a moment to try to memorize the view, beautiful with the rising sun in the background.

Shigeru was also reflective, but more concerned about the future. Ryuu had brought him back. For many cycles he had lived with his soul in the grave, ready to return to the Cycle at a moment's notice. He felt his time drawing near. The boy who had been his rebirth seemed also to be the man who would bring him death. He found now, as he felt his death approaching, that he wasn't ready. He wanted to see how the story would unfold.

He was convinced Ryuu would change this age. He hoped he would be alive to find out how.

It took almost a half-moon to find the path of the army, but after they found it it was easy enough to follow. The army was heading to the Three Sisters, the same as they did every cycle. There was no need and no ability to hide the tracks of thousands of men and horses. A blind man could have tracked them from their scent alone.

Shigeru and Ryuu took the guise of poor travelers, tying their swords low on their backs and hiding them behind clothing. They couldn't draw as fast as they would need to in an emergency, but they trusted their sense to protect them from any dangers.

Their trip took them through territory Ryuu had never been through before. He felt his sense growing in power, extending its reach for hundreds of paces in every direction. It was an unspeakable experience being able to feel the world around him in such detail. If he focused he could sense the bugs and insects which busied themselves beneath him. The world was alive and his greatest danger was losing himself in the information he brought in.

Without Shigeru, Ryuu might have gotten lost. Shigeru was always bringing him back, forcing him to focus on what was essential. Ryuu knew his sense traveled much further than Shigeru's, but Shigeru had the weight of experience on his side. He could identify creatures and events Ryuu couldn't. He could also maintain his focus for longer. Ryuu never saw him lose focus in all the time they had lived together.

After a half moon of uneventful traveling, Ryuu sensed the army. It felt like he was nearing the city, but the city was on wheels, moving and reshaping itself at random. Ryuu had expected columns and more order than what he was experiencing. It cast his sense into doubt.

Shigeru put his mind at ease. "It's the army. An army is in constant flux, stuck between order and chaos. While I'm sure Nori would love to have orderly columns, marching thousands of men over terrain which is not flat prohibits him. I am surprised you can sense them from here. I figure we still have a day or two until we come close enough to meet their rear-guard."

"Can you sense them?"

"Not at all, but if you would rely a little less on your sense, you'd see the evidence of an army passing through here not more than a day or two ago."

Ryuu, chastised, glanced around and saw all the evidence Shigeru was referring to. The path had been trod more recently although the change had happened so gradually Ryuu hadn't noticed it. It did look like the army had passed through in the past day or two.

"Remember, one of the best ways you'll be able to improve is by using your sense in conjunction with everything else you experience. You do it well in combat, but now you need to apply the same principles with every breath you take."

Ryuu nodded. His patience for Shigeru's lectures had diminished since they began this trip. His blood hungered for action, not for learning. It was only through force of will that he remained respectful.

As they resumed their journey Shigeru asked Ryuu about his plan. Ryuu spat out his answer in frustration. "I don't know. Find her and bring her out."

Shigeru stepped in front of Ryuu and stopped him. "Stop. I know you're impatient. But if you are going to get Takako back, charging in won't do. Even you can't hope to fight an army. Even the strongest warriors die if they aren't calm, if they can't reason. You're much too good to die because of a stupid mistake."

Reason and impatience clashed within Ryuu's soul. He knew Shigeru was right, but he didn't care. He tried to step forward but Shigeru laid a restraining hand on his shoulder.

"No."

Ryuu's anger exploded and dissipated like a wave against the rocks. He hated being wrong. He sat down. "Fine. What would you do?"

Shigeru grinned. "I wouldn't be here in the first place. I don't know how you can find one person in an army without going through official channels, and I sure as hell don't know how you plan on sneaking the commander's son's consort out without anyone noticing. But if you pull it off, I'll be very damn impressed."

Ryuu thought about the problem as they continued to get closer to the army. They were approaching the foothills of the Pass and soon it would be impossible to sneak into the army unobserved. Out in the open there were always gaps, places where one could sneak through if they knew what they were doing. In the pass the army would narrow down and there would only be two entrances, the front and the back. If he was going to make his move it would have to be in the next day or two.

The problem became more complicated when Shigeru announced he wouldn't get closer to the army. Ryuu challenged him, thinking it was another ploy to make Ryuu work harder, but Shigeru's mood allowed for no argument.

"Ryuu, I'm a hunted man and there are people in that army who may be trained to hunt me. I am not going to put you in further jeopardy by accompanying you any closer."

Ryuu tried to argue with Shigeru, but he realized it was pointless. Shigeru would not be budged. Ryuu wondered what cause Shigeru had to fear, but it was a question he had held for a long time. He could wait for his answer, Takako couldn't wait for him. They agreed to meet in three days. Shigeru would continue to follow the army's path until it was too risky. If Ryuu could retreat back along it they would meet up without difficulty. They set up a back-up point in New Haven in case circumstances prevented them from meeting up on their first attempt.

The two parted company, and for the first time Ryuu felt like he was alone. Leaving Shigeru felt like leaving a part of his heart behind. Ryuu didn't want to die without seeing Shigeru again, but he was set on doing this, so there was nothing to do but go forward.

Ryuu opened up into the slow trot he had perfected in many cycles of running through the woods chasing after his master. He knew he could keep the speed up indefinitely and it would allow him to cover the remaining distance in the shortest time.

Late that afternoon Ryuu could sense the rear guard and knew if he continued he would be seen. He opted to turn off to the side and approach the army through a parallel valley in the foothills. As night fell and the army set up camp he climbed up to the top of the valley that separated them. He knew he had to act tonight. After tonight the army would be well into the pass and almost impossible to infiltrate. There were sentries posted along the ridge line he was on, but they were spread wide.

Ryuu lay in grass just high enough to cover his body. He was thankful for the new moon. Dark skies meant he would not be seen. He tried to still his heart so he could focus, but he couldn't. It felt tight like he would burst open at any moment, spilling out all his hopes and dreams and plans on the ground with his entrails.

Without his calm, he couldn't focus his senses well. He could tell there were two sentries nearby, but he couldn't extend his search any further than that. He would need a uniform to get into camp. Those two were as good as any.

He thought he had been crawling slowly, but he was behind the two guards in short order. His attempt at stealth was unnecessary. The two were laughing and telling lewd stories from their time in New Haven. He could have walked up right in front of them and not been noticed.

A quick series of blows rendered the two men unconscious, bodies falling to the ground with a muffled thump. Ryuu stripped the guard closest to his size and tied and gagged them both with leather straps he had brought with him. He had just finished throwing the guard's clothes over his own robes when another pair of sentries came over the hill. He had been so distracted he hadn't even sensed them. The sentries were no more than ten paces from the guards he had just knocked out. They were in tall grass, but anyone looking would find them without a problem.

With no options Ryuu stood there, acting how he imagined a sentry would act. As the pair approached Ryuu tried to calm his mind. He would be in a lot of trouble if they were his replacements. The guards walked right up to him and it took Ryuu every piece of focus he possessed not to stare at the guards he had just tied up.

Ryuu noticed the stitching on one of the men's uniforms as he approached. Shigeru had forced him to memorize insignia. This man was a lieutenant, probably the commander of this whole sentry unit tonight. Ryuu cursed. He would know his men. Ryuu looked outward, trying to keep the back of his head pointed at the officer.

Fate was not on his side. The officer stopped and stood behind him, taking in the view of the valley below.

"Where is your second, ensign?"

Ryuu thought fast. "Pissing, sir."

"He couldn't do that here?"

Ryuu grimaced. He hadn't thought of that. Lying wasn't his strongest skill. He'd never had to around Shigeru.

"Said he wanted some privacy, sir."

"Then you should have turned your back, soldier!"

Ryuu fingered his sword with his off hand. He had no answer and wasn't sure if one was expected. He pretended to maintain his vigil, the perfect sentry.

The officer swore. "You are both to report my tent immediately once your relief arrives. I don't know what you're up to, but we're going to get to the bottom of it. Probably trying to sneak women in again . . ."

The lieutenant and his second stomped away and Ryuu let out a deep breath. He hadn't even gotten close to the camp yet!

There was little time to reflect though. As soon as the officer and his second were out of sight Ryuu was racing through the night. Fear focused him and his sense spread out in a protective canopy, warning him of any immediate dangers. When he reached a good vantage point he stopped and observed the camp below him.

Those first few glances were almost enough to convince him to turn around and abandon the attempt. When Shigeru had told him the army would have a few thousand men he had imagined a large group of people, but a camp for thousands was a massive affair which spread out thousands of paces. Hundreds of campfires burned below him.

He had spread out his sense as he ran and now it created the same disorienting effect of being in the city. Ryuu fought against the nausea in his head as he tried to leave his mind open. He needed to find Takako but he couldn't imagine how to go about it. He had thought he could pick her out, but there was too much information. He had hoped she might stand out as a woman, but there were many women present, which also surprised Ryuu. Marching an army wasn't the all-male affair he had expected it to be. He glanced at the moon. Already he had imagined he would be escaping from the camp, not still trying to get in.

Ryuu paused for a moment to think. There had to be a way to make the searching simpler, faster. He couldn't go from tent to tent checking inside. He ran his eyes over the camp again. This was a military camp. There was no way that the tents would be set up randomly. There would be some sort of order to them. If he could figure out the order then he could narrow down his search.

Ryuu tried to think logically. Nori's son would be close to his father for protection and for image. It would make sense then if they were closer to the center of camp surrounded by the entire protection of their army. Ryuu's eyes wandered to the center of the camp again while searching for patterns and exceptions to patterns. His closer examination revealed a likely target. Near the center there was a tent, larger than the others with just a little more space around it. Perhaps it was Nori's tent.

It was too far and far too many people for him to use his sense. If he was going to be useful he'd have to get closer. He thought about trying to plan out his route, but he had no time and he wasn't sure it would do him any good anyway. Whatever plan he had was already in tatters. No point trying to make a bad situation any worse.

Ryuu stood up straight and walked down towards the camp. The closer he got to the camp the more rings of sentries surrounded him. He had worried there would be passwords, but no one challenged him. Either there were none, or the guards were lazy. Ryuu counted himself fortunate to have gotten at least one break.

He relaxed once he was inside the camp. There was no order as soldiers walked throughout the camp. Ryuu paid attention to his surroundings and moved at angles towards the center of the camp. He changed directions while observing the reactions of the people around him. Soon he was confident he wasn't being followed.

He got as close to the center as he could without attracting attention. There was a ring of guards around the innermost tent, but Ryuu cast out his sense and couldn't find Takako within the ring.

Ryuu tried to push out his sense, but there were too many people moving and he was too nervous. He'd have to be close. He started circling the center of the camp, weaving so as not to attract too much attention. Tent after tent and he couldn't sense Takako. Pressure mounted in his chest. He had to find her. This was his only chance.

There was no warning when he sensed her. His sense was too limited by his environment. He needed more training. His intuition, thankfully, had been right. He pushed his stress down as far as it would go, focusing on his surroundings and on his breath. His sense of Takako was strong. She was alone.

Ryuu was able to walk right up to the tent. It was smaller than the tent in the center although still nicer than the tents common soldiers shared. In another stroke of luck there weren't any guards. They were probably assigned to Akio. The consort didn't merit special attention. His hopes soared. He could walk in and sweep her off her feet, rescue her and be out, the hero of the day.

He was still day dreaming as he walked in.

"Get out!"

Ryuu was shocked. Didn't she recognize him? Did she think he was a guard? His eyes adjusted to the dark and his heart fell. He was too late. Takako's clothes were in shreds, one breast hanging out without cover, the other barely hidden. All her legs were visible, long and lean and beautiful. But he could tell. He could sense it. This wasn't the same girl he had left. She had been used.

Ryuu groped around the dark searching for words. His mind had given up on processing what was happening.

"What are you doing here? Akio will kill both of us for sure!"

Anger caught in Ryuu's throat, giving him a voice to speak.

"That bastard can't hurt me."

Takako struggled into a sitting position and Ryuu saw why she had no guards. Her wrists and ankles were bound tightly, tied to the tent. She had nowhere to go.

"I came here to rescue you." The words sounded more pathetic than he had imagined. The day dream of a boy who didn't realize he had walked into the very middle of an army.

"No. Turn around now before he kills us both. Don't be so stupid."

This wasn't what he had planned. She was supposed to jump in his arms, not turn him away. He went to her, trying to explain.

Takako struggled backwards. "No! Ryuu, there's nothing for me or you . . ." Takako's eyes went wide as Ryuu noticed the light of a torch behind him. Takako had distracted him. He had lost his sense again. Shigeru would be very disappointed.

Akio's eyes flared with hate as he recognized Ryuu. In one smooth motion he had placed the torch in a rest meant for it and drew his sword. Akio was quick. He was almost as quick as Shigeru. A sudden step from Ryuu caused Akio's cut to miss by the width of a hair, and Ryuu took two paces back to give himself some space. Akio didn't follow, keeping his balance.

Akio's rage dripped from his voice. "I will kill you for this."

Ryuu didn't respond. He was focusing on his breath, dropping into his stance. He drew his sword.

Akio was on a different level than bandits. He had been well trained since childhood in all the arts of war, and may have had a long future as a swordsman ahead of him. No more. In three moves the duel was decided, and Ryuu sheathed his blade.

Takako couldn't have been more surprised. "Akio was an expert swordsman." Her voice trailed off in shock at recent events.

Ryuu knelt down in front of her. "Takako."

Her wandering eyes focused on him. "I am not what you think, but I will not hurt you. I can take you away from here if you wish it."

He felt her gaze boring through him. He didn't know what he would do if she said no. She looked at Akio's body and back at him, trying to do the calculations in her mind.

"They will kill me if I'm here when he is found. I don't have a choice."

It wasn't a yes, but it would have to be good enough. He leaned forward and cut through the straps tying her. He turned away as she found spare clothing and rubbed life back into her extremities.

"Why were you tied up?"

"He was paranoid about me trying to escape."

With Takako freed, they found another uniform in the tent. Takako dressed quickly, hiding her hair and arranging the uniform so it revealed nothing. Ryuu threw out his sense, but there was no special commotion. The camp was active and busy even in the middle of the night. One guard was stationed outside the tent door, but he seemed to be almost asleep.

Ryuu debated cutting through the back of the tent or going through the guard. He decided it was less suspicious for the tent to be missing the guard than the tent to have a big cut in it. There were many rationalizations for a guard leaving post, fewer for the cut. Ryuu summoned the guard into the tent and knocked him unconscious.

They left the bodies and walked out casually, two guards patrolling the camp. In time they crossed the perimeter claiming to be scouts, and it was over. They walked out over the ridge Ryuu had come up through and managed to get to a safe distance to rest by the time morning light was peeking over the Pass.

Ryuu only allowed them to rest for part of a watch before he urged Takako on. The morning would bring the discovery of Akio's body, and the manhunt would begin in earnest.

CHAPTER 14

Takako followed Ryuu, blind to the events around her. The world seemed to be covered in fog, its ways impenetrable to her vision. She didn't think, couldn't think. Too much had happened in too short a time. All because of some innocent letters to a boy.

When Akio had found them in her rooms at Madame's in New Haven she had been both terrified and excited. Excited by the mere chance Akio would void their contract, terrified at what the alternatives may be. When Akio had taken her, without any fight from anyone, Takako's heart sank beneath an ocean of resignation. Something had seemed so special about Ryuu, but he had not come to her aid at the very moment that she needed him the most. She didn't blame him, she had just hoped he would have been more than he seemed. It was a foolish hope.

When she adapted she found it was nicer not to have any hope. Where there was hope there was sorrow at hope unrealized. But when there was none, when there was only one path forward, it was easy to cope. It was easier not to choose. Easier not to dream.

Akio challenged every shred of dignity and optimism Takako possessed. She had thought her first time would be meaningful.

It had been such a deal in the house. He had taken her roughly on their first night. Takako had studied the art of love-making for cycles in Madame's house, but none of it meant anything when her time came. There was no foreplay, no conversation, nothing resembling even the fake love that permeated Madame's house. He simply ripped off her clothes and rammed himself inside of her until he was finished. When he was done he put his clothes back on and left the tent. Guards came in immediately to tie her up, regardless of whether or not she was clothed. She had learned to dress quickly when Akio left.

Madame had told her about men like Akio, but Takako had never believed her. They thrived on the power they exerted over others. There was no reason for Akio to tie her up. They were in the middle of an army encampment. There was no place that she could possibly go. But it was an exercise in power.

She was fed well and allowed to take care of herself. Besides being tied up almost constantly and having to deal with Akio, her life wasn't difficult. Akio didn't change. He never tried to get to know her or start any sort of relationship. It felt like revenge, and her suspicions were confirmed one afternoon as she overheard him talking to the guards before they came in to tie her again. It was to make sure "she didn't see other men."

Takako had found a numb peace on their days of travel. All she had to do was spread her legs. Akio wasn't creative enough to try anything else. She was alive, and that was enough.

But then Ryuu stepped into the tent. After the immediate shock had passed she had ordered him out. The boy was innocent and kind, and it was generous and brave that he had come for her, but she knew he would die in the attempt. Then she learned a truth about Ryuu that was harder to bear. He had been the one innocent thing in her life she had held on to. But he too was a murderer. He wasn't the boy she had held in her mind. She didn't understand how it had happened. Over the course of her trip she had seen many of the soldiers practicing sword fighting. Akio's father required practice every day, even while on march. But Takako had never seen anyone as quick as Ryuu. She couldn't even see his motions. Everyone at the camp knew Akio was skilled, but Ryuu had killed him without difficulty.

Their escape was a dream that could never come true. She thought they would be stopped, questioned by a guard. The fear in her heart raged, making walking in straight lines a difficult task. Every guard seemed taller, stronger, more aware of their presence than possible. Ryuu was her guide. She kept her eyes on him, allowing the rest of the world to blur into imagination.

Her tension didn't dissipate as they left the ring of guards. Ryuu offered no break. He let them stop for a couple of moments at a time, but he never let her sit, never let her think and plan out her next move. He kept them going, pushing them ever forward. She couldn't believe how calm he seemed. You would never know he had just killed one of the most important people in the Kingdom. He walked with such steadiness. Perhaps it was because of her focus on her own feet, but for the first time she noticed his step was always light and quick. He didn't shuffle around or move from side to side. Each step was precise, targeted. Takako found it so fascinating she almost lost her own balance watching him.

They walked through the night and through the early dawn. Finally Ryuu found the spot he must have been looking for. He closed his eyes quickly and reopened them. Takako couldn't tell if he was trying to think or if he was just tired. It didn't seem to be either. He didn't seem to be tired. In fact, he looked like he could be doing this all day. He spoke in a voice just above a whisper, some of the first words he'd said since the rescue.

"You can rest here for a while. I'll keep watch, but we'll need to be moving again soon. I want us to meet up with Shigeru by tonight. I'm sorry I can't let you sleep for more than a little while. They're going to send search parties by horseback, and I'd like to put as much distance as possible between us and them."

It seemed like an opening to ask questions, to untie some of these mysteries which suddenly surrounded her. But she couldn't find the courage to ask. She settled for the least controversial question she could ask.

"Aren't you tired?"

Ryuu gave her a funny grin, like he had a secret she was close to guessing. He shook his head.

"No, I'm not tired yet. I'll need to sleep tonight for a little while, but should be fine until then. Thanks though."

Takako meant to push the question further, but her level of exhaustion overwhelmed her. She laid her head down in the tall grass and was asleep instantly.

When she awoke Ryuu was still next to her sitting motionless in the grass. She looked around. The sun wasn't too much higher than when she had fallen asleep. Ryuu seemed to read her mind.

"No, you haven't been asleep long, but I was going to wake you soon anyway."

Ryuu startled her. His eyes had been closed, and he had been so still that Takako had assumed he was asleep.

Takako started to get up, but Ryuu laid a hand on her shoulder. It was gentle, a touch she hadn't felt in some time. "There are soldiers coming. They won't see us if we stay still."

Takako strained all of her senses, but she couldn't hear anything, and in the tall grass she was unable to see anything.

It seemed like an eternity passed a moment at a time before she heard the rumble of horses. In the meantime, Ryuu had slithered down on to his belly. Takako followed suit. The horses didn't even slow down. They passed dozens of paces away and kept going.

Some more time passed before Ryuu sat up again.

"They responded faster than I thought they would. I bet they found the guards I attacked earlier first. It will change our travel, but I expect we can still reach Shigeru by tonight. He's not far now." He looked over at Takako. "How are you feeling? We will need to walk quite a ways today."

Takako was sore all over, but didn't want to let Ryuu know. She didn't want to appear weak in front of him. "I'm good."

Ryuu seemed to see right through the lie, but he didn't say anything. He handed out clothing which made them look more like peasants and hid his sword. After putting the clothes on they were up and on their way in no time, keeping the rising sun on their right.

Throughout the walk they would sometimes stop and hide, always due to Ryuu's remarkable senses. Every time it happened Takako couldn't see or hear anyone. Soldiers on horseback crisscrossed the country, but Ryuu always seemed to know they were coming. The tall grass of the prairie was wonderful cover, and they had no fear of discovery.

There was only one conclusion, but the sheer absurdity of it meant Takako didn't come to it until a full day of playing hide and seek with the largest army in the land.

"You're a nightblade, aren't you?"

Ryuu didn't even turn around to answer the question. "Yes."

The matter-of-fact way he answered the question was the only reason Takako believed him. Her history books had taught her that nightblades were long extinct. All individuals who could use the sense were in the monasteries, descended from the dayblades, and Takako knew Ryuu wasn't a monk.

"I thought you were all dead."

"I don't know about that, but to the best of my knowledge, I'm not dead yet."

Takako almost laughed at the sarcasm, but she couldn't believe she was awake. To be in the company of a nightblade. Her life couldn't get any stranger today.

Despite the routine patrols the sun set without incident. Takako was too tired to think about speaking and Ryuu was too focused on everything happening around them for anything meaningful to be said. Takako found she didn't mind the silence. It gave her shattered mind a little peace to process what had happened. The silence felt companionable, peaceful, not awkward.

As dusk fell they met up with Shigeru in a place Takako could only describe as the middle of nowhere. There didn't seem to be any defining marks, any grove of trees or natural features that would have served as landmarks. Takako didn't even know Shigeru was in the tall grass until they were on top of him. The two of them must have sensed each other. Now that she was aware of their secret little details started to make more sense.

Shigeru greeted them both.

"I'm glad to see both of you."

Ryuu bowed to Shigeru. "It's good to see you too." Takako realized his voice was full of relief. He hadn't known whether or not he would succeed. She held on to the information. "Takako needs rest as do I."

Shigeru nodded his assent. "I had figured as much. I'm well rested and can give you the full night. Tomorrow we can split it. Were you discovered?"

"I had to kill Akio. He stepped into the tent just as I reached Takako." Ryuu dropped the news like a rock from a tree.

Shigeru greeted the news with silence. "That's going to complicate things."

Takako thought that seemed liked a bit of an understatement.

"Yes. The patrols are already further afield than I expected. I suspect the guards were found earlier than I had hoped. However, we haven't been seen yet, nor have we gone anywhere near the villages where they might betray us for coin."

"Good. For now at least, luck seems to be on our side. We'll discuss our plan tomorrow. For now, rest."

Ryuu didn't argue. Perhaps he was more tired than he was letting on. Whatever the case, he laid his head on the ground and was asleep right away. Takako thought about trying to ask Shigeru some of the questions swirling in her mind, but she too was tired and the grass made a comfortable bed.

When Takako awoke the two were awake and conversing in hushed tones. She rubbed her eyes and joined them, although there wasn't much to be said. They wanted to visit New Haven. The rumor mill would be in full motion and could provide them information. It was also large enough they wouldn't be recognized. Takako was afraid they were taking her back to Madame's, but Ryuu assured her that wasn't true.

Their journey was slow. Takako felt like a weight dragging the two men down. They seemed immune to weariness, but assented to her repeated requests for breaks without complaint. She had done plenty of chores in the house, but nothing had given her the endurance the two nightblades possessed.

One unintended side effect was that Ryuu began to open up more. Takako could tell he was more comfortable with Shigeru around. Takako had dozens of questions for Ryuu about his life. He answered them all even if his answers were brief. He wasn't used to speaking about himself. The only questions he wouldn't answer were about being a nightblade. In time Takako became frustrated. When one was a nightblade, it seemed like a big deal.

"I'm sorry," Ryuu replied, "but it's like trying to describe different world to you. Everything in our language revolves around the five senses you are used to. There's no language, no frame of reference for me to describe my world. It's everything your world is plus this extra dimension. I simply know the way a blade is going to cut, or that there is a wild horse running in circles over this ridge. This entire planet pulses with life, and I drink it in with every breath. I live in a different world than you."

That night, as all three of them lay in tall grass underneath the stars, Takako asked Shigeru the question that had been bugging her the most.

"Why did you send Ryuu after me?"

Shigeru laughed gruffly. Takako had never heard him laugh before, but decided she liked it. It was a man's laugh, a sound she hadn't heard since she was young.

"I didn't tell him too. Idea was all his."

Takako was taken aback. The entire time she had a picture of Shigeru as a stern master, the one in charge of sending Ryuu wherever he went. It never occurred to her Ryuu might have come of his own accord.

She turned the question on Ryuu.

It took him so long to reply she began to suspect he had forgotten the question, or had fallen asleep. "I needed to use my strength for something, and I enjoyed spending time with you. It didn't seem right, what happened to you."

Takako didn't know what to say to that.

"Thank you."

"You're welcome."

Takako was still a wreck of emotions inside, but she understood Ryuu's simple generosity. She slept peacefully that night.

They reached New Haven without incident. It was easy for them to approach the outskirts of town without being seen. Ryuu could sense individuals long before they could see the fugitives. Within New Haven they blended in with the sea of peasants in town for spring celebrations. Ryuu and Shigeru assumed anyone looking for them would be looking for two young travelers. The three of them were less likely to attract attention.

They didn't need to go far into town before their reconnaissance was complete. The word was all over the streets. Madame's had burned to the ground with all the women inside. Rumors flew on the streets, but the facts seemed simple enough. The army had come and surrounded the building. A handful of men had gone in and a short battle had ensued. It wasn't long before the bodies of Madame's bodyguards were thrown out of the building. In time, the screams of the women were heard.

As the sun set, the men came out of the house covered in blood. Torches were lit. It was only a matter of time before the roar of the flames drowned out the screams of the women inside.

Takako's mind reeled. Even though she was sitting she felt like there was nothing solid to support her. There was no love lost for Madame or her women, but they had never been cruel to her. They had done only what they were supposed to, no more or no less. They weren't saints, but they didn't deserve this.

For a long time Takako wasn't able to cry. Her mind kept running in circles, trying to find some exit, some logical way forward. She was searching for hope and reason but couldn't find any. Finally she broke down in tears. Tears for a new world she didn't understand and felt powerless within. She was caught up in something much larger than herself.

Ryuu and Shigeru watched, unable to connect with the feelings Takako was experiencing. Ryuu knew the pain of losing his family, but it had been so long ago he couldn't touch the emotions that lay dormant.

By the time she had finished crying, Takako only had one thought on her mind.

"I need to return to my family, or at least warn them. If Akio's father got to Madame, it is only one step further to my family. They don't deserve what is coming if Nori believes I am heading there for safety."

Ryuu and Shigeru said nothing. They had no plan, no destination. Hers was as good as any other. They picked their gear back up and left the city without comment, Takako in tow.

Takako's mind kept repeating one thought. She had to get to her family. She couldn't sleep or eat and found the energy to keep the fastest pace Ryuu and Shigeru would set. There was one thing left she cared about and she didn't dare to imagine what would happen if she lost them too.

Fueled by Takako's fear, the journey took just two days. Takako had no trouble finding the path to her house, but Ryuu and Shigeru had to stop her. Their senses knew the truth. The land was dead, confirming their worst fears. They tried to hold Takako back, but she charged forward.

Both Ryuu and Shigeru were shocked by the level of devastation. The house had been burned like Madame's, but the bodies had not been inside. Parents and siblings had all been left outside, hung to trees, their corpses already food for the birds. The villagers walked by every day but took no action to cut them down. Ryuu was disgusted.

Despite the bodies hanging from the trees, Takako seemed unable to grasp the reality of what had occurred. She wandered around the house calling for her family to come out of hiding. Ryuu sat down as a tear crawled down his face. He looked up at Shigeru, composed as ever.

"Who could do this?"

Shigeru couldn't look at his student, his son. He had guessed there would be consequences, but he could not have predicted their extent.

Ryuu wiped away his tear and stood up. There may not be answers, but there was revenge. With Shigeru's help he searched the grounds for clues, seeking the identity of those who had committed the crimes. The villagers all avoided them, so no information was coming from that direction. But Ryuu and Shigeru agreed, only Nori would have had the power to order this kind of punishment.

When Takako's mind caught up to reality she collapsed into the ground, tears streaming down her face. She didn't even notice as Ryuu came and tried to put his arm around her. She threw him off in anger and disgust.

"This is all your fault! Why couldn't you just leave me be? If I was still there, my family would still be alive. It was you that killed them! You!"

It felt good, to be honest, to yell at him, to yell at anybody. It was all she had the power to do. It felt good to cut someone with her words.

Shigeru stepped in, the strength of his voice silencing her.

"Takako, do not blame Ryuu for what happened to your family or to those you knew in New Haven. He did not kill them. He tried only to do the right thing. He was not the one who took innocent lives for one guilty life."

Takako lacked the strength to argue. Shigeru gently took her hand and started to guide her away from the house. Ryuu, perhaps feeling the distance Takako desired right now, went and scouted ahead to make sure their path was safe. Evening would soon be falling and they would want shelter somewhere away from the village.

That night Takako slept restlessly. Her sleep was plagued with nightmares of her family and acquaintances and the imagined tortures they experienced on her account. She tossed and turned, waking in a sweat, struggling to fall back asleep. Finally, she awoke close to dawn and decided that any further sleep was out of the question. Though the evening had passed, it felt like she hadn't slept at all.

She sat up and saw that Ryuu was still on watch. She was confused because he had been on watch last night when she had fallen asleep. He did not look at her even though she knew he was aware she was awake. It would be impossible to surprise him at all, which meant she couldn't throw rocks at him like she desired.

Her anger still simmered, but she was grateful for space. For the first time she had an opportunity to think about Ryuu. She knew more about him now than she ever had during their time as correspondents, but it still seemed like so little. Although he had answered her question, she still couldn't fathom why he had risked everything to come and save her. They had never slept together. They had never done anything besides speak and write to each other. A part of her wondered if Ryuu just wanted her as a prostitute, but there were much easier ways of acquiring one of those.

No, there was something else driving him, but Takako couldn't understand what it was. But Shigeru had been right, it was unfair to judge Ryuu for the consequences of his actions. She knew it, but she still hated Ryuu. She laid back down and debated what to do next.

CHAPTER 15

Life under Orochi was a refreshing and rewarding change for Moriko. Finding his company preferable to that of the monks made her realize how much she had come to detest life at the monastery. He wasn't an easy man to get along with. His size and silence made him difficult to learn more about and his very presence unsettled her even if she did learn not to fear him. The way he moved and the way he avoided Moriko's sense was enough to keep her on high alert even when they were doing something as mundane as sharing a meal.

Once Orochi arrived Moriko was separated from the rest of the monastic community. The only habit that remained was that she still slept in the common quarters. Orochi did not join the monks. He preferred to sleep outside, sitting with his back against the wall. She got the sense that he never slept, not in the manner of normal people.

Even though she slept in the common area, the separation was distinct. The monks no longer spoke to her unless she spoke first. They studied different aspects of the sense. There was no longer a common bond to be shared with those she had spent the past several cycles growing up with. Every day Orochi taught her more about the sense and about fighting than she had ever learned in her time in the monastery. Orochi's knowledge spoke to her, invited her deeper into its mysteries.

Orochi taught her there was more to the sense than she realized. She knew about the distinction between the dayblades and the nightblades, but she didn't know that within each were many different styles and philosophies. Her time at Perseverance had only opened her eyes to one path. Moons ago she would have said it was the only path, but now she understood it was one of many gateways to the sense.

Although he never spoke about it, Moriko was able to discern the skills Orochi had developed were unique even among nightblades. He never spoke about where he learned his skills, but he couldn't have been alone. It meant there were other nightblades. In one conversation she learned Orochi's talents were considered anathema to the other nightblades, a skill against which there was little defense. Orochi's skills were the skills of one who hunted their own kind. What made him an outcast among his own opened the doors to acceptance among the descendants of the dayblades who carried on in the monastic tradition.

It didn't take long for Moriko to understand the depth of the powers she was taught. With skills like Orochi's she suspected she would never again be under the thumb of another individual. Orochi had no fear of the Abbot. Perhaps someday neither would she.

Orochi's training style was unlike anything Moriko had ever experienced. He challenged her to best him both in combat and in use of the sense. She was invited to question and to doubt. Orochi taught her both how to hide her presence and about the limitations of the sense. They would observe the training of the other monks and Orochi would speak to both their strengths and their weaknesses although under his analysis they had far more weaknesses than strengths.

A part of her knew the purpose of her training. With her skills she would be able to hunt down any opponent, dayblade or nightblade. Although she rebelled at the idea she still found a certain pleasure in it. She wanted to exert power over others like the Abbot exerted his power. But one question nagged at her. With these skills she could be a threat to the entire monastery. Why would they teach these skills to someone who had already tried to rebel against the system?

She searched her mind and memory for answers, one day giving in to her curiosity and asking Orochi. "Why are you training me? I tried to kill the Abbot and now you're giving me the skills to do so."

Orochi grinned, a smile which made her think of a large cat ready to pounce on its victim. "When I leave you are welcome to try to kill the Abbot. I don't care. You can even try to kill me. All that matters is strength and skill."

Moriko was shocked. "But don't you work for the Abbot?"

"I don't work for anyone. I go where I'm interested, to places where people will provide me with a challenge. Training you makes me stronger in the teaching. There are few opponents left on the mainland worth my time. Working with you passes the time until another is found. But I work for no man."

Moriko didn't understand, but it she wasn't going to get anything more out of him.

Their training continued and the seasons passed. Although Moriko was never comfortable around Orochi she grew to trust and respect him all the same. In all their time together he never talked about his past despite her continual questioning about it.

Whatever had happened, whoever he had been, he wasn't willing to share it. Moriko guessed he had seen between thirty and thirty five cycles, but how those cycles had been spent she couldn't tell. The only hint she got was that he might have been raised on an island because he always referred to the Three Kingdoms as "the mainland," a phrase she had never heard before.

At night Moriko would think about the person she had become. Before the monastery she remembered running through the trees, taking delight in the life therein. She loved playing with her father, playing hide and seek in the woods closest to their house. In her dreams she wanted to be a ranger, living in the woods and protecting the animals living there. Now her greatest pleasure was a solid strike against Orochi or imagining what she would do to her fellow monks if she ever got the chance.

Late at night, if the monastery was completely quiet, she could hear and sense the sounds of the forest that grew nearby. It was a new forest, lightly wooded, not dense like the forest she held so dear in her childhood. It would trigger a small spark of longing in her, a desire for what she had lost. But then she would push it away. The love of the forest was a childish dream. A dangerous dream for her to hold to now.

As winter turned into spring Orochi focused their training more and more on combat. It felt at times like he was using her to train himself. She did not know his reasons, but she loved the exertion and the effort. She was nowhere near as good as he was, but she was getting better every day.

The pattern of Moriko's life changed late that summer. A messenger arrived in full armor heralding the arrival of someone important. Moriko paid it no mind, assuming it would have nothing to do with her. There was always someone trying to visit the monastery to curry favor with the Abbot. It was pathetic.

But Orochi stopped their practice.

"Do you know whose banner that is?"

Moriko looked. It was a dark red banner with crossed swords clasped in the claws of an eagle. When she saw it she had the impression of a hunter. But she didn't recognize the banner itself. She had never seen it in all the cycles she had been living at Perseverance.

"No, I don't."

"You should. That is the banner of Lord Akira, Lord of the Southern Kingdom."

"He's coming?"

"It would seem that way. I wondered how much privacy he was going to give me."

Moriko shot him a glance. She disbelieved him, but he spoke with no sarcasm or pride. He spoke of facts she knew nothing of and she doubted.

"A Lord would come here to visit you?"

Orochi flashed his menacing grin. "More likely than the Lord coming to visit the Abbot of this dump."

The herald announced the Lord would arrive in two days. The rest of the monastery buzzed with excitement and preparation. The arrival of the Lord was a rare occasion. Orochi shrugged and continued training Moriko. It was entertaining to watch the monks tripping over each other, but Moriko shared their nervousness. Each Kingdom had a Lord, holding the seat of the throne until the Kingdom could be united once again. They held power beyond comprehension.

The Lord's arrival was detected long before he was within view. The Abbot had pushed his sense to the limit to give them all the most advance warning. When the word came down from the Abbot's quarters Moriko and Orochi were sparring. Orochi dismissed her. "Make yourself presentable."

Moriko tidied up, tying her hair back and putting on fresh robes not soiled from her day of training. Orochi didn't bother, but Moriko wasn't strong enough to make him break a good sweat yet either.

The Lord arrived with more people than Moriko had ever seen traveling together. The monastery wasn't even close to being large enough to house all of them so they formed a temporary encampment around the front gate. Moriko could smell the soldiers even though they were behind the wall. It was a combination of crap, dirt, sweat and blood. The stench sickened her. She had imagined a Lord traveling with a retinue of sycophants. Akira traveled with warriors from the battlefield.

When the Lord came into the monastery it was Goro who escorted him to the Abbot's quarters. Moriko couldn't help but notice the dissimilarities between the two. Goro, his back hunched over, unwilling to raise himself to his full height to stand above Akira. Akira walked tall, sure of himself and his purpose in the world. He was clothed well. Moriko noticed the fine material, but also noticed his outfit didn't restrict him in any way. This was indeed a warrior. The Lord did not travel in full armor, but Moriko could tell from how he moved that there were several pieces of armor either hidden under or sewn into his wardrobe.

Moriko's most significant surprise was the age of the Lord. She had imagined a wizened old man. But he was young. He had seen no more than thirty cycles. She had a hard time believing a man so young could wield such power over thousands of people.

Overall, Moriko's first impressions of the Lord were favorable. This was not a man who stood on ceremony or whose power had corrupted his personal discipline. This was a man who still lived by a strict code. Though she knew nothing else about him, it was enough for her to view him more favorably than not.

Akira, several of his guards and Goro entered the Abbot's quarters with little ceremony. Most of the monks milled around, having expected to do more bowing or more demonstrations of their skill. The Abbot hadn't shared Orochi's premonition surrounding the Lord's visit. The clueless monks were awkward enough it made Moriko smile.

After a short conference inside Goro came scurrying out of the Abbot's quarters. To Moriko's great delight, he came to where Orochi and she were standing against the wall, groveling and bowing in a priceless manner. Moriko was starting to wish the Lord would visit more often. It was the most unique experience she'd had in some time.

"Lord Akira demands your presence in the Abbot's quarters, Orochi."

"Fine, let us go," Orochi replied, indicating Moriko was to come as well.

Goro hesitated, but Moriko could almost sense him trying hard not to smile. "I'm sorry, sir, but the Lord only requested to see you."

Moriko's pleasure dropped for a moment before Orochi replied.

"Don't care."

Goro tried to be confident against Orochi. "Sir, I'm afraid I must insist."

Orochi wasn't having any of it.

"Get out of my way, ant. Your life isn't worth a breath of my time."

It was more than enough to get Goro's attention. He bowed and groveled and got out of the way, but Moriko was positive he was hoping for Moriko to meet her death in the Abbot's quarters for her disobedience.

The two of them walked to the Abbot's quarters, entering without hesitation. Moriko was beginning to realize that Orochi held true power in the Three Kingdoms. When one of the three most powerful men in the land was calling for you and you could treat him as an equal it meant you had made something of yourself.

The first difference Moriko noticed when they entered was that the Abbot had toned down his sense aura. Typically when guests were calling he would project it with strength, causing even those who weren't sensitive to the sense to feel uncomfortable and queasy. But around Akira he was keeping it down. Moriko imagined the Lord could still notice it, almost as a sort of background uneasiness, but it wouldn't be as intimidating as for other guests of the Abbot. It was good to know that Akira's power intimidated the Abbot.

The Lord bowed his head slightly towards Orochi and Orochi returned the gesture. Moriko was stunned. A short bow of equal length indicated the two men believed they were on equal ground. For Lord Akira to bow at all should have been outside the realm of possibility.

Lord Akira broke out into a grin.

"Orochi, my old friend, it has been far too long."

Orochi did not return the smile, but replied, "Agreed."

Akira turned his gaze to Moriko. She bowed deeply to the ground, and the Lord favored her with the slightest of nods. Moriko was speechless.

"Who is the girl? Is she the one I heard about in your last letter?"

"She is. She shows great potential to follow the same path as me."

Akira nodded appreciatively. "That is impressive. If her skills are anywhere near yours she will be a formidable ally as she grows older."

Orochi was all business. "What brings you here? During this season you should be closer to the Three Sisters."

The King dismissed the Abbot with a casual gesture. Moriko couldn't believe her eyes. She had never seen the Abbot ordered around by anybody, and the fact he accepted it without argument strengthened her convictions about where the true power in the room lay. She would treasure these moments for the rest of her life.

"May we speak in front of her?" Akira gestured to Moriko.

"Yes. She knows my skills. She should know this as well."

Akira laughed. "So, you plan to create a true disciple in her, don't you? The Abbot must not like that."

"He can piss off. His grabs for power in the region are sickening. You should watch him. He and the girl have come to blows in the past. The Abbot believes that by loaning her to me he can curry your favor."

Akira's enjoyment was apparent. "I should have known. I imagine you came around here brandishing my seal implying this was somehow business of the Kingdom."

"I let the fool draw his own conclusions."

Akira's laughter subsided. Moriko didn't know how to interpret what was happening. Was this what power meant?

"No matter. I'm glad you found a disciple worthy of your training, and if she serves as well as you have, I will be more than delighted to have her be part of my work."

"When the time comes, she will choose her own path, just as I have chosen mine."

Akira's expression became hard to read. He had been hoping for a stronger response from Orochi, but he respected the decision. Moriko concluded that although the two of them had a friendly history, it was one rooted in a mutually beneficial business relationship.

"To the business at hand. I bring news."

Orochi sat down cross-legged in front of the King and closed his eyes. It was apparently a signal to begin.

"One moon ago, General Nori's son was killed and several guards were killed and knocked out."

Orochi didn't open his eyes. "Akio was rumored to be a strong swordsman. His death is a tragedy for his house, but I do not see how my skills are required."

"Patience. There is more. Previous to Nori's departure for the pass he had arranged for a whore for his son in New Haven. A young girl, untouched. Apparently she was one of the most beautiful young girls in the city. Akio went to introduce himself and encountered the girl with a young man whom Akio assumed was a spoiled noble or merchant's brat. Akio gave the youth a beating and took off with the girl."

Orochi didn't move a muscle. If Moriko didn't know him as she did she would have assumed he was asleep. She knew though he was committing everything to memory. He had asked for all the details and was getting them.

"Akio took the girl with him on campaign, apparently used her pretty roughly, but that is of no matter. They were camping two days march from the pass when the assassination happened. A guard on the perimeter was knocked out, and Akio and his attendant were killed. The body was found early the next morning, but no sign has been found of the assassin or assassins. Needless to say, the entire army is disturbed someone was so easily able to infiltrate camp to kill the general's son."

Orochi responded. "It sounds like a skilled assassin. Was the girl involved?"

"This is where I think you will find yourself interested. The girl disappeared, and no trace has been found of her. The scouts in the camp assume she left with the assassin. Nori sent a group on horseback to New Haven to interrogate the whores where the girl was bought. They found some interesting details. The girl had been visited in the past by the same young man Akio found her with. The boy was in the company of an older man named Shigeru."

Orochi's eyes shot up. "Did you say Shigeru?"

"I thought you would find that interesting. You never did manage to track him down, did you? I expect there is a good chance he is the one behind the assassination of Nori's son. I'm not sure why, but perhaps you could ask him when you find him."

"So, Shigeru has a son."

"It seems that way. Your fee will be the same as usual."

Orochi nodded. "You know this might be the last mission I take for you."

"I understand."

Moriko didn't understand. There was a whole history here she had no clue about. These men had known each other for a long time.

Akira indicated the conclusion of the meeting. "I don't harbor the hatred for this man you do. However, the army is nervous. Rumors circulate about the camps and soldiers do not feel safe even in their tents at night. If the situation isn't resolved they will be wiped out on the other side when they meet the Azarians. I need a symbol to keep this Kingdom safe. I need their heads. Shigeru, the boy, and the girl. Everyone needs to know justice reigns in this land. Make it happen."

Orochi was more animated than Moriko had ever seen him before. "I'd be delighted."

With Orochi's declaration of intent, Akira's reason for visiting the monastery was at an end. He shared the rest of the details of his intelligence with Orochi, but even Moriko could tell they had no leads. They weren't sure how the assassination had happened and they had no idea where the assassin and the girl had gone. Their search through the countryside had been as thorough as they could manage, but they hadn't found a trace of the fugitives.

Akira's camp left Perseverance as quickly as they had arrived. Moriko found it difficult to believe such a large group of people could appear and disappear with so little fanfare. Orochi bid Akira farewell and Moriko thought it was the goodbye of two friends who wouldn't ever see the other again.

Orochi was ready to depart just a few watches after Akira left. Moriko had never seen his emotions take control of him. It was reassuring to know he was human. It took her a little pressing, but she was eventually able to get some answers out of him. He had always just been her instructor. Moriko had been trying to piece together his back story for some time. She hadn't imagined it would be so interesting.

"Shigeru was a man I knew in a previous life. We grew up together even though he is several cycles older than me. I looked up to him in my childhood, but he betrayed me, he betrayed our family, he betrayed everything I knew. I was the one who was assigned to hunt him and to kill him and my failure to do so is why I still remain here on the mainland. I had worried he might be dead by another's hand. It will be a pleasure for me to track him one more time if Akira's information is accurate."

"Are we going to be leaving soon?" Moriko knew she was making an assumption, but hoping it would be true.

Orochi shook his head. "I will be leaving soon, but you must stay here."

Moriko's heart dropped through her stomach. Everything she had been through the past few seasons had been related to Orochi. She was still scared of him, but he represented the far lesser of two evils. He did not strike her or abuse her. He trained her and demonstrated respect for her abilities. To leave her here by herself meant life would return to the way it had been before his arrival.

Orochi continued, "For what it's worth, I apologize. Under other circumstances I would have you come with me. However, Shigeru is the only warrior on the mainland I'm aware of who could defeat me. I don't know what his training has looked like since we last met. He may be stronger than me and I won't risk you too."

They were the kindest words she had ever heard from Orochi.

"Have no fear. I will speak to the Abbot before I leave. You will be safe. If I'm successful I'll return. If I don't you must find your own path. In the monastery or outside of it, you are now one of the strongest people on the mainland. You must use the power as you see fit."

Moriko held on to every word, seeking strength and comfort from them. She did not feel like she was ready to face the Abbot and Goro again even though even she believed she'd be able to defeat them in combat if it happened again.

Orochi didn't offer any further comfort. It wasn't his way. In his world an individual survived on their strength. Nothing else mattered.

When he left Moriko felt more alone than she had before, trapped in a life she didn't understand, held in one place by a system designed to control what she could be. She knew what Orochi had done in his time at the monastery. He had made her into a nightblade, one who was capable of tracking, hunting, and killing other nightblades and dayblades. Ironically, she had become the very person the monastery had hoped to train her not to be.

She thought about leaving. She knew she'd be able to avoid any search parties sent out for her. But there was nowhere to go. Orochi was her only connection with the outside world. She would wait for him.

Moriko memorized the walls that surrounded her in the monastery. She paid particular attention to where she had been tortured, tried to hold onto all the hate generated by that spot. The spot focused her determination. She would give Orochi until spring. If he didn't return from his trip or if she expected the worst had happened, she would take off. There would be no deception, no sneaking on her part. She would simply leave, and if it meant another challenge with the Abbot, she would have to be ready. She had to be stronger. By spring her decision would be made.

Surely she could last for a couple of moons.

Chapter 16

The days got longer as summer set in over the Three Kingdoms. While both Shigeru and Ryuu maintained constant vigilance, it was clear the search for them had been called off, or they had moved beyond the scope of the search. There were posters distributed throughout the land detailing the three of them which offered a reward for information, but they were little more than a nuisance. They lived in the wild and only went into villages when necessary. They never went into town all together. They went unarmed and dirty and a wandering peasant did not attract attention.

For Ryuu the days were pleasant. They were up in the mornings hiking through territory he had never traveled through. He was accompanied by the man he regarded as his father and the girl he was obsessed with. Their relationship had been difficult, but Ryuu accepted it with patience. Takako had seen her entire world taken away from her not once, but twice. He could see she still blamed herself and him for the death of her family.

The unspoken accusation troubled Ryuu as well. He worried she was right. He had known Takako had been sold into prostitution. It was one reason he felt her life had been so unjust and had been part of his decision to come to her aid. It never occurred to him innocents might suffer and die because of his actions. Most days his gut told him it wasn't his fault. He had done something just, and the world had responded by doing something evil. But there were nights where he couldn't shake the simple fact that if he had not rescued Takako others would still be alive.

Though he couldn't understand women, it was clear Takako was feeling the same conflict. She would often sit next to him at meals and walk near him if he wasn't scouting ahead, but occasionally her mood would change and she would avoid both him and Shigeru. Fortunately, it seemed to Ryuu that Takako was a natural optimist. Although life was difficult, and she was struggling with what had happened, she seemed determined to make the best of her circumstances. He wasn't sure he would have had the same strength in the same circumstances.

The nights were much the same. Almost all nights she at least slept close to him, for warmth as much as emotional connection, but it never went beyond that. It tortured him, but Ryuu did not press his luck. Although his desire was strong he didn't know what to do and so it was much easier to do nothing and let events take their natural course. The long summer days made him believe he had all the time in the world. He made himself available to talk and was always kind, even when Takako complained about their conditions. He never gave up hope they could become more than whatever they were now.

It would have been easier without Shigeru, who was always nearby. Their safety largely depended on the three of them being together, but even if Shigeru slept in a location not visible to Ryuu and Takako, Ryuu was very aware Shigeru could sense everything he did. Ryuu wanted to bring up the subject, but didn't know how to approach Shigeru. He didn't know if Shigeru had ever loved anybody, if he'd ever been married or been loved. It was the first time in many cycles he didn't know how to talk to his master.

Shigeru didn't seem willing to help either. Their conversation had been minimal since they had picked up Takako. The dynamic was off and Ryuu couldn't read Shigeru's emotions, which were cryptic even at the best of times. Shigeru was tense, but Ryuu didn't know if it was just the circumstances they found themselves in or if something more was bothering him. Shigeru had closed himself off and Ryuu couldn't work up the courage to try to chisel away at his stony exterior.

They continued traveling north although they had no particular destination. Shigeru and Ryuu talked about their plans from time to time but neither could decide on a course for certain. Ryuu hadn't thought of the reality of being chased throughout the Three Kingdoms. They could try to leave through the Pass, but with the army entrenched there and hunting them it didn't seem safe.

The only other viable way out of the Three Kingdoms was by sea, which was north. However, Ryuu and Shigeru weren't sure leaving the Three Kingdoms was the best plan. Ryuu wanted to stay. He argued he and Shigeru had been in a state of hiding for as long as Ryuu had been with him. They could find another isolated place and settle there. Shigeru would respond he hadn't ever killed the son of the most powerful general in the Three Kingdoms.

Ryuu understood the logic Shigeru was using, but he felt there was something else, an undercurrent of fear unspoken driving Shigeru's decision. He wanted to leave the Three Kingdoms and travel as far away as possible, but wasn't telling Ryuu why.

Ryuu didn't dare confide in Takako. He wanted to, but he was concerned that if he expressed worry or frustration with

Shigeru she would become more worried than she already was. He couldn't bring himself to do it.

His indecision grew for almost a moon before he took action. One afternoon as they were walking, Ryuu moved ahead to where Shigeru was scouting. Shigeru noticed his presence but didn't say anything.

"Sensei, what is wrong?"

Shigeru glanced at Ryuu. He looked about ready to come back with a short retort, but thought better of it. They walked forward in silence but Ryuu waited him out. He knew when Shigeru needed to think.

"I don't like the situation we find ourselves in. It. . . reminds me of a situation that happened to me many cycles ago, and I worry that fate will repeat itself."

"What happened?"

"That's not a story for today. Perhaps someday, but maybe not. I would also be fine taking it to the grave with me."

Ryuu lost a step. In the many cycles he had known Shigeru, he had never admitted to having a story he didn't want to share. Ryuu knew Shigeru rarely talked about his past and over time Ryuu had learned to stop asking. But it seemed so close, so essential now that he burned to know the past of his master, the man who had raised him and introduced him to his incredible gifts.

"Shigeru, we are both here. There is very little in the Three Kingdoms that can stand up to both of us."

Shigeru released a grim chuckle. "If only that were true. You are stronger than almost any man I have ever met, but there are still plenty out there who could kill both of us. Please remember that."

Ryuu started to get angry. Whatever was bothering Shigeru dealt both with his past and knowledge he seemed unwilling to share.

"I can't help if you don't tell me what you're hiding from me."

Shigeru also responded sharply. "There is much I haven't told you. Your skills are fantastic, but don't let it get to your head. This world is still a much larger and more mysterious place than you know. I don't know if I've done the right thing in raising you like I have, but I have hope, which is more than I hold out for myself."

"Why won't you tell me what's going on? I want to help. I can help."

"Not in this, Ryuu. I want you to be happy, to lead the life and be the person I couldn't. I worry that if you learn everything that dream will slip away."

With that, Shigeru increased his pace and pulled away from Ryuu. Ryuu, lost in thought, allowed him to do so. He needed his own time to think things through.

Two days later the issue was forced. Ryuu was ahead scouting while Shigeru and Takako followed well behind. Ryuu was high in a tree, allowing his sense to spread out far and wide. They were in new forest, but thick enough that vision was almost useless. The day was hot and his robes stuck to the sweat on his skin. It was a dry heat carried from the prairie to the west.

Ryuu was immersed fully in the sense and didn't notice what was happening to his body. He felt something coming from the south. It felt like a small group of soldiers. They were still a long ways out and difficult to sense. Ryuu took a deep breath and focused his attention in their direction.

There were ten of them. They advanced purposefully, heading almost straight towards where Shigeru was back with Takako. Ryuu's heart began to pound a little faster. It could be a random coincidence they were on the right track, but as Ryuu continued to focus he could tell their path was curving slightly, always pointed towards Shigeru. Somebody in the group was capable of tracking them. Ryuu tried to clear his head to focus. He could feel it, the tentacles of the sense which spread out towards them.

Whoever was sensing Shigeru was better. It wasn't the pattern of the monks in the monastery. The monks used spherical techniques. This was someone trained like Ryuu and Shigeru. He was focused on Shigeru, but he was trying to sense Ryuu too. Ryuu breathed a short sigh of relief. His sense was superior, which gave him a slight advantage. But he couldn't believe someone with the sense was tracking Shigeru. It shouldn't be possible. It put fear into his heart, freezing it and his mind in place.

His fear increased when he tried to pinpoint the individual who was sensing Shigeru. He couldn't. He could tell where the sense was originating, but where there was supposed to be a person, there was nothing. An unnatural emptiness, devoid of all life. Under other circumstances Ryuu would have paid it no more attention than a patch of empty air over a pasture. But it was the source of the sense, and the emptiness continued to move. Ryuu shook with sweat.

He had to get to Shigeru. He realized he had been thrust into a situation far beyond his current understanding. But if he ran towards Shigeru, it seemed likely the other would sense him. The only reason he was safe now was because he was further away. Ryuu thought perhaps the shadow knew Shigeru somehow. Ryuu could sense Shigeru far before he could sense a normal person. Perhaps it was similar to what was happening now.

Too many questions. If he could move Shigeru farther away, it might be safe to get closer, to talk. He knew Shigeru was tuned into him now, so he drew his sword and sprinted away from the approaching soldiers. His efforts paid off. Shigeru followed him, but Ryuu didn't stop until he felt confident he was out of range. He felt a momentary pang of regret for Takako. She was still. Shigeru would have told her to stay put and she would be frightened. But there was no other way.

When he saw Shigeru, Ryuu swore there was panic in his eyes. Ryuu cursed. Shigeru wasn't aware of the danger, but he knew what was pursuing them. Ryuu told him about the soldiers who were tracking him. He tried to judge Shigeru's reaction. Then Ryuu told him about the other that sensed like they did, and Shigeru's face went completely white, like a ghost was haunting him.

"You know what it is, don't you?"

"His name is Orochi, and you're right, he is tracking me. I had hoped this day would never come, but it's too late now. We don't have time. If we live through this, I'll tell you the story of my past. You need to know now."

"What do we do? It's only a matter of time before he picks you up again."

Shigeru was quiet as he tried to come up with a solution. Ryuu, calmer in the presence of his master, tried to think as well. Takako slowed them down. The two of them could have put together a defense, but two against eleven while defending an innocent, there was no way. These men were good, and Ryuu couldn't risk Takako.

Shigeru spoke. "We have to split up. If Orochi is after me, it's only me he will track. You can take Takako. There's a farmhouse I know near here. We can meet there in three days."

Ryuu shook his head. "I can't leave you to fight alone."

Shigeru was firm. "Don't worry, I'm not going to fight. But if we don't split, Takako's life is forfeit. You know it's true."

Without warning, Ryuu started to tear up. "I brought this down on us, didn't I?"

Shigeru smiled, a genuine smile, rare for him. "Perhaps, but this is no time to question fate. I made decisions which brought us to this point too, and you don't know most of them. Let's not worry about how we got here, but instead think about getting out of here. Act in the moment, the way you were taught."

Ryuu nodded, a tear trickling down his face. "Don't die."

Shigeru laughed. "Same to you."

"They're getting close. Time to go."

Shigeru stood and gave directions to the abandoned farmhouse. They embraced quickly and were off. Ryuu ran to Takako, and they started moving to the west while Shigeru took off to the North. Ryuu had never run in fear before. When he thought they were safe he had them stop. He threw his sense out. Five of the soldiers had gone after Shigeru, and the other was with them. Shigeru was running, and they were giving full chase.

The other five were coming after them. Ryuu started to panic. He had to protect Takako, but against five men it would be almost impossible. There was nothing nearby, no place to hide her. He forced himself to breathe, slowly and deeply. He thought about trying to run. But in haste they would leave obvious tracks and would only tire him out. He had to stand and fight. That was fine by him. He had no choice and he could almost hear Shigeru telling him to breathe, to focus on the moment. He was supposed to be one of the best swordsmen in the Three Kingdoms. Five swordsmen shouldn't be a problem. Right?

But he couldn't convince himself. These men were good. They weren't bandits or regular foot soldiers. Already as they approached they began to spread out, to come in on him from all directions.

His breath caught in his throat for a moment when he saw them. Their colors were distinct. Ryuu could remember them from his lessons. They were the honor guard for Lord Akira. They were the best in the land.

Who the hell is chasing us, and what did we do to deserve this?

There wasn't any answer to his questions. There were only the five men in front of him. They were good and well coordinated. For the first time Ryuu touched swords with another warrior in anger. They all moved fast, but Ryuu was quicker and knew their cuts just a fraction of a heartbeat before they made them. When it was done he had been cut, but they were dead.

Ryuu turned to check on Takako. She was fine although shocked. She had never seen the full extent of his ability.

Certain of his safety, Ryuu tried to cast out his sense, but he couldn't make out Shigeru. They were too far gone. With no other options he helped Takako get moving again, and they started making their way to the farmhouse.

They reached the farmhouse in just over a day. Ryuu collected food for them, and for two days the atmosphere was tense but respectful. Ryuu was agitated. Not knowing gnawed at his stomach. He was sure Shigeru would be fine. But doubt crawled within his mind, distracting him from any focused pursuits. He could see Takako wasn't doing well. She had to be even more nervous than him. But he couldn't summon the courage to speak to her.

The days passed with agonizing slowness. Ryuu tried to focus his sense, but he was too distracted to throw it out more than a few paces. He knew he was as good as useless. Takako at least knew how to cook.

The sun rose and fell on the third day. Agitation turned to desperation. It gave him strength and focus. He sat down and calmed his mind, throwing out his sense as far as it could go. He couldn't find anything. No Shigeru, no Orochi, no other warriors. There was nothing approaching the farmhouse. Ryuu had to give Shigeru credit. If nothing else he had certainly picked a remote place.

As night fell on the third day, Ryuu was torn with indecision. He didn't want to stay in one location for too long. Orochi had sent five men after him. Next time he would come himself.

The thought terrified him. He had never been hunted like a common animal. He knew now there were others out there, others like him, with more experience, more training. Before he had the confidence of one who believed he could not be beaten. Now he felt like a child abandoned in the middle of a thunderstorm. Chaos and uncertainly swirled around him, and without Shigeru he had no compass, no light to guide his way.

Uncertainty caused him to stay through the night. He saw Takako observing him closely, but every time she tried to get close to him to comfort him and offer her support he would shrug her away. He didn't want her comfort or her concern. What he wanted was Shigeru back to tell him what to do and to show him where to go.

He spent the evening and the next day given over to the sense. His mind traveled the myriad paths of nature, stretching further than he had ever sent it before. He felt his limits and probed around them, always searching for just a little more. But nothing came. He took no food or drink, content to drink only the information the sense provided him. It was addicting in its own way.

In time he realized the sun had gone down. He allowed himself, slowly, to withdraw back into his own body. When he opened his eyes he saw Takako had been crying.

"I'm sorry. I can't sense him. We need to go, it won't be safe here for long."

Takako shook her head. "But no one has come for four days. Maybe it's safe here. Maybe Shigeru won and is working hard to get here."

"No." Ryuu's voice was firm. "If he is safe, he can find us. If he is in danger, we are too. If he is dead, Orochi is coming after us next, and we aren't far enough away."

Takako looked ready to argue the point, but Ryuu shot her a glare which quieted her. They started collecting the few belongings they had and prepared food for travel. They were ready to leave in a short time. Ryuu had resigned himself. Shigeru was dead and from that point on he would have to find his own path.

Three paces out of the farmhouse, Ryuu sensed him, and a grin broke out on his face. He couldn't remember the last time he had felt so much relief, so much happiness. Ryuu dropped his sack and ran, terrifying Takako. He ran and ran until he found him and caught him mid-stride, hundreds of paces from the house. Shigeru was bloody and ragged, but it looked like at least most of the blood was from others. Ryuu lent Shigeru his support and walked him back to the house.

Shigeru smiled weakly as all three of them met. "I'm glad to find you. I'm sorry I wasn't able to make it on time." With that, the energy seemed to drain out of him and Ryuu had to have Takako help him carry Shigeru to the farmhouse. The two of them worked silently at mending him. Takako found some of the cuts were deep, and they worked on preparing him for rest and healing. It was clear whatever he had been through had almost taken his life.

After he was cleaned and bandages were applied they stood up and washed. Takako was looking at Ryuu with concern etched on her face.

"He'll be fine. The deep cuts will need some time to heal, but he'll live."

Ryuu nodded and finally broke down. He embraced Takako, surprising her. "I can't lose him. He's like a father to me."

Takako gently returned his embrace. "I know."

After two days of rest, Shigeru was up and moving again, even though he moved like an old man. Once Ryuu was sure Shigeru was healthy, he rediscovered his anger. He was upset there was still so much he didn't know, starting with how Shigeru had gotten away from his pursuers.

Shigeru let out another one of his full grins at the question. He was in a better mood than ever. Near-death experiences seemed to agree with him. "I wanted to live more than he wanted to kill me. We played cat-and-mouse for a while in the woods and I managed to take out all his retainers. I caught him with a throwing knife. Then I ran, and he did not pursue me."

Ryuu was confused. "Why not? If he's a strong as you say he is, why didn't he follow you?"

"Because he doesn't want to die and wasn't sure if I'd poisoned the blade. We haven't fought for many cycles. I don't know which of us is stronger. He's a patient man and will bide his time until victory is certain. Or at least until the field is equal."

Ryuu's anger burned brightly. "And he senses better than you do. What's to say he hasn't followed you here?"

"He will. If there is one thing I know about Orochi, he will never give up. If he hasn't given up in this long, he'll never stop until all of us are dead. I don't think he was able to follow me closely enough to find us right away. I may be wrong, but I suspect we have at least a few days before he manages to track us down. If he goes for further reinforcements, we will have even longer."

Ryuu couldn't ever remember being this angry before. "You took a huge risk coming back here!"

It was enough to make Shigeru upset as well. "Yes, I did, but I needed to see you again. I hoped this day would never come, that I could train you, make you strong, and avoid the sins I committed. I thought we had hidden well and that no one would ever find us. I was wrong. Fine. But I have to finish your training, which will happen tonight. Don't let your feelings for the girl get in the way of your rationality!"

That was enough to silence Ryuu. Shigeru was right. He hadn't realized it. He was much less willing to take risks because of Takako's presence, but wasn't willing to give Shigeru the same benefit for wanting to see him again. It was unfair of him.

Ryuu bowed. When he came back up he was calm again. "You are right. I'm sorry, Shigeru."

"It's okay. We're all stressed and I'm afraid it won't be over soon. However, it is how we compose ourselves in these times that determine who we are. The smart thing for me to do would have been to leave you forever, but I didn't. Our feelings will have that effect."

The rest of the day passed quickly. Shigeru tested his body while Takako and Ryuu prepared for the journey, finding as much food as they could and preparing it. As the sun set, Ryuu breathed a sigh of relief. It was good to have Shigeru back again.

The night started out like any other. They enjoyed an excellent meal of game and berries they had found in the vicinity, and Takako had outdone herself in their preparation. The three of them managed to have a conversation that was almost normal, almost like a family who had gathered for a reunion. They kept the fire burning well after they were done with the meal and sat around sharing stories of their lives.

During a pause between stories, Shigeru moved everything forward. "This is good. This is what I have always wanted, and I am glad I've achieved it, now so close to the end."

Ryuu startled. He didn't know what he had been expecting, but not that.

"Ryuu, as you know, twice I have asked you what path you wanted to take. The path I follow, and the one followed by several others, is not an easy one. You were given the choice when we first met, and you were given the choice when you took your first life. The third choice is offered at the end of your training period. Although there is much more for you to learn, even regarding the sense, there is nothing else I can teach you. My own training ended prematurely, and I have passed along all that I was trained and all I have figured out on my own since then."

"Typically, the third choice is as follows. You may follow the path that you have been set on, or you may choose to die, here and now. Once one reaches this level of skill it is unsafe to allow one free rein."

Takako started to cry.

"But, Ryuu, you are my son if I ever had one. I am proud of you. I could never offer you such a choice. Instead, I repeat the offer you've rejected twice. You can continue upon the path you've been set on. I tell you now the truth, that it will cost you the lives of those you love, as it may very well cost you your life. There is no reward, no honor that is guaranteed. Only that you will have a life of hardship, toil, and violence."

"Your other choice is to leave the Three Kingdoms. I know of a place, a place where you could hide with Takako. You could live the life of a normal man, working for a living, enjoying the companionship of another. Raise a family. The choice is yours."

Ryuu looked closely at Shigeru. It was clear now that Shigeru was a torn, broken man. He loved Ryuu and was grateful for the child he had raised. But he also saw the error of his ways, that the child he raised would inherit the sins of his father, whatever those may be. Shigeru wanted him to take the way out. He wanted Ryuu to escape, to leave the Three Kingdoms and live with Takako.

He looked over to Takako. It was the best offer he had heard. She was beautiful and kind. He didn't know whether she would ever love him, but getting to know her was one of the greatest times of his life. The possibility of being able to continue being with her was incredibly tempting.

But he also never would have met Takako if he hadn't followed the path Shigeru put him on. His life hadn't always been easy, and he still had trouble reconciling that he was a murderer. What was the way to show Shigeru the respect he deserved - to continue on the path set before him, or to abandon it now when he had completed training?

Ryuu's mind raced back and forth. There seemed to be nothing worthwhile about the life of a nightblade. It wasn't the life of glory he imagined as a child. Shigeru had made that clear.

He studied Takako, lost in her own thoughts. She hadn't consented to anything, and it was just as likely she would leave when given the chance as stay with Ryuu. She hadn't forgiven him for what happened to her family. Maybe she never would. He wanted to ask her what to do, but knew it was wrong to put the decision on her. She had been pulled into this life. This was his decision to make, and it was his life. Her decision would come later.

The silence stretched on eternally, the only sound between them the crackling of the fire burning down.

He wanted so badly to take the easy path, but something inside of him fought against it. Ryuu looked at Shigeru. He was a good man. He had taken lives, but he had also saved lives. Was there anything greater? He couldn't rationalize it, but he knew that even if he ran away with Takako and she accepted him he would never know peace. There wasn't peace for anyone who had the power he possessed.

He didn't want to.

"I'll continue on the path."

His decision was met with a sad nod by Shigeru and tears from Takako. Shigeru understood his decision, but he couldn't imagine how Takako felt. He had chosen the path of war over the path of peace. He didn't know how to make it clear his decision wasn't to reject her.

Shigeru too, was crying as he continued speaking. "So be it. The choice has been made although I wish it would have been otherwise. You should consider your training complete. I have something that I've been holding onto now for quite some time."

Shigeru dug in his pack and pulled out a small package. He handed it to Ryuu, who unwrapped it carefully. They were a new set of robes, dark as night. Ryuu knew immediately they were the robes of a nightblade.

"These used to be mine, but now they are yours. They are given to students who complete their training. It's my honor to present them to you."

Ryuu held the robes in silence. He loved them but couldn't find the words to say so. Shigeru seemed to understand. He nodded and gestured to the fire.

"Now, build the fire back up, for I have a story to tell. You need to know my story and the time is now. It will explain to you all that you don't know."

CHAPTER 17

The fire crackled around the three of them and Shigeru took his time and held each of them in his eyes. He hesitated. Was telling this story a bad decision? Wasn't it already too late? Shigeru didn't know anymore. He used to have hope. After this moon he knew firsthand how strong Orochi was. He could sense it. Orochi was much stronger than he was. He had lied when he told Ryuu he wasn't sure. Together, perhaps, they could win but he wouldn't risk it. He had built a life for Ryuu and now the journey was Ryuu's.

It saddened him. He had found, after over forty cycles of searching, the peace he had dreamed of as a youth. Not as his masters had intended, but true peace nonetheless. He loved Ryuu and Takako, even though he had just met her. Her spirit was strong. He wasn't sure Ryuu had a chance with her, not after what happened, but he loved her just the same. He could sense fate twisting around Ryuu, and while he had no idea where fate would lead them, his last gift would be the last of the knowledge he could offer.

Ryuu was better than him. His sense was superior and Shigeru knew he wasn't even close to discovering all he was capable of.

His swordsmanship was also superior, and if he didn't hesitate when training against Shigeru he would have realized it himself long ago. He could show better judgment, but it was tough to say. The boy was young. He still seemed too young to be on his own, and Shigeru would try to stay alive for him, but if he could give his life for the boy's he would do so without hesitation.

"It is a good night for a story. The night is cold outside, but we are gathered here around a fire, just like our ancestors were. That is something I should remind you of, Ryuu. In all the stories I've told you, our ancestors wandered. It is a fate I foretell for you as well. Once one reaches a certain power, trouble seems to follow them, and the only way to protect the innocent is to keep traveling. It's a legend among nightblades, but seems to hold true throughout history. I tried to break the cycle, to live the life of a normal man, attached to the land, to a space, but fate has caught up to me as well."

Shigeru saw Ryuu was about to interrupt and held up his hand. "Please, indulge me. I'm feeling sentimental tonight, and I would like to tell this story in one piece if I could."

Ryuu bowed. Shigeru paused, unsure of where to begin. He had hoped for so long he would never have to tell the story he had forgotten how he should tell it.

"The first thing you should know is the history they teach in the Three Kingdoms is incomplete. All histories are, of course, but there are secrets you must know, secrets which people in the Three Kingdoms have never guessed at. You must keep them, for to let them go, to let them slip over too much drink or in a moment of carelessness would bring disaster upon all our heads."

"After the Great War, it was not a good time to be a nightblade. The dayblades had thrived, most of them going into the monasteries and receiving pardons from the governments.

They standardized a curriculum to teach to all those born with the sense, but in devising this curriculum ensured their eventual destruction. The sense is an organic entity. It is an incredible human achievement, the pinnacle of observation and awareness, but it is also natural. The sense is part of a larger whole, a larger fabric even our best philosophers could only guess at. Even you, Ryuu, are only beginning to grasp all you could achieve. It manifests itself differently in people, and people learn it in different ways. A standard curriculum is the lowest bar, but over hundreds of cycles, it is all the monasteries know, and it is why you could defeat their strongest warriors without even breaking a sweat."

"There were those who would not accept what amounted to house arrest. They remembered the way of their ancestors and sought to honor it by traveling the open road. Over time most were killed by the armies, the mobs, and the propaganda. We were meant to go from village to village, maintaining justice and peace. Instead, we became hated, enemies of the commoners thanks to the propaganda of the lords who feared the power we held, the power to support the people."

"But there was a third group, a small group who believed a middle way could be found. A way to achieve some sense of peace and tranquility, and a way to transmit the true knowledge of the sense for generations, to return to the Three Kingdoms when they are needed. Since the Great War they have existed. I was born to them, for they maintain a constant location and have families. Orochi too is one of them and used to be close enough to be my brother in all but blood."

"You know your geography. Far to the north of here, there is the Great Sea, and on that Sea there are many islands, but there is one that holds my people. The islanders of the area believe the island to be inaccessible and uninhabited, but it is not true. There is just one way into it, and that way was discovered by our ancestors after the Great War. It is the perfect location, completely hidden away from the world. Those who live there also die there."

"This nameless community is the last hideout of the old ways, the ways I have been trained in, and the ways you have been trained in. Very, very few people know that these ways even exist anymore, for the secret is jealously protected by those on the island."

Shigeru paused. He could talk about the island for days. He had lived almost all of his formative cycles there, but it wasn't what the story was about. Information about the island would be important, but not as much as Ryuu learning who he was dealing with.

"I was born there to a happy couple, both of whom were gifted in the sense. My parents hoped I would become powerful in the sense due to my heritage. I showed much promise when I was young and displayed many of the hallmarks of one who was gifted. Compared to my peers I had a relentless curiosity, high intelligence, and was mentally adaptable. I could pick up and learn new concepts in a short amount of time."

"Like all children of the island, I trained in the sense from a young age. Even much earlier than you were. For us, learning about the sense was the equivalent of learning to walk here in the Three Kingdoms. It was not always gentle training, but I thrived under the pressure. My skills grew, and I soon was one of the best students on the island despite my young age."

"When I was ten cycles old, two events happened which were the precursors to all that happened later. The first was I became close friends with a girl named Yuki. She was a beautiful girl, and I am reminded of her every time I look at Takako. She was gentle and kind, and like Takako, always seemed to find the bright side of any situation."

"I had been intimidated by her when I was younger. She was two cycles older than me and despite her cheerful demeanor she was well known for refusing the company of any boys who attempted to come close to her. I still believe she knew how dangerous her beauty was. But it wasn't just that. She was beautiful, yes, exquisite, but it was her beauty combined with her gentle nature. That was a rare combination. Boys were always tripping over themselves to be with her, and I think a part of her knew it would lead to trouble some day. . ."

Shigeru's voice trailed off, and Ryuu was about to ask him what happened next, but he continued.

"Anyways, when I was ten, she and I became close. I was a dour child, always working to better myself instead of making friends and playing. Perhaps it was my inability to fawn over her that brought her to me. I think about it a lot, and I still don't know what she saw in me. She was the one who approached me. Perhaps it was because I was the only one not focused on her. I don't know. The other girls on the island were jealous of her status with the boys and perhaps I was the only boy she felt like she could trust herself with."

"Despite my complete lack of effort she eventually won me over, and for a couple of cycles we enjoyed what I would describe as a young, innocent love. There was nothing sexual about it then, at least not for me. I was too young and too focused on my training to consider it. But we spent almost all of our free time together and made childish conspiracies to get some of our training time structured together. She was very quick physically, but otherwise wasn't particularly gifted. Even though I was younger I could beat her at most exercises."

"As my friendship with Yuki developed another new person entered my life. It was Orochi, and although he had only seen five cycles when I met him, he was already considered a child prodigy. I was talented and hard working, but Orochi was something else. The sense manifested in him in unique ways. The first talent he learned, which terrified his parents, by the way, was to mask his own presence from the sense. That skill in and of itself made him one of the most dangerous people on the island, and he was only five. Almost everyone on the island grew up with the sense. Imagine how disconcerting it was that someone could sneak up on you. He caused quite the commotion."

"Orochi's other gifts were unremarkable. He wasn't gifted in any other regard besides the fact he could hide himself, but it was enough. Like me, he was totally dedicated to improving himself, and mastery of the sense is often a matter of effort. Even at the age of five he became the boy to beat. When you can't sense your opponent's movements and he can sense yours, he is a very difficult opponent. It's probably how most swordsmen feel when they encounter a nightblade."

"By the time he worked himself up to challenging me he was starting to reach the limits of his ability. He relied solely on his speed and knowledge. Being five, he couldn't beat anyone on strength. I had to fight blind, using only my sight, which seemed inadequate, but he hadn't gotten quick enough to get past my defenses. I kept my attacks small, no big cuts, so he couldn't dart inside like I'd seen him do with so many others. We fought ourselves to a draw."

"The great thing about that fight, and what impressed me the most about him, was that he wasn't mad. Other children at his age would have been, but Orochi cared about getting better. In me, he believed he had found someone he could train with, even though we were close to ten cycles apart. And I was proud of myself. I had fought to a draw this prodigy everyone else seemed to worship. I became a mentor to him, an arrangement beneficial to both of us."

"Over time the three of us became close. Each of us were outcasts in our community. Not exiled, but we felt different from all the rest. We never could have articulated it at the age we were at, but we did make quite the group. Yuki, of course, was the matriarch, and I do think sometimes she fussed over us like we were actually her children. Despite our age difference, Orochi and I became like brothers. Together, our training took off, and soon we both were without equal among children on the island."

"The next few cycles passed. Our group continued on, getting stronger, growing closer. I noticed my feelings towards Yuki were changing. We were still close friends, and I wouldn't do anything to change that, but I found myself attracted to her. Every time I thought about her I felt warmth fill my body and I found it more and more difficult to carry on normal conversation with her. I could only think about being with her."

"I kept my feelings secret, but I was a boy and I wasn't good at hiding my intents. Yuki and Orochi both picked up on my desire. Orochi made fun of me for being distracted by girls. Yuki's reaction was much more complex."

"I believe now she was torn by my attention to her. On one hand she knew me well, and we were friends with a strong relationship. It wasn't that she disliked me. There had to be a part of her that knew I was different than all the other boys. I was someone who would respect her and care for her."

"But she had sought me out precisely because I wasn't interested in her, and my attentions brought out all the habits I thought had disappeared. Once she was certain of my affections she never let me get too close. We still would talk and train together, but there was an invisible barrier around her I couldn't break. She reminded me of one of my masters, a swordsman known for his incredible defense. He would never strike you. He was an expert at reading the intentions of a warrior before the strike and was always able to deflect your strike. In the many cycles I lived on the island, I never saw anyone land a strike on him."

"Yuki's heart was just like that. She was gentle and never tried to push me away from her, but she never let me get close either. Nothing I tried worked. But I never gave up. I knew she was important and I couldn't let my attraction to her go. And so this difficult tension continued to exist for well over a cycle."

"At the same time, Orochi was getting older and was blossoming in more ways than one. His power lent him a dark edge that he honed over time. In his studies he learned of a clan of nightblades presumed extinct long before the Great War. The clan had created a reputation for powers that manifested like those Orochi had. They could become nearly undetectable, even to other nightblades and dayblades, and created a fighting style built upon the principles of subtlety, stealth, and deception."

"Something in Orochi responded to those principles, and he began to drink deeply of the knowledge offered in those books. While I would never have called him a happy child, he had been pleasant company until the point when he started to emulate the behaviors of the extinct clan. Our instructors were unsure of how to deal with him. The clan which he emulated had enjoyed a mixed reputation among all blades. They were effective, but there is a code of honor among nightblades, and the clan's practices of deception were difficult for many to swallow, even though they were often the ones other clans turned to for solving difficult problems."

"So our masters didn't know what to do with Orochi. On one hand, they recognized his skills could prove invaluable in certain situations, but they tried to encourage in all of us a certain code of ethics and honor which ran contrary to Orochi's techniques. Because they could not reach a definitive conclusion, Orochi ended up being able to continue his studies as he saw fit. One decision among many that led to what happened."

Shigeru stopped again. He took a sip of water and looked thoughtful. Ryuu caught himself leaning forward. An island of day and nightblades? It seemed unreal.

Shigeru cleared his throat. "Those are the facts, the setting. Events unfolded quickly after that. They all happened one winter. I was nineteen cycles old and on the verge of my final stage of training. Orochi was fourteen although he had the size and bearing of a student my age. He and I were still well matched and neither could claim to be the best although the two of us were the most promising of our peers. Yuki had turned twenty-one and reached the conclusion of her training cycle. She hadn't fared well during the final training stages and was released from training without dishonor. She was an available woman and the competition for her hand in marriage had increased ten-fold."

"To this day, I can't explain everything. I can guess Orochi coveted her fiercely. He never let on, or if he did I was too preoccupied with my own obsession to notice I had a competitor. Although he wasn't, not really. He had grown both physically and emotionally, but he was still too young. Maybe that bothered him more than anything else. Perhaps it was because I was closer to her than he was. I don't know why he singled out Yuki, but what I do know is he did."

"Orochi had taken to sneaking around the island at night. He had a fierce pride and was always challenging himself to explore and reach new places. I knew about his night escapades, as he shared many of them with me, but did not report him. He would sneak into shrines, past guards, out onto the coast, all places that were protected. There would always be a souvenir near my bed the next day, a specific rock, part of the shrine, whatever he could find to prove it to me. He always had to prove it, not that I ever disbelieved him."

"However, there were some nights when I would notice Orochi had left, but he wouldn't tell me where he had been. I was confused at the time. Orochi, despite our similar talent levels, had always looked up to me, and I foolishly believed he shared with me all of his exploits, both the legitimate and illegitimate sort. It bothered me that he wasn't sharing, but I decided not to pester him."

"Soon enough my curiosity got the better of me, and one day I asked Orochi where he had been. He looked at me and told me he had been sneaking around the grounds of one of our masters. I suspected he was lying, but I wasn't even sure myself, and I didn't have any evidence. I decided to find out for sure."

"It was a complicated game for us to play as children. I may have been older, but despite everything I told myself, I wasn't mature. Over the next several days we were involved in an elaborate sense-battle. It was a match of subtlety and skill and stealth, not strength, and though Orochi was younger, he was much better at those aspects of the sense, and it felt like I was fighting an uphill battle."

"Orochi, I think now, enjoyed himself more than anything else. For quite a while he had been working at sneaking out and about, testing his skills in real situations on the island. But he had never been hunted, never been tracked by someone who was looking for him and who was familiar with what he could do. It was a new challenge for him."

"During the day everything appeared normal. When it all went so wrong, no one even sensed it coming. Orochi and I pretended to be best friends, and during the day I could almost bring myself to believe it. But the nights were a different story. Orochi was always sneaking out, challenging me to follow him. I didn't know how to proceed. I didn't have the skills he did. If I snuck out of bed at night I would have been questioned. But to not sneak out would be to admit defeat."

"I resorted to lying, claiming I was having nightmares and needed to walk at night to help me fall back to sleep. Our masters bought the lie as it was the only time I ever lied to them. And so I would walk at night, ostentatiously to clear my head, but in reality playing a life-size cat-and-mouse game with the most clever little mouse."

"I could track him a little. I got used to sensing the absence, the black hole he left on the ground he touched. It wasn't perfect, and I would lose him for different lengths of time, but the island wasn't so big and I felt like I had a good track on him most nights. Honestly, I was worried for him. We were a very open community. For someone to be sneaking around felt wrong."

"I caught him one night after almost a full moon of this game. I had pretended to lose him, but in reality I had been sensing him well that night. I knew almost exactly where he was, and I felt confident enough to give him some extra space to see where he would go if he thought he was free. He went to the women's dorms, and the minute he managed to sneak in, it focused my sense like nothing before had done, and I knew, without a doubt in my mind, he was standing over Yuki, watching her."

"Everything clicked for me then. I was furious, but held off confronting him until the next day. After a day of training we got some time alone, and I let him know I had caught him. I was furious at him and threatened to go to the Masters of the island if he ever tried it again. Punishment was severe on the island. At the least he would have lost some fingers. At the worst he would have lost his life."

"Orochi seemed crestfallen, but it wasn't because he had threatened our friendship with his actions, it was because he had gotten caught. I sensed it. I knew that in the way he looked at me, in the way he glared after his disappointment had passed. I knew he was going to try again, but I loved him, and he was like a younger brother to me. I wanted to give him one more chance, a chance to prove he could redeem himself."

"For a while it looked like it worked. He started sleeping through the night. Slowly, very slowly, I began to trust him again. I thought I had saved him. Before long, both he and I were sleeping through the night. But as you can guess, it was all a ruse."

"Two moons later I caught him sneaking out of our dormitory again. It had been a complete coincidence. I had woken up, and he had just been leaving. I know I should have spoken up, but I cared for him. I didn't want to see him suffer the punishment that would have been his. Once again our games began. This time I had the advantage. I knew what his ultimate goal was. He would find Yuki again. I resumed my nightly patrol, always staying within sense range of the girl's dormitory. I thought I could stop him before he came close."

"I will always remember that night. It was a clear late winter's night, crisp and cool with the breeze coming off the sea. On any other night it would have been perfect for staring at the stars because they were all watching us that night. I was bundled in some heavier robes because of how cool it was. I knew Orochi had been tormenting me a little. He was sneaking into warm parts of the island, hiding in huts or near guardhouses where fires kept the cold at bay."

"I don't know how he did it, but I didn't sense him at all, and I wasn't able to notice his sense-absence either. I had thought he was near a guardhouse warming himself by the fire, but he managed to sneak past me entirely. To this day I question myself. Was I day-dreaming, had I somehow failed in my duty to protect Yuki? I don't know. I thought I had been attentive, but I also had been only sleeping a couple of hours a night."

"Anyway, he got past me into the dorm, and all of a sudden he let himself go. He would always hide himself even in day-to-day activities. He claimed it made him stronger, more used to hiding. But he opened himself up to the world, and I sensed him so strongly in that room. It was his claim to victory. He had snuck past me and gotten to the target I had sworn I would protect."

"In that moment I snapped. I was tired and Orochi's sheer insolence had gotten to me. In retrospect, I don't know if he meant any harm. I can't believe Orochi was a bad person. He was just obsessed with her and obsessed with beating me. It was too much for me to take. I broke and charged into the dorms, my sword drawn."

"He was waiting for me. I don't know what he was thinking. Maybe he just wanted to prove himself the best to everyone. But we matched swords for real that night."

"The battle was quick, although from my perspective, it seemed to last a long time. I've told you before we were evenly matched.

Not that night. I was too angry, too focused. I had a rage he didn't have and didn't understand. It had been a game to him. He just wanted to win, but I wanted his life. In that moment I wanted to see the warm blood coming straight from his heart. He didn't take that into consideration as we fought, and in just a few passes I had knocked him back, opening his defenses wide open."

"That moment, Ryuu, is etched permanently in my heart. Sometimes, in my nightmares, it replays itself over and over and I can't stop it from happening. I saw the opening, and I thrust beautifully, a stab right for his heart, meant to kill. But I was so focused, so enraged, I lost all my training, and in a moment, Yuki jumped in front of my strike. I know she woke up and saw us fighting and tried to stop us, but I was too out of control. I should have known she was coming."

"When I first felt my blade penetrate flesh, my heart leapt for joy. I had never taken a life before, but I never thought it would be so rewarding. I had defeated my first monster."

"Although my eyes were wide open, it took me a few moments to realize Yuki was impaled on my blade. I saw my sword, slicing cleanly through one of the breasts I had dreamed so much about. But the part that gets me, that haunts me, is that she was smiling. It's the smile that gets me. Why was she smiling?"

"I went down to my knees. Yuki raised her bloody hand to my face and gently stroked it, once, before she lost control and it dropped. As she fell to the floor, I was all over her, trying to figure out how to heal her. I had been trained to heal, but not like this. I was not a dayblade. I knew how to destroy. Yuki tried to whisper something, but I couldn't hear it. Her lips moved, and her eyes were focused on me, but I couldn't tell if she said anything. I like to believe she forgave me or that she loved me. But I'll never know."

"I was so focused on Yuki I didn't even feel Orochi leave the room. I held Yuki tight until her breath stopped moving, and even then I held her some more. I had never wanted to let her go in life, and I was certain I was never going to let her go in death. I was in shock, but I didn't know it at the time. I only knew I had killed the woman I loved."

"The masters came for me. Our battle had woken the entire island. One problem growing up on an island where everyone was sense-gifted was that nothing was hidden. I was bound and put under guard within moments."

"When the next day came there was a terrible commotion on the island. In over a thousand cycles no one had been murdered on the island. There had been duels, but no murder. I didn't come out of shock. I wanted to kill myself, but I was too cowardly to do it. Yuki's body was burned in that evening. The whole island, including Orochi, came out to pay their final respects, but I was not allowed. I didn't even get to see the last rites of my beloved."

"They didn't feed me or give me water. There was little concern for humane treatment. It was a small and tight-knit community, but one that required adherence. The day and night were miserable, but I didn't complain. I kept replaying Yuki's final few moments, a bit of blood trickling out of the corner of her mouth. I felt I deserved whatever I got and forgot Orochi was the root of all these problems."

"When the sun rose the next morning there was a tribunal of masters who met to decide my fate. There was a fair hearing, and I was given a chance to defend myself, but I did not. I had killed Yuki, there was no denying it. My guilt outweighed the anger I felt towards Orochi. I said nothing, but accepted my sentence without question or complaint. I was given the death sentence, which was carried out immediately."

"It was not a warrior's death, but instead the death of a criminal. I was tied to a cross overlooking the sea. It was death by exposure. I was naked with no way of heating myself. It was a windy day, and the sea lashed against my skin and at night I froze. I was given no food and occasional sips of water to prolong my agony."

"I held on for two nights, but when the sun rose on the third day, I knew I was going to die the next night. My throat was raw, my skin radiated pure anger at the sun and sea and cold. Coughing wracked my body, which only served to heighten the pain. I said my prayers and set myself to surviving the day, ready to give up my spirit to the Great Cycle that night."

"Guilt was my companion. There was Yuki's face, my sword piercing her bare breast, the first time I had seen her naked. And there was her smile which still haunts my dreams. Why did she smile at me? Did she see the next step in the Great Cycle? Did she love me? Did she love Orochi? I don't know, even today."

"The sun set on the final day and I was positive it would be the last sunset I ever saw. It was beautiful, a deep blood red which reflected my mood. I cried when I looked at it. I didn't want to die, but I wasn't ready to live either."

"The sun set, and with it, my wish to live. A strange thing happened, but as my desire to live faded away, as my attachment to life and breath faded, so did my pain. I wasn't happy or content, but I was at peace. I was ready, and my vision started to fade to black."

"Then the pain returned. Suddenly I was on the ground, gasping for air. Everything that had faded came rushing back. The pain in my neck, my throat, my wrists, my hunger and thirst all returned in an instant. It took me a couple of breaths to regain my senses but when it did his voice came to me."

"'You won't die here, not now. You will die at my hands, at a time of my choosing. This island's justice is not sufficient. I want you to live knowing what you did, who you killed. The one person you cared for. The one person I cared for.'"

"I didn't have the words to speak. My mind was slow, like a drowning person finding they had survived the ocean only to find themselves sinking in the mud. I couldn't stand, couldn't get any of my senses underneath me."

"Orochi left me there. I never saw him. But he walked away, and I was left on the ground trying to figure out what had just happened. The guards had regular patrol routes, and I had sensed them earlier in my captivity. I searched for them as my sense began to return. Of course, they weren't around. Orochi never would have chanced it with them near. Not that he would be afraid of sneaking past them, but if he wanted me to live then he would have had to give me a chance to escape."

"Like all inhabitants of the island I knew the paths that criss-crossed the rock like the back of my hand. The guards knew about them too, but they expected me to be tied to a cross. There was a path that would take me to the hidden cove and it would avoid most people as night settled. There would be a boat there and I could take it to the mainland."

"I had one task left to complete, and it wasn't a wise one. I went to the shrine where the possessions of the deceased were kept before being given back to the community. I was looking for one item, driven by an irrational need to possess something of hers. I took her sword and brought it with me to the mainland. It is the same one you carry, made by the finest sword smiths of the island."

"I won't bore you with the rest of the story, although you can imagine how it went. My trip back to the shrine to pick up the sword attracted attention, and although I was weakened, I had enough of a head start I was able to get to the hidden cove faster than my pursuers. The island only had three boats, and I managed to put holes in two before taking off with a third. I have been on the run ever since. I thought I had a new home when I built that cabin, but then on one of my journeys I ran into you."

"There is more to the sense than what I can teach you. Skills that can make you stronger and faster. But I don't know them. I've given you all I can. I had hoped for more for you than the life of a fugitive. I'm sorry I've failed."

Shigeru finished his tale and there was silence in the room. Takako was confused. She hadn't known Shigeru for long, and the story sounded fantastic. She doubted much of it was true. Ryuu was lost in thought. It was so much new information, and some of it he struggled to process. He did not want to believe Shigeru had killed the girl he loved. He looked at Takako and tried to imagine putting a sword through her. His stomach dropped like a rock and he almost threw up. He couldn't imagine it. Trying to do so made him feel sick. For just a moment he saw Takako broken and bloody, almost so real he believed it.

Shigeru observed both of them from a detached standpoint. The telling of the story had drained him. His own ghosts held him back. He realized he wanted Ryuu to be proud of him.

Shigeru, even though he felt it was foolish, almost dared to hope. Takako was a beautiful girl, kind despite all she had been through, and reminded him more of Yuki than he was willing to admit. Perhaps, just maybe they could make it work. If there was some way for Shigeru to sacrifice himself or defeat Orochi, perhaps it could happen. But Shigeru didn't know how.

Perhaps it was possible to outrun and outfight the sins of a father. If anybody had a chance it would be Ryuu. Maybe he could fight for and attain the life his master never had. He knew it wouldn't be easy. Shigeru had murdered the woman he loved and the cost would follow him further than his own life. It was a disappointing, gut-wrenching sorrow and Shigeru struggled to accept it. He had worked hard to prevent this outcome, but fate and the Great Cycle would not be denied their justice. He was thankful that despite his crime he had enjoyed many cycles of happiness with Ryuu. He just wished it could have lasted.

CHAPTER 18

When Orochi left Perseverance it left Moriko rudderless, cast upon a fierce ocean set on destroying her. She had no recourse, no way to safety and a harbor that would shelter her. While he had been at the monastery she had not realized how great of an outsider she was becoming, how separated she was from the normal day-to-day tasks of the monks. There was nothing binding her to the monastery any longer.

Her training with him had a powerful effect. It gave her a confidence she didn't believe possible. She knew she was stronger than any of the monks in the monastery. Where they had once maintained an aura of power, the authority that had once seemed supreme now seemed meaningless. Her only concern, the only unknown in the equations she struggled to solve, was the Abbot.

Moriko understood the skill sets of the monk. Orochi had taught her more about the monastic system than the monks ever had. She knew the strengths and weaknesses of their methods. If necessary she knew how to kill them. She had lost her fear of any of them. Goro was the leader of the pack, not because he was stronger, but because he was the most cruel and most in favor with the Abbot.

The Abbot was a different matter. He possessed an affinity with the sense Moriko didn't understand. She thought she could best him if she understood his powers. But it was rare for him to display his full power so she had little opportunity to assess him. She tried to remember what combat with him had been like, but her mind was unwilling to recall the specifics of a day she'd rather forget.

Her uncertainty and her training with Orochi put her in an awkward position in more ways than one. She desired to leave and was confident she had the ability to leave without worry of pursuit. But she didn't know what she would do if she left. She respected Orochi, but she wasn't sure she wanted to live like him. She was almost of full adult age, but she didn't know how to exist in the world outside of the monastery walls. Her skill sets weren't conducive to finding typical employment.

She used to find solace in the routine and rules of the monastery, but now the rules didn't apply to her. No monk came to order her around, and no monk came to invite her to anything. Every time she saw one of them glance at her, she knew she was outcast. She had been angry at first, but as time wore down her anger she realized the monks were just as uncomfortable as her. She had fought with them and tried to defeat a man they all looked up to. In their minds she was a traitor. A traitor only alive by the grace of the Abbot. She did not belong with them.

For a couple of days after Orochi left Moriko wandered around aimlessly hoping someone would invite her in to their activities. But the monks left her alone, ignoring her as though she was a ghost. She wasn't accepted, but no one reprimanded her either.

In time she began training again. She had to do something and so she continued with the practices she knew. She woke up early in the morning with all the other monks and joined in their morning calisthenics. Afterwards she forced herself to meditate for most of the morning, focusing on her sense-abilities in the manner Orochi had taught her. She focused on being invisible to others and worked on expanding her own sense. Orochi taught her there wasn't any limit to the reach of the sense. It was more a matter of how much information you could train your mind to comprehend. The further out your sense stretched, the more information your mind was forced to deal with. If it could handle it your sense would continue to expand. Once the mind couldn't process all the information the sense wouldn't stretch any further.

Moriko practiced. She focused on sensing everything happening in the monastery, focusing on all life big and small. Once she could handle that amount of information she expanded her sense one pace at a time, tendrils flickering out and reaching new distances. It was a slow process, but Orochi had emphasized patience, and over the course of a couple of moons, Moriko made significant progress. She had learned to reach out several dozen paces further than she had when Orochi left.

She would join the monks for the community lunch and then trained her combat skills. Orochi had opened her eyes to a new system of martial skills and Moriko worked diligently to master them. It was much more difficult without a partner, but she was determined to be strong enough to fight her own battles. She imagined the voice of Orochi in her mind correcting her technique.

As Moriko got stronger life in and out of the monastery continued to participate in the Great Cycle. Moriko didn't think much about events until an incident that occurred in the deep of winter. Goro had left again in a joyous mood. Moriko, who had become an experienced observer of all the patterns of the monastery, suspected he had left to go hunting for future monks.

The search for new monks was never-ending. Monks were always leaving to test new students, but few enjoyed the process of separating children from their families as much as Goro.

Goro's departure made Moriko reflect upon her own life. She thought back to her own arrival at the monastery, how much she had hated Goro and how much she had hated living at the monastery. She had fought against it so hard and had been the last child in her cohort to entertain the idea of escaping the monastery. She realized, with a start, she no longer hated the monastery in the same way. She still hated its practices, but she didn't hate living here anymore. Even though she had the skills to escape she was more comfortable here and didn't leave.

The sudden knowledge surprised her. When had she stopped dreaming of leaving the monastery? It must have been around Orochi's arrival. She had been ready to resist training until death. But he had shown her a new way, a path she had never considered before. She had never imagined she could become so strong.

But by being stronger, her desire to live had increased. She had the power to make change now, no longer helpless in the world.

Her train of thought led her to thinking about the type of girl she had been growing up with her parents, what type of life she had dreamed for herself back when she had only seen five cycles. Her dream had been to be in the deep woods, her first love. She wanted to be among the trees, sensing the mystery of life and death that was so prevalent everywhere in the wilderness.

A couple of moons ago, the thought would have made her chuckle at her foolish youthful ambitions. Today though, watching Goro leave on his task, it made her sad she had lost her dream. She searched her memory, trying to find the love of the wild she had once held, the desire to break all constraints and live within the Great Cycle. But she couldn't find it, the memory erased by the slow passage of time.

In Goro's absence, Moriko tried to forget the realization of her change. She threw herself into her training, focusing only on the task before her. It helped, but there was still the nagging feeling in the back of her mind she had lost something, a key piece of herself that had been erased so gradually she never knew it had happened.

Goro returned two days later. He wasn't alone. He returned with a small girl slung over the back of his horse and tied down. His arrival made Moriko frown. There was rarely any reason to tie somebody up. It lacked a certain amount of confidence. It got everything off on the wrong foot. She observed the situation and threw out her sense.

The girl was boiling with rage. Moriko didn't need her sense to understand that. But she sensed something wasn't quite right with Goro. She opened her eyes and looked. He was moving with some pain and it dawned on Moriko that the girl had gotten the best of him. She had cut him somehow. The thought of a little girl getting the drop on Goro was funny enough she let out a full grin. She already liked the new girl.

The thought cracked Moriko's fragile defenses. The girl was just like she had been, but Moriko had become a part of the system she despised. If the girl looked at her she would see just another monk, not someone separate or superior to the man who had stolen her from her family.

Events transpiring in front of Moriko brought her attention front and center. Goro wasn't just injured, he was furious. He cut the rope holding her to the horse, but he didn't untie her wrists or ankles. She slipped off the horse and tried to land on her feet, but they were well tied and she fell over, unable to break her fall with her wrists tied behind her. Moriko winced.

Goro laughed and Moriko's hand went to her sword. Not today. She wouldn't melt into the background and become another monk who let this happen. She could at least stand up for the girl.

Moriko scanned the monastery. Business was proceeding as usual, and no one was paying any particular attention to Goro and his cruelty. Moriko closed her eyes and took a deep breath. She went deep inside herself, hiding her power, and crept towards him. Worry slipped away as her training with Orochi took over. She wasn't going to be the one to attack. She wasn't sure what her status was in the monastery, but killing Goro would bring things to their inevitable conclusion more quickly than she was prepared for.

Her only goal was to save the girl and remove her from Goro's wrath.

Moriko reached Goro without him sensing her. She enjoyed the power over him as she cleared her throat. She smiled as Goro jumped. He spun around, realization dawning on him. He was about to reach for his blade, but saw she wasn't there to fight, her hand resting on the hilt of her sword. Prepared, but not threatening.

"Untie the girl, Goro."

Goro didn't respond. Moriko thought she could hear his brain running circles around the problem. He had rank on Moriko, but Moriko's tone of voice indicated she didn't care. It had been an order, not a request. If he was going to defy her, he was going to have to fight her, and he was injured. She saw his fear. He knew she was stronger.

He took the coward's path.

"The girl is dangerous! She cut me. If I untie her now she could be a danger both to others and herself."

"Untie the girl, Goro."

"She needs to have an audience with the Abbot. You know the procedure. We can't let her near him if she poses a risk to people."

Moriko didn't respond, her posture strong.

Goro looked frantically about for assistance from some corner, but the monks who had been so conveniently ignoring his cruelty were ignoring his current plight as well. He bent to her will. Orochi had taught her true power. Power was the ability to bend others through persuasiveness, charm, or threats. She felt like she had a preference for threats.

Goro untied the girl, and true to form, she attempted to strike him again the moment she was free. It was subtle, but Moriko caught it, and grabbed the girl's arm.

"He's not worth it. Trust me."

The girl stared with hatred deep into Moriko's eyes. She returned the gaze, hoping the calm pool of her soul would quiet this girl down. She had no malice, no hatred, and even some sympathy for this girl. The girl picked up on it. She relaxed, but Moriko could sense it was skin-deep. Her hatred still burned. Already, Moriko thought, she is working at hiding her true intent. Good.

When Moriko was confident the girl wouldn't strike again she let go of the girl's arm. Goro, clueless as to what had just transpired, started to whimper something about procedure, but was cut off mid-sentence by Moriko's glare. She knew what had to be done and wasn't willing to push the issue more than she already had. She had accomplished enough for today.

She led the girl to the Abbot's quarters to present her to him. Moriko could feel the Abbot starting to show off his strength, waves of energy emanating throughout the monastery. Moriko glanced at the girl. She couldn't tell if the girl noticed the Abbot's energy or not. Whatever the case, the girl was doing her best to hold herself together, and was doing an admirable job of it.

"What's your name?"

The girl was silent.

"My name is Moriko. I want to get out of here too, but it's very hard, and I'll need your help. The people who are here, and the person you are about to meet, are very strong."

It was a white lie. The girl couldn't help Moriko escape the monastery, but if it helped her open up, to trust at least one person, it was worth it. The girl weighed the new information, debating whether or not she wanted to trust Moriko. She was young and desperate for an ally. She trusted Moriko despite her wariness.

"My name is Aina."

"That's a beautiful name, Aina. I have to take you to the person who runs this monastery now. If I don't, I'm going to get into a lot of trouble. He's not a good person, but he's not going to hurt you, ok? I'll be with you the entire time. It will only take a little while, and then you'll be able to go find a spot to rest for the rest of the day."

Aina nodded. Once she made the decision to trust Moriko, it was clear she would do anything Moriko said without complaint. Moriko went back on her own assessment. Maybe there would be a way to use someone who trusted her. She went through possibilities in her mind, but the only solutions she came up with involved betrayal of that trust, which she wouldn't allow.

Her mind embroiled in thought, Moriko went through the procedure of introducing and presenting Aina to the Abbot. The

Abbot, although happy to show off his power to a new student who could sense what he was doing, was otherwise distracted, and went through the formal motions quickly and without fanfare. Moriko had expected a small interview, similar to the one she had gone through when she had been presented, but there was none of that today. Aina was introduced, the Abbot welcomed her, and then she was let go.

Moriko brought Aina to the quarters of the monastery and introduced her to a small room where the youngest of the monks lived. Her introduction to the rest of the trainees made her think that perhaps having Aina's trust wasn't such a good thing for Aina. The moment Moriko walked into the room everything became quiet, and the other students seemed to shy away from Aina.

Moriko took the hint and wished Aina well and left as soon as possible. Hopefully the other girls would look after her despite Moriko's introductions. The girl seemed intelligent, so perhaps she would be able to make her own way. It took time, it always did.

Moriko was lost in thought as she wandered back to her own quarters. She wasn't sure of anything anymore. Even Orochi's training made her feel a little sick to her stomach, now that she looked at it through the lens of her childhood dreams. She wondered how she had become part of the system she had feared and hated so much as a child. Was she any better, or any different than the Abbot, or even Goro?

She had seen children taken and had done nothing about it. She hadn't even cared. She had been too wrapped up in her own problems and her own pain. She had become that which she sought to destroy. She fingered the scar on her abdomen. She couldn't lose her hatred of the monastery even if she knew nothing else.

Never again, she vowed. She had to think, to find her purpose. Orochi and the monastery had given her the training to harness an incredible power. Now she had to figure out how to use it. While she didn't know her final decision, she was certain she would make Goro and the Abbot pay for their sins.

Late that night as the candles burned low, two men huddled together in the Abbot's quarters. Goro was ecstatic. The incident with Moriko brought him closer to the Abbot than ever. Goro had long ago realized he did not have any special powers or abilities and consoled himself with the fact that no one else in his cohort did either. He believed the way to rise above was to befriend and be close to the Abbot.

For so many cycles he had tried, patiently listening to every command, every teaching, seizing every small opportunity to prove his worth to the Abbot, but the Abbot had never seemed to recognize him, never seen him as anything more than a loyal servant. But Goro maintained his vigilance and his dedication.

It all changed the day Moriko had bested him. It was strange that such an obvious, incredible failure would have been the gateway to the fulfillment of Goro's dreams, but it was. Ever since then Goro was the person the Abbot confided in. Their conferences grew in frequency and duration, culminating in regular nightly sessions when Orochi arrived.

Tonight was no different. They thought Moriko was sleeping, but no longer trusted their own senses, even the Abbot, whose command of the sense made him unique among monks. So they huddled together, whispering about the day's events, peeking around to ensure they were alone.

"Master, did you sense what happened today? Moriko, she . . ."

The Abbot interrupted. "Yes, Goro, I sensed the entire thing." He didn't feel the need to add he had lost his sense of Moriko when she went to sneak behind Goro. "What she did was unacceptable."

"What will we do, Master?"

The Abbot flinched at the use of the word "we," but kept himself calm. "I cannot allow this behavior to continue, but she is the favored student of Orochi, who has the ear of Akira. I cannot slay her for any minor transgression as much as I might want to."

Goro hung on to every word. Perhaps he would have some role to play, something that would cement his worth in the Abbot's eyes.

As he hoped, the Abbot looked at him, realization dawning as a plan began to form in his mind.

"Brother Goro, what we need is for her to commit a transgression, an act so heinous that we have no choice but to kill her." He looked meaningfully at Goro. "I think that you will have an important role to play in this, Goro."

"In the meantime, this will take me a while to put into place. Until then, Goro, I'd like you to individually take over the training of Aina. I believe she has incredible promise, and you are the only one I trust in this matter. Train her using whatever methods you deem appropriate."

Warmth flooded through Goro. After all of these cycles, being treated just the same as everyone else, not being unique or special, here was a task he could do. Someday, when the Abbot was ready, he would help get rid of Moriko as well. He left the Abbot's company feeling excited and thrilled.

As he left the Abbot laughed softly to himself. With his hand free to train how he pleased, Goro would attract Moriko's attention. She would kill him quickly and then the Abbot would be left with the perfect excuse for killing her himself. Then he would be rid of Goro and Moriko. Two heads would roll with one strike.

CHAPTER 19

Ryuu, Takako, and Shigeru did not stay much longer at the farmhouse. After Shigeru finished his story they prepared to leave the next day. They no longer bothered to travel at night. All time was valuable to them now. The one who was hunting them could track them day or night.

Shigeru rested and healed for one last night while Ryuu kept watch. Through the entire night all he did was stretch out his sense to detect anything that felt like Orochi. It was a new experience. For the first time in many cycles he felt powerless, naked without the protection his sense afforded him.

That someone could track him, use the same gifts he possessed, and he couldn't do the same, was humbling. He knew what fear was. Enough knowledge to realize what he was up against and how dangerous his opponent was, but not enough knowledge to do anything about it. Ryuu was unable to sleep the entire night.

He came to two decisions through the long hours of the dawn. The first was that if he was ever given the chance he would visit the same terror on those who sought to harm him. Orochi was teaching him how to hunt man, a skill Shigeru had never taught him. Shigeru was a man of honor and principle. He fought in a straightforward manner, always attacking his opponents and challenges head on. But now Ryuu knew a different way. A man who survived and thrived based on his ability to hide, to blend, to be non-existent.

He also vowed that he would continue to train, study, and be diligent. He needed to seek out all kinds of warriors to become a complete fighter. He felt like Orochi was better equipped, better trained and more dangerous than him. He needed to learn more so he could fight Orochi on equal terms, to never be caught off-guard again, to understand everything about the world.

They traveled and they trained. Despite their best efforts they made slow time. Takako was weak and Ryuu was all too happy to plead her case. When they rested Shigeru healed. They were good days. They hiked while the sun was up. Ryuu pestered Shigeru with hundreds of questions, trying to dig out every last piece of knowledge Shigeru held. At night he learned how to prepare food from Takako. Shigeru had taught him, but Takako's skills surpassed both of the men she was traveling with. They would sit around the fire and tell stories.

For a while it felt like they might it out alive. But Orochi found them again.

Ryuu had been sitting watch all night. It had been his practice as Shigeru continued to recover from his injuries. He couldn't do it every night, but he could and did more often than he should. As the dawn began to brighten the sky Ryuu knew. He couldn't sense anything, but he knew.

Shigeru awoke and saw the look on Ryuu's face. There wasn't any need for words to understand Ryuu's expression.

"You could have woken me."

Ryuu stood up, stretching his stiff legs. "I wouldn't have slept anyway. You needed the rest to recover."

Shigeru didn't deny the truth of the statement. "Did you sense anything?"

"No."

Shigeru arched an eyebrow. He knew there was more.

"I know he is on his way here. I can't explain how I know, but I'm certain." He glanced over at Takako, "I'm afraid we can't outrun him."

Shigeru nodded. It seemed to Ryuu that Shigeru had already made a decision and was just waiting for the right time to tell him.

"We aren't going to run from him. He's got our scent. We might evade him for a day or two or experience another narrow escape, but he will never stop. There is no point in trying to prolong the inevitable. We'll wait here and take turns on watch. With his retainers dead, I suspect he will have collected reinforcements, and is on his way back. Fighting him is our only way out of this."

Ryuu wanted to protest, to claim there had to be a better way, but deep down he knew Shigeru was right. This close to his target, a man like Orochi would never stop, would never give up pursuit. Ryuu wished he had never rescued Takako. That he hadn't brought this upon all of them.

Shigeru, as always, seemed to be looking right into him. "Don't blame yourself. It's true these are the consequences of the actions you took. But it's more important that what you did was right. You stood up for someone who needed help. It's more than I can say I've done. If we die, it's as proud warriors. There is no dishonor in that."

Ryuu wanted to scream at Shigeru for talking that way. All he wanted was to go back to the old cabin, to run in the woods and spar with Shigeru. He imagined the spring breeze on his face and the freezing beauty of the nearby waterfall. It felt like he would never go back again.

"What if I'm wrong? What if Orochi isn't on his way and we just sitting here instead of being on the move?"

"You're not wrong. I've trained you well, and honestly, you are and will be a much stronger nightblade than me. I've known for a while now. I can only teach you two more lessons. The first is to trust your instincts. Your mastery of the sense is superb, and if your instincts are telling you something, believe them, because I can guarantee they are right. Second, don't let consequences deter you from what you feel must be done. Saving Takako was the right thing. I won't sit here and lie to you and tell you life will be better for you doing the right thing, but you will be a better person, and that's all I've ever wanted."

Ryuu was flooded with questions and things he wanted to say. There was so much that he wanted to let Shigeru know, how important he was and how much he meant, but there was just nothing that would come out. He nodded and stared into Shigeru's eyes. He knew. It was enough.

Shigeru embraced Ryuu tightly, completely catching him off-guard. Ryuu felt like he was losing his father all over again.

After a few beats of silence, the two separated and got on with the daily chores of living. They went through their morning exercises together and spent some time sparring, both to warm up and for Shigeru to test his recovery. He wasn't quite at his best, but he was strong.

Takako woke up refreshed and Ryuu was delighted to watch her as she set about cooking them a lunch from the food she could scrounge together. The three of them sat around, sharing stories of their lives and laughing. Takako welcomed the rest day. They didn't have the heart to tell her the real reason for the rest.

Ryuu realized Shigeru thought of this as the end. He saw the way Shigeru was trying to squeeze all the enjoyment, all the memories he could out of these last few moments of life, the same way you would twist a rag to get the last few drops of water out of it.

Ryuu couldn't bring himself to accept it. Through all his training, Shigeru had pounded it into his head that warriors needed to embrace death, to be ready for it every day. But Ryuu wasn't. He wanted to live and spend every moment with Takako and Shigeru. He knew Shigeru was right, but it didn't change his feelings. He wasn't ready to die, and couldn't picture a future where he would be.

The sun was setting when Ryuu sensed them. They were on horseback moving fast. Ryuu tracked them with great interest. On the edge of his sense, as far as he could push it out, they had not been heading straight for them. They had been following a meandering course. It was only when their course brought them a little closer that all the horses and men turned to come to them.

It was valuable information. Ryuu's sense extended further than Orochi's. He noted the distances. If they lived through this day it may come in handy.

They came directly for the hut without slowing down. It was another five men plus Orochi. Ryuu turned to Shigeru.

"Why does he only bring five?"

Shigeru shrugged. "He may not have access to more. I suspect though he doesn't intend to overpower us with the other men he brings along. He knows he can only kill us himself. The other men are a distraction so he doesn't have to fight both of us at the same time. He may or may not be stronger than either of us individually, but he isn't stronger than the two of us attacking together."

Ryuu nodded. He supposed the why wasn't really important. A lecture from Shigeru sprang to his mind about not worrying too much about how events had come to be or how they would play out. Both were unknowable and not worth wasting time over.

They directed Takako behind the cabin. Ryuu had to give her credit. She took the news with a surprising calm. The cabin was large enough no one could sneak behind it without notice, but also left her room to start running if she needed. The two of them stood out in front of the farmhouse, waiting patiently.

They didn't have to wait long, and it was clear from the outset their attackers weren't interested in a fair fight. A small flurry of arrows came at them as soon as they were in range. Ryuu and Shigeru could sense them coming and sidestepped the dangerous ones without a challenge.

Then the battle was joined in earnest. As the approaching men became more visible Ryuu saw they had the same armor and insignia as the soldiers they had fought and killed earlier. The observation passed through his mind like water as he moved to defend against the horses bearing down on him.

The men were well trained and their intent was clear. The five soldiers who accompanied Orochi were all bearing towards him and Orochi was going after Shigeru. It was the first time Ryuu had seen Orochi and the sight of him was enough for Ryuu to lose his composure for a heartbeat. He had never seen anyone so intimidating. The man was huge and muscled. It was just a glance, but enough to make Ryuu's heart sink down to his stomach which was tied up in knots.

The soldiers had no interest in fighting one-to-one duels. They kept to their horses and charged at Ryuu. Fear ran through him. He had never had to fight men on horseback. Shigeru had trained him and he was familiar with the theory, but theory wasn't combat.

With just moments to go before they reached him his training took over. His mind went blank. He expanded his sense and drew his sword. As he settled into his stance he had a sensation he had never felt before. Everything seemed to come together in his mind. He saw the strikes and his responses and moved smoothly into combat.

The sensation was a powerful drug. A sense of control flowed through him, and while he didn't feel invincible, he knew he could beat his opponents. He was cut, not deep, but he had known the cuts were coming and knew taking a small cut prevented an opening in his defense later. He didn't feel the blade as it sliced through his skin. He kept pushing forward, always moving, always cutting and blocking.

As he made his final cut, he snapped out of the flow. As he gathered his senses, the first information he processed was that Orochi and Shigeru hadn't begun their fight. He had traveled some distance and was a good twenty paces away from them. They had been observing him, maintaining a safe three-pace distance between themselves. Both seemed somewhat taken aback, but Ryuu didn't know why.

Before he could figure it out, they turned to each other and bowed. Ryuu frowned. After his fight, he didn't expect to see a duel between the two. He flicked his blade, flinging the fresh blood off, and debated moving towards the battle. Fear and curiosity rooted him in place. But Shigeru needed his help. His attitude had been that he couldn't beat Orochi, not alone.

Ryuu tried to attain the same state, the same sense of peace and calm he held when he had fought against the five warriors.

He could feel it on the edges of his ability, but the more he tried to grasp it, the more it slipped away from him.

Ryuu was torn, unable to decide whether or not to help. He desperately wanted to, but he was so afraid. There wasn't enough time to think. He had never shied away from Shigeru's blade or the blades of the opponents he had fought thus far. In previous fights he had been confident, and the confidence gave him strength. He didn't know with Orochi.

Ripped apart by his fear, he couldn't move even as he sensed their duel was about to begin. He couldn't tell what was going to happen. He knew Shigeru was about to strike, could read it in everything from the tension in his muscles to the way his stance subtly shifted.

Ryuu didn't know a thing about Orochi. He couldn't tell if he was about to strike or defend. He seemed empty. Ryuu couldn't tell if his stance had shifted. His stance was neutral and relaxed, poised in a manner that could mean anything. He tried to read Orochi with his sense but couldn't get any information.

His doubts slipped away as they sprang into motion. Ryuu had never seen a battle between two nightblades before. There was no way of seeing his fights with Shigeru from an outsider's perspective. They both moved with incredible speed, but the aspect of the fight that first caught Ryuu's attention was that Shigeru wasn't moving any faster than Ryuu had ever seen. Just for a flash, for a moment, he was proud he had seen Shigeru's best.

But Orochi was faster. It wasn't obvious at first. The difference was by less than a hair, but it would be enough. Eventually Orochi would create an opening Shigeru could not block.

The knowledge moved him forward by one step before he hesitated, unable to move further. His heart and mind screamed at him to move, to save the man who had been his father, but from somewhere deep within, he knew, knew like the sun would rise tomorrow, that it was wrong to step into the fray. No words could describe it, but he felt his soul rebel against the right thing to do.

When the moment came, it came so fast Ryuu barely noticed it, a flicker of the blade in the waning twilight, but then it was over. The two combatants stood in the shadows of the tree, frozen like a painting. As his vision cleared, Ryuu saw the blades, one in Shigeru's chest, one in Orochi's. Then he saw more clearly and saw that Shigeru's wound was fatal, Orochi's wasn't.

Ryuu felt the ground shake underneath his feet, and he fell to his knees. He thought he was crying, but his vision was clear. While his heart broke his mind calmly raced through the facts. He wanted to cry, to break down and weep and curl under a blanket and never show his face to the world again. The world had taken everyone he cared about, everyone he had loved, and had killed them, brutally, in front of him, time and time again.

Shigeru's last act was to turn his head towards Ryuu, and Ryuu saw, or thought he saw, a hint of a grin, the characteristic upturned lip that signified happiness for Shigeru. Ryuu immediately saw his mother, dying, smiling, crystal clear like he hadn't seen her in his dreams for almost ten cycles. He still remembered her, and he knew he would remember Shigeru just as well.

It wasn't what Ryuu saw, but what Ryuu felt that he didn't believe. Although Orochi had won, Shigeru was at peace. His sense was clear, and he had no regrets, no sorrow, no hesitation. It was as if he had been trying to achieve death this entire time and had finally reached his goal. Orochi, who would see the sun rise tomorrow, was filled with terror, anger, hatred, and jealousy.

Ryuu couldn't process it fast enough. As half his mind worked at processing the scene in front of him, the other half was planning ahead. Orochi was wounded, but still strong. Shigeru was dying, dead, and Takako was hiding behind the house, unaware of what had just taken place, scared out of her wits as the silence after the battle descended on the field. She would be waiting for him. He thought he could beat Orochi, maybe, if he attacked now.

Shigeru gestured with his head. He wanted Ryuu to leave. Ryuu shook himself. He couldn't. He wouldn't. But Shigeru repeated the gesture, that damn grin on his face.

The light went out in Shigeru's eyes and Ryuu's decision was made. Shigeru had always been right. He should listen. He stood up and took a long look at Orochi and then turned his back. Orochi's time was not today. Somehow, he knew this. He knew he needed to protect Takako more than he needed to kill Orochi.

Ryuu didn't run, but walked behind the farm, pleasant memories invading the darkness of his heart. He let Orochi watch him take Takako's hand, mount a couple of their would-be assassins' horses and ride away as the darkness fell over the field. He did not know what Orochi would do, but the choice was now in his hands.

Orochi did not pursue.

The pain of the sword was worse than anything he had experienced before, but he was able to push it down and away from his mind. It could be dealt with later. Right now there was the problem of the boy. He, like Shigeru, had felt the boy's powers expand during the fight. The five should have occupied him at least until he could have arrived. But they were dead before he even drew his sword.

The boy was stronger than Shigeru, but it seemed like even Shigeru hadn't known by how much. Perhaps even stronger than him. How had he learned the technique? Shigeru hadn't known it, had never learned it. Or had he, somehow in his cycles of isolation, managed to figure it out?

Orochi weighed his options. He was wounded and not at full strength. If the boy summoned the power again, Orochi would not stand a chance. He had killed Shigeru, and that was enough for him today. Summoning his strength, he cut Shigeru's head from its body. He would present it to Akira as a token of his progress.

The boy's day was another day.

CHAPTER 20

In the midst of the darkness Takako clung to her horse. Like most girls born and raised in her village she had ridden ponies at fairs. But they had been well-tamed and old and wouldn't have galloped no matter the incentive.

The horse she was on now was as different to those ponies as fire was to water. This horse was large and strong and didn't seem to know any other speed than gallop. But Ryuu had rushed her straight to the horse, and she had gotten on without question. Something in the urgency and tone of his voice conveyed how important it was she got on the horse. She was saved by the fact the horse seemed to be well-trained, bearing its unskilled rider with ease.

As branches whipped past her face, her memory returned to the events at the farmhouse. Ryuu's demeanor had done nothing to ease the terror that had been crawling through her mind since the sun had set. Although she couldn't understand Shigeru as well as Ryuu could, it was obvious he was a man on edge. Given his particular skill set, it meant Orochi was a dangerous man indeed.

Hiding behind the house in silence had terrified her. These people could tell where she was without seeing her. What was the point of being behind a house? Ryuu had just had time to tell her it was for her protection. But she didn't understand. How could the house protect her if Shigeru and Ryuu lost? Her life was forfeit.

For just a moment she flashed back to her time in Akio's tent. She had been scared then, but not for her life like she was now. Perhaps it was better to be back there, to never have allowed Ryuu to come and rescue her. She didn't know much of what was happening around her, but she wasn't sure she was any better off today.

The sharp clang of steel on steel brought her attention crashing back to the present. There was no point in worrying about the future until this moment was dealt with. Her urge to peek around the corner of the cabin was unbearable, but Ryuu had cautioned against it. He explained that Orochi would be the only one who could sense her. Even if they failed but killed Orochi, she might be safe from the others with him. If she was out of sight of the battle there would be no way for an arrow to find her either. Takako accepted the logic. Her desire for safety overpowered her desire to see the outcome of the battle.

The sound of the sword fighting rang through the clear, crisp air of the early evening. Without any warning, silence fell over the field, a sacred silence denoting forever that this field grew over the graves of men.

The silence stretched on and on, but no one called for her, no one came for her. It must have only been moments, but each breath felt like she had lived an entire lifetime. Still nothing. She knew the smart action was to hide deeper in the grass, to make herself as invisible as possible, but she could not do it. She had to know what happened, how the story ended.

She picked her way to edge of the cabin, trying to make as little noise as possible in case one of their enemies was nearby.

She crouched down low and moved her head out into the open. Almost immediately she saw Shigeru standing next to an opponent. Although they had never met she knew this man was Orochi. He was one of the largest men Takako had ever seen, and he was built like an outcropping of rock. One glance and she knew they were doomed.

From her vantage point she couldn't see Ryuu. There was no evidence of a battle anywhere in her field of view, and she assumed the battle had happened separate from the match before her. She would have to move further out from the cabin to see the result.

She dreaded the worst. If Ryuu had won, he would be near her, or by Shigeru helping him fight Orochi. The only explanation that made any sense was that he had lost or was unable to move, severely injured. Takako wasn't sure she was up to trying to heal him. Blood and guts had never been her thing.

The movement of swords brought her attention back to matters at hand. Even having watched Shigeru and Ryuu spar, she could never believe the full speed of these men fighting.

She didn't expect it to end so suddenly. In all the adventures she had read the battle waged for what felt like an eternity. Perhaps to those who were fighting, it was true. For Takako, watching the battle, it seemed to go by much faster than she could process it. They moved so fast she couldn't have said at any point in time if someone was winning or losing.

It took her a moment to understand why the fighting had stopped. They had been moving so fluidly, so quickly, it was difficult to understand how it all just ended. It took one of the last rays of the sun striking the scene to illuminate Takako's mind. She saw the glint of the sword in Shigeru's back. He had been run through, the point of the sword sticking straight through his back.

Takako's mind raced and she couldn't grasp onto any one thought. There was the shock of the defeat. Her time with Shigeru and Ryuu had made her a believer, a believer that these two men were the strongest fighters that existed. The belief was punctured by the sword through Shigeru's torso. There was the fear. She still didn't see Ryuu anywhere, and she assumed he had met the same fate as his mentor. It meant she was next. If Orochi was still alive he could find her anywhere. There was no way to hide from him, no way to hide from anyone with the sense.

She breathed, trying to hold on to one consistent thought, something she could wrap her mind around. Unbidden, a memory sprang to the forefront of her mind. Sharing candy with her father in New Haven. She hadn't understood it then, but that was the hardest thing he had ever done. She remembered the sadness in his face. She wondered if he had changed, if he had paid his debts and solved his gambling problem. It was pleasant to think he had.

The grasp of a familiar hand on her shoulder shook her out of her reverie. It was Ryuu, motioning her towards two of the horses that were now riderless. Takako's peaceful reverie had been interrupted so quickly it took her a moment to process that he was still alive, and although he was covered with blood, he was moving without hesitation or any faltering in his step. He was apparently unharmed, or at least not anything serious.

Without the ability to process what was happening, she followed his lead out onto the horses. She took a glance at Orochi, who was watching them but not moving. She saw a glint of steel and saw he too had been impaled. She dared to hope, but Ryuu's attitude led her to believe their plight wasn't over. They were on the horses and moving before she could ask any questions.

The evening was cold, and Takako was not dressed for riding. The dry wind cut through her thin clothes. Ryuu didn't stop to check on her, so lost in his own thoughts. She refused to complain, enduring the long cold ride in silence. Eventually they stopped deep in some woods.

As they were setting up camp Takako got her first glance at Ryuu since the farmhouse. His face showed clear signs he had been crying, but he was doing his best to stay strong. Takako elected not to mention it, nor offer any overt signs of sympathy. Instinctively, she knew that even though comfort was what he needed most, it was also what he would least accept.

In short order Ryuu got a small fire started which Takako huddled close to. She could have jumped into the fire. Shooting pains emanated from her extremities as they warmed up from the edge of frostbite. She didn't understand how Ryuu could be warm, but he maintained a safe distance from the fire, or perhaps it was a safe distance from her.

In the flickering firelight, Takako was reminded just how young Ryuu was. He had only seen seventeen cycles, and although he had killed numerous times, he was still a stranger to the horror of warfare. He had been raised by a man trying to protect him from the world. She wasn't much older, but was more aware of the filth of the world. The actions one person took towards another no longer surprised her.

As the fire continued to burn Ryuu remained silent. Takako thought about going to him and trying to hold him, but his attitude encouraged no kindness and she wasn't disposed to dispense it either. She found out Shigeru had been a rock for her, a shield to protect her from Ryuu's emotions. How would he behave now that his master, his father, was dead? She wasn't sure she should stay to find out.

Despite her indecision it did not take long for the events of the past day to catch up to her. She put her head down and was asleep in a heartbeat.

When she awoke Ryuu was still awake, tending to the fire. Looking around, Takako saw it was mid-afternoon already. Considering she had fallen asleep sometime just before dawn, she had slept for quite a while which explained why she felt so well-rested.

Ryuu looked the opposite. He had visible bags under his eyes and Takako could see the evidence of tears still on his cheeks. She thought he might fall into the fire at any time. He hadn't slept at all. It occurred to her that he hadn't slept at all the night previous either. He had kept the watch all night so Shigeru could get as much rest as possible before the fight. Today was his third full day without sleep.

Takako didn't know what to say. She knew they would be traveling through the night. It was the same pattern they had followed when they were on the run from the army's search. It would mean another night without sleep for Ryuu, but she knew without having to ask him about it they had to keep moving.

As evening came they broke their impromptu camp and got back on the horses. Takako worried about what was coming. She needed to know what was next, what their plan was, whether or not Ryuu wanted to talk about it.

"Ryuu, where are we going?"

He turned towards her as if dazed. She began to wonder, not for the first time since waking, if he was any use to her at all in this state.

"There are some thick woods, very uninhabited, about two days ride northwest of here. Shigeru told me about them once when I was young. It's a very old wood, it will protect us."

His answer did little to reassure her. An old wood would protect them? It sounded like Ryuu was beginning to believe in old wives' tales and myths created to scare children from going into the woods. Perhaps he was too tired to be able to lead them. Could she come up with a better plan?

But then she realized she had been living in an old wives' tale for several moons now. She had accepted the fact that nightblades did in fact exist. She sometimes forgot they had been nothing but legends a cycle ago.

They rode through the night, Takako keeping a close eye on Ryuu. He was slumped on his horse, doing little more than pointing it in the general direction and holding on. Eventually she rode in front of him and tied the bridle of his horse onto the back of her saddle, guiding both horses as he struggled to stay awake.

To her amazement he made it through the night, and as dawn began to break they found another well-hidden spot where they could build a fire without being seen. Ryuu started to move around again, a short, desperate burst of energy to help Takako set up their camp. It was late fall, and even though the days were still somewhat warm, they needed a fire if they were to sleep comfortably.

Ryuu helped get the fire started, lay down and promptly fell asleep. Takako was surprised he had lasted as long as he had. Three straight days he had been up with no food. The thought of food made her stomach growl in anger, but she managed to suppress it. If Ryuu slept through the day, he would wake up able to hunt and catch food. It would be another day, but she would be fine. Despite the hunger pains and the headaches, she knew her body wouldn't give out before then.

Throughout the day Takako kept the fire going and found handfuls of late-season berries scattered around. She ate about half of what she found, which didn't help ease her hunger at all, but still seemed better than nothing. She left the rest for Ryuu when he awoke.

He didn't stir until it was well past dusk. Takako had decided for both of them they weren't going to move this night. They needed time to rest, to recover, to decide what was next. They needed sleep and food. Ryuu was initially upset that she hadn't woken him up earlier, but she stood by her decision, and he came to her way of thinking.

Ryuu went out hunting and came back with two rabbits which were promptly skinned and cooked. Ryuu reminded her to eat just a bit at a time, which was excellent advice. She filled up fast, and it was only then she brought herself to ask the questions which had been on her mind since the hut.

Ryuu told her what had happened, how the soldiers and Orochi had come and how he had managed to take out the five soldiers with little difficulty. But when he got to the battle between Orochi and Shigeru, he faltered. Takako remained silent, allowing him to tell the story at his own pace.

"I couldn't do it. Every single fiber in my body wanted nothing but to go help Shigeru, but I couldn't move. It was like I had stood still for just a breath too long and roots had grown out of my feet. I've tried to rationalize it a hundred ways since then. I don't know if I was scared or if it was something else. I can't even tell if it was fear that rooted me in place. But when Shigeru needed me, I sat back and watched him die."

"You can't think like that, Ryuu. It will do you no good."

Something broke in Ryuu. "But you don't understand. Everything – everything that has happened has been my fault. Because of my actions, your family and everyone who you cared for is dead. Shigeru, the man who gave me everything, is also dead because of what I did. Everyone I care about, everyone I've tried to help, has only ended up dying. If not for me, everyone would be happy and alive right now."

Takako wanted to tell him it would be okay. She wanted to tell him he was right, that he had done the right thing. A part of her respected this boy who had sacrificed everything because he had felt she was wronged. But images of her family flashed through her mind and she couldn't offer the comfort he needed. His actions had killed her family.

She watched in silence as Ryuu struggled through the consequences of his actions. Part of her wanted him to suffer, but part wanted to come to his aid. She hadn't ever felt so torn about her actions before. Her hopeful side won out, just as it always did.

"I forgive you." The words hurt to say, but for a moment she believed them. She couldn't forget, but she could forgive.

A sudden glint of fire sparked in Ryuu's eyes. "I love you," he burst.

Takako held her laughter. Those three words had been uttered often at Madame's, and such men were often the object of ridicule when they were gone. Ryuu had never sounded more like a seventeen-cycle boy. She shook her head. "I know you do."

She stood up and kissed him gently on the forehead. She saw the spark of lust in his eyes, and just for a moment she knew he was thinking of taking her. He had the strength to. She wasn't even sure she'd struggle. But he didn't, and more than anything, that won her over. She embraced him for a moment and went to bed.

Takako awoke to the sound of movement nearby. It was Ryuu just waking up.

That morning they packed up camp, and on the surface everything regained an air of normalcy. Ryuu acted more confident. He had made his plan and could take action.

The next two days went as smooth as running and hiding could go. Ryuu would range far and wide, often leaving the second horse to Takako's care. He would hunt, bring back small game and plants to eat. Takako used the skills she had learned to make the best meals possible considering the circumstances.

Takako attempted to keep a respectful distance from Ryuu. She was uncertain of everything between them and felt it was best not to encourage any affection more than necessary. For his part, Ryuu seemed content not to make any approaches.

As they traveled, Takako realized Ryuu had been right. The forest they were entering was an old forest. They came to areas where the trees grew well above their heads. Ryuu would stop often to rest and to meditate. Takako asked him about it once.

"This forest is more alive than most places I have been. Small animals, birds, the trees release a strong energy. When I sit and meditate, I can sense it all. This place is old, but it is more alive than a city."

Takako begrudgingly admitted that she understood what Ryuu was talking about. Even though she didn't possess the sense there was an atmosphere about this place, an energy she didn't understand but was comforted by. She could see why Ryuu would choose this spot as an area to recuperate.

Just before they entered the heart of the forest, they came upon a small home. There was one family inside, a tree-harvester and his family. Takako was surprised Ryuu had come up to them and didn't work his way around them, but it made more sense when he went to the house and requested to trade. He had skins, some hard-to-find healing plants, and some meat, and was able to trade for a number of necessities for surviving the winter months.

His purchases made Takako wonder how long they were planning on staying in the forest. She had assumed that at most they would be in hiding for a moon as they figured out what their long-term plan would be. It looked like Ryuu might be planning to stay for longer than that. It made her wonder what she would do next.

CHAPTER 21

Moriko was concerned. It had been several moons since Orochi had left and there hadn't been a whisper in the monastery regarding his return. Despite her complex relationship with him she found she missed his guidance. When he had been present she had a purpose. Since his departure she had wavered many times, unsure of the path she was choosing.

Moriko couldn't decide how she felt about the monastery. It perpetrated great harm. The monks took children away from their families forever. It was run by an Abbot obsessed with increasing his political power. And power always attracted sycophantic demons like Goro.

But there were others, and as Moriko struck up conversations with them she discovered a different side to the monastery. No one was overjoyed by having been taken from their families, but many of them believed it was a necessary evil.

When Moriko questioned people about this the answer was always the same. The monks were the first line of defense against the nightblades and the repositories of knowledge and order in the Three Kingdoms. It was a sacrifice, but a sacrifice for the Three Kingdoms. The benefit was worth the cost.

Moriko wasn't convinced the nightblades were as evil as they were portrayed. Orochi was one. She was as well. She didn't think she was any more evil than the next person.

There was something to be said about being the repository of knowledge and order in the Kingdom. Moriko never would have been taught to read outside the monastery, never would have learned the true history of the Kingdom.

Maybe the Kingdom needed the monasteries as it moved into the future. Yes, there were evil people here, but there were evil people everywhere, and it wasn't fair to judge the whole monastery by the actions of the few she hated.

While her thoughts on the monastery fluctuated, her thoughts on Goro and the Abbot never did. Moriko could already see the Abbot's plan. Goro had almost been prancing towards her when he told her the news. He had been personally selected to oversee the training of Aina. The Abbot believed Aina possessed special powers and Goro was the only one in the monastery capable bringing these powers to fruition. Goro might as well have claimed that the sun was brown.

The Abbot wanted her gone, killed most likely, but he couldn't do that without fear of consequence. She was Orochi's student, and Orochi reported to Akira, who could have the monastery razed while the monks slept comfortably inside. So long as she did no wrong, she was untouchable.

The plan was obvious, but Goro had no idea. The poor man believed everything the Abbot said. Some days Moriko wondered if the Abbot was hoping she would kill Goro.

The problem was Moriko wasn't sure the Abbot wouldn't succeed even though she saw it coming. She was on the edge day after day. Goro was cruel to Aina, even to the point of some of the other monks bringing their concern to the Abbot. But the

Abbot fed them all the same story. Goro was chosen because he was uniquely qualified to reach this girl. The monks did nothing to stop the physical and mental abuse Goro gladly heaped upon the young girl. The Abbot's word was final. Moriko was the only example any aspiring monk needed.

One unintended consequence of the Abbot's decision was that it helped bring Moriko back into the fold of the monastery. Several monks came to her to talk about Goro's training. There seemed to be some sort of unspoken belief that Moriko would be able to do something about it.

Moriko was thankful for being accepted back into the community, even if the weakness of the monks angered her. The loneliness of isolation was difficult to bear, and she accepted whatever small inroads of peace were offered to her. She wasn't one of them yet, but every interaction helped.

She didn't know how to proceed. It was clear Aina's trust in her was waning as Goro's training continued unabated. Moriko did everything she could to ease the wounds and the pain, but the girl was coming to the conclusion that Moriko wouldn't actively oppose Goro. In the little girl's mind Moriko was part of the problem, not a part of the solution.

It pained Moriko to think Aina might be right. She hadn't done anything to help the girl besides small, meaningless gestures.

Moriko's dam of emotions finally broke one afternoon in the courtyard. Try as she might, she couldn't always avoid Goro's lessons. It was a cold afternoon, and a thin layer of snow had fallen the night before. Moriko had been off the monastery's premises hunting, a new privilege which she used to her greatest advantage. She came back with a number of small hares, satisfied with her hunt.

She sensed the two of them in the courtyard. Goro was attempting to train Aina in some sword techniques, but to the uneducated observer it probably looked more like he was beating a girl with a stick.

Goro's eyes widened a fraction when he saw Moriko. She had become used to walking everywhere masking herself, but Goro hadn't gotten used to not being able to sense somebody around him. She understood the disorientation. Her first memories of Orochi would never fade.

Goro's shock faded, and he flashed her a malicious grin. He ordered Aina to block his strike. She got into an appropriate position, one any child of her age and training should have been congratulated on. Moriko was surprised to sense Goro's move. He was going to move fast to strike.

The cut wasn't a surprise to Moriko, but Aina had no chance to see it coming. It was a low cut which caught her underneath the rib cage, and she doubled down to the ground, face buried in the snow.

"Block the strike!" Goro shouted.

Moriko was having a tough time trusting her sense, but it all came true. Goro kicked the girl hard in the side she hadn't been struck in. She went tumbling backwards.

Goro spun the wooden blade in his right hand. Moriko couldn't believe, wouldn't believe what was happening in front of her. Although it was too early to sense his intent, her eyes told her more than enough. He would continue beating this girl as long as Moriko was watching.

Moriko wasn't the only one surprised. The other monks saw and sensed what was going on, but no one lifted a finger. No one said a word.

The trickle of anger exploded into a torrent of rage. She knew that taking action was falling right into the Abbot's trap, but she would no longer sit by for her own self preservation. Damn the consequences. If today was the day, so be it.

Goro raised his blade above his head in an attempt to strike Aina, but Moriko reached him first and held the wooden tip of the blade behind him, preventing him from making his cut.

Goro whirled around in anger and surprise. He hadn't sensed Moriko coming and the fury on his face was evident. His spin brought the blade with it, but Moriko was easily able to step to the side.

The two faced each other. Moriko contained herself, the fire in her belly threatening to consume her whole. But if Orochi had taught her nothing else, he had taught her control. It barely held, strained to the limit, but it held.

With anger in every word, Moriko whispered to Goro, "Don't ever touch the girl again."

Moriko was about to turn around, but Goro's pride wouldn't let him stay silent. "You've gone too far this time, Moriko. The Abbot will hear about this!"

It was too much. Moriko couldn't stand the sycophant anymore. She turned on him and grabbed him by his robes. He was taller than her, but she pulled his face down right next to hers. "You will keep your mouth shut. I am stronger than you, and will kill you without hesitation, before you even get a step closer to the Abbot's quarters. You will treat this girl the way you would any other monk."

Moriko turned away. She knew if she continued to talk she would strike him down.

She sensed his strike and sidestepped it. He moved in again to strike, and Moriko stepped into him. She grabbed his wrist and twisted it, disarming him while throwing him down. He rolled to his feet and drew his real blade. A silence descended in the courtyard. No one drew blades, not in the monastery.

Moriko held on to the wooden blade. Her blade was by her, as always, but she hoped that by fighting with the wooden one she wouldn't kill him. She wasn't too worried about Goro hitting her. She could sense each of his moves far in advance, and he couldn't use his own sense to try to block her.

Goro took two cuts. Moriko deflected one and dodged the other. His third cut was a little too hopeful, and he leaned forward slightly following his cut. Moriko used the opening and stepped in with a clean strike to the back of Goro's skull.

Goro tumbled to the ground. It took him a couple of breaths to get back up, but when he did, Moriko could see that he intended to finish it here. He attacked with an energy that sent Moriko back pedaling. She wasn't ready, and with the wooden sword she could only deflect his cuts. She didn't risk a full block for fear of the wood breaking.

Fear and anger started to get the best of her. It was too easy to make a mistake in this situation. She wasn't in control. She tried getting further away from him, but his rage drove him straight into her despite her best efforts.

Goro's blade cut straight into the wooden sword, slicing it in half, leaving a sharpened point where a gentle curve had been. Moriko's conscious mind was no longer in control, just the instincts trained into her over countless cycles. She felt the opening as he came up to strike and drove the wooden sword into his gut, fear and frustration causing her to shove him back as hard as she could.

He fell back to the ground and Moriko could see she had opened a gaping hole in his stomach. It looked like an intestine was trying to leak out, and Moriko knew that Goro was a walking dead man.

Goro hadn't figured it out yet, and that made it worse. She had never killed before, and this was a slow and torturous death. The mask of Goro dropped, and he became the little boy desperate for attention, not sure what was happening to him. He was trying to put the intestines back into his stomach, asking for the Abbot to come and help. A tear rolled down Moriko's cheek. Goro hadn't been an evil man, he had just been pathetic, without the strength to stand on his own.

Goro was nothing but a puppet and didn't deserve a slow death like this. She bent down and cradled his head while pulling out her short blade. She bowed her head in prayer and in a strong clear voice recited the final prayer for the monk who had stolen her from her family.

Goro stopped his blubbering and was looking up at her serenely. He seemed at peace, which was enough for Moriko. She tilted his head back and thrust the blade in under his chin, a quick and painless death.

Moriko saw the moment his soul left his body when the light behind his eyes went out. She had seen death before, but never so close. It sent a shock down her spine, threatening to root her in place.

She looked up and saw a cluster of monks around her. She recognized all of them and knew many of them had come up to her over the past moon to talk about Goro's behavior. As her eyes scanned the crowd she could see one or two monks slowly nodding to her. Perhaps not condoning the act, but at least accepting it as necessary.

She focused on the moment, just as Orochi had taught her. The Abbot was present, but in the heat of the battle she had lost track of her surroundings. The Abbot was the root of all of this. It began and ended with him.

The Abbot was in his quarters, aware of everything that was happening but not moving. He was waiting for her.

Moriko debated. She could call today complete and wait to see what type of justice came to her. On the other hand, delaying could give the Abbot time to bring everyone at the monastery to his side, reminding them of justice and the rules of the monastery. She had killed one of their own, which was punishable by death, but most of the monks were aware of the extenuating circumstances.

Moriko decided to trust in fate. She had rolled the dice by killing Goro, and now she needed to see where they landed. She didn't want to fight the Abbot one-on-one. She wanted him out in public, in front of everyone.

"Abbot!" she yelled at the top of her lungs.

For several breaths there was no movement, but in time Moriko felt the Abbot stir. He released his power, and he burned almost as bright as the sun in the sky. Moriko was prepared. Orochi had taught her how to control herself so the sense of him wouldn't blind her. She focused on Orochi's instructions and stood her ground.

The Abbot came out of his quarters, dressed in the loose fitting robes of the monastery. He walked towards the gathered crowd and paused about a dozen paces away from them. He observed the expressions of the monks, Moriko's stance, and Goro's red blood on the white snow. Moriko could see him taking it all in, calculating his next move. Moriko tried to take it away from him. She knew he hadn't become Abbot because of his strength alone.

"I have killed Goro, sir. I offered advice on his training methods and he struck at me. I disarmed him and he drew his real blade. In the midst of trying to defend myself, I executed a lethal blow. Any of the monks here can attest to the truth of these events."

The Abbot brushed her story aside. "You have killed a monk, and this is punishable by death. Do you wish to take your own life, or shall I do it for you?"

Moriko didn't stoop to his line of thinking. "This incident came about due to Goro's training methods. Methods you knew well about, yet allowed to continue. I attempted to remind Goro the methods of the monastery are as old as this Kingdom and needed to be honored. He attacked me. I defended myself. You foresaw this and yet did nothing to stop it."

The Abbot didn't try to defend himself. He looked among the assembled monks and saw they recognized the truth of Moriko's claim. A malicious impulse twisted the corner of his mouth into a smile.

"I see there are many here who agree with this girl's claims. My answer is thus: I am the power here, with knowledge and understanding which surpasses your own. My path may not be understood by all, but it is the path we must follow, or be lost forever. If any of you disagree, then step forward now!"

At the conclusion of his speech the Abbot let forth a sense-blast like Moriko had never experienced before. Every monk in the courtyard fell to their knees, overpowered by the force of energy emanating from the Abbot.

Moriko just barely stood her ground. Orochi's training had been effective, but she'd never had any practice, just the theory of it. Her first encounter with the Abbot's power was still enough to disorient her.

The Abbot moved in, blade in hand. Moriko fought, but her sense was overpowered by the sheer energy radiating from the Abbot. She was forced to fight by sight alone, and while she was well trained, the Abbot was in charge of the fight.

Moriko fought against overwhelming waves of helplessness. This battle was for her own life, but she couldn't focus enough to take control. She was left blocking by reflex the movements of the Abbot's blade, and she knew it would only be moments before the strategy failed.

She succeeded in putting some distance between her and the Abbot, and they each took a moment to appraise each other. The Abbot was still confident in his powers and had good reason to be. She hadn't done anything against him.

Moriko took a breath and focused herself. The Abbot's power was blinding, but she knew it could be worked around. She pushed the sense out of her mind, focusing on the present moment, dropping into a waiting stance. The Abbot didn't give her long to wait.

He sprinted forward, confident in his position. Moriko moved out of the way and cut at him. It was a hesitant cut, and the Abbot was able to deflect it, it had been a true counter attack. Moriko wasn't as helpless as she seemed. He gathered himself, and they began in earnest.

In three moves Moriko found an opening and struck, cutting deep into the Abbot's left arm. It wasn't a fatal cut, but it was painful, and the Abbot hadn't been cut in a very long time. He howled with rage and frustration, and without warning the full power of his energy struck Moriko.

She had thought she had seen everything the Abbot could do, but she had never seen him in a true rage. The waves of energy she had been able to push aside redoubled and filled her mind with fire. The other monks, already prostate on the ground, groaned and started having seizures. It took all her focus just to remain standing. She tried to advance, to step forward, to end it all, but it was hopeless. She couldn't think well enough to move.

The Abbot stepped near her, and with one move brought the hilt of his sword down hard on her head. Moriko's world, which had been filled with light and energy, abruptly went dark.

She was surprised when she awoke. She hadn't expected to be alive at all, but a small part of her knew being alive wasn't necessarily a good thing. Her belief was reinforced as she took a mental inventory of her body.

Overall, she wasn't in too bad of shape. Her head felt like it was ready to split open any moment, like her mind was too large for the skull it inhabited. But that wasn't going away anytime soon, so she'd have to deal with that.

One leather strap had been tied tightly in her mouth, gagging her. Her arms were tied behind her, tight enough she couldn't move at all. Not just her wrists either, but they had also tied her elbows close together. She tried flexing her muscles, but was completely incapacitated by the leather straps. The Abbot wasn't taking any chances. He knew she was stronger than before. Likewise, her legs had been tied both at the ankles and above the knees. Bearing the pain of looking down, she saw that the straps around her ankles were tied to a ring on the monastery wall.

It appeared running away wasn't going to be an option.

Glancing around, she saw that she was also under guard. Two of the monks stood a couple of paces away, watching her. There was hesitation in their eyes. The gag indicated she wasn't supposed to be speaking to them. The Abbot must have been worried about her inciting a bit of rebellion.

Moriko resigned herself to her situation, at least for a time. There was nothing to be done, and her head was ringing too much to be of any real use. Best to recover as much as she could for whatever was coming next. She knew it wouldn't be pleasant. He'd kept her alive to kill her in his own time, make her a symbol.

She didn't have long to wait. The next day the Abbot came forth and with the help of several monks, placed her up against the wall. They didn't even untie her legs, just her arms to tie her to the wall again. Her robe was ripped off, exposing the mass of scar tissue on her back, and the Abbot went to work.

The pain came over Moriko in waves, fire lashing up her back with the caress of the Abbot's work. Her scars re-opened, trickling blood down into the white snow. He never went in to finish the job. He just stood there, methodically tearing her back into shreds until her world went black yet again.

When she awoke she was in the Abbot's quarters. She was not gagged, but tied the same way she had been when she awoke the time previous. Her back was on fire, a situation not helped by the way her arms were tied behind her. They hadn't bothered redressing her. When she looked around, she knew why she wasn't gagged. The only person nearby was the Abbot who was bringing her stew and water.

He knelt in front of her and brought her mouth to the bowl. Moriko wasn't sure what the Abbot was up to, but she was so hungry and her mouth so dry she didn't care. She accepted without question.

The Abbot fed her the entire bowl and gave her plenty of water to drink. When she was done there was only one question. "Why?"

"Because, my dear, I want you to get better, to heal. Once you do, I will do it again, and heal you again, until some part of you breaks. Maybe it will be your body, maybe your mind, but you will break, and then I will have my satisfaction."

Moriko wanted to throw up, wanted to rid herself of the food, to starve herself instead of partaking in the torture, but she couldn't. The food was warm in her belly, and for a moment at least, she was somewhat content. The Abbot went back to his daily duties, taking one last look at Moriko. She could feel his eyes crawling up her skin.

The Abbot smiled. "It's a shame really, to destroy you. You are a rather beautiful girl. Perhaps I would have taken you for a wife someday."

Anger and despair washed over Moriko. The Abbot was a careful man. Escape was going to be next to impossible, and there was nothing she could think of. She missed the woods, and she missed her father. She didn't want to let the Abbot see her tears, but she couldn't hold them back.

CHAPTER 22

They had been fortunate to find a large tree rotted out near its core. With some digging, Ryuu had been able to create a space just large enough for Takako to lie down and Ryuu to sleep sitting up. It wasn't as comfortable as the places they were used to, but it was warm and kept them dry while it snowed around them.

A full moon of peace and quiet gave them enough time to get into a routine. Ryuu spent a lot of time hunting, collecting as much food as he could before the winter made it more difficult to find. Takako spent her days preparing the food, preserving as much as she could. When she had spare time she made small improvements to their tree, such as making herself a bed of twigs and needles that was almost comfortable. Ryuu was amazed by her ability to dedicate herself to creating a home given how transient they were.

They were both in the tree, watching a heavy snow fall around them, when Ryuu sensed something he had never before experienced. It felt like the sun had exploded on the horizon. Someone had released an incredible amount of energy, energy like Ryuu had never experienced before. Even more perplexing, it was at least a day's journey away. There was no way he should be able to sense anything at that distance.

Takako had seen his face go pale when it occurred and asked him what the matter was. Ryuu tried to explain it to her, but he didn't have the words to describe it. Every living thing gave off energy, but not like that.

That night he didn't sleep well. He spent much of the evening attempting to sense anything else that would give him some clue as to what had happened. Whatever it was, it seemed important that Ryuu figure out what had caused it. The past few moons had made it obvious there was still too much he didn't know. If he was going to live he needed more knowledge. He would have to get closer to find out more.

He debated his course of action through the night, but when the sun rose he had a plan.

When Takako awoke he had already made breakfast for her.

As she ate he broke the news of his plan.

"I need to leave for a few days."

She looked at him, shock on her face.

"You're leaving?"

"Just for a few days, but I need to find out what happened yesterday. If I don't know what it is, someday it may be dangerous to us. I'd like to leave you here, where it's safe, and come back in a few days."

Takako had some strong objections.

"Why would I be safe here? Orochi can sense me. It doesn't much matter if I'm in a tree."

Ryuu shook his head. "Not here. This forest can hide people even from the sense."

Takako didn't have to ask for clarification. Her expression was obvious enough.

"I don't know if you can tell, but this forest is alive with energy. I'm very strong in the sense and I know your aura well. I could recognize it in a city hundreds of paces away. But here, in the forest, there is so much life I would have to be almost on top of you to notice you. I promise you, hiding here is going to be much safer than coming with me. It could be dangerous."

Takako did not want to be left alone. Ryuu insisted. He didn't want the responsibility of watching Takako. She slowed him down. He gave her instructions if he wasn't back in a few days, but he wasn't worried. She could take care of herself.

He packed light, bringing just enough dried food for a couple of days on the road. He did everything he could to reassure Takako, but he recognized in the end he'd just have to move forward.

With a tight embrace he was off. He didn't look back.

Ryuu moved towards the source of the disturbance. He kept up a trot that lasted throughout the day, eating up the leagues between him and his destination.

As he drew closer, Ryuu sensed he was approaching a small village. He drew a cloak over himself to hide his sword and entered the village as a wandering traveler. He traded some of his skins for food, and the friendly street merchant was happy to tell him more about the area. The piece of information that Ryuu found most interesting was the piece about the monastery nearby.

Although Ryuu didn't dare press the merchant with direct questions, it seemed as though nothing out of the ordinary had occurred in the village. People were going about their business as they would any other day. No one seemed nervous or fearful. Whatever had happened hadn't happened here. His stomach dropped a bit. The event had to have come from the monastery.

Ryuu went to another merchant to purchase more goods and acquire more information. He found what he was looking for in an elderly gentleman selling trinkets of the Faith.

"Good morning, sir."

"Morning, lad. Come to see some of my relics?"

Ryuu tried to give him a genuine smile, as he hoped a believer would. The old man had as many relics as Ryuu had wives, but it didn't hurt to humor him. "Yes, actually, I was hoping to visit the monastery."

The old man furrowed his eyebrows. "What would a young man like you want up at Perseverance?"

"Well, sir. I'm the son of a scribe, and my father asked me to travel this way to copy some of the sacred texts they keep there."

The old man's suspicions dissipated. "I see. Well, be careful. The Abbot up there is hungry for power and has the strength to match."

Ryuu digested all of this information. Perhaps the Abbot was the source of the event he had sensed. He thanked the man for his information and directions, traded a few of his remaining skins for a trinket and went on his way.

He didn't have to follow the old man's directions for very long. Soon after he left the village he began to sense a power unlike anything he had come across before. Someone in the monastery was giving off an incredible power.

Shigeru had always cautioned him about going anywhere near monasteries. Their purpose was to seek out those who might be sense-gifted. Shigeru also told him they were often above average warriors as well. It was about the worst place for a nightblade to be.

Ryuu also knew the monks had trouble sensing he was a nightblade. Shigeru had held on to some theory the sense manifested itself in different ways and that monks were only trained in recognizing and working with one manifestation of the sense. Ryuu wasn't sure about the why but he hoped his luck around monks would hold.

He stopped in his journey and got off the path. There was a small copse of trees a couple of hundred paces off to the side where it looked like he could remain hidden. If he was going to be approaching a monastery, it seemed much more sensible to do it at night.

Ryuu worked himself into the trees and laid down. The best course was to get some rest. Approaching a monastery seemed like it would take all his energy.

He awoke in darkness, and as he looked around and took in the moon he determined he had slept into the early evening. The moon would have to go much further across the sky before most people would be asleep. The night was crisp and clear. He approached the monastery with caution and sensed the two guards long before he got to the walls.

They both seemed to be located close to the center of the compound. Ryuu smiled to himself. Of course they wouldn't need to walk the perimeter, or be anywhere near it. They could sense anyone coming without having to expose themselves at all. It also meant they would be hard to sneak up on.

Ryuu considered the problem. They hadn't noticed him yet. There was no activity in the compound. He didn't trust that he would be able to sneak up right to the walls though. They might not be able to detect him from here, but they certainly would notice anyone right next door.

Finally he decided there was nothing for it. If he was going to get into the monastery, he'd have to do it the old-fashioned way. He gathered his cloak around him and pictured himself as a weary traveler. He did his best to allow his sense to settle, to rely only on his eyes and ears.

He shuffled up to the gate. Ryuu reached up and gave a timid knock, but he sensed the two guards were already coming to the gate. He relaxed. They didn't approach expecting trouble. They walked casually, talking between themselves. It was clear monasteries were not used to being infiltrated. They unlatched the gate, not even bothering to see who it was.

Ryuu didn't give them time to ask him a question. The very breath that the gate was open and he could see both of them he struck out with his hands. Within moments they were both on the ground unconscious. He wasn't interested in killing them if he could help it.

Ryuu closed his eyes and took a deep breath. He let his sense expand and fill up the small compound. One building was younger monks all sound asleep in their beds. Training to kill him someday, Ryuu reflected. The thought caused his heart to sink. Another building was full of older monks, more seasoned experts. They too were asleep.

But the building in front of him was the source of the energy. Ryuu forced himself to finish scanning the monastery. There was a small stable with a few horses and another building whose purpose Ryuu couldn't discern. There was nobody in it though.

Ryuu's interest was the building in the center. He walked straight towards it and entered through the front door, unprepared for what he was about to encounter.

His first shock was that there was a girl in the room, about as old as he was. She was gazing at him curiously, and Ryuu returned the gaze. She was gorgeous, but not just because of her looks. Even bound on the floor, Ryuu could see the poise and power she possessed, the willpower and the energy. But the most interesting fact about her was that he hadn't sensed her there.

It put Ryuu immediately on his guard. He thought the only person who could do that was Orochi. An accomplice perhaps? If so, he should be grateful. A closer inspection revealed she was in pretty bad shape. She had been beaten and was covered almost from head to toe in bloody welts and cuts.

Although Ryuu did not step any closer, he spoke to the girl, his tone cautiously neutral.

"Who are you?"

"My name is Moriko."

"What happened to you?"

"I disobeyed the laws of the monastery," She paused, but then saw Ryuu was waiting for more. "I killed a monk who was abusing a young girl."

Her answers stoked Ryuu's ever-present curiosity. A girl who was strong enough to kill a monk, whom he couldn't sense, but killed for good reasons? She seemed interesting.

"Do you know Orochi?"

The girl's reaction was subtle, but unmistakable. She knew the name. She didn't lie. "Yes, he was my master."

Some pieces fell into place for Ryuu. His revenge started tonight. He drew his blade and stepped towards her. He had already sealed her fate in his mind.

"A student of Orochi's does not deserve to live. Be at peace." He rose the sword to strike when two events happened simultaneously.

The first was Moriko's reaction. She looked at him, smiled gently, and said, "Thank you."

The second was that the great power source began moving in the building. Ryuu had pushed his thoughts of it aside while the girl was the focus of his attention. Now that it was on the move it came back to the forefront of his awareness.

He lowered his sword into a defensive stance and turned to look on the source of the energy. It was another monk, but dressed in different robes than the others. If the information of the villagers was to be believed, Ryuu supposed this was the Abbot.

The energy radiating off his body was incredible, and if what Ryuu had sensed a couple of days ago was any indication, the man was showing only a portion of his strength. Just his normal presence was debilitating. It was so bright it blinded the sense. Ryuu realized even untrained people would recognize the power in front of them.

Ryuu relaxed the same way Shigeru had taught him when they first went into a city. It was the same lesson. If your sense is about to be overpowered the best thing to do is let it go. It was a tool and nothing more. If it isn't working, you drop it, and focus on all the other training you did.

Relaxed, his sense suppressed, Ryuu was surprised to note the Abbot no longer had any strong effect on him. His other senses were sharp and clear. He silently thanked Shigeru for training him well.

The Abbot didn't seem to pay Ryuu any mind, like having a stranger with a sword in your receiving room was as common as the rising and setting of the sun. His only reaction seemed to be disappointment Ryuu hadn't killed Moriko yet.

"Please, don't stop on my account. I just wanted to watch the end of her life, as well as observe you, my friend. I can only imagine you are the young one Lord Akira wants dead so much."

Ryuu didn't respond as he processed the new information. It was Lord Akira that wanted him dead then. It was logical, given he had killed Akira's top general's only son. Orochi was just a sword for hire then, albeit one with a personal score to settle.

The Abbot continued. "Please continue. If you kill her, you'd be doing me a great favor. She'll be dead and you'll be my present to Lord Akira."

The Abbot's self-confidence grated on Ryuu. He had come too far in his training and had fought too many strong opponents to be intimidated by a man who only knew one trick. He wouldn't be captured here. Ryuu turned to face the Abbot.

The Abbot laughed. "Really? I dare you, boy. I'm very curious what has Lord Akira and Orochi so worked up."

Ryuu moved in to strike. He could feel the Abbot's energy flare, the same way it had felt when he had first sensed it. But with his sense pushed down, it was nothing but an uncomfortable gut-twisting moment, disconcerting but little else.

Ryuu made his cut. The Abbot, caught in his moment of pride, was much too slow in drawing his own blade to block. Ryuu's cut passed through the Abbot unopposed. In an instant, all his energy vanished into oblivion, the Abbot dead before he even had time to be surprised by what had happened.

Ryuu turned to Moriko and let his sense open up again. She was surprised as well, but managed to control her reactions. She looked at him calmly as he turned to face her. He knew he didn't have long before the entire monastery was up in arms, but he had to know more about Orochi.

"Who is Orochi to you, and where is he?"

Moriko examined him. He could tell she was weighing her options, deciding what course to take. To his relief, he saw her shoulders relax, and knew she would tell the truth.

"Orochi was my master. He taught me how to be a nightblade, but since he left to hunt you and your friends, I do not know where he has gone."

Ryuu took a moment to weigh her words. Although she did not have all the information he desired, she was telling the truth.

"Why are you bound?"

"I killed a monk."

Ryuu raised an eyebrow to invite further explanation.

"He had no honor and was abusing a young girl new to the monastery."

Despite himself, Ryuu was beginning to like Moriko. She was strong and honest, qualities he found himself attracted to.

"Who is Orochi to you?" He had to know more.

"My way out."

Ryuu could sense the monastery waking up. To live for cycles upon cycles in the presence of the power of the Abbot, waking up without that presence would be disconcerting, like waking up to discover your right arm had detached itself while you slept. It would take them some time to orient themselves and decide on a course of action, but it wouldn't be long.

He studied Moriko carefully. She had been beaten severely, close to the edge of her life, but she lay there, open to whatever happened next. Despite his opinion of Orochi, he seemed to have trained her well. Ryuu decided to trust her, hopefully not just because he found her attractive, he thought to himself.

"What would you have me do?"

The question clearly surprised her. She must have been expecting death. "Well, cutting these bonds would be a good start."

"Will you continue the mission your master started, to kill me and those close to me?"

She looked at him venomously. "Orochi may have trained me, but I am my own. I am not his lapdog."

Ryuu shrugged. It was good enough for him. With a quick flick of the wrist, he cut through her bonds. She took a moment to rub her wrists and ankles and then slowly moved to her feet. She was strong, but just as clearly injured. Ryuu wasn't sure how well she would fare on her own.

"Come with me. I can take you to where I am hiding. You can recuperate and decide what you wish to do."

Moriko didn't appear to be in a place to say no to a gift. "Thank you."

The words had barely escaped her lips when the first of the monks came rushing in. Moriko seemed to surprise them, but Ryuu had to remind himself they couldn't sense her either.

As Ryuu stepped forward to meet them, he was surprised to be joined by Moriko. She grabbed the Abbot's sword and stood next to him. He glanced at her dubiously, but her return glance stifled any warnings he may have given.

The monks were strong. They were fast and well trained, but they weren't nightblades. The sense provided just the smallest of openings which made him stronger and faster. They did not fall easily, but they did fall, either by his blade or by Moriko's.

Ryuu glanced over at Moriko again. Many of her cuts had opened and blood was oozing from old wounds, but it didn't look like she had been cut. She was exhausted though, rocking back and forth on her feet in her efforts to remain standing. Ryuu felt a wave of admiration for the girl, fighting despite the suffering she had experienced.

The second wave of monks came in, this group less experienced than the ones before them. They halted when they saw their comrades on the ground. Then they saw Moriko, covered in blood, looking like a demon set forth on the monastery. They were ready to bolt.

Ryuu seized the moment. "I do not wish to kill you all. I only wish to leave in peace."

One of the younger monks pointed at Moriko. "With her?"

"Yes."

"She has killed one of our leaders! She must pay with her life."

Ryuu tried to think of a diplomatic solution and failed. He was too tired from travel and from combat. "She is under my protection. If you wish to fight her and kill her, you must come through me first." He tilted his blade so all could see the blood along its edge.

The monks scampered back a step or two, looking around the room and seeing the bodies of their elders scattered over the floor. They looked at Ryuu, who still hadn't been cut, and none of them stepped forward to challenge him, but they didn't get out of the way either.

Ryuu decided to keep moving forward. He wasn't going to be able to talk his way out of this. He watched the monks. None of them stepped forward to challenge him, and almost all of them moved back in response to his movement. He held his sense out, focused on them, but though one or two were hesitant, none intended to move forward to strike them.

Ryuu and Moriko stepped out of the Abbot's quarters. He was worried about her. Although an outside observer might think she was fine he could see her steps were uncertain. She wasn't going to last long before she passed out from her injuries. He looked to the stables.

Decision made, he led them there and started saddling two horses. Not being experienced, it took him longer than he would have liked, and in the time he was saddling them the entire monastery came out to watch. He did not sense an attack from any of them. Their emotions ran from angry to confused to upset and sad.

They mounted in silence and moved to ride off, but despite the crowd's uncertainty about attacking, there seemed to be an unspoken consensus not to let them through. Ryuu drew his sword and spoke in a low voice that carried in the winter's night.

"I came here because the power of your Abbot drew me here. But when I arrived I found dishonor and threats. I am not proud of the violence done here tonight, nor do I regret it. Those who seek to do harm will be duly rewarded. Your Abbot was killed in one cut, and your elders' blades never even kissed my skin. Despite your training, those who draw their blades against me will die."

A monk near the back of the milling assembly spoke up. "But you are a nightblade. We must stop you."

Ryuu shook his head. "I am a nightblade. And you are dayblades. Know, brothers and sisters, we all walk the same path. You are welcome to visit me at any time."

Ryuu took a moment to let his statement and claim sink in. It felt right to let the world know he was a nightblade. For so long he had hidden. His had been a life of shadows and deception. Honesty was refreshing, like letting sunlight into a part of his soul he hadn't dusted in a long time.

Ryuu didn't wait for the monks to rationalize his argument. He started their horses forward, and the crowd parted. Once he sensed a monk almost draw his blade, but fear overtook him at the last moment and he faltered.

As they made it out the gates of the monastery, Ryuu released a deep breath he didn't even realize he had been holding. He looked over at Moriko, who was struggling to stay upright in her saddle. Ryuu shook his head. This was going to be a long journey.

They rode the horses back as far as they could, but Ryuu made them get off a fair distance from the edges of the forest. He didn't want to be leaving tracks.

Ryuu tried a couple of times to get Moriko to open up, but she was deep within herself dealing with the pain and exhaustion. Ryuu also noticed that as Moriko grew more and more exhausted he was able to sense her. Even her presence was beautiful. She exuded the sense in the same manner he did, tendrils of awareness flitting to and fro all around her. It was a beautiful, intricate pattern, invisible to all but him in this world.

When she became too tired to walk on her own he supported her. When she couldn't even stand on her two feet, he carried her. Ryuu had predicted correctly, the journey was long. It was only because of their time on the horses that they made it back to Ryuu and Takako's campsite by the rendezvous time.

When they reached the camp, Takako was unhappy about the situation. Ryuu didn't know what to say, so he didn't say much. He said he had rescued the girl. He settled the senseless nightblade into their tree. Then he sat in his customary spot, asleep the moment he was still.

CHAPTER 23

The forest was a terrifying place without the company of another. Takako had never been in the woods alone. Ryuu had been right. These woods were alive. One didn't recognize it at first, but the variety of sounds was astounding. After Ryuu left she found a dead branch on the ground light enough she could pick it up and swing it with ease, heavy enough she could convince herself it was a weapon.

During the day she managed to keep herself busy, ranging as far from their tree as she felt comfortable to find food. Ryuu had left her with an ample supply of meat, but she enjoyed the variety of berries to break up the monotony of dried meat.

The nights were difficult. With nothing to do but hide in the tree it was too easy to jump at every sound, to imagine that every twig that snapped was an assassin. She wished she lived in a world where that was as ridiculous as it sounded. The sounds of the forest kept her awake each night.

Takako could feel her shoulders relax when she saw him return. But now that she was safe her anger blossomed. He had taken her from all she cared for and left her in the forest alone. He owed her better treatment.

The girl didn't make her feel better. At first Takako had thought it was a body. There was so much blood. But the girl was alive and Ryuu wasn't willing to say much about her. He just laid her down and went to sleep himself, not even asking how she was. Men.

Takako looked over the new arrival scornfully. She reminded Takako of Ryuu. She was of average size but there wasn't any fat on her. She was strong. She had shoulder length dark hair, and an incredible set of cuts and bruises over her entire body. Takako was surprised she was still alive. It was no wonder Ryuu had been covered in blood.

Ryuu didn't sleep long. He seemed to have the ability to wake up at will. After he was up he made a fire and asked for Takako's help in taking off the woman's clothes. Takako was close to making a remark about Ryuu being a pig, but saw the seriousness in his eyes. It was the same look she had seen after their last encounter with Orochi. Takako let the remark die on her tongue and helped him.

They got to work, peeling the clothes off the girl with as much gentleness as they could manage. Blood had caked the clothes to her body in several places, and Takako grimaced every time she tore off congealed blood with the clothes. They washed the wounds and tried their best to dress them, although they didn't have enough bandages to dress all the cuts. They had to choose those which looked most dangerous.

The work was exhausting but gave Takako a sense of satisfaction. Healing was a worthwhile endeavor, and she felt optimistic about her work. If they could prevent infection the girl should recover without too many problems. As they worked Takako noticed many of the new scars were laid over old scars. Whoever the girl was, she had been through some severe beatings.

Ryuu was strangely silent the next few days. The woman, who Takako learned was named Moriko, developed a fever after the first night. She and Ryuu took turns caring for their patient while the other focused on survival. Ryuu would hunt and skin, and Takako would cook and dry the meat and gather food from the forest. Though all of their time was spent in relative proximity to each other, Ryuu never gave more than vague, one-word responses to Takako's inquiries.

His silence angered Takako. After all they had been through she deserved honest answers from him. Something had happened on his trip, more than him bringing back an injured woman. She was tired of feeling like she didn't have the slightest sense of the world around her.

Takako did her best to put the questions aside until Moriko awoke. Then she would have answers. Until then she kept a respectful distance, not trying to push herself into Ryuu's thoughts. It angered her that he wasn't as concerned about her well-being as he was Moriko's. The days without him had been difficult, and his return hadn't made anything easier.

Moriko awoke after three days and slowly but steadily regained her health. All of Takako's hopes that Moriko would clear up the situation were dashed quickly. Ryuu had brought home the only person quieter than he was. Takako had thought they would be on the move as soon as Moriko was up and about. No one else seemed to share her opinion. They both seemed content to rest where they were.

All of this built up Takako's frustration. She didn't want to live in the woods and she didn't like being stuck in the limbo she was in. She wanted to know what they were going to do. Her mood wasn't helped as Moriko's story came out in bits and pieces.

When it did, Takako understood why Ryuu hadn't mentioned anything to her. Moriko was a nightblade known by Lord Akira, trained by Orochi. And Ryuu had killed another person of importance in the Kingdom. It was as though he was trying to bring the full might of the military down on their heads. And not just the military, but the entire monastic system as well, which spanned all Three Kingdoms.

But Ryuu didn't rise to her anger and continued to be nonchalant about their potential danger. His attention was on Moriko and her healing. She was furious at being thrust into a fight that wasn't her own, angry at becoming a hunted criminal when she had done nothing wrong. She was angry because she was afraid, and she wanted Ryuu to share her fear and anger.

As Moriko got healthier she and Ryuu spent more and more time together, fueling Takako's rage. Moriko had been watching Ryuu's training and had asked to join in. Ryuu accepted as if he had forgotten Moriko was Orochi's student.

All day long Takako listened to the sound of wood smashing into wood. Neither of them trained with swords, preferring to give it their all with wooden weapons, which Takako wanted to remind them were still weapons. Both of them would come back bruised, sweaty, and happy.

Conversation at meals focused almost exclusively on technique and their shared history as nightblades. To their credit, Takako supposed, they did attempt to include her, but even though she had known Ryuu longer and had been through so much with him, the bond he and Moriko shared was stronger.

Her jealousy surprised her. She had spent the past few moons trying to stay apart from him. Now that the separation was actually happening she found she missed his presence. The old adage of not knowing what you have until you lose it was proving to be true. The two of them also shared something that Takako couldn't touch. They saw the world in the same way with their sense. Ryuu had tried to describe it to her, but Moriko understood it. Takako was losing her last connection to the world.

It was a cold morning when Ryuu gathered them all around a roaring fire. He had a lot of wood sitting nearby and Takako rightly assumed it was time to make a decision.

"We need to decide how to move forward." Takako laughed softly to herself. That was one thing she appreciated about Ryuu. He never went about things in a roundabout manner. He struck straight to the heart of the matter.

Moriko looked up from the fire. "You assume I'm with you. What if I want to leave?"

Takako flared her nostrils and stared daggers at Moriko. Ryuu had risked everything in his rescue of her. She owed him nothing less than her life. How dare she question they stay together? Takako caught herself. What had happened to her jealousy? Maybe it would be better if she and Ryuu were alone.

Ryuu spoke slowly, choosing his words with care. Takako could see him struggling with the mantle of leadership of this small group. "You will be hunted for what happened at Perseverance, just as we are pursued for my actions. Although your mobility will be hampered by having company, I believe we are all safer if we stay together. However, your path is yours to choose. I make no claim on your life."

Takako was surprised. She was familiar with the traditions of the warrior class. Often a soldier who was saved by another considered his life in debt to the other. Ryuu was relinquishing his most powerful hold on Moriko right away.

Moriko was equally surprised. "Why release your claim? You have every right."

"I do. But I believe everyone makes their own choice. If you stay with us, I want it to be because you choose to do so. If you don't want to remain, I would rather you leave. Shigeru was fond of comparing life to combat. Either commit fully or die half-heartedly."

Moriko nodded, offering no more.

Ryuu pressed the point. "Your path is your own. Do you choose to stay with us?"

Moriko did not answer right away and Takako found the silence unbearable. It felt like a long time passed before Moriko spoke. "I suppose I'm with you. Let's see where this goes."

Ryuu nodded. It was good enough for him.

"I've been thinking about it for a few days now and I see two options. The first is that we run. We find a hiding spot no one will ever find us. Maybe it's outside of the Three Kingdoms, but we keep running until no one is chasing us anymore."

Takako liked that idea. She was convinced bloodshed only led to more bloodshed. For them to try to do anything besides run would only continue the larger cycle of bloodshed and violence they had already experienced.

"Our second option is to take the offensive. To take out Orochi before he can kill us."

Moriko was staring at Ryuu and Takako's heart dropped when she sensed the determination in Ryuu's voice. Whatever her choice was, it was clear he had an idea of what he wanted to do.

Moriko spoke up. "Orochi has the backing of Lord Akira. If you decide to go after him you may end up against an entire kingdom. Orochi is possibly Akira's most valuable asset. He's more than an incredible warrior, he is capable of hunting down other nightblades. He alone could guarantee the continuance of Akira's reign."

Ryuu returned Moriko's piercing gaze. "The thought had occurred to me."

Moriko looked uncertain. "I have mixed feelings about Orochi, but I do want to bring down the monasteries."

Takako stared at both of them, mouth agape. One of them wanted to attack an entire Kingdom head on, and the other wanted to take on a system which spanned all Three Kingdoms. Neither of them would ever be criticized for a lack of ambition, but someone had to talk some sense into them.

"Do you two even realize what you are talking about? Ryuu, you want to take on a Kingdom, and Moriko wants to take down a system that all three Kingdoms depend on. Don't you realize you'll only sow more chaos and bring more pain and destruction down, not just on you, but on everyone who lives in the Three Kingdoms?"

They both looked at her, startled by the emotion of her outburst.

"Can't you see how violence only begets more violence? Ryuu killed a young man to rescue me and Orochi came and killed Shigeru. Now Ryuu wants revenge. Moriko, the Abbot struck out at you and you killed Goro. The Abbot would have killed you, except Ryuu killed the Abbot. Violence brings about more violence. Almost everyone I have ever known is dead because no one could step back and see the pain their actions caused!"

Takako finished, leaving a surprised silence behind her. It was clear neither of them had thought about their actions in that light.

After what felt like a whole cycle, Ryuu spoke. "Shigeru often lectured me about the dangers of violence. He believed there were times when violence was necessary, but it should be avoided if possible. He never framed it the way you did, Takako." He paused, collecting his thoughts, testing them before he spoke again. "I do believe violence is a necessary part of the world. We will never exist without war or conflict and it becomes the duty of those who are strong to minimize it as much as possible."

Takako looked over at Moriko, who was also reflective. "When I was a little girl, I spent all of my time in woods much like the ones we are in now. What I keep thinking about is the concept of harmony. I think Ryuu is right when he says there will always be conflict in the world. However, I think it is everyone's duty to live in harmony as much as possible. The wolf may kill the deer, but he doesn't hunt more than he would need to eat and stay alive. In the same way, violence may be necessary for survival, but we should never seek to do more than is necessary."

Takako's spirits lifted. Perhaps these two warriors could be persuaded to see the wisdom of her cause.

Ryuu spoke up. "I don't think we are safe as long as Orochi is alive. He was able to hunt us down even though we left no traces. His ability is superb, and he does not strike me as the sort of man who will give up now. Now that Moriko is with us he will redouble his efforts."

Moriko agreed. "He is not an evil man. Intimidating and intense, perhaps, but he does not cause pain for the sake of pain. He is a man who needs purpose. Now that Shigeru is dead, his purpose will come from Akira, and he will never stop as long as the purpose is not fulfilled. He is driven."

Ryuu looked closely, again, at Moriko. "If it came to it, could you fight him? Could you kill him?"

Moriko averted her gaze. "I do not know. That is a question I will need to answer for myself. I do not love him, but he is also the man responsible for me being alive and as strong as I am. There is a debt which must be acknowledged."

Takako wanted to press the issue, but Ryuu shot her a warning glance. It was good enough for now. Takako didn't fully trust Moriko yet, but Ryuu did. She would have to be on her guard to make sure he wasn't taken by surprise too.

For a number of long, drawn out moments, there was silence around the campfire, each occupied with their own thoughts. It was Ryuu who broke the silence.

"I don't like it, but I think we need to hunt down Orochi. Only once we have settled with him will there be any chance of safety."

A thousand objections rose in Takako's throat, but none of them made it out. He was probably right, but that didn't make her feel any better. She felt like an insignificant pawn in a grand catastrophe, a catastrophe that she could almost see coming, but with no evidence to back it up, she felt like she had no choice but to go along. Even if it meant death for all of them.

CHAPTER 24

High above the plains and the forests of the Southern Kingdom Akira sat in his castle as the snows fell. His castle wasn't grand or showy. It was a fortress on a hill with a commanding view of the surrounding land. Some of his advisers claimed it was the highest hill in the Southern Kingdom not connected to the mountains, but Akira saw no way of proving that. His castle was not there to make a statement, it was there to keep his family safe.

It was the height of winter and the bone-cutting wind drove snow against the walls, which shook as if battered by the rams of an opposing enemy. Visibility was nonexistent and messengers and traders struggled to reach the safety of the castle walls. Akira glanced down at the letter in front of him, unwilling to accept its contents, wishing but not believing them false.

Orochi had been wounded during his fight. He had managed to make it back to camp and his guards had brought him to a town where there was a proper healer. Orochi had taken a fever, and the doctor wasn't sure if he would make it. However, the message was dated a full moon ago, and by now whatever had happened, had happened. Akira couldn't imagine Orochi succumbing to something as simple as a fever. He couldn't see Orochi dying at all.

Akira meandered around the rooms at the center of his castle which served as his war rooms. He'd given orders to be left alone. Today he had received reports that General Nori was livid upon his return from campaign in the fall. He had barely held his units together during the campaign, his thoughts dedicated to revenge. Advisers stationed with Nori's army had written Akira with warnings that the man was unraveling, falling into drink as the winter blocked his army in. Akira was thankful for the snow. If winter hadn't come with the strength it did Nori might have moved his entire army to find the boy who killed his son.

The same boy also wiped out almost half a monastery. Even the Abbot of Perseverance had been killed. It wasn't public knowledge. The monasteries had elected to keep the matter private. Akira was almost more worried about the repercussions of that action. Doubtless they'd send out a task force, but who was to guess what their next actions would be? He made a note to have a conversation with the Chief Abbot. Whoever this boy was, he was strong and ruthless and throwing systems into chaos.

Akira worked through his knowledge backwards. They had all been surprised when a warrior of such skill was found in the kingdom. Akira had inherited from his father an extensive collection of records which detailed all the important warriors in the kingdom. Anyone with an uncommon degree of skill was listed and their students and family tracked. In this way Akira always knew who was in his kingdom and who might someday pose a threat.

There was nothing on this boy or the man who had raised him. Orochi had given him some clues, but knew more than he would say. It connected to his past. That much was certain. What Akira was puzzled by was why the pair would come out when they did.

They must have been in hiding for at least ten to fifteen cycles. Why now?

He created a story he felt fit the pieces he had, but he had no evidence. The older man, Shigeru, had escaped from some place that trained nightblades. Akira had suspected of such a place since he had met Orochi. He had tried to find it, but if it was in the Southern Kingdom they were much more clever than him. He had sent out spies every cycle to no avail, and Orochi wouldn't speak about it. Akira was disturbed that such a place existed without his knowledge, but Orochi was much too useful to torture for the information. If they could even manage it.

Shigeru and his son had lived in hiding. Akira suspected that although Shigeru trained his son, they did not seek out conflict. Everyone knew the nightblades were hunted. So they hid in peace. But something had caused that to change, and Akira guessed it was Nori's son. Shigeru's boy had been flirting with Takako. This much was known from what Nori's soldiers gathered. When Nori's idiot son grabbed the girl the boy went after. An old story, really. But the boy succeeded, and by purpose or accident killed Nori's son, which led Nori to report to Akira, which brought Orochi into the picture.

Orochi. After all this time, Akira had begun to hope Orochi would never find Shigeru. Akira had debated telling Orochi, but he wouldn't compromise his honor. Orochi had served him well. It was his duty as a ruler to return the favor.

Akira glanced at a map which hung on the wall. It didn't detail all the information his network of spies brought him, but it was a constant reminder of the delicate balance the Three Kingdoms existed in. The treaty gave them peace, but it was tenuous. It was a miracle it had lasted as long as it had. Only because of the shared fear of the nightblades.

The Southern Kingdom shared borders with both the Western and Northern Kingdoms. Either would be delighted to have sole access to the bountiful resources of the Southern Kingdom. Lumber, ores, grain, all of it was produced in the Southern Kingdom. They traded with the other two Kingdoms in return for the finances which kept Akira's military fed. Akira's kingdom had the only passage through the mountains, so Akira needed to maintain the largest military of all the Kingdoms.

If either of the Kingdoms got wind of the trouble which was brewing in the south, they wouldn't hesitate to make advances. As it was, Akira's northern border was lightly defended. Fighting in the pass was taking the bulk of his men. The Azarians were up to something as well, and Nori's performance in the pass had been dismal as he remained distracted.

In a perfect world he could leave his northern borders undefended. In theory those kingdoms were his allies and he should be able to leave them open. However, they were allies only as long as it was mutually beneficial. As soon as there was a chance for anything more, any one of them would seize the opportunity.

The Three Kingdoms needed to be reunited. Akira recognized the truth, but it would never happen without suffering and bloodshed. None of the Kingdoms would relinquish their illusion of control even if it meant sacrificing a chance for lasting peace. Only together would they be strong enough to create a peace which was permanent.

He had dispatched Orochi and the entire house had started to fall around him. If one nightblade could take out a monastery, what could two of them do? Akira couldn't imagine the fear if the public found out. The monasteries were supposed to be the protection against nightblades. He began to understand why they had been so feared. As advisers and warriors they must have been invaluable allies, and the number of them would have guaranteed some degree of safety because one could always be dealt with by another. But with only a handful of them running around, nothing short of a dozen squads of soldiers could take out one of them. It was ridiculous how much they altered the balance of power.

Akira was balanced on the edge of a sword. On one hand, the boy was a threat. He had taken out the monastery and killed an official's son. What bothered Akira was that he didn't know why the boy had attacked the monastery. Had he tracked Orochi there? Did he come to rescue the girl? Her name had been, what, Moriko? He couldn't think of a reason why he would rescue her. Maybe to take her as a hostage against Orochi?

He shook his head. It was dangerous to make assumptions without information. He knew the boy represented a threat to his Kingdom. But he wasn't convinced the boy wouldn't simply return to hiding if the threat to his life disappeared. He had lived his entire life in hiding and had only come to light when the girl was threatened. It seemed logical to assume the boy would return to the state he knew best.

But Nori needed a head. Otherwise he would become unhinged. From every report he was already close to losing everything that made him a valuable asset. But if Akira allowed Orochi to continue, he made an enemy out of a nightblade who had already proved he could disrupt major operations.

Akira's head swirled with the complications of the situation. There wasn't an option without risk, but to not make a decision was even more dangerous. He did the best he could to protect his people, but the constant stress of knowing one wrong decision could mean the death or enslavement of his people haunted him every moment.

After completing another circuit of the rooms, he stopped again at the map. He couldn't help but think that if he had two nightblades in his employ his position against the other Kingdoms would be strengthened. It was against the terms of the treaty, but the risk seemed worth the reward. Commanders who would never fall for an ambush, assassins who knew exactly where they would never be seen. The uses for them were endless and the temptation was strong.

He tried to resist the temptation. His father had cautioned him about the dangers of power. Akira had always tried to live by his father's advice, never wanting to do anything more than rule the Southern Kingdom well. To try for more was to risk it all.

Nori was the problem. His descent into alcoholism was concerning. Akira insisted on discipline among his troops, and an army was a small family. Word of his behavior would spread. If it affected the army the pass and the Kingdom were at risk. Nori's position was of vital importance and something had to be done to ensure he stayed in one piece.

Akira considered the distances and the risks. Perhaps he could allow Nori a personal leave and have him meet up with Orochi. Even for his age, Nori was one of the top swordsmen in the country, and Akira knew he had kept his skills as well-honed as his blades. He might be an asset to Orochi, just as Orochi may temper Nori's rage. It also gave Nori the purpose he was looking for. That purpose would draw him out of his alcoholism and set him on a straighter path.

With a set of horses, Nori could make it to where Orochi's last reported location was. If the hunt was completed soon, Nori could be back with the army moons before it was ready to march south again for the spring. The plan wasn't without its risks, of course, but it also seemed like the best option.

Akira left his main room and went to his private offices where he started drafting out two letters. The first was to Orochi, ordering him to stay in one place until General Nori arrived. Akira did not attempt to use any guile. Nori was an exceptional swordsman and had a strong personal hatred of the target. He was to assist Orochi in any way possible, and Orochi was to defer to him in matters of strategy.

The second letter was to General Nori. It explained to him that Akira's top assassin had been assigned to the mission of avenging Nori's son. He was waiting and Akira was sending Nori to assist him. Nori was to travel with no more than a small group of men.

After writing the letters, Akira sealed them and pushed away from his writing-desk. He hesitated just a moment before calling for a messenger. He had trained himself many cycles ago to learn that at a certain point a man simply had to act. He had to make the best decisions possible with the information available to him. Once committed, he just had to accept the consequences.

Akira called for his secretary, asking that the messages be sent that day. He hoped both made it in time. He felt as though his Kingdom was unraveling in front of him.

Chapter 25

It took Orochi a moment after he woke up to remember where he was. It took only the barest shifting of his weight for his memory to come back to him. Shigeru had cut him deep. If his cut had been just a bit faster, Orochi would be as dead as Shigeru. It had been closer than he expected.

Just as he had every day since he had come upon the farmhouse, Orochi replayed the fight in his mind. It had happened fast. In some part of his mind he had built up his expectations for the confrontation into epic proportions. But it had just been a few moves. Shigeru must have figured out Orochi was faster, just a little stronger. A couple of more passes and Shigeru knew that he wasn't going to be able to get past Orochi's guard.

In hindsight, Shigeru's decision was brilliant. Orochi had never seen a move quite like it before. Shigeru had left a small, minuscule opening in his guard, the sort of opening only an expert swordsman would be able to see and take advantage of. Orochi hadn't even questioned it. He moved in, the killing strike happening within the space of heartbeat.

But it had all been a ruse. In the moment Orochi attacked Shigeru's blade had turned in. It was a sacrifice, taking advantage of the moment without defense to strike. Orochi had seen the blade coming and had managed to shift his weight slightly, just enough that the cut wasn't fatal. It had still almost killed him. He had attempted to field-dress the wound, but he hadn't done very good work.

The fever had been devastating, and it was only due to the assistance of others that he was alive today, a fact that grated on him. Ever since he had left the island he had depended on no one but himself and had done well.

Worse, the fever had taken almost a moon to break. He had been unable to move, unable to use the sense, unable to do anything that made his life worth living. He had considered giving it all up, letting the fever take him or ending his own life. He had killed Shigeru. He had taken his revenge. It was all that he had wanted for as long as he could remember. Now that it was complete, he felt an emptiness he didn't know how to fill.

The only thing that kept him going was the thought of the boy, whom he assumed was Shigeru's son. The boy made Akira's honor guard, perhaps the best swordsmen in the Kingdom, look like children with sticks.

Orochi's curiosity kept him going. He wanted to know how the boy had managed to reach such a high level without training. His first thought had been that Shigeru had discovered training secrets without the masters on the island. But Shigeru hadn't discovered the secrets. If he had, Orochi wouldn't have had a chance in their duel. Even with Orochi's skill at suppressing the way the sense encountered his life, he was still confident that with those skills Shigeru would have killed him.

Somehow the boy had learned, and Orochi wanted to know how.

The wind and snow howled outside and Orochi couldn't help but think of the legends of the elemental dragons that commoners still told. It was easy to imagine the wind swirling around his ankles as the tail of the dragon attempting to trip him up, and the ice which struck all over his body, the frozen breath of the beast.

Orochi pushed his thoughts aside as he approached the command tent. He had heard stories of the general he was about to meet. A swordsman who could hold off a squad of men with no more difficulty than a woodsman raising his axe. A man who, it had been rumored at one point in time, was the reincarnation of Morehei, the legendary nightblade of old. Orochi snorted to himself. If nothing else, the man knew how to build a reputation.

But Orochi had also heard the rumors of the old man's weakness. When the boy had killed his pathetic excuse of a son the general had broken like a dry twig. Orochi had nothing but contempt. The man may have been great once, but a man who allowed adversity to triumph over him had no place in Orochi's world.

Orochi had considered destroying Akira's letter or killing the messenger and striking out on his own again. He had killed Shigeru and his life's purpose had been fulfilled. But his own code held his hand from his blade. Akira had always been honest with him and had wielded him well. If he left Akira's service he would do so to his face.

Orochi was also troubled by the sense he had of the boy, and not just the power he displayed. There was something, a current underneath the surface of reality surrounding him, but Orochi couldn't put his finger on it. It was like trying to catch a feather falling from the sky. The more he tried to catch it, the further he pushed it away. He felt it was important, vital even that he understand it.

Orochi shook his head. Some mysteries wouldn't be solved today. He pushed aside the tent flap and stepped in, the heat hitting him like a blow to the face. It was a simple tent unfit for a general of Nori's stature, which was why it had been chosen. But the heat within was unbearable, especially for Orochi.

Orochi knew Nori wasn't much older, but the two of them were separated by much more than just a few cycles. Nori was by the fireside, a cup of whiskey in his hand. Orochi didn't need his sense to tell the man was dying whether he realized it or not. His hand shook almost imperceptibly. His sword wasn't even within reach, marking him as careless as well.

He had been a true warrior once. Orochi's eye took him in. The calluses on his hands, the defined muscles, slightly the worse for age. But it was the recent decay which was the most obvious. The disheveled hair, the bags under his eyes. Nori's weakness made him sick. Orochi knew firsthand the pain that came with losing a loved one. In his case it had been partly his own fault Yuki had died. Nori didn't even have that to deal with, yet was finding refuge in drink instead of in warfare. Orochi suppressed his rage. He had seen it before, the toll that living took upon those still alive.

Nori looked at Orochi with open contempt. Orochi had half expected this sort of reaction. Nori knew nothing about Orochi whereas Orochi knew almost all about Nori. Orochi suspected Akira would have described him as little as possible to his general to keep his secret. It gave him yet another advantage over the decaying man.

Orochi kept himself at a relaxed attention. He didn't approve of Akira's orders even though he understood his motivation well enough. He would follow them out of respect for his word, but he didn't have to like Nori or show this man any more respect than he deserved.

The moment Nori opened his mouth, Orochi knew for sure he was drunk even though the sun had recently risen over the tops of the trees.

"So you are the man Akira sent after the murderer of my son!"

Orochi raised an eyebrow in surprise. To refer to Akira without his title could be considered treason in some areas. To show contempt for a man of Orochi's size was downright foolish. Either the man had a high opinion of his abilities or was more drunk than Orochi suspected. Either way, he kept his silence.

"Our Lord has sent me here to finish the job you could not. I'll need all the information you have on the whereabouts of our targets. Once we have found them, I will show you what it means to be a warrior."

In other circumstances, Orochi would have removed his accuser's head. But Nori was in such a pitiful state it would have dishonored his blade.

"Yes. May I ask what your plan is?"

Orochi grinned at the anger on Nori's face. The general did not appreciate Orochi's lack of manners. He didn't come here expecting to be treated as an equal. Nori was a man used to deference, used to fear. He wouldn't find either in Orochi.

With effort, Orochi swallowed his pride. Killing Nori would gain him nothing and potentially lose him everything. His arrangement with Akira had been beneficial to this point and a drunken general wasn't worth losing it.

"I'll prepare my notes and bring them to you by first light tomorrow."

Nori nodded. "Good." His attitude made it clear their meeting was over.

Orochi shook his head as he turned around and walked out of the tent. He preferred his life simple. He did not care for court intrigue or desire power. He had wanted revenge, and with that complete he found he wanted peace and to be left alone.

It had been so warm in the tent Orochi had forgotten the blizzard outside. The cold wind cut right through his robes and for a moment Orochi relished the sensation. It felt more real and more right than anything happening in the tent behind him.

He scanned the surrounding area. There had to be someone around worth talking to. He saw the man standing guard at the perimeter of the camp. Despite the freezing temperatures and wind, he stood relaxed but firm in his post. His insignia marked him as a higher ranked infantryman, not an officer. But Orochi guessed besides himself and a sober Nori, this man was probably the best swordsman of the bunch, as well as the most intelligent. Just what he was looking for.

Orochi walked up to the soldier, remaining in the soldier's field of vision so as not to give any indication of stealth. He noted the soldier slightly shifted his stance so he was facing Orochi. Although he didn't bring his hand any closer to his sword, it was clear he was ready for combat.

Orochi saw the shift, and the soldier saw that Orochi had seen it. They both broke out in a small smile and Orochi bowed his head slightly, a token of respect to the other man.

The soldier was eager for company. "So you're the assassin?"

Orochi grinned. Such forthrightness was rare but appreciated. "Yes."

The soldier's eyes took in Orochi. "Good?"

"Yes."

The soldier nodded. "I thought as much. You're certainly intimidating, even from a distance. Would you care to spar sometime when I'm not on duty?"

Orochi liked this man. "As time permits, yes."

The man lived and breathed swordsmanship because from the man's glances Orochi could tell he was about to ask about Orochi's blade. He spoke quickly to interrupt the process before it started. He jerked his head at Nori's tent. "How long as he been like that?"

The man glanced around, although no one was anywhere near earshot with the blizzard howling around them. "I'd rather not say, sir."

"I need to know if I can depend on him when the moment comes. I'm not out to ruin his reputation."

The guard thought for a moment. "You can always depend on him. Just needs a little action to remind him why he's alive. Moping around like he is now, he can only think of his boy and that causes him to drink. All this traveling, with nothing to do, he's only gotten worse. But get him out hunting and he'll be back sure as the sun will rise."

Orochi digested the advice, trying to determine if he trusted this opinion. To be a member of an honor guard meant loyalty, an unwavering devotion to a lord. But most men were not fools, biased they may be. Nori had been formidable before. Perhaps if the alcohol were to leave his system he may be again.

He was surprised to find he wanted to believe it. The man had lost a son and that would impact any man's soul. For the son to be so near when it happened, to be protected by the very army that defined the man had to bring a unique pain. There was no honor to be found in the bottom of a wine cup, but it was a cold man who wouldn't mourn the loss of a son.

Orochi shivered. Such dark thoughts depressed him although they came more often since his fight with Shigeru. It was if

Shigeru's blade had struck him not to kill, but instead to fester, thoughts of remorse and loss crawling their way to his heart.

He shook his head. Thinking such thoughts would get him nowhere. Better to act than to reflect. He strode to his tent, already looking forward to his routines. One could never practice forms too much, and the purity of movement often burned away the thoughts of his own past.

When the sun rose the next morning Orochi was prepared. He woke light and refreshed. His kata the night before had stripped him of his fear and concern.

Orochi stepped out of his tent to greet the new day. The blizzard had passed through in the night and a virgin snow lay all around him, undisturbed except for the path of footsteps left by the few sentries overnight. The air was crisp and chilled his throat, but there was no wind, and his robes kept him warm enough.

He walked to Nori's tent to let the guards know he would request another audience as soon as the General was prepared. They let him know they would pass along his message, but in a confidential tone, one whispered to Orochi it may be some time before Nori was prepared to entertain visitors. Orochi nodded his understanding and looked around for something to do.

In the center of the camp, a group of soldiers was beginning to mill about, warming up their bodies by practicing their martial arts. Orochi walked over to observe their movement. He had heard Nori trained his soldiers with some unique skills and he was hopeful he might be able to observe.

If the soldiers were disturbed by his presence they didn't show it. They went about their daily routine in the manner of those who have gone through it hundreds of times before. Few words were exchanged as a captain of the guard led his men through their initial stretches.

From the stretches they moved to techniques, choosing sparring partners based on equal ability. Orochi watched and was impressed by what he observed. Honor guards were skilled, but even among the skilled there were levels of ability. Everyone here was good.

As Orochi observed, he began to notice patterns in the soldier's movements. The strikes and cuts they practiced were very directional, with moves tending to favor quick stabbing motions and close blocks over swinging cuts and blocks. It was a style suited to fighting in the close quarters of the passes. Orochi approved. It was a dangerous style because the guard was closer to the body, but a group of skilled warriors could use it in enclosed spaces without fear of striking an ally. Orochi had never fought as part of an army before, had never been in combat without a wide freedom of movement, and so the moves were different than the ones he preferred. None of the soldiers would be fast enough to deflect his blade, but they were good.

He sensed Nori approaching behind him, but took care not to display the knowledge. He didn't trust Nori and did not want him knowing he was a nightblade.

"Are you impressed by my soldiers, assassin?" Nori did not bother to hide the disdain in his voice.

"They are skilled."

"Do you wish to test your skills against them?"

Orochi considered. Sparring would be a good stretch and relaxing. A part of him burned to demonstrate to Nori just how good he was, but he restrained himself. He held to the belief that the less potential enemies knew about him, the safer he was.

The belief had guided him well thus far despite temptations. He shook his head. "Perhaps some other time."

Nori nodded as if some long held suspicion of his had been confirmed. Orochi shrugged it off. Let the man challenge him and he wouldn't be alive long enough to be surprised.

Nori invited Orochi into his tent. Orochi noted Nori wasn't drunk this morning. Hopefully it would last. Orochi wanted to respect this man who had accomplished so much.

The tent wasn't as warm as it had been the night before. Nori was moving with a vigor Orochi hadn't seen before, which was good to see. In front of him was a detailed map of the South Kingdom. Orochi ran his eyes over it, impressed despite himself.

Nori had mapped out all the places where conflict had arisen. Where his son was murdered and where the monastery Perseverance was attacked. Nori observed Orochi looking at the map and knelt down next to it. "Where did you fight the nightblades?"

Orochi knelt down as well and pointed out the location. "They had been hiding in an abandoned farm house near here."

Nori marked the spot and then looked over the entire map. "I've been trying to determine patterns which might help us find them. But there aren't enough sightings of them to determine a pattern."

"True, but we don't need a pattern. Sometimes all you need is a story, a story which explains the facts and helps predict the future."

Nori looked at Orochi skeptically. "But any number of stories could be made up to explain any set of facts."

"Also true, but certain stories will make more sense and are more likely to be correct."

Nori continued his look of disbelief.

"For example, we know why your son was murdered," he looked up at Nori, who was doing his best to control himself. "And tracking them out of the pass wasn't too difficult, which led to the fight in which I killed the older one. After I was wounded the boy took off with the girl heading to the north. I suspect the direction was chosen because it was the way they had already been traveling. However, that path would have taken them close to Perseverance."

"This is where I start to guess, but I would suspect the boy attacked Perseverance because he was looking for me."

Nori looked at Orochi quizzically.

"Perseverance had an Abbot who was very strong in the sense. The boy may have thought I would take shelter there with my injuries. He would have investigated, and he would have found the Abbot and killed him."

Nori's uncertainty was still plastered on his face. "Why would the boy believe you were hiding in a monastery?"

"The boy is a nightblade. He knows the monasteries serve the kingdom and they would be the safest place for someone to hide from a nightblade."

Orochi kept his face straight. The boy would have gone to Perseverance because of the stuck-up Abbot releasing his powers there. It would have attracted him like a moth to flame. Orochi would have given up much of his gold to know what happened to Moriko. He hadn't heard anything.

Nori finally nodded his agreement. "That make sense. Why didn't you?"

"Because I knew he would be looking for me there." The lie came easily to Orochi, but it was a story that made sense, and the truth behind it remained. The boy would be coming for him. The knowledge resided in the core of his body and he didn't deny it.

He ached for the challenge of a new opponent, especially one as strong as the boy might be.

Nori again pored over his maps. "So if your story is correct, what do we do next to track them down?"

"We do nothing. We find a defensible position and wait for them to come to us."

"How is the boy supposed to find you?"

"You underestimate him. If he is a nightblade he will find us. There is no place in the Three Kingdoms we could hide."

Nori brought his gaze to bear on Orochi. "I want you to know that killing them isn't enough for me. I want them to suffer for the pain they have brought. If we can take any of them alive, my orders are to do so. They will live to regret their decisions."

Orochi's stomach twisted at the man's suggestion. Torture for information was one thing. Torture for pleasure was without honor. He did not approve, but gained nothing by fighting it. He would have to find them first and kill them cleanly. If his hunch was correct, they were fighting because of the situation they had been put in, not for any malicious reasons. It was survival.

Orochi left the tent discontent. He had offered service to Akira because he had believed it would lead him to Shigeru. Over the passing of cycles, he had come to realize Akira was a ruler equal to the task put before him. He knew how to lead men and he was just, and Orochi had seen him make decisions over and over again which protected the people of his land. Orochi respected him.

Nori was a different man, weaker, addicted to power and the abilities that came with it. Akira's decisions were based on the greater good while Nori's were based upon that which brought him pleasure and respect. It was unacceptable.

Orochi wandered the campground, lost deep in thought.

CHAPTER 26

It was, Ryuu reflected, the nature of life to seek patterns, from the movement of a flock of birds in the sky to the daily actions people took every day. Every morning he and Moriko awoke before the sun rose in the sky. They would condition in the woods: running, climbing, lifting rocks and logs. Then came combat training and instruction. Moriko was teaching him how to hide his strength and Ryuu was teaching her new sword techniques and a more natural use of her own sense.

By the time the sun was near the tops of the trees, Takako would wake and the three of them would be off again, heading northeast. Deciding how to track Orochi had been a difficult decision. Moriko and Ryuu had combined their knowledge and intuition. Moriko knew the locations of all the military instillations in the Kingdom. They assumed with his injuries Orochi would have to return to one for healing. They also assumed he wouldn't give up on his mission and would choose the military base closest to his current location, or the location he assumed Ryuu and Takako would be heading. From there he would move north, the direction he had seen Takako and Ryuu take.

They decided their best bet was a small outpost near the northern edge of the Kingdom. It was a local garrison which served as a training ground for the local militia. Moriko said it contained a small contingent of regular military but had enough beds and supplies to contain a full company of men. It felt right. Shigeru's last advice to trust his instincts resonated in Ryuu's mind.

The three of them traveled at a slow pace. Moriko, while strong, was still recovering from the abuse she had suffered at the monastery. Ryuu suspected the lasting damage was more in her mind than in her body, but she still hesitated just a moment too long in swordplay. A typical opponent may not notice it, but her hesitations were as deep as ravines in Ryuu's mind, and they rendered her defenseless against a skilled swordsman such as Orochi.

Moriko knew it and she knew he knew it, but they had an unspoken agreement not to discuss it. Ryuu couldn't judge her and only knew a little of what had happened to her at the monastery. But whatever had passed had scarred her enough to fail to commit to her sword. Fighting most people it wouldn't be an issue, but if the sun rose on a day she had to fight or defend against Orochi she would be at his mercy.

Ryuu also didn't know how to approach Takako. She had been distant ever since he had returned from the monastery and he couldn't piece together why. A part of him wanted to find someplace safe for her and hide her. She didn't belong in this struggle between the nightblades of the age, but had fallen in due to Ryuu's own bungled morals.

But there was no place she could hide that was safer than with the two of them. Ryuu desperately wanted to comfort her and to be present for her, but she wouldn't let him. He had tried to speak alone with her a couple of evenings but had been firmly rebuffed.

Without better options he gave her the space she hesitated to ask him for. He couldn't shake the knowledge he was still responsible for all that had happened to her. He just didn't know how to make the situation any better.

As the sun rose above the horizon, Ryuu could see evidence that winter was beginning to pass. The ground they walked on was no longer snow covered, although often muddy and slippery, wet from the melting. It slowed their progress further, but a part of him didn't mind. He knew that once they reached the outpost it was unlikely their little group would stick together. They were united by purpose and necessity, and some days it seemed like little else.

Ryuu pushed his thoughts aside as he got up and began warming up. He could sense Moriko getting up about a hundred paces through the woods. He was beginning to sense her naturally, the way he had once been with Shigeru. But she was much more difficult. She had managed to adopt a very slight, consistent shield against the sense. While most people burned brightly, she did not, a dim candle in a forest fire.

Ryuu had learned to hide himself to a degree, but hadn't internalized the technique the way Moriko or Orochi had. But although she was hidden, she wasn't invisible, and it gave Ryuu hope he would be able to defeat Orochi when the time came.

Although he couldn't see her from where he was standing he could sense her move in unison with him as they grabbed the wooden swords they had made. They walked far enough away that their practice wouldn't wake Takako in the early morning hours and they began to spar.

Moriko managed to keep up with him well. She was fast and strong and had a good sense of improvisation. Their wooden blades snapped through the air, meeting and disengaging in ever-faster conflict. The tension built, and as was often the case, Ryuu could feel Moriko start to fall back against the speed of his cuts and thrusts.

With a quick snap of his wrists, he was inside her guard. He stepped in, wooden blade against her neck, her back against a tree, his face so close to hers he could smell the fresh sweat on her skin. She breathed heavily from the exertion of the combat. Ryuu held his cut close, his face close, and recognized for the first time his attraction to the dark haired mystery standing in front of him.

It was an impulse, a moment's lack of reason, and he kissed her.

It was a mistake.

With incredible force, she shoved with all her might, throwing him back a good three paces. Off balance, he had no ground, and fell backwards, his feet tripping over a root.

Ryuu was speechless, his mind tumbling over a series of strong feelings. He loved Takako. He was sure of it. Why would he do that? His mind raced for answers but only found confusion.

Moriko wasn't making things easy for him either. She regarded him in silence, her face neutral but her stance defensive. If Ryuu was going to try to get close to her again he would be experiencing a wooden blade to the face if not a steel one.

Ryuu searched for words, but his mind couldn't hold onto them. He had never considered this, never thought the woman he had brought back from the monastery would have this power over him. He didn't know what Takako thought of him, but this wouldn't help his case. He should ask her to not tell Takako.

Finally his mind snapped into place. He may have made a mistake, but Shigeru had taught him lying to friends, to family, was inexcusable. No more. He stood up, brushed himself off and looked Moriko right in the eye.

"I'm sorry, Moriko, that wasn't appropriate."

Moriko returned his gaze without saying anything, allowing the moments to hang like stones between them. But then she let out just a bit of a grin, and Ryuu thought for the first time that she was the most beautiful woman he had ever seen. She didn't have the looks of Takako, but she was primal, and Ryuu was entranced.

"Let's continue" Moriko said, as she stepped into a defensive crouch.

Ryuu shook his head and grinned. No forgiveness, no absolution, simple acknowledgment was the extent of what he was going to get. He supposed it would have to be good enough. They continued their sparring practice, but Ryuu was never able to get inside her guard again.

They returned to camp and Ryuu woke Takako up. He couldn't help feel a pang of guilt as he greeted her, but he kept his peace. He didn't know what was going to happen to the two of them, but he still cared for her, and he couldn't bring her any more pain.

As Takako awoke Moriko packed up the few items that constituted their camp. For once Ryuu appreciated Moriko's less than verbose nature. He didn't need another complication right now. Orochi was enough.

Moriko and Ryuu determined what direction they wanted to be moving, and the three of them took off. The sun against his face cheered him and brought him out of the depression he hadn't even realized he was feeling.

He knew he felt guilty about Shigeru's death. Although he knew that in one way he wasn't responsible, that Shigeru had died at the hands of another, he also knew he bore some responsibility for what happened. That guilt had gnawed at him since he had felt the grief start to dissipate.

But spring was coming and Ryuu could feel the renewal of the Earth. The quiet pressure on his sense which he lived with most of the cycle was returning, softly muted over the winter. Birds and squirrels were starting to flit throughout the forest again and there was an atmosphere of expectation as the earth returned to life.

Moriko sensed the guards before he did, which only confirmed how distracted he was. For all of her skills the monastery training was not as good as the training Shigeru had given Ryuu and his sense was much better developed than hers. But there were two guards in the trees ahead of them.

Moriko gestured for Ryuu to follow her away from the guards. They met with Takako, who was staying as far behind them as she could and retraced their steps. Ryuu threw his sense out in every direction to search for others. Once they were satisfied they were out of earshot, Ryuu broke the silence.

"Are we there already?"

Moriko seemed uncertain. "Maybe, I would have guessed it was further away."

Ryuu tried to contain his frustration. He wouldn't have done any better. Neither of them had experience navigating these distances. It was testament enough they had even stumbled upon the camp.

"I didn't sense anyone beyond the two guards."

"Neither did I."

Ryuu brought his hand to his chin and thought. The odds of running across two guards in a tree stand in the middle of the woods were pretty low. It indicated a larger, static force nearby.

But they didn't know which direction or what the force may consist of. If it was the camp they were looking for there could be dozens of soldiers waiting for them somewhere within a day's walk. But there was also a chance the soldiers were there for another reason, such as being an advance lookout or rear guard for a company on the move.

Moriko was thinking many of the same thoughts. "We need to know more before we decide what to do."

Ryuu closed his eyes and reached out with his sense. He could still feel the guards on the very outside of his range. They hadn't moved.

"I agree. We need to move back and set up a place for Takako. Then tonight we scout."

Takako glared at Ryuu. "I don't want to be left alone anywhere near an enemy camp. I've been in one of those before, and I don't care to repeat the experience."

"We'll move quite a ways back and we'll hide you. You won't be able to light a fire tonight, but other than that you'll be fine. We'll make sure we choose a safe spot."

Takako nodded, but she didn't look convinced. As they started to move back to find a campsite for Takako, she grabbed Ryuu's arm and held him, waiting for Moriko to go away.

"Ryuu, I have a bad feeling about this. The two of you need to stop hunting Orochi now. I know he killed Shigeru, but if you keep this up, something bad is going to happen."

Ryuu looked down at Takako's lovely face, a tear streaming down her face, and his heart dropped from him. He knew he loved her, which only solidified his resolve.

"I know it's dangerous. But it's the only way we're ever going to be free of him, free from all of this. If I thought there was any other way, any way at all, I would pick you up in my arms and run all night and every night after until we found a safe place where we could spend the rest of our days in peace. But I can't do that knowing we'll be hunted forever. I can't live like Shigeru did."

Takako's shoulders sagged as she realized her arguments didn't have any weight. "But I don't want you to die like him either."

They walked in awkward silence until they reached the location Moriko had chosen. Ryuu found his voice again.

"You know I will do everything I can to protect you."

"I know that, but it doesn't make my feeling any less horrible."

"I'm sorry, but this has to be done."

Takako couldn't control herself any longer. She whispered violently, "I know that! I know we are stuck here on this path, but it will lead us all to ruin. I know it doesn't make sense, but it's what is in my heart."

Ryuu held her like it was the last embrace he would ever be able to give her. He wanted to give her peace but didn't know how. "I will be back. I promise it. We're just going to go scout it out and decide upon our next steps." He let her go and walked away. "I love you, you know."

Takako nodded wearily. "I know you do. Please come back."

Ryuu nodded and turned away. He wasn't sure he could keep going if he stayed near her.

He met with Moriko and they moved through the woods towards the scout outpost. Ryuu was thrilled by the feeling of hunting with another nightblade. As they drew within visible range of the scouts they halted and whispered. They had sensed other outposts as well, each having overlapping areas of visibility. If they were going to sneak by they would need to wait until dark.

With nightfall near at hand they sat and waited. Ryuu took the time to calm himself and focus his sense. He crawled through the outposts searching forward. He lost the sense of his immediate surroundings in favor of understanding what lied ahead. He didn't worry, Moriko was alert to changes in their vicinity. He continued forward and found what he was looking for, a garrison, a bright glow of life at the edges of what he could reach with his sense. It was small and seemed to hold less life than he had expected. But they were active, pacing back and forth. They were nervous.

He came back to himself and to the state of awareness which brought in information from nearby. It was a difficult transition to make, and he did it slowly. As soon as he had the attention to spare, the question came full force to his mind. Why would seasoned warriors be nervous when they were on guard duty?

The answer came right after the question. They knew Ryuu was coming. But did they know that he was here? If so, they had already walked right into a trap.

Moriko caught his excitement and raised an eyebrow.

"They know we're coming, or maybe even that we're here," Ryuu said. He explained what he had sensed.

Moriko listened and took a moment to think. "It doesn't change the situation. We still need to get close enough to know what we're up against. Orochi is the only one with the sense in this area besides us and I haven't felt his presence at all."

"Would you?"

"Probably. It seems more likely he anticipated you coming after him and is set up in a defensible position, or is using it as a decoy to attack you from behind. Either way, he's around, and we need to know what's in front of us."

Ryuu reluctantly agreed with Moriko. A part of him wanted to go back to Takako, to ensure she was safe. She might be in greater danger than he had thought. But the facts were still the same and their decision had to be carried through.

Fortunately, as the sun fell the clouds rolled in and the almost full moon was covered by a blanket of darkness. Moriko and Ryuu moved like ghosts through the woods, passing between guard posts without raising an alarm. They moved into a short clearing where all the tress had been cut down. Ryuu pushed forward with his sense and felt a second ring of guard posts on the other side of the clearing.

Ryuu approved of the simple genius of the plan. Whoever had designed this outpost knew their strategy. They needed wood for the building, and cut it all down in a perimeter around the outpost, creating a clearing that archers could see through. Any attacking force would have to walk through a potential rain of arrows with no cover.

The clearing was filled with tall grass which Ryuu and Moriko knelt in crawled through. The grass wasn't tall enough to hide a man, but it provided sufficient cover on the pitch-dark night. Moriko and Ryuu made it through and found a concealed place in the forest. Both of them could sense the number of guards around them, but no one seemed to have noticed them.

They slipped into their roles. Ryuu pushed his sense outward and Moriko focused on their immediate surroundings. There were no surprises and plenty of information. Ryuu's sense traveled up and down the outpost, making quick calculations as to the number of people present, the size, and the layout of the fort.

But where was the snare? Ryuu continued questing with his sense and found it in the middle of the town. Or more accurately, he found nothing. In the middle of everything he found a hole of nothingness, an emptiness and a blackness against his consciousness.

Ryuu retreated back to himself. "He's there, right in the center."

Ryuu related everything he had sensed. "Why is everyone so afraid? Who do they think we are?"

"It's not who they think we are, it's what they believe about us. You attacked a monastery and killed a fair number of the monks inside. I'm sure the story has grown by now. I don't think you understand the reverence the common people hold for the monks. They probably view you as a monster."

"Well, that's comforting."

With just a trace of regret in her voice, Moriko responded. "You haven't spent much time in the world. I haven't either, but I am familiar with the power of the monasteries, having seen it firsthand."

For a while the two sat huddled together whispering about a plan of attack. They couldn't reach an agreement, but every so often Ryuu would return to his meditative state, focusing on the fort. The pattern of the guards was a standard army movement with about twelve day watches and twelve night watches. With the limited number of soldiers it felt like many were pulling multiple watches, which would make them less observant.

The sun was just beginning to rise when they decided they had enough information, and Ryuu was focusing his sense one last time on the fort when he felt the disturbance. Violent actions by the gate. He threw out his sense as far as he could and just barely touched a white-hot ball of anger and fear. His sense collapsed around him as he lost focus and he felt like throwing up. It couldn't be true, yet he was certain.

Takako was down in the fort. She had been found and captured.

There wasn't any way.

Ryuu's mind raced. It could be a trap of some sort. He didn't know if it was possible, but perhaps it was possible to simulate the sense of someone else. He wished Shigeru was alive to tell him what was possible, what was logical.

The whole army was up and drilling in the pre-morning light. Orochi was awake, the darkness deep in the center of the town. They couldn't attack now. They would all be killed, and Ryuu didn't know if it was even Takako. He was unwilling to believe his own sense. He needed to know.

"We need to get back to the camp right away."

Moriko didn't question him, even when he got up and began running with abandon. He ran right up to the nearest tree stand and climbed up in three graceful paces, pulling himself up smoothly even as the archers were beginning to react, startled by the presence of another person. His blade flashed twice and all three people dropped from the tree. Two bodies struck lifelessly on the ground while Ryuu landed softly on his feet and sprinted through the grass.

Moriko followed him. One archer in a nearby stand attempted to take a shot, but Ryuu and Moriko were moving fast at a difficult angle, and the arrow passed harmlessly between them. Within a handful of breaths they had fallen into the second ring of trees, pursued only by the sound of alarm bells ringing throughout the forest. If nothing else, Moriko thought, they had lost their element of surprise.

Both Ryuu and Moriko noted the guards in the trees in the second ring had disappeared, but Ryuu did not stop to investigate. He charged forward, fear for Takako lending him a speed he didn't know he possessed.

They reached the camp and Ryuu dropped to his knees. The camp looked orderly, but it was deathly quiet.

Takako was gone.

Chapter 27

Takako was at a crossroads, torn apart by indecision. Her feelings towards Ryuu were complex. He was a good man and she knew he always meant well. He could be trusted to take the action he believed was right. Perhaps there wasn't much more she could ask for in this world. Perhaps there was a future with him.

But she could not shake her anger at Ryuu. She knew he was doing his best, but his decisions had brought death to her family. As much as she understood, she couldn't bring herself to forgive. She wasn't sure she ever could.

Takako had stayed with Ryuu because it was the easy way out. All she had to do was follow. But this wasn't her life. She had loved adventure stories growing up, but in reality they were brutal and dark, not as great as the stories made them sound.

She was laying down against a rock which provided a solid back rest. As her thoughts ran away, the evening sun came out, warming her cold body. It brought her thoughts into the light again. She had always been optimistic and her time with Ryuu was ruining her.

In a single moment she knew she was going to leave. There wasn't any need for doom to follow her. She was a beautiful, well educated lady. The last cycle had been a cycle of change, but there wasn't any reason she couldn't start her own life anew. She didn't owe Ryuu anything.

Her mind raced with possibilities and she felt lighter than she had in many moons. She would want to leave the Southern Kingdom, but there wasn't anything for her here. Maybe she could start a restaurant. Everyone liked her cooking.

Takako packed up what little she possessed. In a moment of hesitation she decided to write a short note. It read, "Thank you, Ryuu, for everything, but this isn't the life for me. Please don't search for me. This is what I want, and I will always be grateful."

It wasn't all true, but it was a kindness she could leave him. He deserved that much at least.

With one last glance at the camp Takako took off, her footsteps light and her heart excited. Ahead of her lay a myriad of options. She chose to go north. If her understanding of their position was correct it would send her to the Western Kingdom. There she would start a new life.

The moon was high in the sky when she walked across a wide path, paying little attention to her surroundings. She heard the shouts of recognition and turned and there was a squad of soldiers walking right into her.

Takako moved to run, but the soldiers were well trained. Despite her rush of adrenaline, she was apprehended before she could take three paces. The soldiers found two leather straps and tied one tightly around her wrists and one connecting her ankles. She would be able to walk without problems, but she would not be able to run. Without a word they started marching towards the fortress.

The soldiers did not seem to bear her any particular malice. They kept their pace slow so Takako wasn't stumbling over the roots and bushes in the last light of the evening. She was grateful for that much, but wasn't able to focus her emotions on much of anything. The fear churned her stomach and made her legs numb, threatening her ability to walk. There was only death within the fortress, which made taking every step up to it that much harder.

When the fort came into view, she finally lost her determination, her pride. She fell to the ground, and although part of her wanted to have the spirit to walk into the fort on her own two feet, she couldn't do it. She couldn't will her legs to move, and she began crying, hot tears running down her face, oblivious to anyone who might see or might care.

She couldn't see the pained look on the soldier's faces, but she did feel the strong hands lift her and place her on a soldier's shoulder. She was carried like a sack of rice into the fort. She couldn't summon the strength or the will to resist, but she did leave a trail of tears and rage behind her.

Once inside the fort the soldiers took her to a short, stout building with thick, solid walls. She deduced it was a prison of some sort, built to hold deserters and criminals until justice could be dealt. She was deposited in a small room, her bonds left on. A thick, stout door was shut behind her and Takako could hear the sounds of a thick bar being shut behind it. It was almost enough to make her laugh. They were afraid enough of her to make sure she wouldn't escape. Or, she supposed more hopefully, they were more afraid of who may come to get her.

The hope buoyed her spirits. If Ryuu was scouting the fort he would come for her. But what if he wasn't? She had been walking for quite a while before she'd been captured. If he went back and saw her note, maybe he wouldn't search for her. She couldn't bear the thought she had doomed herself. Ryuu would come. It was the only hope she had.

That thought, Ryuu would come, became her mantra. She repeated it to herself, over and over, and was repeating it when she heard movement on the other side of the door. She couldn't hear any orders being given, but she could hear the bar being lifted and the door being unlatched.

She didn't expect to see Orochi standing there, his large frame filling the entire doorway. He stepped in and motioned for the guards to shut the door. Takako did not hear them latch it or put the bar down, which made her wonder what Orochi intended. The fear began to grip her again, but she kept it under control by continuing to think about Ryuu coming.

Orochi looked at her, studying her for a couple of moments. It was as though he was in her head. "It is good you think of him. If you plan to live, you must keep your hope. It will be what keeps you alive in here."

Takako blinked away her surprise. She had never heard Orochi speak before, and although he had a deep, booming voice, it sounded more like he was trying to comfort her than threaten her. This from the man who had killed Shigeru in cold blood.

Orochi continued to peer into her thoughts at will.

"I suspect there is more to me than you realize. When we are confronted with an enemy, we often seize the opportunity to dehumanize them. I know Shigeru was a friend of yours, but he wronged me."

Takako found her voice. "So he said."

Orochi tilted his head in interest. "Did he? I would have loved to hear his accounting of events."

Takako decided that retelling the story from Shigeru's perspective wasn't in her best interests as a captive, and so she remained silent.

"You know he was responsible for the death of someone I cared for."

Even here, imprisoned, Takako couldn't believe the justifications the men around her used for killing each other. "Your violence only begets more violence. Now that you have killed him, his student will come for you. All of you create a cycle there is no escape from. For as strong as you all are, you are too weak to find a different path."

Orochi nodded. "That may be true. Some would argue we are fated to it."

"A person makes their fate. They can always choose a different path. The paths that doom you are of your own choosing."

Orochi leaned back against the door of her cell. "You are intelligent. I have respect for Shigeru's boy and the power he possesses. I see the company he keeps is indicative of his quality as well. For what it is worth, I am sorry it has come to this."

He paused and then continued. "I have come to offer you an option, a way out."

Takako's heart leapt for a moment, unable to think of what such a way may entail.

He motioned for her to calm down. "It is not what you think. I am honor-bound to an oath I made to Lord Akira. You will die today, have no doubt about it. What I come to offer you today is a quick death, a warrior's death. General Nori is taken with alcohol and has not been able to shake the demon which poisons his mind. He is, literally, mad with grief over the death of his son, and I suspect you will become the victim of that anger unless you take action."

"I consider myself to be an honorable man. To protect his realm, Lord Akira ordered your death, and I shall see that through as I promised him. But torture and whatever Nori has planned for you this afternoon, is not honorable. It is the product of a weak mind. I will take your head, right here and now, if you wish it."

Takako's stomach felt like it had dropped from her body. To choose death over torture seemed like the worst two options she could choose between. She thought of her father, stuck between selling his daughter and losing everything. There had to be a way out of this cycle. She had to hold out hope that Ryuu would come for her. She had to hold on and be strong. He would be here before that happened.

Orochi shook his head. "I sense your hope. The boy will come. Of that I have little doubt. He fights as an honorable man must. He will come after you, but he will have to wait until nightfall. There is no way to approach this fort by day. There are too many archers, and even with his skills he will need the cover of night to reach the fort. By then, it may be too late."

Takako wanted to call him a liar, to throw his words back in his face as Ryuu strode through the door to her cell at just that moment. It was an attractive, beautiful dream, but she recognized the ring of truth in his voice. He believed in Ryuu, but he also knew Ryuu was smart and would be forced to wait until nightfall to attack. So her choice was before her. One day of torture or immediate death.

Despite her desire to lay down and cry, she held her head up. She wanted life, and she chose hope. She couldn't afford not to hope, not here. If she needed to survive torture, survive she would. It was better than giving up.

She didn't have to answer. Orochi read the decision in her face and in her bearing. He gave her a short bow as a measure of respect. "I did not think the consort of a warrior of Ryuu's strength would be weak, but it seemed appropriate for me to make the offer. I hope you are not offended. From one warrior to another, I offer you my respect. May your journey to the Great Cycle be sweet."

Takako barely managed to keep her head up as he left the room. She didn't have the energy to tell him she wasn't Ryuu's consort. As soon as he left she collapsed in a heap, her body unable to support her any longer. The time in her small cell seemed to inflate and slow down until each footstep of the guards felt like an entire cycle had passed. She lost any objective measure of time.

When Nori came, Takako felt like she had suffered an entire lifetime in waiting. She moved slowly, reacted slowly. The air around her seemed as heavy as water as she attempted to struggle, attempted to escape her captors.

Nori brought her into a different room with a high table. She was thrown on the table without ceremony, and she could feel the leather straps being tied tight around her wrist and ankles. Her clothes were ripped off, and she was left naked on the table, unable to move.

Takako was prepared to experience lust, to experience the desire of the men who saw her. She had become well enough used to her body to expect it. She didn't expect Nori's reaction, or lack thereof. There was no arousal in his face. He stood in a corner and looked at her. He was not excited and made no move to take her by force despite her vulnerability.

It was more disconcerting to realize he was just watching her, examining her. She wasn't an object of lust so much as an animal to him. Something to be taught the error of its ways. Takako could almost feel the disconnect from his humanity, and that scared her more than anything had before.

The fear in her body melted her down. Even if she hadn't been tied to the table she was confident she wouldn't be able to move. She had experienced the paralysis of true fear before, but nothing that had ever permeated through every single part of her body.

The first feelings of pain were almost a relief from the fear. Nori had brought with him only a few tools, but his experience was evident. Takako at first tried closing her eyes, but it was worse not knowing.

Nori didn't hurry, working alternately with an extremely sharp knife and a hammer. He always took his time. The pain and the waiting were unlike anything Takako had ever experienced. She had been burned and injured before, but she had never known the world of pain that existed beyond that, white-hot, agonizing, and unending. She had resolved to be strong, but that resolution was broken within moments. She cried for mercy, screamed in pain until her throat was raw. She would have told him anything to make him stop. But he continued without emotion.

Twice she passed out from the pain and twice Nori brought her back with smelling salts. Then he would begin again, slowly, building the pain up to yet another unbearable crescendo. The third time she passed out Nori did not wake her up, and she slipped into the blissful realm of unconsciousness.

When she awoke she saw through the open door that evening was beginning to fall. She didn't even bother trying to move. Something, deep within her, had finally snapped. The hope which had sustained her for so long, the belief everything would be okay, was gone. She didn't have the mental strength to catalog her injuries, but some part of her knew her body would never heal from this, would never work again.

She knew both her legs were broken as was one arm and probably a couple of the bones in her torso. Skin was missing from small sections of her body, including her face and breasts. If she did survive the day she would never have her beauty again, never be able to walk normally. Her dreams of making her own way had disappeared. She did not know everything Nori had done between her legs, but she knew she would never enjoy making love, she never had enjoyed it.

It was the never part that got to her. She would never do many of the things she had dreamed of. That hurt more than the physical pain itself. Some part of her had always believed everything would turn out. Setbacks and challenges were temporary and could be overcome. But what had happened to her ended that. Even if Ryuu rescued her, she wouldn't be the same.

A single tear rolled down her cheek and shattered upon the table as it dropped from her face. Little droplets had spread out from the point of impact. There wasn't anything left.

Takako figured out the truth. She had heard of people who had reached this stage in their lives, but the thought of getting here had always terrified her. Aging had never scared her, but the process of giving up, of not having anything to look forward to froze her heart. She believed in the Great Cycle, perhaps now more than ever, because it was the only hope she had remaining.

She heard slow footsteps outside her door and closed her eyes. If she could feign unconsciousness, perhaps they would just let her lie here for a little while longer. That was all she wanted. Just to lie there and let the darkness overcome her.

Somehow she knew from the footsteps. He moved like Ryuu and Moriko. She imagined she could sense the shock from him as he looked over her and cataloged her injuries. She knew he didn't look at her lustfully, not because of her injuries, but because he saw her as a person. It was refreshing, in a way, but she still just wanted to be left alone, to be allowed to sleep once and for all.

"Your sleep will come soon enough. But not now, and not by my hand."

If Takako could have summoned any movement to spit any words of hate out at him she would have, but she had nothing left but resignation.

"There's no need. You hate me, and with good reason. I would wish you would rejoin the Great Cycle without malice in your heart towards me, but I understand if that's not possible. Take comfort. I sense the end of this journey is near. I cannot sense him, but I can sense this world beginning to change. We are on the verge of a new age. I know he will come tonight. I will challenge him, and I do not know who will win. He is stronger than Shigeru, but I suspect he never told you that. I will let him see you before we meet."

Takako imagined herself nodding to Orochi's statement, and he seemed to sense her agreement. It was nice not having to physically move to communicate.

"I will leave and shut the door behind me. You have my word I will guard it until he comes for you. Nori will not be allowed back in. Your suffering is almost over."

Takako once again imagined agreeing, and once again it was enough for Orochi. He left, and as the door shut behind him all the remaining light faded, leaving her in complete darkness.

Takako closed her eyes and could feel the life in her blood draining out of her. She was ready. She wanted nothing more than to die quietly without hope.

CHAPTER 28

Moriko sat as still and quiet as a statue as the sun rose high in the sky. She had to compensate for Ryuu's inability to do anything but pace with his hand on his sword ready to cut down anything that moved. Someone needed to be the calm one. Ryuu was angry, scared, determined, and uncertain. He wasn't thinking straight. He couldn't hold on to a single thought long enough to follow it to its conclusion. He was jumping back and forth faster than a jackrabbit in danger. He was a danger not just to himself but to her as well.

A part of her went out to him. She couldn't imagine his pain. But if he didn't focus he wouldn't last. Moriko didn't suspect an attack. Nori and Orochi's strategy was simple, obvious, and effective. They weren't going to come out and lose men in the woods. They would wait for them to come in, determine the field of battle. It was a significant advantage. Moriko was tempted to just walk away from it all.

As she watched Ryuu, Moriko allowed her thoughts to wander. He wasn't the only one involved. She was reaching the point of no return. If she went with Ryuu on the rescue her course would be set.

She didn't know where she stood. She wanted to believe her situation was different than Ryuu's, that Lord Akira and Orochi wouldn't hunt her down the same way they had Shigeru and his student. She was only an escaped monk, far less dangerous than a full fledged nightblade. She wanted to believe she could walk away without fear of consequence.

The rational part of her mind knew it was a lie. Orochi and Akira had no reason to view her as anything other than another nightblade who posed a danger to the realm. Her only chance to convince them otherwise would be to go straight to Orochi and plead with him. He knew her well, perhaps he would believe her.

It would be a tough sell. Orochi knew of her disdain for the monasteries. It would be difficult for him to believe she hadn't some choice in the matter. Perhaps he wouldn't believe her at all and would kill her where she stood.

Joining Ryuu on his attempt would firmly place her in Ryuu's camp, and she wasn't sure she wanted that either. She liked Ryuu but she wanted to maintain her distance. If she wasn't close to anybody, if she wasn't responsible to anybody, she wouldn't suffer like Ryuu did.

He was an interesting man, not just because he was a nightblade in a world where they were nearly extinct, but because of his innocence. His emotions were so raw and pure. He wasn't cynical or disillusioned. He saw the world as it was and sought to change it, thought he could change it.

He was also immature. There was clearly a relationship between Takako and Ryuu, but he had the gall to approach her. She didn't compare to Takako at all. Takako was a good woman and beautiful beyond compare. Her skin was smooth and soft unlike the scars which criss-crossed Moriko's body from her time in front of the Abbot. She knew how to bring pleasure to a man, a set of skills Moriko had never even imagined having the time to learn in her situation in the monastery.

But Ryuu was also attracted to Moriko, and Moriko was cynical. She didn't believe Ryuu was malicious. He just found himself with two women he liked and didn't know how to act. He would have to choose, but didn't. He was too young to realize he couldn't have it all.

Moriko's reverie was interrupted by Ryuu stopping his pacing right in front of her. "We need to leave now. She could die at any moment!"

"She's not going to die."

"You don't know that, don't say that," Ryuu spat back, his emotions almost literally carrying him away.

"I do. She's bait. I don't know if they were searching for her or found her by chance, but Nori and Orochi are using her to draw you in. They get to choose the ground, they get to set all the traps and all the kill spaces they want. Bait is no good if it's dead. They want you dead, and for that to happen she needs to be alive. So stop worrying."

Ryuu shook his head at the last comment, but kept his silence. He knew she was right, it was just difficult for him to admit it. She softened her tone.

"Look, I know the waiting is horrible, but we have to wait until nightfall. We both know there's no way we can cross through that grassy patch without getting stuck like a shooting target. We need the cover of night to make our advance."

Ryuu collapsed in exasperation. "I know. I know they will keep her alive. But it doesn't stop me from wanting to go in and get her." He made no effort to hide the tears that started streaming from his eyes. He looked up at Moriko. "They could still hurt her."

Moriko didn't have anything to say. That statement was most likely true.

"Did you know all this was my fault? When I first met Takako, Shigeru had hired her to teach me how to interact with women and girls, how to act in society. Nothing more. We became friends. When she was taken, I didn't feel like I had any choice. I had to stop it from happening. But look at all the pain it's caused. Her entire family is dead and now she's captured, enduring whatever they have in store for her, all because I tried to stop things. Shigeru is dead. All because of me. I should know to leave well enough alone."

Moriko's heart went out to Ryuu in that moment. "It's not your fault. Yes, many people are dead, but that doesn't make your actions wrong. You did the best you could with what you knew. The ones who are responsible are the ones who swung the sword. Not you."

Moriko's decision was made. "And I will help you. But you have to know something. I will not help you in any fight against Orochi."

Ryuu looked up, rage flashing in his eyes.

Moriko stepped back. She had never considered Ryuu hadn't anticipated her dilemma. She assumed he would have thought it through. She regained her confidence and returned his stare with all the willpower she could muster.

"I understand he killed Shigeru, and I'm sorry for the pain he caused you. But you are forgetting two things about him."

Ryuu's gaze pierced her like a blade.

Moriko stepped forward, hands relaxed at her side.

"First, I can't believe Orochi is an evil man. He is intimidating, scary, and unapproachable, maybe even misguided. But he is not a bad man. He disdained the monastery and its systems, and to my knowledge he has never broken his word. I will not be responsible for helping kill a decent man."

Ryuu's face was a mask of anger, but he made no move against her.

"Second, Orochi was a teacher and a mentor to me. If not for him I would have been killed at the monastery many cycles ago. He was the one who trained me as a nightblade. He was the one who made me as I am today. I will not attack the man who did that for me even if I disagree with his actions."

Moriko had underestimated the depth of Ryuu's emotion. He drew his sword and Moriko knew she was no match for him. His speed was incredible. He had guarded his intent well, and she never sensed it coming. She couldn't even react before he had his blade to her throat.

The cold steel bit into her flesh, but she refused to move, refused to show fear, even when Ryuu spoke softly in her ear, his voice full of menace. "You are talking about the man who killed my father."

She looked Ryuu straight in the eyes. "I know. And you are talking about killing mine."

It was exactly what he needed to hear. Ryuu's eyes went wide, and he deflated as if he had been punched in the stomach.

Ryuu couldn't find his words. He looked up at Moriko, eyes filling with tears, and Moriko could see he was at the end of his rope. He had done everything he could to protect everyone he loved, and it was all slipping away.

"I'm. . . I'm so sorry." Ryuu turned and started shuffling away, his body boneless as it slumped down against a tree.

Moriko didn't know how to react, but Ryuu needed help. If he was going to go into the fort in this mental condition, Orochi would destroy him. In his current state, Orochi might not even have to do the work. A child with a stick and a grudge could probably kill Ryuu right now.

She came to him and sat down next to him and cradled his head against her chest as he sobbed. It was the first time she had held a man. She embraced him, emotions flooding her senses as well.

Eventually Ryuu's breakdown subsided, and Moriko could see that everything had burned away. He was a man on a mission. Moriko nodded her approval and cleared a space in the dirt at their feet. With a stick she sketched out the compound, making corrections as Ryuu brought them to her attention. Much of it was guesswork, albeit educated. They weren't able to sense walls or buildings, but only the people in them. It was guesswork to determine which collections of people represented which types of buildings, but they felt reasonably sure of their efforts.

They discussed several ideas for entering the compound, from a direct walk up the main road to attempting to sneak in through the tree tops without being detected. A simmering tension lay beneath the surface, as Moriko's ideal attempt kept them completely unnoticed, while Ryuu preferred an approach that left a trail of corpses in his wake.

Like all great plans, they ended up deciding on a compromise. Ryuu would attempt to enter the compound directly. His goal was to divert attention to himself. While Ryuu was the distraction, Moriko would sneak in and pull Takako out by approaching and leaving from a different direction. It was as good as they could come up with. Ryuu was the better swordsman and Moriko could get in and out without Orochi sensing her.

It was also a plan which pitted Ryuu against Orochi. Ryuu was happy about it, Moriko unspeakably sad. She knew she was going to lose at least one of them if not both. She cursed fate for putting her in this position.

Moriko looked up at the horizon. "They'll be expecting us to attack in the middle of the night."

Ryuu glanced at the horizon as well. By a quick judgment it looked like they still had a couple of watches before the sun was down. "That's why we are attacking as soon as the sky is dark."

She almost protested, but realized it was the most logical decision. Many guards would be sleeping in preparation for the night watch and wouldn't recover quickly. It would give them an advantage in the opening moments of the attack.

They decided to take turns sleeping and keeping watch. Moriko was exhausted and fell asleep in an instant. When she was awoken, the sun was just dipping below the horizon.

"Three watches and then wake me." Moriko nodded at Ryuu's command.

Like Moriko, he fell asleep instantly. Considering the emotional strain he was under, it was surprising he could sleep at all. She smiled to herself and kept watch, reflecting on the turn of events which had very likely brought her to the last day of her life.

CHAPTER 29

Ryuu awoke the moment Moriko moved to wake him. Again Moriko was reminded of just how different Ryuu's training had been from her own. Sometimes it didn't even seem like he slept. His sense was so well-tuned he was able to pick up movement towards him even while asleep. He had attempted to teach the ability to Moriko, but she hadn't been able to get the hang of it. She suspected it wasn't so much an issue of technique or ability, but more the repeated conditioning of waking up to an imagined threat. Ryuu had mentioned in passing once that Shigeru had often tested him with midnight attacks.

They prepared without speaking. Words weren't necessary. They knew what they were doing, knew there was nothing further to be discussed. They each practiced some cuts and made sure their edges were sharp.

Moriko couldn't help but stare a little as Ryuu went through his kata. She could see the small differences in his swordsmanship that made him better than anyone she had met. His moves and cuts were perfect. She had considered her own training to be rigorous, but his had been more intense. For over ten cycles he had done nothing but train every day with a man who was one of the best swordsmen in the Three Kingdoms.

Even more impressive, Moriko was convinced she had yet to see his true skill. He had dispatched the Abbot with so little effort, Moriko was positive she had never seen his full potential. In all of their training, he had always been able to block or dodge every single one of her attacks. It was sometimes only by the smallest of distances, but she had never struck him. To an untrained eye they may be close in skill, but Moriko suspected a vast plain separated them.

Having known both Ryuu and Orochi, she didn't know who would win in a duel between the two of them. She had never seen the true strength of either of them. She hoped she would never have to find out. She still wanted both of them to live through the night although she knew that she would lose one of them to the Great Cycle before the sun rose.

As he finished his movements his eyes locked with hers, and she didn't need her sense to understand the turbulence of his emotions. His eyes flashed with anger, compassion, and determination.

Silence stretched between them, and Moriko imagined for a moment that even the forest which sheltered them had gone quiet in expectation. In an uncharacteristic moment, she felt like she needed to fill the silence with something, but there was nothing she could say that he didn't already know.

Ryuu glanced in the direction of the fort. He could feel the tension and the fear emanating from that direction. The soldiers there knew. After their dramatic exit from the premises at sunrise, they knew they were hunted. There was a predator in the woods much more dangerous than them. Ryuu grimly smiled to himself. They had no idea how right they were. He had to save Takako. After all the pain and suffering he had put her through she deserved a better life.

The secret fear gripped his heart. The rational part of his mind knew she was alive. They intended to kill her as surely as they intended to kill him, but not yet, not now. She would die after he was committed, after he was in their trap. He needed Moriko to save her. He just had to make sure that he was fast enough and strong enough he could disrupt their plans before they blossomed. Still, he couldn't help but fear it was already too late, that they had killed her regardless of the consequences.

He wasn't sure he could live if Takako died. There would be no redemption for him. Already he felt like he had caused so much suffering in her life. Every day he wondered what would have happened if he had just let her be. She might not have had the best life, but her family would still be alive, her suffering earning their freedom. It wasn't much, but it seemed to Ryuu it was more than she had now.

Ryuu had come to a resolution. He would save her and make sure she was safe. He would hide her so far away no one would ever be able to find her. Takako could live out the rest of her cycles in peace, maybe even rebuild a new life. It was her best hope. So long as she was away from him, she would be safe. He would have to deal with Lord Akira, but he felt certain he could elude and fight off any pursuit.

All he needed to do was rescue her tonight. All that stood between him and her was Orochi. His anger burned, but he managed to wrap it all inside of him, taking comfort in the strength it gave him. Kill Orochi, save the girl, get her someplace far away, and then leave her in peace. It was the only way she would be safe.

His purpose was set, and although his anger burned through him and warmed his blood, he was calm. Shigeru had taught him well. He motioned to Moriko, and they began their walk towards the fort. There were no sentries on the outer perimeter as there had been that morning. They had brought everybody in to the inner ring of defenses. It was a smart move. The outer ring had been too spread out. It was good for detection of a typical intruder, but Ryuu and Moriko could have taken out a guard post, or several posts, without anyone being the wiser.

When they were almost to the clearing Moriko split off. Ryuu tried to quest out with his sense, but the fort was still too far away. He could sense the archers around the perimeter. Orochi had stationed a lot of them out there. Ryuu admitted Moriko was right. It would have been impossible to cross the clearing in the daylight. With so many archers he would have been shot down no matter how many arrows he might have tried deflecting or dodging.

The men he sensed were nervous but competent. They didn't let their fear control them, and Ryuu respected that. But if they stood in his way tonight, they would die. He could sense their arrows nocked in their bowstrings, their bows held in relaxed awareness. They were professionals.

When he judged enough time had passed, he hugged the ground and began slithering forward through the grass. There was a slight breeze on the air, and he tried to time his movements with the upcoming breeze. It was slow, agonizing work. His heart wanted him to stand up and challenge all comers, but he knew even with his skill he couldn't stop a barrage of arrows. Despite all of his power he was still just a man.

When he was about half way through the tall grass, he took a break and rested, sitting on his calves in a tall clump of grass.

He focused his mind and reached out with his sense. The archers were all still there, in a relaxed state of readiness. No one gave any hint of detecting him. He sought out further and found what he was searching for. There was the outpost with the darkness inside. And Takako was near him.

Ryuu was surprised to sense how weak she was. He was still far away, but he could barely sense her. She was in pain, she was dying. The realization hit him without warning, and he had to snap back to his own reality to prevent himself from jumping up and sprinting towards her. There was no way he could fail. Takako was counting on him, expecting him to save her.

He still had time. She was weak, but her will was strong. She would hold on until he got there.

Ryuu redoubled his efforts. It was essential he make good time to the fort. He went back to hugging the ground, moving one agonizing pace at a time. What had taken him only a handful of breaths earlier today was now taking an endless stretch of infinite moments.

By the time he had passed from the grass back into the woods every part of him was on fire. He had never expected that simple crawling would take so much out of him. But he had not been seen. He was keeping his sense close, but even where he stood, hidden in the dark shadows of a tree, he could tell he was surrounded by enemies. Fortunately, most of them were focused on the grass, looking out. Now that he had passed the first ring he could move more freely.

In short order he was only a dozen paces away from the perimeter of the fort. He examined it and was pleased to see it fit with the estimations he and Moriko had made under the afternoon sun. He took a moment to sense the watch patterns of the sentries that patrolled the wall, and with certain decisiveness, he ran at the wall, planting two feet against it as he reached to the top. In his mind's eye he flashed back to the first time he had seen Shigeru climb the tree stand. He used his momentum to swing his body up and over the pointed timbers. He landed silently on the top wall as two sentries had their backs turned. Without pausing he rolled off the wall and into a clump of bushes on the other side.

He took a deep breath. He had been prepared for combat, but he was grateful it hadn't occurred. The closer he could get before he was discovered the better. It meant fewer enemies he'd have to fight through. Fortunately, there weren't many people in the fort proper. Most everyone was stationed on the walls or in the forest surrounding the fort. Once penetrated it was soft and ripe for the picking.

Ryuu threw his sense out and he found everyone in the fort itself. Two people stood out above the rest. One was Orochi, whom Ryuu could sense clear as day from this distance. Orochi had to have detected him by now. Ryuu wondered why he hadn't started the alarms yet. Whatever the case, he wasn't moving, which at this point in time was enough for Ryuu.

The other individual was new, but Ryuu felt like he had sensed him somewhere before. It wasn't coming to him though. He was an older man filled with anger. He was strong, an excellent swordsman, and his rage fueled him. It bothered Ryuu that he couldn't identify him, but he pushed the thought out of his mind. Whoever he was, if he was important, Ryuu would have known who he was. He would push forward.

Ryuu noticed that at that very moment there was no one looking at the path between him and Takako. Only Orochi was in the way. Ryuu didn't hesitate, didn't even give himself time to think about it. He darted forward, every step as silent as the grave he planned to send Orochi to.

He found the door to the building without difficulty and slid it open, revealing a long hallway with rooms off to the side. But his attention was grabbed immediately by the figure sitting cross-legged against the wall at the end of the hallway.

It was Orochi, every bit as big and strong as Ryuu remembered him. His heart quickened, and he grabbed his sword, but had enough control to not draw.

Orochi looked up with a curious expression. If Ryuu hadn't known, he would have guessed he was being studied. Orochi's gaze lingered on him for what felt like an eternity. He did not move or even flinch at Ryuu's presence. The man was as cool as anyone Ryuu had ever met.

Orochi broke the silence. "She trained you in my techniques."

Ryuu was caught off guard. He had expected anger, some form of evil, something dark. Instead, he felt a calm sense of strength and purpose. Of honor, even. It deflated all the anger he had brought into the hall. He shifted his stance into one less aggressive. He nodded.

"You are an apt pupil. You haven't had long to study, but even I wasn't sure until you stepped through the door."

Ryuu didn't know what to do. Here Orochi was complimenting his study skills, which was just about the last event he had expected to happen upon encountering Orochi for the last time.

"Did Shigeru talk about the techniques he had never mastered?"

Ryuu was shaken. The mention of Shigeru's name almost caused him to draw his sword, but he restrained himself. His anger was overridden by his curiousness, but not by much.

"A little."

"How did you learn them?"

"I haven't."

Ryuu realized it was silly to be having this conversation, admitting there were skills he didn't possess. It was as if he and Orochi were solving a puzzle together.

Orochi nodded as if Ryuu had confirmed something he had long ago known. "I had wondered if that may be the case." He patted his chest. "Underneath my tunic, I have a letter for you. I wrote it. It gives directions to the island where Shigeru and I grew up. They would be very interested in meeting you if you survive the day. As a hidden refuge, it is hard to find, but I expect you'll manage. Do not trust them, but they may be able to offer you some guidance. I suspect their aims are different than your own, but they may help you harness your strength. If I'm right you have more raw talent than anyone currently alive."

With that Orochi stood up. Apparently the conversation wasn't going to last all night. Ryuu tensed and dropped into his stance. Orochi let out the hint of a grin. "Not now. I will wait here. You should say good-bye to the girl."

Ryuu was shaken to his core. Here was the enemy he had driven himself to hate the past few moons freely offering what he most wanted.

Like Shigeru, it seemed like Orochi could read his thoughts.

"Did Shigeru tell you about me?"

Ryuu nodded, unable to form the words to converse.

"Killing him was personal. I am sorry for your loss, but I am not sorry I killed him. He had taken that which I loved."

Ryuu found his voice. "He would have said the same about you."

Orochi nodded. "I don't know if he would have been wrong in saying so. I was young and headstrong, but she didn't deserve what happened. She didn't need to save me. Anyway, as I said, it was personal. If I had not given my word, I would leave you in peace. If you are what I think you are, it will be a very interesting fight. I can't break my word to Akira. I made the same deal with the girl, but I want you to know it would have been clean. Not like this. That," he gestured in the direction of the door, "is an abomination. It is not the mark of a warrior, and for that you have my sympathy. I would have struck him down myself."

Ryuu understood what Orochi left unspoken. He was bound by honor. Ryuu found the name he had been missing. General Nori. He had been the father of the scum Ryuu had killed in the camp. This was personal for everyone. He was the strong swordsman Ryuu had sensed on the way in.

Ryuu found he trusted Orochi. He walked up to him and moved past him, completely open. Orochi did not attack and muttered another apology as Ryuu walked past. He stepped into the room and fell to his knees at the sight that greeted him.

Ryuu had slain before. It had been a gut-churning experience, but it had been necessary and defensible. He could never imagine doing something like this, something so grotesque.

Takako was on the table tied by each wrist and ankle, but she was almost unidentifiable. The calculating portion of Ryuu's brain took over to compensate for what he was seeing, trying to catalog the injuries. Broken fingers and toes. Fingernails pulled. Skin flayed from all of her sensitive areas. Burn marks. The thick bones in her legs were broken as were some of her ribs. She was covered in blood, and Ryuu had to suspect she had been raped as well. She was breathing, but barely.

It finally dawned on him that he was too late. He had always been too late. She was dead right now, her body just hadn't figured it out yet. Even if he did manage to kill everyone here and carry her out, her body was in no condition to move anywhere. She would breathe her last before he could pass the walls of the fort.

He should be angry, but he didn't have the strength anymore. It was unbearable. The world continued to conspire against him, to take away everything good he had encountered in his life. His parents, Shigeru, Takako, all of them shared the distinction of dying in front of him as he watched helplessly. All his power, all his strength, was nothing but the greatest joke the Great Cycle could play on him.

The tears streamed freely from his face, and his body was wracked by sobs. He knew Orochi could sense him, and he felt the corresponding sorrow in Orochi's aura. It was comforting, but not enough. It would never be enough.

He almost didn't hear her over the sounds of his sobs.

"What are you crying for?"

Despite himself, he laughed as he cried. He could feel her spirit had been broken as well as her body, but he appreciated the effort.

Ryuu crawled over to her, unable to summon the strength to stand. His robes picked up Takako's blood on the floor, but he didn't care, didn't even notice. He knelt at the table and made a move to comfort her, but couldn't find a spot he could touch without causing her more pain. He laid his head down next to hers and let himself cry.

The two of them laid there, silent except for the sounds of Ryuu's sobs and Takako struggling for breath. Outside, Ryuu could sense Moriko had begun her attack on the other side of the compound. Men were dying, and the other strong presence, Nori, was rushing headlong to attack her.

The action calmed Ryuu's mind as he focused on action he could not see. Moriko would be able to hold out for a while, but not for too long. He knew she was trying to give him time, not knowing he was safe for now. Their plan had gone to hell. He was supposed to be fighting Orochi, not crying in the middle of a fort.

Outside of blood, the room was bare. Every time he glanced back at Takako, his mind reminded him of the truth, even if his heart couldn't accept it. Takako would never leave this room alive. The thought brought him right back to the edge as red swam in his vision.

"Takako, I'm so sorry, so sorry for everything."

Takako managed to open her eyes and look at him. Her mouth moved slightly, trying to form the words, but as she did she coughed up a thin stream of blood. Her lips moved, but Ryuu couldn't make out the words. He wasn't sure she was even making the words she was trying to.

Ryuu leaned close. "Takako, I love you. I love you so much, and I'm so sorry for everything. I only wanted you to be happy."

Takako smiled, an effort that seemed to take all of her energy.

So he had come after all. Takako wasn't surprised. He was that kind of man. He would never give up, always try to make things right.

He didn't touch her, and for that, Takako was grateful. Everything hurt. If he tried anything, she would give up completely. She was ready and blackness was already beginning to cloud the edges of her vision. She didn't want to die, but she was ready. She would get to see her family again. She tried to tell him it was okay. She forgave him. She cared for him and was fine, but she couldn't hear her own voice. Hopefully he'd heard her.

Through the cloud of her thoughts and the pain, she heard his voice again. Claiming he loved her. Saying he was sorry, over and over again.

And then she couldn't focus on his voice anymore. She could hear him talking, like the buzzing of a fly around her ear, but she couldn't make out what he was saying. The pain had gone away as well. That was nice.

She realized then, at the end of all things, that she was content. Her time with Ryuu hadn't been wasted. She hoped he would realize that. She smiled then and gave up the fight. Darkness rushed in on her vision, and in the very last moment before the end, she felt the presence of all life surrounding her, embracing her.

And then she joined the Great Cycle.

He wanted one last word, something he could remember her by. Some aspect of forgiveness, some sense of closure. But as she smiled, he knew it was over, that her smile was her goodbye.

And then he felt her energy leave her, and he was no longer looking at Takako, but the shell of the body that once held her. He collapsed into her, ready now to touch her, to try to comfort her. His tears mixed with her blood as he lay there against the table, unable to move, unable to forgive himself for the pain he had brought into the world.

Moriko sneaked inside the camp before she was noticed. The sentries had been professional, but there were always gaps and it had been a simple, if physically challenging, job to enter the premises. Their plan had been for Ryuu to be the distraction, to draw the attention of the guards and warriors.

When she made it into the camp, she waited for a moment and let her sense expand. What she sensed made her doubt all her abilities. The camp itself was awake and alive as they had expected, but she swore she felt Ryuu and Orochi, talking. Everything else in the camp was as she had expected.

Moriko focused her sense on a guard she could see. Everything about him felt right. She returned her focus to the center of the camp where Orochi and Ryuu were, and the two of them were still not fighting. Despite herself, she believed it. Perhaps they would all live through the night.

She settled back in the shadows. There was no reason for her to announce herself if there was no need. She would sit and wait and see how the situation developed. She kept her sense focused on Ryuu as he walked past Orochi. When he reached the room with Takako, Moriko wasn't prepared for the wave of anger and despair she felt from him. It almost knocked her senseless.

Her curiosity wanted to see what he saw, to know what could generate such feelings. But she knew better. She knew Takako had been broken by her experiences here. Maybe as a rape victim. Whatever the reason, she felt like she had seen enough and more pain would be unnecessary.

She sat confused as Ryuu refused to move and Orochi patiently waited for him. She had never felt Ryuu so inactive before. Moriko shifted her attention from him to Takako and she understood everything. Takako was in incredible pain and was dying. It had been torture then.

Moriko's own experiences flashed through her mind. Being beaten and stabbed by the Abbot, tied to his floor. Takako had suffered through worse torments during her one day here. And she was innocent, having done nothing more than be loved by a nightblade. Hardly worthy of the pain and suffering she had undergone. It had cost her her life, and unlike Moriko, Ryuu had not come along in time to save her.

Moriko's anger took hold of her then, a fiery grip that squeezed all the rage out of her. She was stronger than those who were here, and it was time to let them know the nightblades were not dead and would not be hunted like this. Her hot fury froze as cold determination, and she used her sense one last time to get the lay of the place.

She took just a moment and waited for a roving patrol to come too close to her hiding spot. She slid out as they walked by, and with two quick, clean cuts, she severed the life from their bodies. They didn't even know death was coming until it embraced them, a stranger reaching out from the shadows.

Moriko gave the guards a small amount of credit. Even if she had hoped to, she wouldn't have been able to return to her hiding space. The alarm was raised in an instant, and she could feel the entire attention of the outpost being turned in her direction. She felt even Orochi's sense as he noted her presence. Her greatest satisfaction was the small sense of surprise she felt from him. He hadn't been able to detect her, not even this close.

All thoughts flew through her mind and left without the slightest disturbance. She let them go as she fell into her favorite stance and focused on the present. She kept moving, both to avoid archers and to prevent the guards from trying to box her in. She focused on another pair of soldiers leapt towards them.

The guards may have been prepared, but fear still emanated off them like a stink. Their defense was slow, unfocused, and Moriko moved through them as easily as she would pass between two trees. They fell behind her, but Moriko was already moving on to the next pair.

When Takako died, even Moriko, in the midst of combat, felt it. It felt like a flickering but bright candle had just gone out. The darkness flooded the edges of her vision, and the distraction was almost fatal. Moriko deflected the cut just in time and grimaced as she took stock of her situation. More and more soldiers were converging on her location, and within moments she would no longer be able to pick them off one at a time.

At that moment Moriko sensed someone new approaching, someone stronger than the other soldiers. Perhaps this was the general that Ryuu had mentioned. She backed up a few paces to buy herself time to focus. It gave her the time to sense him clearly. He had Takako's presence all over him, and in a moment, Moriko knew this was the man who had tortured and killed Takako.

Once the moment of rage passed, his presence gave Moriko pause. She knew Ryuu would want to be the one to kill this man, especially if he was the one who had committed the violence against Takako. She almost held back her attack, but she wanted blood. He was here now and had to be defeated. He felt strong enough to be able to turn the tide of the battle.

The other soldiers halted their attacks in deference to their general. They knew this was personal for him and had the respect to draw back. Moriko took the moment to collect herself. He was strong and his rage ran deep. It would either be the death of him or make him stronger than he had ever been.

With his draw, she saw it would be the latter. His iron control had hardened over his rage, forming a core that would not accept defeat. He was strong and smart. He came in with small controlled cuts, never committing himself to a stroke. Moriko dodged and parried, but did not provide the opening he was hoping for.

The pass concluded in the space of a couple of heartbeats and they separated. Moriko suppressed a shudder of concern. He was strong and fast and controlled. He wasn't afraid, and he was more than ready to die so long as she came with him. Short of having the sense, he was the most dangerous opponent she could have encountered.

It took an extreme effort, but she pushed all thoughts out of her mind. She settled into her stance and brought all of her focus to the moment. He would make a mistake, and she would make the one cut that would end this.

The world called him back. It had been blissful to lose himself in his grief, to allow the tears and the anger to flood over him, to shut out the outside world in a way his gift, his curse, never allowed him to. Ryuu missed his parents, the vaguest of memories against the relentless tide of time. He missed Shigeru and Takako. He knew that when they joined the Great Cycle they had taken a part of him with them and the only way to be whole again would be to follow them on their journey.

But Moriko kept moving forward, and the battle raging outside the room crashed through even his shut-down sense. Despite an initial attempt, he could not block the sounds of battle coming through the walls. With a deep breath he opened himself back up and felt the world flowing around him, the same as it always did. He imagined, just for a moment, that Takako brushed against him too.

Nori was approaching Moriko. It would be a difficult fight for her. He didn't even have to focus to feel the absence that was Orochi. He was outside the building, guarding against intruders and watching his protege. No one else knew Ryuu was in the tent.

It dawned on him then that Orochi was guarding him. He was giving Ryuu the time and space to mourn his loss.

Orochi's actions sealed up Ryuu's heart. Moriko had been right about him. A killer, yes, but an honorable man who followed his own conscience. Ryuu's anger transformed and cooled into ice, an indestructible calm. He would kill Orochi. But not in anger. Not in vengeance. For justice. For being part of the plan that caused Takako such pain.

He stood up and readjusted his blades. He ran his fingers over the hilt, almost believing he could feel the feminine grip of their original owner. Today was the culmination of almost thirty cycles of waiting and vengeance.

He looked one last time at Takako's body, but he didn't feel anything. It was only a shell, an empty vessel, broken like a clay pot, its contents dispersed to the four winds. He knew she was around him, just like every other living thing. He bowed deeply to her body and walked out the door.

Orochi was right where Ryuu expected he would find him. Across the yard, Moriko and Nori had paused their fight momentarily, and Ryuu's unexpected presence created a commotion throughout the yard. Nori wasn't in command of himself, unable to spread his focus beyond the point of Moriko's blade. One loose arrow came in towards Ryuu, but he swatted it away with his bare hand with such a dismissive gesture the other archers on the wall held their shots.

Ryuu stopped in front of Orochi, just out of the range of a quick strike. He hadn't realized how much bigger Orochi was. Ryuu's head only came up to his chest. He bowed, more deeply than he had before. "Thank you."

Orochi nodded. "It was not my way. But Akira placed me under his command. He could not see beyond his son's death."

Ryuu felt a surge of respect for this enemy. He may have killed Shigeru, but he was a good man. He was the most worthy opponent he had faced.

Ryuu made to reach for his blade, but Orochi held up his hand. "A moment, please. I have two items to discuss."

Ryuu dropped his hand back to a ready position.

"The first is a favor. If I win today, I would like your permission to take your swords. If I lose, I would ask that you bury me with your own, and take mine as an offering."

The request confused Ryuu until he spoke again. "They were hers."

Ryuu didn't even hesitate. "It will be as you say."

"Thank you. Second, on my person I have a map back to the island Shigeru and I are from. Should I die today, I ask that you would consider going there. I sense a strength in you that is undeniable. They may help you." He paused, grinning just a moment. "They might also try to kill you or convert you, but that's a challenge you'd have to face on your own."

Ryuu agreed and drew his blade. One way or another, everything ended today.

CHAPTER 30

Once Ryuu left the building it was as if a truce had been called on the battlefield. All the soldiers who had rushed to attack Moriko found the warrior they were supposed to be fighting turn up right behind them. The soldiers did not know what Orochi was, but there had been guesses. Where knowledge failed, superstition grew, and it was already believed, despite any evidence, that Orochi was the best swordsman in the camp.

Moriko did have to admit to herself that the two of them threw off a presence. If she had not been used to both of them, she would not have believed it herself, but everyone in the camp could feel the power emanating from the two nightblades. Everyone put down their swords, knowing they were spectators in a clash of steel far beyond their abilities.

Everyone but Nori, so blinded with rage and anger he had shut out everything besides his battle and his target. He moved in quickly, but Moriko could sense him coming, and his conservative strikes couldn't get near her. If he wanted to win he would have to commit, and once he did he would leave one opening which she would exploit.

His cuts came fast, almost blurring with the speed of his strikes. But his skill was to no avail. Moriko saw every move clear as day before he had even started. Those she couldn't sidestep she deflected with the side of her sword. She wasn't in any danger, but she also wasn't creating any openings for him. He was playing too conservatively for that.

Finally, Nori lost his edge. The rage took over and overwhelmed his control, just for a moment. He wanted so badly to kill her, to maim her. Moriko saw it all. He thought he saw an opening and his cut was strong and committed, everything he would have needed for a victory. But Moriko sensed it, nudged his cut aside and took the opening, cutting deeply through his abdomen.

She didn't wait or gloat. The strike had surprised him, but he could still be dangerous. In his momentary surprise, the very breath he realized he had been cut fatally, she turned and cut again, slicing through the side of his neck.

And with that, Moriko's battle was over. It took him a few moments to die, but there was no change in his soul. He died angry and full of rage, a man who had lost his honor.

Moriko didn't spare the time to watch him die. She wiped her blade and turned around to join the soldiers watching the fight between Ryuu and Orochi.

The first time he had seen Orochi outside the farmhouse, Ryuu had frozen in fear, unable to help his master, the man who had become his father. He had watched, helpless as Shigeru had given his life in an attempt to take Orochi's. Up until this moment, he had worried it might happen again, that at his core, beneath all his strength, he was a coward.

It was one thing to face men who were not his equals. Mistakes could be made which would end his life, but he was strong and smart and the odds were always in his favor. It was something else entirely to face an adversary just as strong.

Shigeru's lessons floated somewhere in the back of his consciousness. "Every time you draw your blade, you must be prepared to die. A warrior who goes into battle expecting to live will always be weak. Only by willing to face death is victory possible."

As with many lessons, Ryuu didn't understand until later. In this case, it was today. Takako's death had seen to that. Life or death held no particular distinction for him any longer. His only thought was his blade and how he could direct it against Orochi.

Orochi sprang forward to attack. The movement just barely caught Ryuu by surprise. Orochi contained his intentions so well it was difficult, if not impossible, to sense him. Ryuu simply reacted, giving ground to gain the time necessary to block, parry, and dodge Orochi's strikes.

When the world snapped, Ryuu hardly noticed it. Somewhere in the back of his mind he realized he still could sense Orochi. He stopped giving up ground, and with a quick cut of his own he drove Orochi back and they disengaged, taking the measure of each other.

Moriko couldn't believe her eyes or her sense. The engagement hadn't lasted more than a couple of breaths, but she had never seen swordsmanship of this quality. She had always known, somewhere, both Orochi and Ryuu were better swordsmen than her, but she had always thought herself close. That wasn't true.

An untrained observer would be hard pressed to tell the difference, but their cuts were just a heartbeat quicker, their reactions faster. Even though she wasn't fighting she had a hard time tracking their movements.

Ryuu was cut, but he had driven Orochi back with his last move. Moriko had never seen Orochi driven back before.

As her sense wandered over the battlefield, she realized there was something different about Ryuu. The world and all of its energy and all of its life seemed to envelop him, to move through him in a way she had never observed before. He almost didn't feel human anymore.

Orochi focused his sense on Ryuu and felt the way energy moved through him. Orochi had glanced it before, back before his fight with Shigeru. It had been but the work of a moment and had been gone. But now it had settled on the boy.

He had never thought the stories had been any more than old wives tales. A legend designed to motivate the Warriors of the Path. He had even known some who had claimed to have the power although he had never known for sure.

He knew now. He had never experienced anything like this. The boy had a gift and probably didn't even realize the extent of his power. Orochi couldn't shake the feeling that the world had worked its magic to its own ends to create this boy. Too many coincidences. Shigeru had stumbled onto something much greater than he ever could have imagined although maybe he had known all along. It all felt preordained.

Orochi shook his head. He had never believed in anything beyond his own ability. It seemed like a poor practice to start now. Regardless of his own feelings on the subject, he had his honor and his word to uphold.

He smiled to himself. This should be interesting.

Ryuu wasn't able to process what was happening. The world was different, more vibrant. He could sense the blood flowing from the cut on his chest, but he also knew it was clean and posed no threat to him.

Everything swirled about him. The attention of the onlookers, the cool breeze which passed through the compound. Everything moved and breathed as one. He sensed Orochi's intention before he started moving, and he didn't even pause to consider how unusual that should have been.

He sensed how every muscle in Orochi's body was screaming, pushed to the utmost from a lifetime of difficult conditioning. Idly, he realized Orochi was coming at him with unprecedented speed and power, but it didn't faze him. Their swords met and met again, and there was going to be an opening, as clear as day, right there.

Ryuu's cut was true, and though Orochi was quick, the cut moved through him, almost without resistance. Alone it wouldn't be fatal, not unless it wasn't treated in the next watch. But it caused Orochi to disengage for the second time, and Ryuu was content to watch him retreat.

Moriko was without words. She hadn't even sensed the two of them. Their movements were too quick. It had lasted but a single heartbeat, but they each must have made four or five moves. Moriko didn't even know. She couldn't tell what had happened. She could have sworn they had blurred they were moving so fast.

Orochi had disengaged again, and Moriko could see the cut on the right side of his abdomen. She glanced at Ryuu, and there was no new blood. She went back to Orochi, and her heart went out to him. Despite everything, he was a good man.

He must have sensed it because he turned to her and bowed his head. He knew her thoughts, knew her well. And he accepted her choice. It was enough.

He was incredible. Orochi still had one trick up his sleeve, and the fight wasn't over, but the boy was the best he had ever seen. He had the gift.

He felt sympathy and glanced over at Moriko. The girl was torn, Nori's body at her feet. That pleased him. She would pull through, despite everything the monastery had done to her. Orochi was proud. He had created one good thing in his time here. That was enough. He bowed to her and resumed his focus on Ryuu. It was time.

Orochi came again, but Ryuu was ready. He could tell, once again, Orochi was giving all he had, the way a warrior should. He held nothing back, ready for death to claim him.

The moves were quick, and there was the obvious opening. Ryuu took it, plunging his sword deep into Orochi's belly.

Orochi almost smiled. Shigeru had taught him this trick the last time they had fought. He pushed the pain down, his sword held above his head, ready to make the killing blow, even as he began to die.

Ryuu knew it was too obvious, had known before he even made the cut. He focused his will through a single empty handed blow. His right hand held on to his sword while his left made the strike. He wasn't prepared for the result.

Orochi never saw or sensed it coming. Ryuu's palm struck his chest with unimaginable force and shoved him off Ryuu's blade. He had never seen a strike with such power or speed.

Ryuu watched as Orochi tumbled end over end, off his blade, across the field. He had never expected that to happen. He had just planned on stunning Orochi, not knocking him backwards several paces.

With that thought, his world snapped back to normal, and Ryuu realized something inside of him had changed. He pushed the thought aside, focusing on the present. Orochi was still alive. The cut had been fatal, but not immediately. He approached Orochi with caution.

As he did, Orochi struggled to his knees. Like a true warrior, he had not dropped his sword. He set it on his right side, the blade pointing towards him. It was a gesture of peace. Respect for Orochi flooded through Ryuu and he sheathed his sword, though he didn't drop his guard.

Orochi looked up at him. "You have the gift."

Ryuu let the comment wash over him. Orochi had known more about Ryuu than Ryuu had. It was best to accept it. It was not the time for questions.

Orochi looked over at Moriko. "Will you take care of her?"

Ryuu shared his gaze. She was, literally, all he had left. "I will."

Orochi nodded as blood started to trickle out of his mouth. "Good." He looked up at Ryuu again. "Will you honor your word?"

Ryuu knew that he was referring to the swords. He glanced at them and then at Orochi. "I will."

Orochi nodded. "Good." He was starting to have difficulty speaking, but he managed to get one last phrase out. "A warrior's death, please."

Ryuu stepped behind him. He felt Orochi settle down on his knees and gave him a moment to say prayers and make his final peace. A small twitch of the head was all the sign he needed, and with one smooth, perfect stroke, he drew his blade and took off Orochi's head.

Moriko glanced about herself, attempting to maintain the same calm that was frozen upon Ryuu's face. Orochi had been killed. Her mind was still attempting to catch up with what her eyes had seen. As she glanced around, she saw she wasn't the only one.

The entire compound was silent. Every man here was highly trained and every one of them was aware of the significance of what they had just seen. There was no hiding the truth now. It would be loosed upon the land, to what ultimate end no one could guess. It was as if a boulder had been thrown into a pond, stirring up the very fabric of existence. No one alive had seen two nightblades duel.

It didn't take the sense to understand that the place was filled with awe and fear. Although Ryuu and Moriko were outnumbered ten to one, not one soldier attempted to renew the attack. Archers held their bows loosely knocked at their sides and some soldiers were sheathing their blades.

When Ryuu spoke, it even made Moriko jump. He seemed to speak quietly yet his voice was heard throughout the fort.

"We are not here for you. We came for the girl and for your commander. I have no wish to kill more today, but if any would stand in my way, come, and let me finish this so I may bury my dead."

He was greeted with silence. The soldiers glanced from one to another, and as a group silently chose life over death at Ryuu's blade. Once the sound of the first sword being sheathed reached the ears of the rest there was mutual consent.

Ryuu nodded and sheathed his own blade. He looked over at Moriko inquisitively and she nodded her head. She was fine.

Ryuu went back to the center tent and came out a while later with Takako's body in his arms. Moriko could see the tears trickling down the side of his face.

Moriko went over to Orochi's body, deciding what best to do. She motioned a soldier to her, who came despite his obvious reluctance.

"Do you have a cart I may use to transport his body? I can return it later if you wish, but I need to give him a proper rite of passage."

The soldier's face was full of questions, but he didn't ask them. "Yes, sir."

Not long after that, Ryuu and Moriko left the fort through the front gates. Moriko had offered the use of her confiscated cart for Takako's body as well, but Ryuu declined, opting instead to carry her all the way back to their camp.

The journey was uneventful. Each of them built a funeral pyre and each of them placed a body on top. They worked in silence, each of them too wrapped up in their own thoughts to spend time speaking to the other.

When the work was finished they stepped back, each of them hesitating to speak.

Ryuu was the one who broke the silence. "I think that maybe she was right."

Moriko didn't have to ask what he was referring to. "Maybe, there's no way of knowing. I don't think we were wrong though."

"Even at this cost?"

Moriko fixed her gaze on the bodies of her friend and her mentor. "No."

Ryuu changed the subject. "Orochi was a good man."

Moriko agreed. "He was hard, but he was honest and he was fair. He held to his code and did what was asked of him."

"He had a purpose."

"Yes." Moriko read into Ryuu's thoughts. "And now you need to find one. The word will get out. You won't be able to hide again."

Silence settled over the two of them like a comfortable blanket. They were both lost in thought

Finally he spoke again. "I would rather not draw my blade against another again."

Moriko studied him. Her heart went out to him, but she suspected there was a deeper truth he didn't understand quite yet. "I hope you're right."

They lit the pyres and watched in silence as a love and a master went up in flames. Moriko would have done anything to get an idea of Ryuu's thoughts, but he was closed down, and it was only sorrow she sensed.

As she watched the flames dance against the evening sky, Moriko felt a lightening of her spirit. Although she knew it wasn't true, she finally felt free. She had escaped the monastery, and although she mourned Orochi, a part of her was also aware that he had been the only one who was capable of tracking her down. Since he had rejoined the Great Cycle she knew she was more free than she had been since she was a child.

As she stood next to Ryuu, she knew she wanted to be with him on his journey. There was an understanding between the two of them that she had never shared with anyone before. She acknowledged that it might not be quite fair, as they were the only two nightblades in the world they were aware of, but she also knew him as an honest, kind man. Maybe that was enough.

As the pyre burned low to the ground, Moriko turned to Ryuu and spoke softly. "So, what do we next? It's all over."

Moriko was delighted as Ryuu smiled at the use of her "we."

"Not quite yet. There's one more thing that we need to do."

Moriko looked at Ryuu quizzically, but she couldn't tell what he was thinking.

EPILOGUE

Lord Akira was pacing in his castle, staring at the maps in his study.

For almost a full moon he had been distraught, not eating as usual, nor as calm and confident as was his manner. Rumors had become something more. Not quite fact, but not fiction either. At times it sounded like everyone in the kingdom knew he had a nightblade in his employ.

The news from the fortress had come just days after the battle, delivered by a messenger who had worn out multiple horses and had almost killed himself to bring the news as soon as possible. Despite the attempts to preserve secrecy, too many people had witnessed the events at the fort and the word was out in public.

It caused him to go back through the entire chain of events, trying to find the mistakes, trying to find where he should have acted differently. But what frustrated him was that he wasn't convinced he should have done anything different. He had gone all the way back to when Orochi first came through his doors, outsmarting and out-fighting his entire guard.

Perhaps he should have turned Orochi away. But the greater part of him believed he had made the right decision. The knowledge that a nightblade existed combined with his offer of services had been a moment not to pass up.

Akira had lost more than an ally. From the first day they had met, Orochi had made his position with Akira clear. He wanted to use Akira just as Akira wanted to use him. There was no pretense, no hidden agenda. Orochi was not a power-hungry man. He already had power and knew what he hoped to gain from it.

As one of the three Lords it had been a blessing. Akira had fathered no sons and the plots against his reign ranged from silly to subtle. But almost everyone born with ambition was trying to play some angle. Not Orochi. He had been as straight as they came.

Akira looked at the map of the Three Kingdoms arranged before him. He seemed to be the only one who understood that the world was larger than their Three Kingdoms. Yes, there was limited trade with the outside world, but geography and weather had made the Three Kingdoms almost immune to a serious attack the past few hundred cycles. There were the attacks through the southern pass, but Akira and Nori had suspected for some time they were at most a diversionary strategy. Something wicked was brewing in Azaria, but he knew not what.

The Three Kingdoms held sheltered, fertile, and mineral-rich land. They were an ideal location for invasion. Their own legends told of invaders from lands unknown in the days of the One Kingdom. Akira suspected it was only by chance they hadn't been seen since. But it was too much to ask that they never return. As the Three Kingdoms stood now, they would fall to any organized invader. The majority of troops for all Three Kingdoms were stationed along their own borders with the other Kingdoms, not towards the outside world.

Akira knew the other two Lords also had dreams of unifying the Three Kingdoms and becoming King. But Akira also knew that he was the only one of the three who wanted to do it for the good of the Kingdom.

Despite Nori's weaknesses he had been a capable general and had seen the bigger picture surrounding the Kingdom. He had been willing to hold the pass with fewer and fewer troops over the past few cycles, knowing that by diverting troops he was preparing for the success of future wars.

Akira wasn't sure any of his other generals had the same foresight. Toro maybe. They were all capable commanders, but the real promise lay in the generation below them. The generation of Nori's son and of the new nightblade. They were young and hungry and several were brilliant. Akira's scouts within the army reported on the progress of several of them. His hope was to have them in command of his armies within three cycles, time to make a killing strike upon the other Kingdoms.

He looked at the map one final time and suppressed the urge to wipe everything off it. He knew what the kingdoms needed to survive, and he knew he possessed the ability to make it happen. He had the leadership, he just didn't have the resources developed yet. And now two of his most valuable assets had been taken from him by a boy.

As soon as the thought ran through his mind he knew he was not alone. He couldn't say how he knew, perhaps some vestigial part of the sense everyone possessed. There was only one person who had the slightest chance of getting in here. Deja vu struck in force, and he knew the fear for his own life. He turned and drew his sword with one lightning quick move.

The man, the boy, Akira corrected himself, was leaning against a corner, studying the map Akira had just been looking at. He was of average height, and while obviously strong, didn't look like the sort of person who could kill Orochi. He looked remarkably average and young. He was still several cycles away from full adulthood. But his robes were as dark as night and caused him to blend into the shadows.

Disbelief almost made Akira laugh, but he knew already what this boy had accomplished. Perhaps he was lucky, but no one had the luck to create the results this boy had. He was the most dangerous man alive inside his kingdom, all three kingdoms, at this moment.

The boy looked up at him. "Bad time?"

Akira held his sword steady and level. He was facing the boy who was bringing his Kingdom to the brink of collapse. Maybe where others had failed, he could succeed. The boy was unarmed. He would be easy to kill. Akira moved in to attack while the boy watched.

Akira didn't know how to describe what happened next. As he went to strike it seemed like the boy blurred out of his sight. He couldn't track the motion of the boy's body. The next thing he knew the sword was out of his hands with the back side of the blade tight against his throat.

Understanding washed over him. The boy wasn't here to kill him. If he had been he just missed out on the easiest opportunity he had.

The back side of the blade was removed from his throat, and Ryuu handed the sword back to him. "I'm not here to kill you." He paused. "I don't think."

Akira raised an eyebrow. "You sound uncertain."

"I suppose it depends upon the outcome of this meeting, but I only see it going one way."

"Are you seeking employment to replace the skills Orochi brought to this Kingdom?"

"No."

Ryuu turned and gazed over the map. "I've never seen an accurate map of the Three Kingdoms. How good is this?"

Akira fought down his warring emotions. A small part of him felt he should be angry. His castle infiltrated, his life threatened, spoken to like a peer of a young man. But the greater part of him couldn't resist the sheer audacity of the boy and his complete lack of understanding regarding court etiquette. It was a refreshing change from the sycophants and plotters he spent most of every day with. It was much the same appeal that Orochi had possessed.

He couldn't quite hide the pride in his voice. "I believe it to be the most accurate map of the Three Kingdoms in existence. I have taken extraordinary measures to ensure its accuracy and detail."

"You want to take over all three Kingdoms." It was more of a statement than a question.

Akira was startled. How could the boy have known? But he stopped his denial. It was self-evident. There weren't many other reasons to build the most expensive, accurate map in the Three Kingdoms. It was also a pretty open secret.

"Yes, but so does every Lord. I just believe I'm going to be the one who succeeds."

"Why?"

Akira stepped back. Such blunt questions were socially shocking, if refreshing. He had never spoken so openly about his plans. But somehow he felt the boy needed to know. If he could convince the nightblade he could convince anyone. He still thought he could convince the boy to work with him.

"Order, strength, discipline. My citizens are generally happy. They may complain about the harshness of the rules we've set, but there is little crime and little to fear outside of the normal risks of existence. Our military is strong and fast and we are always on a war footing, unlike the other two Kingdoms, who have begun their fall into decadence. Their peace has made them weak. I also had the service of the best assassin in the Three Kingdoms. He would have been instrumental in a clean campaign."

Ryuu grunted. "Why take over the other two Kingdoms if your own is going so well? Aren't you content with the power you possess?"

"I am. But I see a greater responsibility ahead. The Three Kingdoms are part of a larger world, and although geography has helped us remain independent, it will not always be so. We have a rich land here, a land which would mean a lot to other people beyond our shores and ranges. If we don't unify under a strong hand, we will all fall."

"Considering the cost it seems like a thin justification for a grab for greater power ."

Akira gazed at Ryuu with a hint of anger. "I am well aware of the shortcomings. I understand that the safety of the whole sometimes overwhelms the needs and lives of more than a few people. That knowledge doesn't make anything easier, but it doesn't make it any less necessary."

Ryuu was angry as well now. "No Kingdom is worth the lives of my master and my friends."

Akira transfixed him with a steely glare. "The Kingdom is worth that, and much more besides. If I can keep hundreds of thousands of people safe, but must kill a handful of people to make it happen, it is a sacrifice I am more than willing to make."

Ryuu's hand went to where his sword would have hung if he had one, briefly, before he took it away. Akira noticed the gesture but didn't flinch. "You burned down an innocent family, killed my master, and tortured my friend to death. If those are the actions your peace is founded upon, war seems like a more pleasant alternative."

Ryuu saw the look of sadness flash upon Akira's face and was surprised.

Akira held his gaze. "I ordered your death, the death of your master, and the death of the girl who started this whole mess. General Nori took his orders further than he should have." Akira rose his hand to silence Ryuu's retort. "He was an officer under me, and like all officers in the military, I am responsible for his behavior. I am sorry her family was killed in addition to the women in the brothel, and I have received reports about the torture she suffered. For all these actions, I owe you more than an apology. But I will not apologize for the deaths of your friend and your master. They were the correct order then, and they are the correct order now, even with you here ready to take my life."

"Why?" Ryuu was barely able to get the question out through his clenched jaw.

"Because your very existence threatens the Kingdom and all the work that I have attempted to perform over the past few cycles. You know better than anyone alive how nightblades are demonized in popular culture. I'm sure by now you realize it's not accidental. The nightblades split our great Kingdom in three, and that must never be allowed to happen again. Now that the public knows about you, there is no telling what will happen. Everyone is scared, uncertain how the balance of power may be shifted. You are safest dead."

With a supreme effort of will, Ryuu managed to hold his anger in check. "We were never a danger to anyone."

Akira raised an eyebrow. "Don't delude yourself. The first time something happens that threatens you, you attack. When Takako was taken, in a perfectly legal transaction, I'll remind you, you went into the camp and killed an officer of the army. Not the actions of a peaceful man. When your master was killed, you attacked both a monastery and an army base. Any time something has happened to you, you have responded by sowing disorder and chaos, elements that will tear my Kingdom apart. When you're unhappy with me, you come personally into my chambers. Hardly the actions of a typical peace-loving citizen."

"Everything I did was to protect someone who couldn't protect themselves."

"Which is exactly what I'm doing, just on a scale you can't seem to comprehend."

The steel and frustration in Akira's voice penetrated through the haze of anger surrounding Ryuu's thoughts. He thought through all his actions and tried to assume Akira's perspective. In a flash of insight, he realized that Akira's actions weren't much different than what he would have done. If he had to choose between mass chaos and the death of a few individuals he would have chosen the same path. Abruptly, his anger cooled.

"I see."

Akira, not being able to track Ryuu's thoughts, was surprised at the concession. He was surprised at himself as well. He realized he had been expecting to die, and had spoken much more openly than he was used to, even with his closest advisers. He had inadvertently created a bond with this boy.

Ryuu was still muddling through his thought process, and Akira turned it to his advantage.

"So, what are you going to do?"

Ryuu looked up. "Well, I came to you to tell you to stop hunting us. If you weren't going to listen, I was going to kill you."

"That was your solution?"

"Not perfect, I admit, but it would have gotten the job done."

Akira shrugged. He enjoyed the blatant disregard for authority the boy held. "It might have. Everyone will be searching for you now."

Ryuu examined him. "I think the plan still holds out. I have no ambition for power, nor any desire to serve a master other than myself. I would like to lead a peaceful life and explore the origin of the sense to greater degree. Orochi gave me some leads before he died."

"He spoke to you then."

"Yes. He seemed to believe I was a lot stronger than I think. He gave me some directions on how to continue my training."

"To what end?"

The question paused Ryuu for a moment. "I guess I've never really thought about it. I've always trained to be stronger simply to be stronger. I suppose it's for times such as these when strength is necessary to protect those who I care about."

Akira nodded. "You haven't yet figured out a purpose for your life then?"

"I'm not sure there is a purpose to an individual's life."

Akira glanced from Ryuu to his map back to Ryuu. "We all have purpose, whether we pursue it or not." He paused. "Would you consider working for me under the same conditions I had with Orochi? They were generous terms."

Ryuu shook his head. "Not just because of how I personally feel about you. I've seen decent men be party to horrible actions because they tied their honor and their obedience to another man. The peace of a Kingdom isn't worth the suffering Takako experienced. I think being party to that helped kill Orochi in the end. Better to be free and responsible for your own actions."

Akira found himself liking the boy more and more. He was reasonable, if perhaps too young to understand the ways of the world. He found himself more curious. "Do you believe you will be able to live in peace even if you and I part today less than enemies?"

Ryuu shrugged. "I hope so, but it would be naive to assume that just because I hope so it will be. Shigeru often worried that those who lived by the sword would be fated to die by it. Perhaps it is true. It is pointless to predict the future. What is important is that what I want at this moment is peace."

"Are you sure you won't consider working for me?"

Despite himself, Ryuu grinned just a little. It was nice to be appreciated for one's talents. "Yes."

"Where will you go, and what will you do?"

"I wouldn't tell you for the world."

"You know I will send spies after you. You are far too dangerous a man to leave wandering around my Kingdom."

"I may not stay in your Kingdom. But you are welcome to send any spies. They will risk their lives, and I suspect they won't be able to track us anyway."

"What if I need to contact you?"

The corner of Ryuu's mouth turned up just a bit as if he found the idea amusing. "Akira, I leave you alive today because you have convinced me you are not out to kill me or Moriko, and you will leave us in relative peace. But we are not allies. If your claims are true about why you rule and what your goals for ruling are, then you are a man best left alive, and perhaps are best suited to pursue a Kingdom for all. But that will not be my fight."

Ryuu turned to leave, but Akira spoke before he could begin his egress. "Do you really think you'll be able to do it?"

Ryuu glanced back quizzically.

"Do you think that as a warrior, you'll be able to find a life of peace?"

As Ryuu looked at Akira, he couldn't help but think that this young man, just barely of the legal age of a soldier, had the eyes of a man who had seen much, much more. "No. I suspect the sword will continue to find me. But we are defined by our actions, and what kind of man would I be if I didn't at least attempt to live in peace?"

Akira nodded. He understood this boy, and somehow, this boy understood him better than a whole reception room full of nobility and courtiers.

"I wish you the best of luck. While I will try to keep track of you, you have my word that no harm will come to you or the girl on my account. Perhaps you'd do the kindness of not killing any messengers I may send."

Ryuu grinned and suddenly went from a sage to a young man in an instant. "Depends on how good-looking they are."

With that he was out the door. Akira started to track him but found that he had disappeared into the emptiness. It was a pretty impressive skill.

Akira grinned despite himself. He and Orochi had understood each other and respected each other, but he liked that boy. He had a feeling that some day he might see him again. Perhaps not. Either way, from the bottom of his heart, Lord Akira hoped he would find peace.

Author's Note

Before you go, I just wanted to take a moment to say thank you for reading. If you liked the story, please take a moment to review the book wherever you purchased it, or on social media. Small independent authors like me rely on reviews to help spread the word about our work.

Finally, if you're interested in being among the first to know about upcoming releases, get behind-the-scenes glimpses of the company in action, and get FREE STUFF, please head on over to www.waterstonemedia.net and sign up for our newsletter. We'd love to see you and hear from you.

Thank you,

Ryan

Made in the USA
San Bernardino, CA
25 October 2016